D1187746

PUSS IN BOOTS

LADY KILLER

ED McBAIN

Puss in Boots

Lady Killer

GUILD PUBLISHING LONDON

This omnibus edition published 1988 by
Guild Publishing
by arrangement with Hamish Hamilton Ltd

Photoset in Great Britain by
Rowland Phototypesetting Ltd, Bury St Edmunds, Suffolk
Printed and bound in West Germany
by Mohndruck, Gütersloh

CONTENTS

Puss in Boots

This is for George Greenfield

1

She thought she heard a sound.

She looked up sharply from the flatbed, listening.

The palm fronds outside the studio rattled with a fierce November wind. A bird called inanely to the night.

Nothing more.

She kept listening.

Lots of expensive photographic and sound equipment in here, you had to be afraid of junkies breaking in. The heavier stuff like the Bell & Howell projector, synched to the mag recorders and dubbers, would be difficult to haul away unless you backed a truck in. But all the lenses and all the smaller cameras like the Nikons and the Hasselblads, even the Pageant projector could be packed easily into the back of a car, driven up to Tampa or St. Pete, sold there in a minute.

Kept listening.

The wind again, palm fronds whispering.

A car going by, tires hissing on asphalt.

Hardly any traffic, this time of night. This was cattle country, or used to be. The studio was set back some three hundred yards from what was still called Rancher Road, surrounded on either side by acres of land already yielding to the developers' bulldozers. Ten o'clock at night, you'd think it was two in the morning, everything as still as death except for the bird again, calling, calling, and the wind, and the clicking whisper of the palms.

She shook a cigarette free from the package of Benson & Hedges on the blue Formica surface of the flatbed editing machine. The Steenbeck was worth at least twenty thousand, but nothing a junkie could pack in a duffel bag. She picked up a plastic lighter the color of the cigarette package, and thumbed it into flame. She took several puffs on the cigarette, and then immediately stubbed it out. There was work to be done.

She'd shot a bit more than nineteen thousand feet of film in twenty-eight days, figuring a burn ratio of six-to-one in order to get the ninety-minute finished film she was going for. The dailies came back from the lab in New York on eight-hundred-foot cores that fit onto the Steenbeck's revolving stainless steel plates. She'd carried two of those cored rolls to the studio tonight, and had already run one of them through the machine several times, taking notes, marking film and magnetic sound tracks. The second roll was now on the machine, together with her A and B tapes. She checked her synch marks again, to make sure the film and the mag tracks were in absolute synch, and then moved the control lever to roll all three at twenty-four frames per second.

One of the two screens above the editing surface flashed the first image.

The speakers on either side of the screens erupted with sound. It was almost ten-thirty when the last frame of film rolled through the machine.

She lighted another cigarette, threw the control switch to fast reverse, and sat there smoking while the work print and the mags whirred back through the machine, savoring the cigarette this time, a satisfied smile on her face, pleased with what she'd seen but realizing there was still a great deal of work to be done before the first of the month.

The negative was what she'd be taking with her to Mexico. Plus the workprint and the synchronized sound tracks. Find a lab down there to do the rest of the work. Plenty of work down the road. Assuming all went well. Assuming Jake came up with what she needed down there. Assuming Henry didn't start getting . . .

Well, no sense getting itchy herself.

This was no time to panic.

She stubbed out the cigarette, lifted the cores from the plates, made sure film and sound rolls were tightly wound, and then taped their ends. She put the two cores of film in a sixteen-millimeter film can, one on top of the other, put the lid on it, and closed it securely. She packed her four sound rolls in plastic bags, and then put them into an aluminum carrying case together with the can of film. She carried the case to the back door, set it down just inside it, and then went around the studio turning off all the lights except the one just inside the door.

She picked up the carrying case.

She hesitated near the light switch.

Went back to the flatbed to make sure she'd put out her cigarette.

Went to the door again.

Looked back into the studio, her hand on the burglar alarm panel beside the door.

Put down the carrying case for a moment while she searched in her shoulder bag for her keys.

Picked up the case again, hit the three-digit code on the alarm pad, opened the door, snapped out the last of the lights, and stepped outside.

It was twenty minutes to eleven.

A light bulb in a cage hung over the back door to the studio.

It cast her long shadow on the white gravel of the parking lot.

She locked the door, located her car keys in the illumination afforded by the light bulb, and was walking toward the car when she saw a second shadow on the ground.

She was turning, starting to turn, when the knife plunged into the meaty part of her back, just above the shoulder blade.

She felt only searing pain as the blade penetrated.

She screamed.

And then she was turning, *being* turned, a hand clasping onto her right shoulder and spinning her around to meet the knife as it plunged again. She dropped the aluminum carrying case. She screamed again. The knife kept coming at her. She screamed as blood bubbled into her mouth, spit blood as she screamed, kept screaming until she could no longer scream, the front of her yellow blouse covered with blood welling from her wounds, her face covered with blood, her throat, her hands covered with blood as she fell to the white gravel and the gravel turned red.

And she stared up sightlessly at a star-drenched Florida sky while the palm fronds whispered and the blood continued to run from her torn and lifeless body, touching at last the aluminum carrying case with its cores of film and sound tapes.

At eleven-thirty that night, in a bar called the Goat's Head, some sixty miles north of where Prudence Ann Markham leaked her blood onto a white gravel driveway, two girls in aerobic costumes were playing darts and drinking beer. One of the girls was a blonde and the other was a redhead. The blonde was wearing black tights, a yellow leotard and yellow leg warmers. The redhead was wearing blue tights, a green leotard and green leg warmers. They were both nicely color-coordinated. Neither of the girls was wearing aerobic shoes. They were both wearing shoes with extremely high heels. Black patent leather on the blonde, blue patent on the redhead. The snug costumes, the leg warmers, the stiletto heels made them look like Bob Fosse dancers.

Or hookers.

The girls had just come from an aerobics class, though they probably hadn't been wearing the high heels while they exercised. They kept talking about the class being too crowded, and there being hardly any space near the mirror, meanwhile throwing darts at the board and occasionally hitting it. Each time one of their darts flew out of control, they wiggled their pert little asses and giggled. They were making a big deal out of playing darts like beginners.

Tick and Mose figured the show was for them.

They had been coming on with the girls for the past half-hour now, from the minute the two of them pranced into the place like racehorses. So far, Tick and Mose were batting approximately zero. This was because they had started off by telling the truth. They had told the girls they were in the movie business. The girls thought this was a line. The girls were both in their early twenties and hip to the ways of the world. You met two guys in a Tampa bar that looked like an English pub—all mahogany and brass and leaded windows—they told you they were in the movie business, you had to figure they were full of shit. That had been the first mistake Tick and Mose made, telling the girls the truth about their line of work. They should have said they were in the construction business. The next mistake was giving the girls their true and proper names, which the girls thought were phony.

George Ticknor had said, "My name is Tick."

The blonde girl had said, "What's your friend's name? Tock?"

"Mose," Mose had said. His full name was Mosely Jones, Jr. His father was also in the movie business, in Atlanta where Mose was born, but he didn't think it was wise to bring up the movie business again.

"What do you girls call yourselves?" Tick asked.

14

"*Women* is what we call ourselves," the blonde said, and bent over to pick up another dart, exhibiting her fine feminist ass and causing Tick to wet his lips.

For the past half-hour, they'd been making a game of trying to wheedle the girls' names from them. The girls kept playing darts and wiggling and giggling. Tick and Mose sat at the bar, watching them, trying to make conversation over the noise of the TV set blaring the late night news.

"I'll bet your name is Trudy," Tick said to the blonde.

"Ick, Trudy," she said, and pulled a face.

"But close, right? Judy?"

"No way."

"I'll bet you ten dollars your name has an 'oooo' sound in it."

"My mother taught me never to gamble with strangers."

"Who's a stranger?" Tick said. "I already introduced myself."

"Tick, right," she said skeptically, and pulled another face.

"You're ticking us off, Tick," the redhead said. "Take a walk, okay?" But she wiggled her ass again.

"You must be Eileen," Mose said to the redhead.

"Nope."

"Or Maureen."

"Nope."

"Or Colleen. All redheaded girls have Irish names."

"Wrong," the redhead said.

"So what's your name?"

"Revlon," she said, and threw a dart.

The dart missed the board by a mile. It almost missed the *wall*.

"Revlon?" Mose said.

"Figure it out," the redhead said.

Mose tried to figure it out.

"So you guys are in the movie business, huh?" the blonde said.

"That's right," Tick said. At *last*, he thought. A little fucking progress at last.

"Big movie producers, huh?" the redhead said.

"Dir*ec*tors," the blonde corrected. "Looking for starlets. How come you don't have your casting couches with you?"

"I'm a sound man," Mose said. He was lying now. He was a grip.

The blonde picked up her beer mug and licked at the foam, unimpressed. There was a fine sheen of perspiration on her face and on the sloping tops of her breasts. Tick wet his lips again.

"I'm a gaffer," he said. He was lying, too. They were both grips.

"Oh?" the redhead said. "And what's a gaffer?"

"I do the lighting," he said.

"Lights, camera, *action*!" the redhead shouted, and pointed her finger at the blonde, legs spread, ass jutting, one hand on her hip. Both girls giggled again.

"That's not the way it works," Tick said.

"That's not the way *what* works?" the redhead asked.

"Lights, camera, action. That's not what a director says."

"I told you," the blonde said. "He's a director."

"No, I'm a gaffer," Tick said.

"Okay, so tell us what a *director* says," the redhead said, and winked at the blonde.

"First tell us your names," Tick said.

"I already told them mine," the redhead said. "You figure it out yet?" she asked Mose.

"Sure. Revlon."

"Sure *what*?" the redhead said.

"Revlon," Mose said, and shrugged.

"Come on," Tick said. "How we gonna get to know each other if you won't even tell us your names?"

"Who says we *want* to get to know you?" the blonde asked.

"Well, we're talking here, that's getting to know each other, isn't it?" Tick said. "Come on, what's your name? I'll bet it has an 'oooo' sound in it."

"No, it's Rachel," the blonde said, almost shyly.

"What's your friend's name?"

"Gwen."

"Nice to meet you both," Tick said, and got off the bar stool and walked to where the girls were standing near the dart board, hands on their hips.

"Is your name really Tick?" Rachel asked.

"For Ticknor," he said, and nodded.

"Actually, that's kinda cute," she said. "Tick."

"So what does a director say, Tick?" Gwen asked.

Tick was trying to figure out which one he wanted. The blonde had bigger tits, but the redhead had legs that could make a grown man cry. She reminded him a lot of Connie. The red hair, those spectacular wheels. But no one in the world was like Connie.

"Well," he said, "first your A.D. yells for quiet. He'll say . . ."

"What's an A.D.?" Gwen asked.

"Assistant director," Tick said.

"Okay, he yells for quiet."

"'Quiet, please,' something like that."

"Then what?"

"Then the director says, 'Stand by . . .'"

"Okay."

"And then, 'Roll camera . . .'"

"Which is when your cameraman starts the film running," Mose said.

"'Rolling,' is what he says," Tick said.

"The cameraman," Mose said.

"Then your director says, 'Roll sound . . .'"

"Which is when your sound man starts his recorder and says, 'Speed.' Me," Mose said, "I'm a sound man." Still lying.

"Then your A.D. says, 'Mark it,'" Tick said.

"For the guy on the clapstick."

"And *that's* when the director yells, 'Action'," Tick said.

"So at least I was right about the action," Gwen said, and looked them over with what Mose hoped was new respect. "So you're really in the movie business, huh?" she said. "A sound man and a . . . what'd you say you were?"

"A gaffer," Tick said.

"What the hell's a gaffer?" Rachel said.

"I told you. A lighting director."

"Well, at least you're *some* kind of director, right?"

"I'm a whiz with lights," Tick said. He had decided she was the one he wanted.

"Listen," Mose said, "we're gonna be perfectly honest with you."

"Go hide the silver, Rach," Gwen said.

"No, seriously," Mose said.

"He's being serious, Rach."

"I am."

17

"Weren't you being serious before?"

"Well, yes, but . . ."

"Or honest?"

"What he means . . ." Tick said.

"You figured out where the Revlon comes from?" Gwen asked Mose, playing to him. Good, Tick thought. No problems about who gets who.

"Of course I figured it out," Mose said.

"So where'd it come from? The Revlon."

"Where'd it come from?" Mose asked.

"A bottle," Gwen said.

Mose looked at her.

"He still doesn't get it," Gwen said.

"I get it, I get it," Mose said.

"You were talking about redheads, remember?"

"Sure. Listen, I get it."

"So what is it?"

"Revlon," he said, and shrugged. "Listen, I get it, Revlon."

"I think I picked the dumb one," Gwen said. "So let's hear your big honesty pitch, okay?"

"Well, the minute you girls walked in, I said to Tick here . . ."

"Wait, let me guess. You said we oughta be in pictures."

"No. I said you were gorgeous. Both of you."

"We are," Gwen said. "So?"

"I know you are. That's what I told Tick."

"So?"

"Let me take it from here, okay?" Tick said.

"Here comes the whiz with lights," Rachel said.

"I'm gonna give this our best shot, okay," Tick said, "and if you tell us to walk, we'll walk. But we'd like to get to know you better. I've got a nice place right nearby here, with a good stereo system and some very good pot, and if you'd like to come there with us, I think we can maybe have a good time together. If you say no, we'll thank you for your kindness in listening to us and go our merry way, sadder but wiser. So that's it, our best shot," he said, and smiled in what he hoped was a boyish manner.

"What are you?" Gwen asked. "The dumb one's agent?"

"We're just two nice guys hoping to spend a little time with two nice girls."

"He thinks we're hookers," Rachel said.

18

"I do *not!*" Tick said, sounding offended, but wondering about it nonetheless.

"We're not, you know," Gwen said.

"I didn't think you were."

"I mean, we're *not*."

"So what do you say?" Mose said.

"Listen to Speedy here," Gwen said. "It's a good thing you're handsome because you sure are dumb." She turned to Rachel. "What do you think?" she asked. "You want to go listen to some stereo with these two nice guys who're hoping to spend a little time with two nice girls?"

"Gee, I don't know," Rachel said. "I'm a little stiff from exercise class."

Tick held his breath.

The girls exchanged glances.

Tick waited.

It seemed to take forever.

"Well," Gwen said at last, "I'm game if you're game."

"Well, maybe for a few minutes," Rachel said.

"Good," Tick said at once. "Let me settle the tab, and we'll . . ."

And that was when he heard what the television announcer was saying.

The television announcer was saying that a woman identified as Prudence Ann Markham had been found stabbed to death outside a movie studio in Calusa, Florida.

Tick looked at Mose.

Mose was staring open-mouthed at the television set over the bar.

"So are we getting out of here or what?" Gwen said.

On Friday morning, November 28, the day after Thanksgiving, Matthew Hope went to see Carlton Barnaby Markham at the county jail. Markham was wearing dark blue trousers, a pale denim shirt, black socks and black shoes. A handsome man— lean and muscular, with blond hair and blue eyes—he was rendered anonymous by the institutional clothing he wore and the jailhouse pallor he'd acquired in the four short days since his arrest.

Markham had been charged with violation of Section 782.04

19

of the Florida Statutes which read: "The unlawful killing of a human being, when perpetrated from a premeditated design to effect the death of the person killed . . . shall be murder in the first degree and shall constitute a capital felony, punishable as provided in Section 775.02." In Florida, even a person accused of a capital crime was entitled to bail, the State Attorney's burden being to oppose bail by showing that the evidence in hand was legally sufficient to obtain a verdict of guilty. The Court, in its sole discretion, had the right to grant or deny bail.

Markham had been denied bail.

According to the Grand Jury's indictment, he had "coldly, calculatedly, and premeditatedly" murdered his wife Prudence "in an especially heinous, atrocious and cruel manner," the latter language setting up for the State Attorney a request for the death penalty as defined in Section 775.02.

"Did you kill her?" Matthew asked.

"No, I didn't kill her," Markham said.

Important to Matthew in that when he'd decided to specialize in criminal law, he'd also decided he would never take on anyone he believed was guilty. Since July, when he'd begun his new career (*some* career, so far) he'd represented only two clients (well, almost two) who'd been charged with criminal offenses. The first was a lady schoolteacher who'd been arrested for violation of Section 316.193 of the Florida Penal Statutes, defined as "Driving, or being in physical control of, a vehicle while under the influence of alcoholic beverages or a chemical or controlled substance, or with a specified blood alcohol level" and commonly referred to as DUI, for "driving under the influence." The violation was a misdemeanor that could net a $500 fine and up to six months in jail for a first conviction.

There were four county court judges in Calusa, and two of them had come up with an innovation regarding punishment for a DUI conviction. If an offender was placed on probation, a bumper sticker was affixed to his automobile and the sticker read:

CONVICTED DUI
Restricted License

The license restriction meant that the driver could only use his automobile for business purposes or for routine chores like grocery shopping or visits to the doctor. Matthew had argued the case unsuccessfully: the lady was fined $250, and her car wore the DUI bumper sticker for the full six months.

His second client—the *almost* client—was a man charged with violation of Section 893.135, "trafficking in cannabis," a first-degree felony punishable by three years in prison and a fine of $25,000. He admitted to Matthew, up front, that when he was arrested he was indeed carrying in his pickup truck five hundred pounds of very good Mexican gold, but he insisted that a good criminal lawyer should be able to beat the rap. Matthew had no reason to believe he was a good criminal lawyer who could beat the rap; he would have refused the case, anyway, because the man had already admitted his guilt. (He also called Matthew a no-good turd as he left the office in high dudgeon, but that was *after* he learned Matthew wouldn't represent him.) One and a half clients since July. Back to real estate closings, divorce settlements, will probations, property liens—until Carlton Barnaby Markham called from the county jail.

"Want to tell me why they arrested you?" Matthew said.

"They arrested me because they couldn't find anybody else to arrest," Markham said.

Somewhat petulant mouth, sudden anger flashing in the blue eyes, as though he suspected Matthew of having baited a trap. Voice tinged with a faint Southern accent. probably born right here in Florida. When you thought of Florida, you visualized beaches and water and sailboats and cloudless blue skies, and palm trees and oranges, you conjured a *resort*. The resort, though, was a part of the Deep South—as far south as you could go, in fact, without falling off the continent—and there were millions of people here who weren't on vacation, and who knew damn well that this was Dixie.

"Even assuming the police were wrong . . . " Matthew said.

"They were."

"Even so, the State Attorney wouldn't have gone to the Grand Jury without what he believed was sufficient cause for indictment."

"I'm sure he thought he had a strong case."

"And so did the Grand Jury when they returned a true bill,

and so did the circuit court judge when he denied bail. Mr. Markham, why were all these people so sure you killed your wife?"

"Whyn't you go ask *them*?"

"Because you're the one who's asked me to represent you."

"What do you want me to tell you? Why it *looks* like I killed her?"

"If you will."

"Whose side are you on, anyway?"

"Nobody's. Not yet."

"All they've got is circumstantial evidence," Markham said.

"Well, that's all they *ever* have, unless someone's caught in the act, or unless someone else witnessed the actual killing. They didn't catch you in the act, did they?"

"Of course not!"

"And I'm assuming no one witnessed the murder."

"Only the killer."

"So why'd they arrest you? Why'd they charge you?"

Markham was silent for several moments.

Then he said, "The blood was the main reason."

"What blood?"

"On my clothes."

"There was blood on your clothing?"

"Yes."

"*Her* blood? Your wife's blood?"

"So they say. Her *type* blood."

"You were wearing this clothing, with your wife's blood on it—her *type* blood—when they arrested you?"

"No, I was asleep in bed when they came to the house with their warrant. I was wearing pajamas."

"When was this?"

"Four days after the murder."

"They came to the house with an arrest warrant . . ."

"Yes."

"What time of night?"

"A little after eleven."

"And you were in bed, wearing pajamas."

"Yes."

"Then what?"

"I got dressed, and they took me downtown and questioned me."

"Who was present at the questioning?"

"A detective named Sears, from the Sheriff's office, a police detective named Morris Bloom, and a man named Arthur Haggerty, from the State Attorney's office."

"If they requested someone from the State Attorney's office, then they already thought they had real meat. Did they show you this clothing with bloodstains on it?"

"Yes. They asked me if I recognized it."

"Did you?"

"Yes. It was mine. A jacket and a shirt and a pair of pants. And my shoes and socks."

"The clothing belonged to you."

"Yes."

"And there was blood on it."

"Yes. Well, *dried* blood. And a lot of dirt."

"Dirt?"

"Earth."

"Did they say where they'd got this clothing?"

"They dug it up in my backyard. They came to the house the day after the murder—with a search warrant. They began digging, and they found the clothes and the knife."

"A knife? What do you mean? You didn't mention a . . ."

"A butcher's knife. They said it was the knife I used on Prue."

"Had you ever seen that knife before?"

"Yes."

"Where?"

"In my kitchen."

"It was *your* knife?"

"Well, *our* knife. It was a kitchen knife. A butcher knife. It hung on a rack in the kitchen."

Matthew stared at him.

"Mr. Markham," he said, "I guess you realize that's pretty strong circumstantial evidence. Even if they've got nothing else . . ."

"They know the clothes were stolen," Markham said. "The knife, too."

"Stolen?"

23

"Someone broke into the house and stole them. Took a lot of other things besides."

"When?"

"Ten days before the murder."

"Did you report the burglary?"

"I did."

"To the police?"

"Well, of course to the police."

"Did they investigate?"

"They sent some detectives around. Bloom and his partner, a black cop named Rawles."

"And this burglary took place ten days before the murder?"

"Yes."

"Where were you when it happened?"

"At a friend's house. My wife was working, she's a . . ."

He hesitated, catching himself.

"She *was* a filmmaker," he said, switching to the past tense. "She made commercials, industrials, an occasional documentary."

"Here in Calusa?"

"Well, all over. But she rented studio facilities here. She was working out on Rancher Road the night of the burglary. And also on the night she was killed."

"Working?"

"In the studio there."

"Doing what?"

"Editing."

"Editing a film?"

"Yes."

"What kind of film?"

"I don't know."

"Well, was it a documentary, a commer . . . ?"

"She didn't tell me. She got that way sometimes."

"What way?"

"Secretive about her work. Protective of it."

"So . . . she was at the studio on the night of the burglary."

"Yes."

"And you were at a friend's house."

"Yes."

"From what time to what time?"

"Oh, just for a few hours. We were planning a fishing trip. I got there at about nine, it must've been, and left at eleven."

"Got home and found the house burglarized."

"Yes. Around eleven-thirty."

"Was your wife home yet?"

"No. She was still out at the studio. Didn't get home till around one, one-thirty. The police had already left by then."

"What else was stolen that night?"

"A clock-radio, and a camera, and a small television set."

"In addition to the clothes they later found buried in your yard."

"Some other clothes, too. Some of Prue's clothes."

"And the knife."

"Yes."

"Just the one knife?"

"Yes."

"Did you list these missing items for the police?"

"Yes."

"During the interrogation—after they arrested you—did anyone mention this burglary?"

"Yes, I did. I told them those clothes and that knife had been stolen from the house."

"Did anyone make any comment about that?"

"Haggerty said, 'That's *your* contention, Mr. Markham.'"

"It's more than just that," Matthew said. "A burglary *did* take place and you reported it to the police. If the clothes and the knife were stolen from your house ten days *before* the murder . . ."

"They were."

"Then what the hell are they hoping to prove?"

"That I killed her," Markham said. "You see . . . I have no alibi for the night of the murder."

"Where were you *that* night?"

"My wife had work to do. That's what took her to the studio. I went to the movies alone."

"Which theater?"

"Twin Plaza I. In the South Dixie Mall."

"Meet anyone you know?"

"No one."

"In the theater?"

"No."

"In the mall?"

"No."

"What time did the movie start?"

"Eight o'clock."

"What time did it end?"

"Around ten-thirty."

"Did you go directly home after the movie?"

"No. I wandered around the mall for a while, and then went to a bar named Harrigan's."

"What time did you get there?"

"Around ten to eleven."

"How long did you stay there?"

"I just had one drink."

"What'd you drink?"

"A Tanqueray martini. Straight up. Very dry. With two olives."

"How long did it take you to drink that?"

"Well, I was watching television. There's a television set over the bar."

"So you left the bar when?"

"Around . . . twenty to twelve? A quarter to twelve?"

"And got home when?"

"Around midnight. The police got there about twenty minutes later." Markham sighed deeply. "I know how it looks. I've got no real alibi for where I was when somebody was stabbing her, and the police have only my word for the burglary." He shook his head. "So if you don't take the case, I can't blame you much. I can only tell you again, I didn't kill her."

"I believe you," Matthew said.

2

Matthew's demand for discovery listed twelve essentially boiler-plate items—plus an added typewritten one for "any police reports made in connection with this case"—and concluded with the words, "WHEREFORE, said Demand for Discovery by the Defendant being material and relevant to the proper defense of Defendant under applicable rules, cases and constitutional provisions, Defendant requests that this demand be answered in all respects."

The demand was delivered by hand to the State Attorney's office on the first day of December.

On Wednesday morning, December 3, Arthur Haggerty, the Assistant State Attorney who was handling the prosecution's case, had his response delivered by hand to Matthew's office.

It read:

IN THE CIRCUIT COURT OF THE TWELFTH JUDICIAL
CIRCUIT IN AND FOR CALUSA COUNTY, FLORIDA

STATE OF FLORIDA
     VS.   CASE NO.   <u>84-2207-CF-A-S9</u>
CARLTON BARNABY MARKHAM

STATE'S RESPONSE TO DEFENSE DEMAND FOR DISCOVERY

1.   *Names and addresses of persons with
    information relevant to offense: 3.220 (a)
    (1) i.   <u>See attached</u>
    <u>witness list</u>.
2.   *Written or taped verbatim witness
    statements made to police: 3.220 (a) (1) ii.
                               <u>See attached</u>.

---

3. Defendant's oral, written, or taped statements: 3.220 (a) (1) iii.
                                    See attached.

4. Co−defendant's oral or written statements: 3.220 (a) (1) iv.   Not applicable.

5. Grand Jury testimony of accused: 3.220 (a) (1) v.   See attached.

6. Tangible papers (objects obtained from defendant): 3.220 (a) (1) vi.   None.

7. Whether State has confidential informant: 3.220 (a) (1) vii.   None.

8. Whether State has used electronic surveillance: 3.220 (a) (1) viii. None.

9. Whether there has been a search and seizure (with documents, if any): 3.220 (a) (1) ix.
                              Yes.   See attached.

10. *Expert reports and statements: 3.220 (a) (1) x.   Yes.   See attached.

11. **Tangible papers and objects to be used at hearing and trial: 3.220 (a) (1) xi. Knife, clothing, photographs, autopsy report, diagrams of scene, statements, cassettes.

12. Similar fact evidence. Florida Rule of Evidence 90.404 (must be provided at least 10 days prior to trial.)

13. Police reports made in connection with this case: 3.220 (a) (1) xii.   See attached.

*Defense must reciprocate within 7 days.
**Defense must reciprocate within 15 days.

The prosecution has (   ) has no (X) knowledge of evidence tending to negate defendant's guilt.

I HEREBY CERTIFY that a true copy of the foregoing has been furnished by hand to: MATTHEW HOPE, ESQ., Summerville and Hope, 333 Heron Street, Calusa, Florida on this 3rd day of December, 1986.

> SKYE BANNISTER
> STATE ATTORNEY
>
> by _Arthur Haggerty_
> ARTHUR HAGGERTY
> Assistant State Attorney

Matthew had his work cut out for him.

"I have to tell you frankly," Frank Summerville said, "I don't appreciate your having taken on this case."

"It's the first real case I've had since July," Matthew said.

"By that, I assume you mean the other petty little legal matters that have been occupying your time here are all *fake* cases."

"Frank, this is an important one."

"Every case we handle is important."

"Yes, I recognize that preparing eviction papers for the owner of a condominium . . ."

"His tenant stopped paying the rent. In that respect, the eviction papers are important to him. And if something is important to a client, it's important to us."

Matthew knew many people who maintained that he and Frank looked alike. He figured these were the same people who insisted that married couples of many years standing (or sitting, or lying abed) resembled twins. Actually, he could see no resemblance between him and Frank but their dark hair and brown eyes.

Matthew was thirty-eight years old. Frank had just turned forty. Matthew was an even six feet tall and weighed a hundred and seventy pounds; his partner was two and a half inches shorter and twenty pounds lighter. Frank's face was round— what he himself called a "pig face"—and Matthew's was narrow,

29

a "fox face" in his partner's lexicon. Moreover, Frank was originally from New York, and Matthew's home town was Chicago.

"Suppose you lose it?" Frank said.

"I don't intend to lose it."

"What'll you do then? Take an ad in the paper? Matthew Hope, Attorney at Large, desperately seeks clients charged with sundry misdemeanors or felonies . . ."

"No, I won't take an ad in the paper."

"Why not? Desperate dentists take ads," Frank said.

"I'm not a dentist. Desperate or otherwise."

"I know. You're a *criminal* lawyer." The emphasis was on the word "criminal" as though Frank felt there was something criminal about being a criminal lawyer. "Even unemployed actors take ads," he said. "In *Variety.*"

"And *remain* unemployed," Matthew said. "And I'm not unemployed. And when did you start reading *Variety*?"

"Leona subscribes to it."

Leona was Frank's wife. Another difference. Matthew was divorced.

"Well, I'm not going to lose it, so I won't have to take an ad," Matthew said. "In *Variety* or anyplace else."

"Zack Norman takes ads in *Variety.*"

"*Is Zack Norman a dentist?*"

"He's an actor. The point is, Matthew, if a person suddenly decides—for no apparent reason that I can discern—that he wants to specialize in *criminal* law . . ."

"I didn't *suddenly* decide," Matthew said.

"That's right, you were dabbling . . ."

"Not dabbling."

"That's right, *flirting* would be the more appropriate word. Flirting with murder cases that took you away from real estate, and probate, and all the other petty concerns of the legal profession which, I'm sure, must seem terribly humdrum to Mr. Perry Mason."

"Is Perry Mason a dentist or an actor?"

"Matthew, I'm trying to make a point here," Frank said. "You may think it was enough to start studying the Criminal Laws and Rules book as if it was the Bible . . ."

"*Were* the Bible . . ."

30

". . . and having lunch with every criminal lawyer in town, picking their brains . . ."

"Picking *his* brain . . ."

". . . but just between you and I . . ."

"You and *me* . . ."

"Well, all right, if you want to repeat everything I say instead of listening to me . . ."

"I *am* listening to you, Frank. And I hear what you're saying. I have not been a raging success, I know that"

"That's right."

"But this is a big one . . ."

"Homicide? No kidding? A big one?"

"And if I can get Markham off . . ."

"I'm concerned about what might happen if you *don't* get him off. What repercussions will that have for the firm, Matthew? Will a potential client automatically assume we're lawyers who *lose* cases? Lawyers who *lose* cases don't make money, Matthew."

"If I wanted to make money, I'd become a dentist," Matthew said. "And take an ad in the paper."

"All of a sudden, money doesn't matter to him," Frank said to the air. "All of a sudden, he doesn't care about alimony payments, or the private school for his daughter, or his tennis club, or his . . ."

"I care about *all* of those things, Frank. But . . ."

"*All* of a sudden, those of us who are concerned with the finer things in life are all of a sudden crass and grasping . . ."

"You said it, not me."

"Matthew, listen to me, okay? Ask Benny Weiss to take over, okay? Or Jim Willoughby. They're both fine criminal lawyers, and I'm sure either of them would *love* representing a pauper who . . ."

"Markham isn't a pauper."

"From what I understand the man owns a *clock* shop."

"Clocks are important, Frank. Everybody has to know what time it is."

"In Calusa, nobody gives a *damn* what time it is. Calusa isn't New York, Matthew."

"Noplace is, Frank. We all know that."

"In New York, it's important to know what time it is. In

31

Calusa, does anyone take a clock to the beach? Selling clocks in Calusa is like selling ice cubes in Nome, Alaska."

"Or refrigerators."

"Or refrigerators, right. What I'm saying . . ."

"I know what you're saying."

"What am I saying?"

"You're saying don't lose it."

In Calusa, there are two local law enforcement agencies. The Calusa Police Department handles any crimes committed within the city limits. The Calusa County Sheriff's Department handled any crimes committed beyond the city limits but still within Calusa County. Uniformed Police Department cops are called officers. Uniformed Sheriff's Department cops are called deputies. Plainclothes detectives from either department are called just that: detectives.

Carlton Barnaby Markham lived in the city of Calusa, but his wife had been slain out on Rancher Road, well beyond the city limits, and the homicide had been investigated by the Sheriff's Department. Among the discovery papers supplied by the State Attorney's office was a report written by a Sheriff's Department detective named Jonas Crier:

INVESTIGATIVE REPORT	
Calusa County Sheriff's Department	
INVESTIGATION AT: Calusa County, FL	**DATE THIS REPORT:** 11/20/86
TITLE: Prudence Ann Markham 1143 Pompano Way Calusa, FL	**CLASSIFICATION:** MURDER
	FILE: 86–51175

SYNOPSIS:

Writer, the on–call detective supervisor on 11/20/86, was phoned by Det. Sears at 2307 hours, and advised that he was responding to a stabbing incident at 8489 Rancher Road, Calusa.

Writer did respond to the incident location and met with Cpl. Gandy and Det. Sears at 2315 hours.

Stabbing victim was DOA white Caucasian female, app. age 30–35, app. height 5'7", app. weight 125, hair blonde, eyes blue, wearing yellow skirt and blouse, brown sandals, no handbag, no identification.

Victim was lying on back in gravel parking lot outside Anvil Studios at above address, 15'6" from entrance door. Door locked, burglar alarm activated, no sign of forced entry. Caged light over door only illumination in parking lot. Blue 1985 Honda Civic locked and parked 12' from body parallel to cyclone fence surrounding studio. (Sketches of scene attached.)

Medical Examiner J.E. Ritzig pronounced victim dead at 2331 hours, probable cause multiple stab and slash wounds.

Ford Econoline van from Criminalistics Unit on scene at 2335 hours.

Radio call at 2340 hours yielded Honda registered with Div. Motor Vehicles by Prudence Ann Markham, 1143 Pompano Way, Calusa.

Phone call at 2345 hours to number listed in Calusa directory under name C.B. Markham, 1143 Pompano Way, yielded no response.

Body removed to Southern Medical mortuary at 2350 hours.

Writer, in company of Det. Sears, arrived 0020 hours, 11/21/86, at 1143 Pompano Way in subdivision named Sunrise Shores. Mr. Carlton.

Barnaby Markham answered door, agreed to accompany Sears and writer to Southern Medical for possible identification victim.

Positive ID made at 0050 hours, victim Prudence Ann Markham, wife of Mr. Markham, age given by him as 28 years old.

Mr. Markham stated his wife was working on a movie, renting editing space at Anvil Studios. Last saw her alive when she left house at 1900 hours. Stated that he himself left house a half-hour later, 1930 hours, drove to Twin Plaza I, where he saw motion picture starting at 2000 hours. Movie let out at 2230 hours. Markham says he wandered mall, went to a bar named Harrigan's for a drink, drove home from there, arrived at ''a little before midnight.''

(See transcribed statement for exact details of statement.)

Writer did then respond back to Calusa P.D. and met with Det. Morris Bloom where together the attached P.C.A was drafted.

Writer did then give Det. Bloom taped statement described above.

Writer has had no further involvement in this case and/or investigation other than what is described above.

COPIES TO: Det. M. Bloom, Calusa P.D.

REPORT MADE BY: Det. J. Crier #53, Deputy Sheriff Calusa County, Calusa, Florida.

REPORT APPROVED BY: Gregory Younger, Sheriff of Calusa County, Calusa, Florida.

At ten o'clock on a bright December morning, it was difficult to believe that the parking lot at Anvil Studios had been the scene of a violent stabbing not two weeks earlier. The white gravel driveway glistened like snow in the sunshine, the pink stucco building behind it reflecting a hue that touched the ground like a blush, echoing more deeply in the hibiscus bushes and bougainvillea that crowded the walls. The words ANVIL STUDIOS, fashioned of wrought-iron letters, were affixed to the front side of the building above a wrought-iron, black anvil logo. Matthew parked his Karmann Ghia in a space just below the anvil, and then walked to the front door and opened it.

Wood-paneled reception area, bookshelves on one wall, white Formica-topped conference table, four black vinyl covered chairs around it, white decorator filing cabinets on another wall, a small decorated Christmas tree in a stand on top of one of them. A young girl sat behind a desk just inside the door, telephone receiver to her ear. She looked no older than seventeen, a round-faced brunette with a stunning figure, sparkling blue eyes, and hair cut in bangs on her forehead and molding her head like a sleek black helmet.

"Yes," she said into the phone. "I understand that," and rolled her eyes at Matthew, taking him into her exasperated confidence. "But we ordered the stock two weeks ago, and if we don't have film we can't shoot, now can we? Wouldn't you agree with that? That a person can't load a camera with promises of delivery?" She rolled her eyes again. "No," she said, "we're not Twentieth Century-Fox, that's true. Why? Is Twentieth Century-Fox one of your customers? Oh, I see, I didn't think so. We're just an itty-bitty little film company here in teensy-weensy Calusa, and all we're shooting is a ninety-second commercial for a furniture store on the Trail, but you guaranteed delivery by the first, Mr Peyser, and today is the third, and it'll be Christmas before you know it, Mr. Peyser, so when are you going to deliver the fucking *stock*?" She looked at Matthew, shrugged elaborately, and then said into the phone, "Oh, forgive me, I didn't realize you were perhaps a Baptist minister. I thought you were perhaps a person accustomed to dealing with eccentric motion-picture types who occasionally pepper their speech with obscenities especially when they are so fucking aggravated they could *scream*! Just tell me when we're going to

get the stock, okay? Give me an exact date and an exact time."
She picked up a pencil and began writing. "Okay," she said.
"Thank you ever so much, Mr. Peyser, and it had better be *here*
by then." She slammed the receiver down onto the cradle,
looked at Matthew, grinned angelically, and said, "So. What
can I do for *you*?"

"I have an appointment with Mr Andrews," Matthew said.
"My name is Matthew Hope."

"I'll buzz him," she said, and lifted the receiver and hit a
button on the base of the phone. "Mike," she said, "there's a
Mr. Hope here to see you." She listened a moment, said,
"Right," and then put the receiver back on its cradle. "You can
go right in," she said. "It's right through the door there, you go
into this big room looks like a mausoleum. He's in the projection
booth." The phone rang. She picked up the receiver, said "Anvil
Studios," and then waved him on toward the door at the far end
of the reception area.

The room Matthew entered was perhaps forty feet wide by
sixty feet long. He had never been inside a movie studio before,
but this one couldn't possibly be mistaken for anything but what it
was. Hundreds of film cans were stacked on shelves lining the
room, each can bound with a white adhesive strip upon which
a title had been lettered with a black marker. Two huge angled
consoles with buttons, switches and dials on their faces sat before
a glass-paneled room containing what Matthew guessed was
sound equipment. Open boxes of cables were strewn everywhere
on the floor. Aluminum carrying cases were stacked against the
walls. Several cameras on wooden tripods stood in the underfoot
debris like wading birds in shallow water. A large white screen
dominated the far end of the room. The projection booth faced
it. Matthew climbed a short flight of steps, knocked on the
closed door, and then opened it.

A man in his early thirties was sitting behind the projector,
rewinding a reel of film. The film came off the takeup reel, its
leader flapping. He put his hand up to the still-moving reel,
slowed it with his palm, removed the reel from the spindle, put
it in a can, and only then turned to face Matthew.

"Mr. Andrews?" Matthew said.

"Yes." He rose, extended his hand. "Pleasure to see you."
His face was square, the cheekbones high, the nose a trifle

too large. He had long curly red hair that sat on his head like a fright wig. He was wearing wrinkled lime green trousers, white high-topped sneakers with red stripes on them, a purple shirt with narrow yellow stripes, a tiny blue clip-on bow tie, and a pink polyester jacket flecked with random black tufts of fabric.

If he'd stepped out of a tiny automobile, he could have been a circus clown. If he'd stepped off a banana boat, he could have been an immigrant. But his eyes were the eyes of a robot programmed to kill. Pale blue. An eerie feeling of transparency about them, suggesting that if you looked hard enough you might see through them into the circuitry buried in the skull. The mouth, too, seemed etched onto the emotionless face, a thin line that attempted a smile as he shook hands with Matthew —but the smile was programmed and it came over as false.

"It's an honor to meet one of Calusa's most illustrious criminal lawyers," he said. The words may have been spontaneous, but they sounded rehearsed. Moreover, Matthew was not one of Calusa's most illustrious lawyers, criminal or otherwise.

"It's good of you to make time for me," Matthew said. "I know you must be busy."

"I'm usually here from seven in the morning till ten at night," Andrews said, and sighed heavily. "It's a long day, believe me, but hard work never killed anyone. I sometimes think my partner and I inadvertently chose the correct name for our little enterprise. Anvil Studios. In that we keep hammering away against steely resistance in an attempt to forge some small appreciation of quality here in the boondocks."

The thin false smile again.

Matthew was sure he'd spoken those very same words a thousand times before. Hit the robot's HARD WORK button and out came the anvil metaphor.

"Actually," Andrews said, "the name is an acronym of both our surnames. My partner's name is Peter Villiers, he's of French ancestry. We put together the first two letters of my name and the first three of his, and came up with Anvil. It's fortuitous that our names aren't Sheen and Itkin."

Again the narrow smile.

Again, the feeling that he'd told this same little anecdote many times before.

"Mr. Andrews," Matthew said, "I have the Sheriff's report

made on the night Prudence Markham was murdered . . ."

"Terrible shame," Andrews said. "An extremely talented person, hard to come by here in Crackerville, U.S.A. Cultural pretensions abound in Calusa, Florida, but everyone here spells culture with a K, as in cat. A wonderful person, Prue. I'll miss her."

"Did the police contact you that night?" Matthew asked. "There were no reports in the file . . ."

"Well, I wasn't here," Andrews said at once.

"You weren't working your usual long hours that day, is that it?"

"My usual . . . ? Oh. Seven to ten. No. At the time of the murder, in fact, I was in bed with a little bitch from Sarasota."

The words irritated. More so in that they were accompanied by the android smile. There was about Andrews an air of self-importance entirely out of keeping with the fact that he was a small-time filmmaker in a city not particularly noted for such endeavor. One would have expected such a bloated attitude from a production chief in Los Angeles, though even there it might not have been tolerated. To find such an ego here in Calusa was unimaginable. To find it in someone so *young*—

"Then they didn't telephone you?" Matthew said. "To ask you to come out here?"

"No, they didn't. The building was locked and the burglar alarm on. The killer couldn't possible have been hiding inside. Therefore, why the need to drag me out of bed? Elementary, my dear Watson," he said, and smiled again.

"Had you ever worked with Mrs. Markham?" Matthew asked. "You said she was extremely talented . . ."

"An exception here in Calusa. Ex*treme*ly talented. I should know. I'm a shrewd judge of talent and a man of little patience for dilettantism."

"Then you *did* work with her."

"On several films, yes. We did one, oh, it must have been six months ago, I would imagine . . . yes, in June sometime . . . at the beach on Sabal Key, an educational film for showing in schools, an attempt to introduce adolescent shit-kickers to the beauties of the omnipresent and largely ignored natural splendor surrounding them here in Florida."

Period.

Another rehearsed speech.

Or was he really so bright that his mind, computerlike, fashioned pearly strings of words and spewed them instantaneously?

"Were you working with her on her current project?" Matthew asked. "The film she was editing on the night she was killed?"

"No. On occasion, Prue adopted an air of unbecoming secrecy about her work. My partner and I prefer *discussing* creativity, as did the American expatriates at Deux Magots in Paris all those years ago. You may consider it odd that I think of myself as an expatriate, when surely Calusa is within the territorial limits of the United States. But anyone here who is concerned with quality filmmaking *is* an expatriate, believe me. I often feel like Samson among the Philistines."

Or Hercules in the Augean stable, Matthew thought. Incessantly shoveling horse manure.

"She once did an educational film on child abuse," Andrews said, gathering steam. "A fine film, as it turned out. But you would have thought she was Woody Allen, the *security* surrounding that project! A closed set, just herself, the actors, a cameraman, a lighting man, a sound man, and a few grips—all of them sworn to secrecy. Edited the film here all by herself, at night, in a locked room. Never left a scrap of film around for anyone to see, God knows where she was hiding it, perhaps under her mattress. And then the unveiling! Ta-ra! Ran it right here in this room, this very projector, that very screen. A marvelous film, as I said, I believe it even won a small prize later on. But why such theatrics? I despise pretension in art."

"But you liked Mrs. Markham."

"Yes, very much."

"What was her new film about, do you know?"

"I thought I made it clear . . ."

"I'm sorry, I must have . . ."

". . . that she often worked in secrecy."

"Yes, but . . ."

"By extension, I was alluding to her new project as well. I had no idea what it was. A documentary about the horseshoe crab? An advertising campaign for one of Calusa's illustrious jewelry stores? She never said."

"Did you ask?"

"I knew better than to ask Prue anything when she was in her *auteur* mode."

"But she was using editing space here . . ."

"Yes. Renting it at a thousand dollars a month. My partner and I are forced to rent some of our space, the price one must pay for attempting to make films of distinction in a backwater village. Peter and I came here from Pittsburgh, we're both graduates of Carnegie Tech. We'd decided to forsake the Hollywood route, littered as it is with car chases and special effects. We decided instead to make quiet little films, establish our reputation *here* as quality filmmakers, and then move on when the establishment was ready to recognize the superiority of our work. But one must eat. Hence the rental of space. We have fine facilities here, and we're not above allowing lesser mortals to use them."

"Did you consider Mrs. Markham a lesser mortal?"

"I consider almost everyone a lesser mortal." The smile again. "But not Prue, no. As I said, she was extremely talented."

"Mr. Andrews, this editing room she was using . . ."

"Yes?"

"May I see it?"

"Why?"

"On the night she was murdered, the police found only her body and her automobile outside there in the parking lot."

"A terrible tragedy."

"The car was locked. Nothing in it. No handbag, no identification . . . certainly no film."

"I'm sorry, I don't seem to be following your drift."

"Well, she was here editing *film*, wasn't she?"

"I would assume so. I have no idea why she was here."

"Her husband says she was here editing film."

"Well, yes. But her husband is a murderer."

"I don't believe that, Mr. Andrews."

"Which, of course, is why *you're* here."

"Yes. That's why I'm here."

"But I still don't know why you want to see that editing room."

"Because if she was here editing film, there has to be film. Do you have a key to that room?"

"Certainly. But I don't like violating the privacy of anyone renting space here at Anvil."

"Mrs. Markham's privacy has already been violated," Matthew said flatly. "In the worst possible way."

"I suppose your point is well taken," Andrews said. "Let me get the key."

The editing room door opened onto a six-by-twelve-foot space with a fluorescent light centered on the ceiling. A machine Andrews identified as a Steenbeck occupied most of the room. A chair on wheels sat in front of the machine. Behind the chair was what appeared to be a canvas sack hanging from a metal frame. Andrews identified it as a film bin, and explained that film to be discarded was usually dropped into it. The bin was empty. So were the hangers over the bin, where Andrews said the editor usually hung film or sound tape he or she planned to use. There was nothing on the surface of the editing machine. Not a scrap of film, not a hint of tape.

"Any other keys to this room?" Matthew asked.

"Only the one Prue had. And the master I just used to unlock the door."

"Then where's the film? If she was editing film . . ."

"She may not have been editing, you know," Andrews said.

"Then why would she have rented . . . ?"

"She may have been looking at what she'd already shot, selecting the best takes, marketing the film, deciding how she would cut it later on. *Part* of the editing process, certainly, but not editing *per se*."

"Even so, she needed film."

"Yes."

"So where is it?"

"Did the police check out the automobile?"

"Thoroughly."

"No film in the trunk?"

"Nothing."

"That's decidedly odd," Andrews said.

"Is there anywhere in the studio she might have stored the film? Before she left?"

"We do have a storage room," Andrews said, "but I was in there straightening up last night, and I didn't see anything that might have been hers."

"How do you know?"

"The reels are marked for identification," Andrews said. "A tape around the can, with the working title of the film lettered onto it."

"And all those titles were familiar to you?"

"All of them."

"Were any of the cans untitled?"

"None of them."

Matthew was silent for a moment. Then he said, "Do you have any idea how long she was here that night?"

"None."

"You weren't here when she arrived were you?"

"No."

"What time did you leave the studio?"

"At around six. As I mentioned earlier . . ."

"Yes, your friend from Sarasota. Was *anyone* here when you left?"

"I was the last one out."

"Did you set the burglar alarm?"

"I did."

"And locked the door?"

"Yes."

"Did Mrs. Markham know the alarm combination?"

"Yes."

"I assume she had a key . . ."

"Of course."

"This film she was working on," Matthew said. "Would you know who was working with her?"

"I'm sorry, I don't."

"Who does she *normally* use? As cameraman, as grip . . . what's a grip?"

"A grip is a person who moves things around the set. Grips come and go, they're relatively easy to find. But Pru used the same cameraman, lighting director and sound man on most of her films."

"I'd appreciate their names," Matthew said.

3

Henry Gardella considered himself a man of exquisite taste.

"I want this to be tasteful," he'd told her.

"It will be," she'd said.

"That's why I came to you," he'd said. "There are hundreds of people in Miami who can shoot this movie, I could've gone to any one of them. I picked you instead."

"Thank you," she'd said.

This was back in September.

Very serious girl, he'd thought. Been shooting movies for years now, good reputation. Interested in making a buck, though, who wasn't? Move out of the penny-ante documentary shit she was doing into the big time. He was putting up a hundred and seventy-five grand to make the movie. Plus she'd be getting ten percent of the gross, which wasn't meatballs.

"A movie is like a bullfight," he said, "the same ritual each time out. Raw stock to dailies to assembly to rough cut to final cut to first answer print to second answer print to release print. Every day of the shoot, you ship your exposed film to the lab, and get back your one-lights the next day—everything you asked the lab to print. Ritual. Routine." He looked across the desk at her. "I could get this movie done for a hundred grand, maybe less," he said. He was lying. "I know guys in Miami who can grind it out in a week." Still lying. "But then I'd get the usual cheap product, and what I'm looking for is taste. I'm looking for something, if we do it right, it'll be like a first-class Hollywood production, not something we shot in some sleazy hotel room on Collins Avenue with a tattooed sailor and a couple of hookers. There are more hookers in this town than you can shake a dick at."

He smiled.

Prudence Ann Markham did not smile back.

Very serious girl. Sitting there in a gray skirt and a white blouse, low-heeled shoes, hands folded in her lap, blonde hair caught in a bun at the back of her head, looked like a minister's

43

ED McBAIN

wife. He wondered what kind of panties she was wearing.

"I'm looking for style," he said. "Class. I want the kind of taste I saw in that movie you did on child abuse. Understated. Powerful."

"Thank you," she said.

"Don't misunderstand me," he said. "I want to see everything there *is* to see, we're not doing Donald Duck here."

"I know that."

"But there's a cheap way of showing sex, and there's a classy way, and I want the classy way."

"You'll get class," she said.

He wondered if she had blonde pubic hair.

"And style," he said.

"And style."

"And taste."

"Of course."

"Did you see *Behind the Green Door*?"

"No," she said.

"There's a slow-motion shot in it, that's the kind of thing I'm talking about. Very classy. The man ejaculates in slow-motion for what must be five minutes. It's like a snowstorm on the screen. Very beautiful. That's the kind of class I'm looking for. You should get the video, take a look at it."

"I will."

"You should also take a look at *Deep Throat*. That played in legit theaters, do you realize it? Grossed fifty million dollars. What you saw was this gigantic *edifice* on the screen, husbands and wives in the audience, guys with their girlfriends, a regular movie theater, not one of these cheap porn houses, and Linda Lovelace swallows it to the hilt. That's what I'm looking for, a tasteful movie like that, where maybe we have a chance at getting into a legit house. The video I'm not worried about. We'll make a lot of money on the video. Also, you'll do two versions—when you're cutting it, I mean. So we can sell the soft one later on to cable. Cable," he said, and shook his head sadly. "On cable, you never see any real action. You *know* what they're doing, but you never really see any close shots of what they're doing. I want a lot of close shots, there's nothing more beautiful in the world than two people making love, don't you agree?"

"Yes," she said.

44

"We can make a lot of money on this movie, if we do it right," he said. He paused, looked her dead in the eye. "Do you think you can do it right?"

"Oh, yes, I know I can."

Eager. Smelling the money. He was willing to bet her thighs were sweating under her serious gray skirt.

"Because a hundred and seventy-five thousand is a lot of money I'm putting up."

"I know."

"When can you start?" he asked.

"I thought the end of the month."

"And when can you deliver a final cut?"

"By Christmas?" she said.

A question mark. She wasn't even *sure* it would be Christmas.

"That long, huh?"

"Well, we want to do it right," she said.

"How many days do you figure? For the actual shooting?"

"I thought thirty-five."

"Make it twenty."

"Twenty?"

"Figure a four-to-one burn ratio . . ."

"I was thinking ten-to-one."

"Make it six-to-one."

"Still, twenty days . . ."

"That's all you should need."

"I don't see how . . ."

"Thirty-five days is out of the question. There are people could do this in ten, fifteen days."

"Twenty still feels . . ."

"All right, make it twenty-*five*, that should do it."

"Twenty-eight," she said. "Because, you see . . ."

"Okay, twenty-eight, I'm not gonna argue three days. Can you get the people you need in Calusa?"

"I don't want to use my regular people," she said.

Running scared already, he thought.

"Who will you get?" he asked. "I don't mean your actors, that's up to you, provided you don't use hookers."

"I've got some good people in mind," she said.

"And no junkies looking to make a fast buck unzipping their flies."

45

"No, no."

"I want this to look real. Real people doing it. With taste, of course. So who have you got in mind?"

"For the actors, do you mean?"

"No, I told you, that's up to you. I don't want to mess here with artistic control."

"I appreciate that."

"So who have you got in mind?"

"Some people in Tampa."

"Experienced movie people?"

"Oh, sure."

"Don't hire anyone in Miami. I've been running this dinner theater here for ten years now, I don't want word to get around that Henry Gardella is financing a dirty movie. Not that it'll be dirty."

"It won't, I promise you."

"And I don't want the boys to get wind of this, either. Do you know who I mean by the boys?"

"No. Who do you mean?"

"The boys," he said, and brought his fingers to his nose, and bent the nose sideways. "The ones who'll shoot you in the kneecap if they think you're moving in on their territory. Keep this quiet, keep it discreet, keep it tasteful."

"I will,"

He wondered if she'd object to his throwing up her serious gray skirt, teach her what he meant by taste.

That was back in September.

Now, on the fourth day of December, he sat in his office at the Candleside Dinner Theater, and wondered what had happened to the goddamn film.

Prudence Ann Markham dead, and nothing to show for his money.

He'd personally budgeted the movie at a hundred and seventy-five grand. He'd figured five men—camera, lighting, sound and two grips—at twenty-eight days, a ten-to-twelve-hour day, for about thirty-five thousand. He'd figured another twenty-five for the actors. Renting the equipment would cost seventeen. The sixteen-millimeter stock, processed and printed, would cost about ten thousand, figuring a six-to-one burn ratio, though Prue kept saying ten-to-one would be better. The quarter-inch sound stock would cost another six to seven hundred bucks. He had to figure something like ten bucks a day per person to feed the crew and the actors. Federal Express charges for shipping the negative to a lab in New York or Atlanta and the dailies back to Florida would come to something like fifteen hundred. All the later lab work—quarter-inch to mag, sixteen to thirty-five millimeter, opticals and so on—would be another forty to fifty grand. A hundred and fifty grand in all, give or take a penny here or there, with an additional twenty-five going to her as a bonus on delivery of the final cut.

Being dead was her own business. Dumb husband decides to kill his wife, who the hell knew why? Maybe she was playing around outside the marriage. You got these quiet, serious types, they turned out to be screamers in bed. Not their own beds. Always somebody else's bed. Screamed loud enough to wake up the whole neighborhood.

He'd written checks to her production company—The Prudent Company—each and every week of the shooting. Wrote the first one on the third of October, wrote checks every damn week after that, kept writing them right up to the Friday before she died.

So where was the film?

What the hell had she done with the film?

He figured he'd have to drive over to Calusa, do some looking around.

He didn't like the idea.

Calusa was boring, except when dumb cunts were getting themselves killed.

Matthew would have gone to Otto Samalson, but Otto Samalson was dead.

He would have gone to May Hennessy, the Chinese lady who'd been Otto's assistant at Samalson Investigations, but Otto's family had dismantled the business and sold off the furniture and equipment the moment his will was probated, and the last Matthew had heard, May had moved to Hong Kong.

There were only a dozen detective agencies in the city of Calusa, population fifty some-odd thousand, and so the choices were limited. The private detective he decided to use was a young black man named Warren Chambers, recommended by Benny Weiss who was indisputably the best criminal lawyer in town.

Warren had been a police officer in his native St. Louis, and had been living in Calusa for the past three years, where he'd done security work for several firms before opening his own agency. He was a soft-spoken man in his mid-thirties, his shy, reserved manner and his horn-rimmed glasses giving him the look of an accountant rather than what one imagined a private eye should look like. Beanpole tall, a former basketball player for the University of Missouri, which he'd attended for two years before joining the St. Louis P.D., Warren still moved like an athlete, and seemed uncomfortable in the lightweight business suit he wore to his first meeting with Matthew. His eyes were the color of his skin, as dark as loam, and they watched Matthew intently as he spoke. Matthew liked people who *listened*. Warren Chambers was a listener. Which perhaps accounted for his reputation as a careful and accurate investigator.

"The cameraman's name is Vaughan Turner," Matthew said. "the lighting man is Lew Smollet. The sound man is Mark Wiley. That's the nucleus crew she normally used. Here are their addresses, they all live right here in Calusa." He handed a sheet of paper across the desk. "I'm also giving you copies of the State Attorney's witness list and the witnesses' statements—I'll need your help there, too. There are only two of them. Both of them live right next door to Markham. Velma Mason lives in the house on the right. Her statement says she saw Markham breaking the glass on his own kitchen door on the night of the burglary. Positive ID, she's been living next door to him for seven . . ."

"What kind of visibility that night?" Warren asked.

"That's one of the things I want you to find out."

"Okay, who's the second witness?"

"Man named Oscar Raddison. Lives in the house on the left. Claims he saw Markham burying something in the backyard on the night of the murder. That was what gave them probable cause for the search warrant."

"Where does our man say he was?"

"At the movies. Twin Plaza One, the South Dixie Mall. And later on at a bar."

"Got home when?"

"Around midnight."

"Is that when this guy saw him?"

"No, he saw someone at eleven-fifteen."

"Burying the clothes and the knife?"

"No, just burying *something*."

"Didn't identify the something as bloody clothing? Or a bloody knife?"

"No."

"Again, you want to know whether a positive ID was feasible. I'll get on that right away. Did the police find any bloodstains in Markham's car?"

"There's nothing in the lab reports about bloodstains in his car."

"How do they figure he drove all the way from Rancher Road to his house without leaving bloodstains in the car? I mean, if he was wearing these clothes soaked with blood . . ."

"I don't know what they have in mind," Matthew said. "They're not obliged to disclose how they plan to hang him."

"They'll have to work pretty damn hard to explain his car being clean."

"The best way to explain it is to say he didn't kill her."

"Anybody see him at the movies?" Warren asked. "Or later in the bar? In his *blood*stained clothes?" Light sarcasm in his voice. Matthew smiled.

"Not that he knows of."

"So we're still looking for an alibi."

"Anyone who might have seen him on the night of the murder, yes."

"That'll be like searching for a needle in a haystack," Warren said, "but I'll do my best. Do you have a picture of him?"

"Just this one," Matthew said, and opened the top drawer of his desk and took out an eight-by-ten black-and-white photograph of Markham standing alongside his wife on a beach someplace. "I had it enlarged from a recent snapshot."

"I wish we had one without his wife in it," Warren said. "Her picture's been all over the papers, it might scare off a potential witness. But let's say we *do* come up with somebody who'll say,

'Yes, I saw this fellow buying a ticket there at Twin One,' or 'I saw him eating a hot dog later there in the South Dixie Mall,' or having a drink in the bar . . . what's the name of the bar?"

"Harrigan's."

"What'd he drink? Did he tell you?"

"A Tanqueray martini. Very dry, straight up, with two olives."

"Just the one drink?"

"Just the one."

"So, okay, suppose somebody says, 'Yeah, I saw him.' I'm not so sure that'll stand up. The prosecution'll tear into him, remind him that the murder took place back in November and can he be *sure* this is the man he saw, can he be positively *certain* because we are dealing here with a brutal murder, sir, and I know you understand the gravity of the charge against the defendant. *That* kind of legal bullshit."

Matthew smiled again.

"Anyway, it's perfectly reasonable to believe that the man went to a movie alone because his wife was working, and stopped for a drink later, and *didn't* see anyone he knew or anyone who knew him. There's nothing wrong with that story." Warren picked up the witness statements, read both carefully, and then looked across the desk at Matthew again. "Judging from this lady they've come up with, they're gonna claim Markham *faked* the burglary," he said. "Lady saw him breaking into his own house, that's what they're gonna try to show. The man stole his own clothes and the knife because he planned to use them in a murder ten days later. Where'd he say he was on the night of the burglary?"

"A friend's house."

"From when to when?"

"Nine to eleven."

"And got home when?"

"Around eleven-thirty."

"And this lady says she saw him breaking in at *ten*-thirty, right?"

"According to her statement."

"So if we can show Markham was with his friend—what's the guy's name?"

"Alan Saunders, lives out on Whisper Key."

"Have you talked to him yet?"

"On the phone. He seemed vague about the exact time Markham left him."

"Uh-oh."

"Yeah."

"Okay if I take a run at him?"

"I'll give you his address," Matthew said.

"Because if we can nail down these times, we're home free regarding the burglary. Either that, or we have to find the burglar. Maybe if we find the burglar, we also find the killer."

"We're not obliged to find the killer," Matthew said.

"But it sure wouldn't hurt," Warren said. "Let me ask around downtown. I've got a few friends in the police department who enjoy schmoozing with a former big-city cop. Maybe I can come up with some other unsolved burglaries, same M.O., who knows? It's worth a shot. Who'll be talking to these two witnesses? You or me?"

"I planned to drop in on Mrs. Mason later this afternoon."

"Maybe I'll have something on what she could've seen or not seen by then. I'll check the papers, find out what the weather was like, what kind of moon there was, anything that might have affected visibility. I may even run over to the house tonight, see if there's a street lamp, or floods in the backyard, or a light over that kitchen door. Be nice if we could knock out her identification that way, wouldn't it?"

"There's something you should ask Mrs Markham's crew when you talk to them," Matthew said.

"What's that?"

"What they were working on. And where she stored the film."

"Okay, let me get started." Warren said, and rose suddenly, unfolding the long length of his body from the chair. He extended his hand. "Let's keep in touch, Mr. Hope," he said, and smiled. "It's gonna be nice working with you."

They shook hands.

"Call me Matthew," Matthew said.

"And you call me Warren," Warren said.

CALUSA POLICE DEPARTMENT

WITNESS STATEMENT

Case No: 84–2207–CF–A–S9
Date: 11–21–86
Time: 0120 hours

I, Velma Judith Mason, residing at 1141 Pompano Way, Calusa, Florida, do hereby make the following voluntary statement to
Det. Morris Bloom #714 and _____ who have/has identi-
fied themselves/himself to me as Detective(s) of the Calusa Police Department.
I make this statement without having received any reward, nor have I been made
an offer of reward for making this statement. No threats, force or promise have
been made to induce me to make this statement.

Q: November 21st at 0120 in the morning. Would
you please state your full name?

A: Velma Judith Mason.

Q: Mrs. Mason, are you familiar with the people
who live at 1143 Pompano Way? That is the
house next door to yours, isn't it?

A: Yes, it is.

Q: Do you know the people who live there?

A: Yes. Prue and Carlton Markham. I know them.

Q: How long have you known them?

A: I've been living there for seven years now. I
met them shortly after I moved in.

Q: Seven years ago. You've known them all that
time?

A: Yes.

Q: And, of course, you would be able to recognize
either one of them . . .

A: Oh, yes.

Q: If you saw them on the street, or in a restaurant or . . .

A: Anyplace. They've been my neighbors for seven years. We were in and out of each other's houses all the time.

Q: Now Mrs. Mason, can you tell me in your own words what you saw on the night of November 10, that was a Friday night. Were you home that night?

A: I was.

Q: What were you doing at approximately ten—thirty on the night of November 10?

A: I was watching television.

Q: Do you remember what show you were watching?

A: Yes. A movie on cable. A murder mystery. I like murder mysteries.

Q: Where is your television set located, Mrs. Mason?

A: In the living room.

Q: Is your living room on the side of the house that faces the side door of the Markham house?

A: Yes.

Q: That would be the south side of your house, would it not? Facing the north side of the Markham house.

A: I'm not good at directions. My living room . . .

Q: Well, would it be correct to say that your living room windows open on the side of the Markham house where the side door is located? The door leading into the Markham kitchen?

A: Yes, that's correct.

Q: And if you looked through one of your living
    room windows, could you see the side door of
    the Markham house?

A: Yes, I could.

Q: All right, please tell me what you saw and
    heard on the night of November 10.

A: The first thing I heard was glass breaking. I
    thought it was coming from the television
    set, because there was a lot of action going
    on. But then I realized it was coming from
    outside.

Q: Outside your house?

A: Yes. The sound of glass breaking.

Q: What did you do when you heard the sound?

A: I went to the window and looked out.

Q: Looked out where?

A: Toward the Markham house.

Q: Toward the side door of the Markham house?

A: Yes.

Q: Are there glass panels on the side door of the
    Markham house?

A: Yes. Well, on my house, too. These louvered
    panels in the upper half of the door.

Q: Louvered glass panels.

A: Yes.

Q: Could you clearly see the side door of the
    Markham house from where you were standing at
    the window?

A: Oh, yes. It's only ten, fifteen feet away.

Q: And what did you see?

A: I saw Carlton Markham standing at the side door. With a hammer in his hand.

Q: Are you sure it was Carlton Markham?

A: Well, of course. I've known the man for seven years.

Q: What was he wearing?

A: Gray trousers and a blue sports jacket. And a hat. One of those little straw snapbrim fedoras.

Q: What color was the hat?

A: Same color as the jacket. Blue.

Q: What was Mr. Markham doing?

A: Just standing there. At least for a minute or so. Then he reached into where the louvered panels were broken, reached inside the house . . .

Q: When you say the panels were broken . . .

A: That must've been the glass I heard breaking.

Q: But could you *see* the broken panels on that side door?

A: Oh, yes.

Q: And you say Mr. Markham reached in where the panels were broken . . .

A: Yes. Reached in with his hand.

Q: Was he wearing gloves?

A: No. I didn't see any gloves.

Q: What happened after he reached in?

A: He opened the door.

Q: And then what happened?

A: He went into the house.

Q: Did you see any lights go on after he went into the house?

A: No, I didn't.

Q: Did you see Mr. Markham *leaving* the house?

A: No. I went back to the movie. I figured he'd lost his key or something and had to break the glass to get in.

Q: You didn't call the police, did you?

A: No, why should I? It was Carlton going inside his own house.

Q: But there *were* police cars later on, weren't there?

A: I don't know. I understand there was a burglary, but I went to bed right after the movie went off. I didn't see any police cars.

Q: Okay, thank you, Mrs. Mason. (tape stops)

Signature: *Velma J. Mason*   **Witnessed by:** *Det. Morris Bloom*

Time completed: _0145_   **Witnessed by:** *Det. Cooper Rawles*

Christmas in Florida never felt right to Matthew. They decked out Main Street in holly and pine, and hung a big Santa Claus in a sleigh over the three-way intersection at the Cow Crossing —which actually *had* been a cow crossing back when the town was incorporated—but without snow it didn't mean a damn. He realized the very *first* Christmas was celebrated in a climate not too much different from Florida's, but to *his* way of thinking

56

Christ should have been born at the North Pole. Today was the fourth day of December, and Velma Mason's house was already decorated for Christmas. Wreaths in the windows facing the street, lights strung in the Norfolk pine on the front lawn, little plastic Rudolph the Rednosed Reindeer sitting alongside a small hibiscus bush. She answered the doorbell on his third ring, stood just inside the closed screen door, peering out at him.

"Mrs. Mason?" he said.

"Yes?"

Woman in her late sixties, he guessed, wearing eyeglasses, a flowered housedress, and sandals. She looked startled. Faded blue eyes opening wide behind the thick-lensed glasses, the better to see you, my dear. Behind her, a Christmas tree winked its lights near a screened lanai at the back of the house, and Matthew heard a television set blaring a game show at four in the afternoon.

"My name is Matthew Hope," he said. "I'm the attorney defending your neighbor."

"Yes."

Still defensive. Screen door closed. Arms folded across her chest now. Keep the big bad lawyer out of the house.

"I've read the statement you made to the police . . ."

"Listen," she said, "have you got some kind of identification?"

Matthew took out his wallet, opened it, and extended his card to the closed screen door. Mrs. Mason opened the door, took the card, and squinted at it. On the unseen television set inside the house, someone seemed to have won six thousand dollars.

"All right to come in and ask you a few questions?" he said.

"I guess," she said, and opened the screen door wider. She did not give him back his card.

He followed her into the house. It smelled of Florida mildew, old age, and stale cigarette smoke. The Christmas tree near the lanai looked pathetically scrawny and severely underdressed. Rattan furniture. Soiled throw pillows. Beyond the lanai, another house in the development was scarcely hidden by bougainvillea. Mrs. Mason looked at the television screen, her back to him, and then turned off the set.

Silence.

"Well, have a seat," she said, managing to sound reluctant, suspicious and rude, all at the same time.

He sat.

"I want you to know right off," she said, "that I think Carlton killed her. I also want you to know that what I told the police is the absolute truth." She hesitated, and then said, "I liked Prue a lot." She took a package of cigarettes from the pocket of her dress, shook one loose, lighted it—nicotine-stained fingers, Matthew noticed—and let out a stream of smoke. "So what do you want to know?" she said. "I'm not about to go back on anything I told the police, if that's why you're here. I can never understand why lawyers take on cases defending murderers, anyway," she said, and shook her head.

"Well," Matthew said, "everyone's entitled to a fair trial with a proper defense. Which is why we have to ask these questions, even though you've already answered most of them."

"Yes, well, let's just get it over with," she said, "I don't want to miss any of my shows."

"Yes, ma'am, I'll be as brief as possible," Matthew said, and immediately opened his briefcase and took out his tape recorder. In what he felt was a seamless introduction, he said, "I know you're familiar with these gadgets," and smiled, and started the tape going, and immediately said, "Mrs Mason, on the night of the burglary at the Markham house, did you . . . ?"

"There wasn't any burglary," she said.

"Well, a burglary was reported to the police," Matthew said. "Did you happen to . . . ?"

"That doesn't make it a burglary," she said, "it being reported."

"Did you talk to any policemen that night?"

"No, I did not."

Defiantly. Aiming her words straight at the recorder, chin jutting. Good, he thought.

"A detective named Morris Bloom didn't interview you that night, did he?"

"No, he did not."

"So you didn't have an opportunity to discuss what you'd seen until much later, is that right?"

"Not until the night of the murder."

An assertive nod. Another puff on the cigarette.

58

"Were you questioned here at the house?"

"Well *first*, yes. Then I went downtown with Detective Bloom, and he taped what I'd already told him here."

"Did you *volunteer* information about what you'd seen on the night of the burglary?"

"No, Detective Bloom asked me about it. And it wasn't a burglary."

"He knew a burglary—or whatever you choose to call it—had taken place, is that right?"

"That's right."

"And asked you if you'd seen or heard anything that night?"

"Yes."

"Before that—before Mr. Bloom asked you about it—had you discussed what you'd seen with anyone else?"

"No, I knew there'd been some kind of fuss next door, but I supposed Carlton had straightened it out with the police who came around. I mean, explaining to them it was him breaking into his own house."

"You're sure it was Mr. Markham?"

"Positive."

"You saw him clearly?"

"Plain as day."

"He was standing at the side door, is that right?"

"Yes."

"With a hammer in his hand."

"Yes."

"He'd just broken the louvered glass panels, isn't that what you said?"

"Well, if you hear the sound of breaking glass, and you look out your window, and you see someone standing at the door with a hammer in his hand, then you've got to figure he's the one who just broke the glass, don't you?"

"And that's just what you figured."

"That's just what I figured."

Another nod. Pleased with herself, pleased with the way she was handling this.

"Did you call over to him?" Matthew asked.

"What do you mean?"

"Did you open your window and call over to him?"

"No. Why should I? It was a man getting into his own house. I knew who he was, it was none of my business."

"You didn't open the window?"

"No."

"The window was closed, is that right?"

"Yes, it was very chilly that night. It started getting cold down here in October, the end of October. All my windows were closed."

"But you were able to hear the sound of breaking glass? Even with all your windows closed?"

"I have very good ears, thank you."

"So when you looked through this closed window, you saw a man facing the door, is that right?"

"I saw Carlton facing the door, yes."

"With a hammer in his hand."

"Yes."

"And he was wearing gray slacks and a blue jacket and a blue straw hat."

"Yes."

"Had you ever seen him wearing those clothes before?"

"Except for the hat."

"You saw him wearing gray slacks and a blue jacket."

"Oh, sure. Lots of times."

"Did you ever see him wearing a blue hat?"

"No."

"Or *any* kind of a hat?"

"I really can't say. I didn't watch Carlton day and night to see what he was wearing."

"Did you notice the color of his hair?"

"No, he was wearing a hat. I just told you."

"You know that Mr. Markham is blond, don't you?"

"Of course I know. I've lived next door to him for seven years."

"Was this man blond?"

"I told you, he was wearing a hat. But he was Carlton, all right. I ought to know Carlton."

"How can you be so sure it was Mr. Markham?"

"His build, his height, his weight, his posture, the way he was standing, the way he moved . . . it was Carlton, all right."

"Did you see his face?"

Mrs. Mason hesitated. She stubbed out her cigarette, lighted a fresh one, blew out a stream of smoke.

"Mrs. Mason? Did you see his face?"

"Yes," she said.

"When?"

"What do you mean when? I saw him standing there . . ."

"Yes, but you said he was facing the door, didn't you? He'd just broken the glass louvers, and was facing the door. I'm assuming that when he reached in to unlock it, he was still . . ."

"I know I saw his face."

"When?"

"It was Carlton."

"Mrs Mason, did he turn away from the door at any time? Did he turn to look at you? While you were standing at the window?"

"I know it was Carlton."

"Mrs. Mason, at any time while you were looking at this man, did you clearly see his face?"

"I saw him clearly *all* the time. He was standing about where the Christmas tree is, only about that far away."

"I asked if you had clearly seen his *face*."

"If I recognized him as Carlton, then I must have seen his face, isn't that so?"

"Are you asking *me* whether or not you saw his face?"

"I'm just saying it's common sense . . ."

"You're saying if you identified the man as Mr. Markham, then you must have seen his face. You're not saying . . ."

"That's right."

"You're *not* saying that you saw his face and were therefore able to identify him as Mr. Markham."

"That's the same thing, isn't it?"

Not the same thing at all, Matthew thought. "Mrs. Mason," he said, "were you wearing your eyeglasses while you were watching television?"

"Yes. And I was wearing them when I saw Carlton, too."

"Didn't take them off when you went to the window, did you?"

"I *never* take them off. They're bifocals."

"Are they new glasses?"

61

"New? I've been wearing glasses since I was twelve years old."

"A new prescription, I meant."

"If you're trying to say these are new glasses I wasn't used to or something, then you're barking up the wrong tree. I've been wearing these same glasses for the past three years now. And I see fine with them, thank you."

"Mrs. Mason, do you remember if there was a light burning over the Markham kitchen door on the night of the burglary?"

"First off, there *wasn't* any burglary. It was Carlton going into his own house. And next, they *always* left a light on over that door. That's the door they usually went in by. There's no garage, just the carport, and they walked right from there to the side door."

"Is that what Mr. Markham did on the night of the burglary?"

"What do you mean?"

"Walked from the carport to the side door?"

"I don't know what he did. I only saw him when he was standing there outside the door. And it wasn't a burglary."

"Did you see his car? In the carport?"

"I didn't look for his car."

"Well, you would have noticed a car if it was there, wouldn't you?"

"I didn't notice a car. I wasn't looking for a car."

"Not Mr. Markham's car or anyone's car, is that right?"

"Not any car at all. I heard glass breaking and I looked out toward the side door. I didn't look toward the carport."

"Which is close to the side door, isn't it?"

"Close enough, but I wasn't looking for a car. I was looking to see who it was broke the glass on that kitchen door."

"What time did you go to bed that night, Mrs. Mason?"

"Right after the movie went off."

"Which was when?"

"I don't know when. It was when the movie went off. Eleven o'clock, I guess."

"You went directly to bed at eleven o'clock, is that right?"

"Directly to bed, yes."

"Did you hear a car coming into the Markham driveway at any time after you went to bed?"

"No, I didn't. I'm a sound sleeper. Fall right off to sleep, and stay dead to the world till morning."

"You were asleep at eleven-thirty?"

"*Sound* asleep."

"Then you wouldn't have heard Mr. Markham if he came home at that time."

"He *didn't* come home at that time. He came home around ten-thirty. And broke the glass on his side door. And went into the house."

"Did you hear any police cars arriving later that night?"

"No."

"Did you hear Mrs. Markham's car when she got home later that night?"

"No."

"All you saw or heard, then, was the sound of breaking glass and a man entering the . . ."

"It wasn't just *any* man," Mrs Mason said firmly. "It was Carlton Markham."

Whose face you never saw, Matthew thought.

4

A sure indication of progress in the city of Calusa, Florida was the new sign outside the Public Safety Building. It stated—in bold white letters on a blue field—that this was the POLICE DEPARTMENT, a blunt admission for staid Calusa, whose citizens chose to believe their elected place of residence was as crime-free as Eden had been before the serpent did his number.

Nor was the large sign hidden, as had been its smaller predecessor, by the leaves of the pittosporum bushes that flanked the brown metal entrance doors of the building. It stood on a metal post close to the sidewalk and perpendicular to the building, so that it could be seen from either direction of approach, clearly visible during the day and illuminated at night. POLICE DEPARTMENT; it shouted. Here we are, folks. You got troubles, come on in. Matthew had troubles. He nodded in brief approval, and then walked into the building and directly to the elevator bank.

Detective Morris Bloom was waiting for him on the third floor. Today was the eighth of December. The men hadn't seen each other since the end of last May, a long time between drinks. Their handshakes, their smiles of greeting were genuinely warm. It wasn't until they were seated in Bloom's office (hung with photographs of his derring-do in Nassau County, where he'd worked before moving south) that Bloom said, "I hear you had a run-in with Rawles." He was referring to some heated words exchanged between Matthew and Bloom's colleague, Cooper Rawles, back in June while Bloom was on vacation.

"I guess you might call it that," Matthew said.

"I'm sorry to hear that," Bloom said.

He did look extravagantly sorry. Then again, he always looked sorrowful, his mournful brown eyes—overhung by shaggy black eyebrows and straddling a nose that had been broken more than once—seeming perpetually on the edge of tears. Bloom dressed as though he were an undertaker in a cold climate, favoring dark suits that hung forlornly on his huge frame. He was an inch over six feet tall, and he weighed easily a solid two-twenty, with broad shoulders and the oversized knuckles of a street fighter. Matthew had learned only recently that he'd worked as a detective out of New York's Ninth Precinct, no garden spot, before he'd moved to Nassau County. He could visualize Bloom tossing Alphabet City dope dealers on their asses. Bloom had taught him everything he knew about the so-called "manly" art of self-defense. Matthew now knew how to break someone's arm without working up a sweat. Maybe that was manly. In any event, he would have entrusted his life to Bloom without a second thought.

"Coop told me you were sticking your nose in a narcotics case, is that right?" Bloom said.

"A good friend of mine was killed, Morrie. I was trying to find out why."

"Well, I don't want to compound the felony, Matthew, but . . ."

"Then please don't."

"But investigating homicides is police business."

"So I was informed."

"You're getting sore again, right? Don't. I'm your friend. But Coop's a friend, too, and I wish you two would get along better."

"He's going to like me even less after today," Matthew said. "I'm about to stick my nose in again. Officially, this time."

"The Markham case, right? I hear you've taken him on."

"I have."

"I wish you hadn't. He's guilty as homemade sin."

A Southern expression. Detective Morris Bloom was going native.

"Morrie, I have a few questions to ask you."

"Shoot," Bloom said.

"The Markham murder took place in Calusa County . . ."

"It did."

"But not in the city of Calusa."

"That's right."

"The Sheriff's Department detective who filed the original report was a man named Jonas Crier."

"Good cop," Bloom said.

"And his report indicated that he met with you here at the Public Safety Building after he'd taken Markham's statement on the night of the murder."

"He did."

"And that he gave you a taped copy of that statement."

"True."

"Why?"

"Because we were investigating a burglary that had taken place at the Markham house ten days before the murder."

"How did he know that?"

"I told you. He's a good cop."

"Come on, Morrie."

"Okay. One of our cars was patrolling Sunrise Shores on the night of the murder. Saw a Sheriff's Department car in front of the Markham house, stopped to see what the trouble was, thought an assist-officer might be called for. He spoke to Crier, mentioned there'd been a burglary there a week or so ago. Crier picked up on it, called me, and then came to see me after he'd talked to Markham."

"Did he turn the homicide investigation over to you at that time?"

"No."

"Did he turn it over to you at *any* time?"

"No."

"Morrie, you were present at the Q and A on the night Markham was arrested . . ."

"Together with Haggerty from the State Attorney's office, and Detective Sears from the Sheriff's Department."

"The one who caught the initial squeal out on Rancher Road."

"Yes. Crier was his supervisor. When Sears figured he was looking at a homicide, he called back home, asked Crier to come on out."

"Was Sears officially in charge of the investigation?"

"Right."

"Then why were you present at the Q and A, Morrie?"

"Because I was the one who handled the burglary investigation."

"Why was your presence so essential? No one even *asked* my client about the burglary."

"He volunteered the information, that's correct. I was there to ask specific questions if it came to that."

"But it never came to that."

"No, it never did. What are you looking for, Matthew? A

technicality? I had every right to be there at the Q and A. You know I handled the burglary, I'm sure Haggerty sent you my report when you filed for discovery."

"He did. He also sent me the witness statement you took from Mrs. Mason. Why were you assigned to take her statement?"

"Because I handled the burglary."

"Oh, I see, the burglary had become your specialty, is that it?"

"Matthew, never get sarcastic with a native New Yorker. He can beat you at it in spades."

"Since you're the burglary mavin," Matthew said, ignoring the advice, "then I'm sure you know my client claims the clothes you later found in his backyard were stolen from his house ten days before the murder. Together with the murder weapon. He stated that at the interrogation."

"He did. But Matthew, that's not going to help you, believe me. We've got him cold. Those clothes, that knife . . ."

"They were stolen ten days before the murder, Morrie."

"So your man says. But we found them buried in his backyard the day *after* the murder."

"Any fingerprints on the knife?"

"I'm sure your discovery demand asked for any reports from experts . . ."

"It did."

"Well, didn't you read the report from the lab in Tampa? The knife was wiped clean, blade *and* handle both. But that didn't stop the techs from finding bloodstains—it's almost impossible to get rid of *all* traces of blood on a knife with a wooden handle. Those stains match the stains on the clothes, Matthew, your *client's* clothes, and the stains are Prudence Markham's blood type, Matthew, type B, Matthew. If ever there was a . . ."

"How'd you happen to go digging in the backyard?"

"Matthew; what kind of game are you playing with me here? Didn't you demand documents relating to search and seizure?"

"You know I did, Morrie. My client told me Sears went in there with a search warrant."

"He did."

"On the strength of what a next-door neighbor claimed to have seen?"

"That was enough for the judge who granted the warrant,"

IN THE CIRCUIT COURT
CALUSA COUNTY
STATE OF FLORIDA

AFFIDAVIT FOR SEARCH WARRANT

BEFORE ME, A JUDGE of the entitled COURT, Personally came:
Det. Ralph Sears   , **a POLICE OFFICER of the CA-LUSA COUNTY SHERIFF'S DEPARTMENT, to me well known, and who being by me first duly SWORN, made APPLICATION for SEARCH WARRANT, and in support of this APPLICATION on OATH, says:**

That he has REASON TO BELIEVE, and DOES BELIEVE that the LAWS of the STATE OF FLORIDA, particularly:

FLORIDA STATUTE(S):	782.04
to wit:	Murder

have been violated by: Carlton Barnaby Markham,

and it is the AFFIANT'S BELIEF that EVIDENCE or FRUITS OF THE CRIME are presently to be found in the following described location, to wit: 1143 Pompano Way in subdivision named Sunrise Shores, located within the city limits of the City of Calusa, County of Calusa, State of Florida. 1143 Pompano Way is located approximately 100 feet east of Flanders Avenue and 200 feet north of the intersection of Flanders Avenue and 12th Street. The structure is a one-story building, beige in color with a darker brown color trim. Its front door faces west and is of aluminum construction. The number 1143 is on the wall of the structure to the right of the door. The structure is on a lot approximately 60 feet wide by 100 feet long. To the right of the lot is 1141 Pompano Way, owned and occupied by Velma Judith Mason, a widow. To the left of the lot is 1145 Pompano Way, owned and occupied by Mr. and Mrs. Oscar Raddison.

Affiant specifically requests warrant to

search a flower bed approximately 4 feet wide and 12 feet long, planted with gloxinias and gardenias and located approximately 20 feet from the rear wall of the structure at 1143 Pompano Way, approximately 6 feet from the easternmost property line marked by a row of wax myrtles.

THAT THE REASON FOR THE AFFIANT'S BELIEF IS AS FOLLOWS:

1. On 11/20/86 at 2245 hours, affiant responded to a radio call from Deputy Sheriff Cpl. Gandy and proceeded to 8489 Rancher Road where the body of a stabbing victim later identified as Prudence Ann Markham was lying in the parking lot outside Anvil Studios, a motion picture studio.

2. In the company of Det. Supervisor J. Crier, affiant proceeded to 1143 Pompano Way, arriving at 0020 hours, 11/21/86. After consultation with occupant, Carlton Barnaby Markham, affiant proceeded with him and Det. Crier to Southern Medical Hospital where positive identification of victim was made.

3. Det. Crier then proceeded to Calusa P.D. Affiant drove Mr. Markham home, arriving at 1143 Pompano Way at 0115 hours on 11/21/86. Affiant then interviewed neighbors on right and left of Markham house.

4. Oscar Raddison, occupant of 1145 Pompano Way did state as follows: (See witness statement attached.)

   That on 11/20/86 at 2315 hours, he was awakened by the sound of someone in the backyard of 1143 Pompano Way. He went to his window, looked out, and saw Carlton Barnaby Markham digging in the flower bed behind the house.

That on 11/20/86 at 2320 hours, he saw Carlton Barnaby Markham burying something in the flower bed and then shoveling earth over it.

WHEREAS, AFFIANT PRAYS that a **SEARCH WARRANT** be issued, according to **LAW**, commanding all and singular, the **SHERIFFS** and their **DEPUTIES, POLICE OFFICERS** acting within their jurisdictions, and **STATE ATTORNEY INVESTIGATORS**, acting within their judicial circuits of the **STATE OF FLORIDA**, either in the day time or the night time, or on Sunday, as the **CIRCUMSTANCES** of the occasion may demand or require, with the proper and necessary assistance, to **SEARCH** the previously described location, and **SEIZE AS EVIDENCE**, any of the following:

Any and all evidence that may relate to the murder of Prudence Ann Markham,

in order that such EVIDENCE may be used in the PROSECUTION OF THE CRIMINAL LAWS OF THE STATE OF FLORIDA.

Pit R. Sears

AFFIANT

SWORN AND SUBSCRIBED before me, the <u>21st</u> day of <u>November</u>, **A.D., 19**<u>86</u>.

Salvatore N. Monello

ACTING AS MAGISTRATE

IN THE CIRCUIT COURT

CALUSA COUNTY

STATE OF FLORIDA

STATE OF FLORIDA, COUNTY OF CALUSA
I hereby certify that the foregoing
is a true and correct copy of the
original filed in this office.
Witness my hand and seal this:
NOV 21 1986

_____

D.N. Terrill, Clerk of Circuit Court

_____ *H. Lackler* Deputy Clerk

Bloom said, and sighed heavily. "Matthew, this was a very brutal murder, the M.E. counted fourteen stab and slash wounds, that's *rage*, Matthew, that's pure, unadulterated *rage*. I wish we weren't on different sides of this one, I really do."

"I don't think he did it, Morrie."

"I'm sure he did," Bloom said, and sighed again.

Matthew was just leaving his office that Monday afternoon when the telephone rang. He muttered "Shit," put down his briefcase on the table inside the door, crossed to his desk, lifted the telephone receiver, and said "Hello?"

"Matthew, hi. It's Susan."

His private line. His former wife.

"I hear you've taken on a big one," she said.

"Who told you?"

"Eliot McLaughlin."

The attorney who had handled the settlement agreement for her. The man responsible for siphoning off a goodly amount of Matthew's income each and every month of the year. Matthew bore him no ill will. He merely wished he would get hit by a bus.

"When can I see you?" she said.

Last spring, while Matthew was "sticking his nose into a narcotics case"—as Bloom had so delicately put it—he and Susan, for reasons still not clear to either of them, had begun seeing each other again. "Seeing" was a euphemism. They had, in fact, begun sharing each other's company in a manner a good deal more

71

intimate and passionate than when they'd been man and wife. Go figure it. He hadn't seen her since Thanksgiving Day, when together they'd placed a long distance call to their daughter Joanna at her boarding school in Massachusetts. The Simms Academy. It sounded like a military school for recalcitrant girls. Actually, it was quite good, and Joanna—after more than two months of bitter complaining—seemed genuinely beginning to enjoy it. This may have had something to do with the fact that she'd met a seventeen-year-old quarterback named Thomas Darrow, and they had become what Joanna called "a thing." Joanna was fourteen years old. Matthew could only hope "a thing" wasn't another euphemism.

He and Susan had become "a thing," too.

In provincial, gossipy Calusa, there were not many people who didn't know that Matthew and Susan were seeing each other again. Some people cynically maintained that Matthew's fresh desire had less to do with Susan's obvious charms than with an urgent need to get rid of his onerous alimony burden. Other people genuinely wished that the sound of wedding bells would be heard again in the not too distant future. Still others gave the new (or old, or both) lovers two, three months at the most. But Matthew had been seeing Susan for six months now and when he heard her say, somewhat breathlessly, "When can I see you?" there was an odd little stirring in his groin that he could not attribute to indigestion.

"Tonight?" he said.

"We have a lot to talk about," she said.

"What time?" he asked.

"What time do you get out of there?"

"I was just leaving the office. I'm running out to Sunrise Shores to interview a witness."

"What time do you think you'll be finished?"

Matthew looked at his watch.

"Four o'clock?" he said.

"Come directly here," Susan said. "Do not pass Go, do not collect two hundred dollars."

Oscar Raddison was a man in his late fifties, his blue tank-top shirt bulging with the muscles of a weight lifter, his red running shorts revealing thighs like oaks, his body resplendently tanned, his brown eyes sharp and intelligent. He admitted Matthew to the house, showed no reluctance at all to having their conversation taped or to later giving the same information in a deposition. He even offered Matthew a drink. This was at two-thirty in the afternoon. Matthew declined and Raddison went to the refrigerator to get himself a Heineken beer.

He popped the can, and then said, "I'd like to be finished here before Lou gets home. Louise. My wife. We're going out to an early dinner."

"I won't take much of your time," Matthew said, and started the recorder. "Mr. Raddison, according to the witness statement you gave Detective Sears of the Sheriff's Department . . ."

"Nice feller," Raddison said.

"I haven't met him yet," Matthew said.

"Smart, too," Raddison said. "When I told him about that flower bed, he knew right off he'd find incriminating evidence there."

"You told him this when he came back to the house on the night of the murder, isn't that correct? Well, it would have been morning by then, about a quarter past one in the morning."

"Yes."

"About the same time Detective Bloom was talking to Mrs. Mason."

"I wouldn't know about that."

"Well, her witness statement was taken at twenty after one that morning."

"I still wouldn't know anything about it. Did *she* see him, too? Out there in the garden?"

"What did *you* see?" Matthew asked.

"Carlton. With a spade in his hands. Digging up the garden."

"What time was this?"

"I woke up around a quarter past eleven . . ."

"Was it the sound of the digging that woke you up?"

"No. I had to pee. I wake up two, three times a night to pee. A side effect."

"Of what?"

"I've got a high cholesterol problem, the doctor put me on medication. One of the side effects is excessive urination. I usually go to bed around nine, wake up around eleven, eleven-thirty, then again at two, then again at five, then sleep in till eight, when

I get up and go over to Nautilus. Flatulence is another side effect."

"I see," Matthew said.

"I guess I shouldn't be saying all this with that machine going, but it's the truth."

"So you woke up to go to the bathroom at eleven-fifteen . . ."

"Right. And that's when I heard someone digging in the yard next door."

"Someone. Not Mr. Markham."

"Well, I didn't know it was Carlton till I took a look."

"When was that?"

"After I finished peeing."

"Looked from where?"

"The bathroom window."

"Was the light on in the bathroom?"

"No, I never turn it on, it'd wake Lou. I just find my way there in the dark—I've got this little night light in the hall, I never have a problem."

"So the bathroom was dark."

"Yes."

"And you looked from the bathroom window over to the Markham backyard, is that right?"

"That's what I did."

"Where *is* the bathroom, Mr. Raddison?"

"Just down the hall from the bedroom."

"At which end of the house?"

"Right there," Raddison said, and pointed.

"That would be the southern end of your house, wouldn't it? The end farthest from the Markham house."

"The southern end, right. But it's not all that far. And I've got good eyesight, check with my doctor if you like. Never wore glasses in my life, still don't. I saw Carlton plain as day. Digging there in the flower bed."

"With what?"

"Well, with a spade. Or a shovel. Either one, I couldn't tell you which."

"He had a shovel, or a spade, in his hands."

"Yessir."

"And was doing what with it?"

"Digging a hole in the flower bed."

"How large a hole?"

"Big enough to hold them clothes and the knife, I reckon."

"You didn't *see* clothes or a knife, did you?"

"No. I just saw him burying something. But when they came to dig it up . . ."

"But you didn't actually *see* Mr. Markham burying *clothes*, did you? *Or* a knife?"

"I saw him digging a hole in the flower bed, and putting something in it, and shoveling dirt back over it, and then putting the flowers back in place on top. That's what I saw."

"*Not* bloody clothing or a bloody knife."

"That's what they found in that hole, isn't it? So that's what Carlton had to be burying."

"Did you at any time clearly see what he was burying?"

"Nossir."

"*Whatever* he buried . . . where was it while he was digging the hole?"

"On the ground."

"You saw it on the ground?"

"Nossir, I didn't see it. His back was to me, it must've been at his feet there on the ground. The clothes and the knife. He didn't go back into the house for it, so it had to be on the ground."

"You didn't see him going back into the house?"

"Not specifically, no."

"What do you mean by 'specifically?'"

"I mean I didn't see him actually going back into the house. But he was headed for the front door. Later on. When he was finished out there."

"You said a moment ago that his back was to you while he was digging."

"Yessir."

"Then you didn't see his face."

"Not while he was digging."

"What did he do when he finished digging?"

"Picked up this stuff on the ground and dropped it in the hole."

"Was his back still to you? When he picked up the stuff on the ground?"

"Yes, it was."

75

"And when he dropped it in the hole, was his back still to you?"

"Yes, it was."

"Then you didn't see what he dropped into the hole . . ."

"I already told you that."

"And you didn't see his face, either."

"Not then."

"Did you see his face when he was shoveling the earth back? Or when he was replacing the flowers?"

"No, not then neither."

"When *did* you see his face, Mr Raddison?"

"When he was leaving the yard."

"You saw his face as he was leaving."

"Yes. Turned toward me for a minute, and I saw his face."

"For a minute?"

"Yessir."

"Exactly a minute?"

"Well, a minute, more or less."

"Which was it, would you say now? More or less?"

"I didn't time it."

"Could it have been less than a minute?"

"It could've, I really can't say. He turned away from the flower bed and started walking toward the side of the house . . ."

"Going where?"

"Well, I don't *know* where. I guess back to bed."

"Walking toward the side of the house, you say?"

"Yes, the space between our two houses."

"Leading toward the street?"

"Well, he could've got to the street that way. But he could've got to the front door of his house, too."

"Did he have the shovel with him? Or the spade?"

"He did."

"But you don't know, do you, whether this man you saw— let me rephrase that. When this man finished digging, did you see him enter the Markham house?"

"No, I didn't. He passed out of my line of vision. When he started walking between the houses."

"Toward the street."

"Or the front door."

"Well, did you hear a door opening or closing?"

"No, I didn't. I went back to bed."

"Were you in bed when Detective Sears came to talk to you?"

"I was."

"Asleep?"

"Asleep, yes. I pee, then I go right back to sleep."

"Didn't you find it strange, though? Mr. Markham digging in the flower bed at that hour?"

"I thought it was a little peculiar, yes. But they were peculiar people, anyway, you know. Man runs a clock shop, woman makes movies." Raddison raised his eyebrows. "Besides, at the time, I didn't know she'd been killed. I didn't learn that till Detective Sears got here."

"And you felt it important to tell him what you'd seen in the Markham backyard."

"Well, sure. wouldn't *you* think it was important? Man's wife is stabbed to death, and then you see him burying clothes and a knife? I mean, that's . . ."

"But you *didn't* see what he was burying."

"Well, that's what they dug up."

"A few minutes ago, Mr. Raddison, you said you thought Mr. Markham might have gone back to bed after he finished whatever he was doing there in the backyard. Do you . . . ?"

"He wasn't out there taking a leak, that's for sure. He was burying the clothes and the knife."

"But do you have any reason to believe he'd been in bed *before* he started the digging? He wasn't wearing pajamas, was he?"

"No, he wasn't wearing pajamas."

"What was he wearing?"

"Dark clothes. Pants and some kind of windbreaker, blue or black, but dark anyway."

"Was he wearing a hat?"

"Nossir, no hat."

"Did you see his hair?"

"Yessir."

"What color was it?"

"Yellow as corn," Raddison said, and Matthew's heart sank.

He could not concentrate on what Susan was saying.

They were sitting out by the pool of what used to be the house he shared with her, the house he was in fact sharing with her more and more frequently these days, sipping martinis and watching the tail end of a glorious sunset, and she was telling him that Joanna would be coming home from school on the nineteenth, which was less than two weeks away, and they had to figure out what they were going to tell her about themselves because Joanna was a smart cookie who would realize in an instant that these weren't the same two lively antagonists she'd left back in September when she'd gone off to school.

He was thinking there were too many things missing in this case.

He was wondering how the State Attorney planned to account for all those missing things.

"The trouble, of course," Susan was saying, "is that until *we* know what the hell we're doing, how can we explain it to Joanna? Do *you* know what we're doing, Matthew?"

"I know what I *wish* we were doing," he said.

"That isn't true," she said, and looked him dead in the eye. Full pouting mouth that gave the impression of a sullen, spoiled beauty, brown hair worn sleek and long again after her experiment with a wedge cut, dark eyes somber in a pale oval face, studying him now. "You're a million miles away, aren't you?" she said. She put her hand on his arm. "Tell me."

"No, no," he said. "Let's figure out the Joanna thing first, I know you . . ."

"We've got eleven days before she gets here. What's bothering you, Matthew?"

"Too many things missing," he said, and shook his head.

"Are you talking about the Markham case?"

"Yes."

"What's missing?"

"Do you ever go anyplace without a handbag?"

"Yes."

"Where?"

"Exercise class. I throw my wallet in the glove compartment."

"Anyplace else?"

"Yes. The beach. Same thing."

"But around town . . ."

"I carry a bag. Why?"

78

"Why isn't the State Attorney concerned about that missing handbag?"

"What missing . . . ?"

"They find a woman dead in the middle of nowhere, fourteen stab and slash wounds. Her car is parked twelve feet from where she's lying dead on the gravel. The car is locked, the police have to break into it. Her handbag isn't in the car. It isn't in the studio, either. So where is it?"

"Was there a wallet in the car?"

"No. Nothing. No film, either."

"Film?"

"She was editing film out there on Rancher Road. So the film is gone and her handbag's gone, and her keys are gone, so I have to assume the *killer* took all those things, am I right?"

"Well, yes, that sounds reasonable."

"So why doesn't it sound reasonable to Haggerty?"

"Haggerty?"

"The man who's handling the State's case."

"I'm not following you, Matthew."

"I mean, *he's* got to assume the same thing I'm assuming, doesn't he? That's the *killer* took those things."

"Yes?"

"But he thinks my *client* is the goddamn killer! So what happened to all that stuff my client had to have taken if he *is*, in fact, the killer? Where is it? If Haggerty had it, he'd have listed it on his response. So he hasn't got it. So where is it? And where's the shovel or the spade or whatever the hell my client allegedly used to bury his clothes in the backyard? I have to assume he hasn't got that, either."

"So? Can't he make a case without . . . ?"

"Oh, he's sure as hell going to try. But why isn't it *bothering* him?"

"Should it be bothering him?"

"It's bothering *me*. Because it makes me wonder what he's *got*, Susan. Never mind what he *hasn't* got. What has he *got*? What has he got that makes him feel so confident he can send Markham to the electric chair? He hasn't got the missing handbag, the missing keys, the missing film, the missing shovel. The killer's got those, Susan. But Haggerty doesn't seem to give a damn. He's got two witnesses and he's got some bloody clothing and a bloody knife, and he seems content to be going with that alone. Why?"

"Why don't you *ask* him what else he's got?"

"He's already told me what he's got. My demand for discovery specifically listed tangible papers or objects."

"Well . . . is he allowed to hide anything?"

"No, he can't do that."

"He's required to tell you . . ."

"Yes. Required by law. He doesn't have to tell me how he plans to try his case, of course, but . . ."

"But he does have to tell you what evidence he has."

"Yes."

"Well, *has* he told you?"

"I have to assume so."

They were silent for several moments. The sun was all but gone.

She said, very softly, "I wish I could help you, Matthew."

"I'm sorry to bother you with this crap," he said.

They fell silent again.

"What else is bothering you?" she asked.

He sighed deeply.

"Tell me."

"I may be in over my head, Susan. I may be sending an innocent man to the chair because I don't know what the hell I'm doing."

"You *do* know what you're doing," she said.

"Maybe."

"*Is* he innocent?"

"I have to believe that."

"But do you?"

"Yes."

"Then you won't let them kill him, Matthew," she said, and took his hand.

In bed with her, the case was still with him.

The reflected light from the pool outside flickered on the ceiling. In his mind, there was the same elusive wavering of light, slivers of evidence fitfully moving at the whim of the wind. Her long hair fell over his face, her mouth covered his. His eyes were closed, the splintered light danced behind them. She lowered herself onto him.

And for just a little while, he forgot the handbag, forgot the keys and the film, forgot the shovel, forgot all the missing things, and there was only the here and the now, and the remembered heat of this woman he once loved and perhaps now loved anew.

And then he thought again. The *killer* has those things.

The sign on the wooden post read:

ORCHIDACEOUS
Exotic Orchids

There was an address lower on the post: 3755. A dirt road to the left of the post ran off Timucuan Point Road through thick clusters of cabbage palm and palmetto. The place used to be a cattle ranch, and the entire property—a thousand acres of it—was still fenced with barbed wire.

The dirt road ran past a lake shrouded by oaks.

There were alligators in the lake.

The dirt road continued along the side of the lake for half a mile, where it ended at the main house. The greenhouses were set back two hundred yards from the main house, across from what used to be the stables when there were still horses here. Situated catty-wampus to the greenhouses was a windowless, unpainted cinderblock structure that housed the generator. The building was perhaps fifteen feet wide by twenty feet long. It had a dirt floor. It had a louvered ventilating slit high up on one of the walls. A naked light bulb hung in the center of the space, operated from a switch just inside the thick wooden door. There was a padlock on the door.

He unlocked the door and snapped on the light.

She was wearing only high-heeled red leather boots. Soft red leather. The kind of boots that looked rumpled at the ankles. Tall boots that folded over onto her thighs. She had long red hair a shade darker than the boots. A tuft of even darker red hair curled in a wild tangle at the joining of her legs. She sat in the dirt in one corner of the room, behind the generator, her hands tied behind her, her legs bound at the ankles. A three-inch-wide strip of adhesive tape covered her mouth. Her eyes flashed green in the dim glow of the hanging light bulb.

"Evening Puss," he said.

He closed the door behind him, and set down the shopping bag he'd been carrying.

"Miss me?" he asked.

He came toward her, walking around the generator, and she cowered away from him, trying to move deeper into the corner. He looked down at her. He shook his head, clucked his tongue.

"Look at how filthy you've got," he said, "sitting here naked in the dirt. Shame on you. Woman who always took such good care of herself."

He kept looking down at her.

"Maybe I ought to take that tape off your mouth," he said. "You're not gonna scream if I take it off, are you? Not that anybody'd hear you. You promise you won't scream if I take off the tape?"

She nodded.

"You're sure now? You won't scream like you done last time?"

Another nod, green eyes wide.

"Well, then, let's just take off the tape," he said, and crouched beside her. He smiled, twisted her head, found the end of the tape, and with one violent tug ripped it free. She bit her lip, stifling a scream.

"Hurts, don't it, when I pull the tape off that way?" he said.

She was still biting her lip.

"You hear what I said? Hurts, don't it?"

"Yes," she said.

He nodded, got to his feet again, and went back to the door where he'd left the bag.

"You hungry?" he asked.

"Yes," she said.

He carried the bag back to where she sat in the corner.

"Bet you're hoping there's a sandwich in here, ain't you?" he said.

"Yes," she said.

"Bet you'd eat scraps I spit on, wouldn't you?" he said.

She did not answer.

"I asked you a question," he said.

"I'm not *that* hungry," she said.

"Don't get sassy," he said.

"I'm sorry, I . . ."

"Did you hear me ask you a question?"

"Yes, and I'm . . . I'm sorry I was . . . if I sounded sassy."

"Or maybe you don't want me to feed you, is that it?"

"No, I want you to."

"Want me to what?"

"Feed me."

"Even scraps I spit on?"

"No, I . . . I don't want to eat anything like that."

"You getting sassy again?"

"No, I'm not, really. I'm sorry. But . . ."

"'Cause you better not get sassy with me, Puss."

"I won't, I'm sorry."

"I thought you was a woman'd take just about *anything* in her mouth," he said. "Isn't that so? That thou hast transgressed against the Lord thy God, and hast scattered thy ways to the strangers under every green tree?" He scowled and looked at her mouth. "Just about anything in that mouth," he said. "And here you are turning down good, wholesome food."

"You didn't say it was . . ."

"Woman who enjoys *eating* as much as *you* do," he said. He was still scowling. He kept looking at her mouth. And then his gaze suddenly shifted to her breasts. "Oh my, are you cold, Puss?" he asked. "Or just scared?"

"Cold," she said.

"But not scared?"

She did not answer him.

"Is that why you're all puckered up like that?" he asked, and suddenly pinched the nipple of her left breast between his thumb and forefinger. "Because you're cold? Or is it because you're scared?" He squeezed the nipple hard. "Does that hurt?" he asked.

"Yes," she said.

"Oh, excuse me," he said. "So which is it?" he asked. "Cold or scared?"

"Both," she said. "Please let me go."

"You mean let you go *here*?" he said, squeezing harder. "Or let you go *period*?"

"There," she said. "Please."

"Because I *will* let you go, you know. Sooner or later. When I'm finished with you."

"Please," she said.

"Hurts, don't it?" he said.

"Yes! Please oh *please*!"

He released his grip on her.

"There," he said, and smiled. "What do you say?"

"Thank you," she said. She was gasping for breath.

"Bet you wish you had a sweater," he said, "the way this building stays so cool and all. Maybe there's a nice warm sweater in this bag. Wouldn't it be nice if I brought you a sweater?"

"Yes," she said.

"Why?" he asked.

"Because I'm cold."

"Oh. I thought maybe you were modest."

"No, I'm just . . ."

"You mean you're *not* modest?"

"That's not what I meant."

"What did you mean? Are you modest or aren't you?"

"Whatever you say," she said.

"Am I hearing sass again? Answer my question!"

"I meant . . . if *you* think I'm immodest, then . . ."

"Yes, I do."

"Then . . . then I think I'm immodest, too."

"But you don't *really* think so, do you? Not really. Thou hadst a whore's forehead, thou refusedst to be ashamed." He smiled suddenly. "Are you cold, too?" he asked.

"Very."

"And scared?"

"A little."

"Only a little? Aren't you scared I might hurt you again?"

"Yes."

"But only a little. Maybe I didn't hurt you enough. Maybe if you're only scared a teeny-weeny little bit . . ."

"I'm very scared," she said.

"You will be," he said. "You'll be very scared before I'm finished with you." He smiled again. "Poor little Puss," he said, "all naked and shivering and cold in her sexy red boots. Withhold

84

thy foot from being unshod, Puss, and thy throat from thirst. Are you thirsty?"

"Yes."

"Sure wish I had something for you to drink. Sure wish there *was* a sweater in this bag, too, but there isn't. I burned all your clothes last night."

"You didn't."

"Oh, but I did. You won't be needing clothes anymore, will you?"

"What . . . what does that mean?"

"When I let you go."

"When . . . when will that be?" she asked.

"When I'm ready," he said. "Stand up."

She leaned away from the wall, eased herself onto her knees. Struggling, she managed to shove herself into a standing position.

"Move here," he said. "Around the generator. Under the light."

She half-hopped, half-shuffled to the center of the room.

"Shall I untie you?" he asked.

"Yes, please," she said.

"No, I don't think so," he said. "Are you wondering if there's food in the bag?"

"Yes."

"There isn't."

"You said . . ."

"I said I bet you wished there was a sandwich in this bag, that's what I said."

"Yes, that's what you said."

"Something to eat."

"Yes."

"Because poor little Puss is *so-o-o* hungry, isn't she?"

"Yes."

"And thirsty."

"Yes."

"But there's nothing to eat or drink in the bag," he said. "There's only a towel and a pair of scissors."

She looked at him. He was smiling again. And suddenly she began trembling.

"Are you scared?" he said.

"No," she said.

"The towel doesn't scare you, does it?"

"No."

"Then what? The scissors?"

"Nothing."

"Then why are you shivering like that?"

"I'm . . . cold."

"No. You're scared."

He reached into the shopping bag, took a rolled beach towel from it, and unfurled it like a flag. He draped the towel over her shoulders, arranged it over her breasts.

"Modesty, modesty," he said, "naked, and ye clothed me," and reached into the bag again.

The blades of the scissors caught the feeble light from the overhead lamp.

"We don't want you getting all covered with hair, do we?" he said.

"What . . . ?"

He opened the scissors.

"And he shall pluck away his crop with his feathers," he said, and clutched a tangle of long red hair in his left hand.

5

Oh my oh my oh my, all the hurly-burly, all the hustle-bustle, all the bullshit of a movie set. Once, when Warren was still walking a beat in St. Louis, he'd pulled duty where they were shooting a movie on location, sergeant must've been paid a C-note to keep order in the streets, maybe more, but none of it filtered down to the grunts.

Man, those movie people!

He never in his life had seen people act so much like walking gods. Strutting around all puffed up with the glory and the wisdom of what they were doing. Citizens standing around goggle-eyed waiting for the star to appear. The "star" was somebody on one of the television series, you blinked your eyes he'd be gone next season. Warren had the feeling that if the director asked some lady to take her baby out of its buggy and smash his head on the sidewalk for the cameras, she'd have wet her pants and said, "Oh, yes, sir, thank you, sir, in a minute, sir, just let me comb his hair."

Same thing here.

Smalltime shit here, but the same damn thing.

Must've been something about making a movie that gave the people involved the feeling that they were rearranging the universe.

Big truck outside the house on Sabal Key, cars parked all over the street and even the sidewalk. Not a police car in sight, though any zealous cop could have handed out ten thousand summonses. Movie people didn't care. They'd park right on top of a cop's *hat*, you gave them the opportunity. Cables and lights in the truck, all kinds of heavy equipment. Warren walked right past it, up the driveway and into the front door of the house.

Never ask, never explain, that was Warren's motto.

Walk in like you belonged there, Mr. Cool, bit of a strut on, dark glasses helped.

Oh my oh my oh my, here he was back again in downtown St. Louis, except that this was the backyard of a Sabal Key

7

house and all the cameras and lights were set up around a swimming pool, and all the people running around frantically doing their godlike things were shooting a commercial for patio furniture. Didn't matter. They could've been in Rome shooting *Cleopatra*.

"Help you?" somebody asked.

"Nope," Warren said, without even turning to see who was talking to him.

"This is a movie we're shooting here," the voice said, and a body materialized in front of him, hulking, threatening.

Warren lifted his shades onto his forehead and beamed a cold, brown-eyed stare at the man. Big gorilla wearing blue jeans and a blue, sweat-stained T-shirt. A grip, no doubt. They called them grips. Lotsa muscles, no brains, the longshoremen of the movie business. Warren reached into his pocket, took out his wallet, and flipped it open to the police shield they'd given him when he retired from the St. Louis P.D. A fraction of an inch smaller all around than the buzzer he'd worn for five years, but looking like the real McCoy when you flashed it fast.

"Checking," he said, and snapped the wallet shut, and turned away from the man, and over his shoulder said, "Where's Vaughan Turner?"

"Setting up a shot there," the man said. "Is there some problem?"

"No problem," Warren said, and walked away from him, skirting the edge of the pool, which did not look too terribly inviting on a December day with the temperature at fifty-six degrees. Sunny Florida, he thought.

He knew better than to interrupt any of these shakers and movers when they were setting up a shot. Very temperamental, movie people were. You told them a hydrogen bomb had just been dropped over Calusa Bay, they'd say, "Move aside a minute, we have to adjust this flag."

They were adjusting flags now, trying to get the lighting right. He'd picked up a lot of jargon back there on location in St. Louis, you hang around all day scratching your ass, if you had any brain at all in your head you began to understand the language these Martians spoke. They were shooting with an Arriflex on a tripod, what they called "sticks" because the legs were wooden. The man looking through the viewfinder was

Vaughan Turner, one of the men Warren was here to see, Prudence Ann Markham's usual cameraman (or cinematographer, if you wanted to get fancy). Turner looked through the viewfinder, and then looked up and said, "Flag it on this side."

He was talking to the lighting director, Lew Smollet, another man on Warren's list. Smollet attached a square of white fabric to the gobo, cutting the light, and turned to look at Turner, who was peering through the viewfinder again. "Take it up to the top," Turner said, and Smollet adjusted the flag again, and Turner nodded, and said, "Okay, I want all these cables to go."

A pair of grips began lifting and moving the cables that were snaked on the terrace. A girl in a bikini stood looking bored and chilly near the outdoor lounge chairs that were the *real* stars of the show. Smollet went over to her and held a light meter to her face.

"What've you got?" Turner asked.

"Eleven-sixteen split," Smollet said.

"Okay, I'm ready," Turner said. "Where's Bud?"

"Right here," a man said.

Obviously the director. Chief of all the Indians. Wearing jeans and a white, long-sleeved Ralph Lauren sports shirt with a little blue polo pony and rider on the left pec. Smoking a cigarette which he ground out on the terrace now. Turner stepped aside as he looked into the viewfinder.

"Looks fine," he said, "I'm ready. Jane?"

"Ready," the girl in the bikini said.

"Danny?"

A man in swim trunks, standing near the diving board, signaled with his hand.

"Okay, let's go for it," Bud said.

"Quiet, please," the assistant director said.

A man sitting behind a sound cart—this had to be Mark Wiley, the third man Warren was here to see—took off his headphones and said, "Are we doing playback?"

"No," Bud said. "Stand by, people."

It was suddenly very quiet. Out beyond the pool, a pelican swooped in low over the gulf.

"Roll camera," Bud said.

"Rolling."

"Roll sound."

"Speed."

"Mark it," the A.D. said.

A man holding a clapstick and standing just in front of the actress in the bikini said, "Thirteen B, take six," and brought the black-and-white clapper down onto the slate on which the same information was chalked.

"Action," Bud said, and the actor in the swim trunks began walking toward the actress in the bikini, who eased into one of the lounge chairs. As the actor approached her, he said, "Hi, honey," and leaned in to kiss her. "Ready to relax on our Tropical . . . ?"

"Hold it, hold it," Wiley said from behind his console, and looked out over the gulf. "Is there a plane out there?" he said. "A motorboat? Something?"

"Cut it, cut," Bud said.

"Yeah, it's a boat," the A.D. said.

Bud sighed. "Okay, let's wait," he said.

Warren sighed, too.

They waited until the boat had gone by, and then they went through the same "Quiet please, standby, roll camera, roll sound mark it, action" rigmarole another time. Bud cut again to tell his actors that he wanted the dialogue between them *before* Jane sat in the lounge chair. They rolled again, and again Bud cut to tell Smollet he wasn't getting much of a shot, and would he please take another reading? Smollet put the light meter on the actress and gave him a new reading of eleven. They rolled again, and cut again, and rolled again, and cut again, and finally got the shot on the twelfth take.

"Okay, let's move all these toys," Bud said, and the grips started struggling the camera and the lights to the other side of the terrace.

Warren walked over to where Turner was telling one of the grips to "head wrap" something.

"Mr Turner?" he said.

The thing Mose and Tick liked most in the whole world was money.

They also liked girls and dope, but they figured if you had money the girls and the dope followed as the night followed the day.

PUSS IN BOOTS

Ever since they'd heard about Prue's murder almost three weeks ago, they'd been following the case with more than casual interest, reading the newspapers, watching all the television coverage. It seemed that her wimpy husband who ran a clock shop had done the lady in. It seemed this very same wimp was being held without bail and being defended by yet another wimp who, from what Mose and Tick could gather, had hardly ever handled a criminal case in his entire career. It seemed that the State Attorney's Office was going for the death penalty, and it further seemed they had a damn good chance of getting it.

None of this interested Mose and Tick.

Money interested them.

Which was why the *omissions* in the news coverage captured their singular attention.

When a good-looking, twenty-eight-year-old blonde gets murdered in staid Calusa, that's headline news, man. Especially if the murder is a stabbing. Knives are scary. Hardly anybody knows what it feels like to get shot, but *everybody* has cut himself accidentally and knows how that can hurt, man, and knows how the sight of all that blood welling up can turn you pale with fright. Stabbings made good headlines. Newspapers loved headlines dripping blood. Television reporters loved talking about stabbings, too. They could show pictures of pools of blood soaking into the ground, and they could show the bloody knife, or a reasonable facsimile of the bloody knife, turning slowly under a harsh light that sent little pinprick reflections of terror darting out into the viewer's living room. Brutal stabbings brought out the very best in news reporters.

Which is why Mose and Tick found it peculiar that none of the newspaper or television reporters had once mentioned that the good-looking twenty-eight-year-old blonde who'd been found floating in her own blood had been directing a skin flick.

It seemed to Mose and Tick that such news was the stuff of excellent headlines, especially in this day and age when the Attorney General's Commission on Pornography had decided there was a definite link between obscenity and violence. Was it possible that no one *knew* she'd been engaged in lighting and framing and shooting delicate footage on the intricate art of tickle and grab? Could that possibly be *possible*? Or were the police and the State Attorney's Office simply playing it smart?

91

Neither Tick nor Mose had ever met anyone in Florida law enforcement who could be considered smart. Still, *were* they withholding the skin-flick bombshell till they could explode it to startling effect and great astonishment at the trial?

Mose and Tick strongly doubted this premise.

Their conclusion was that no one in law enforcement knew about the movie Prudence Ann Markham had been working on since the twenty-ninth day of September.

Which meant that no one in law enforcement was in possession of either the negative or the work print.

Which meant that a very valuable property was kicking around out there someplace in Calusa.

Which was what interested them about the murder of Prudence Ann Markham.

Which was what brought them to Calusa on the afternoon of December ninth.

To find Connie.

Because maybe *she* knew where the film was.

Warren was upset.

He came to Matthew's office at two o'clock Tuesday afternoon, and began telling him what was bothering him. Together, the two men had a lot of things bothering them.

"To begin with," Warren said, "she didn't use those three guys from Calusa. The crew you gave me. I went out to see them this morning, they're shooting a commercial out on Sabal Key, using some guy's house with a swimming pool there. You ever been on a movie set? It's a madhouse. But I finally managed to talk to all three of them in bits and pieces. None of them worked with her on this film she was shooting. Only one of them —the cameraman, Vaughan Turner—even *knew* she'd been working on a movie. I think he was annoyed that she hadn't hired him. But he didn't know what the project was, thought maybe she wasn't even shooting it here in Calusa. The other two were surprised to learn she'd been working on something without them. *And* annoyed. *More* than annoyed. Outright *pissed*, in fact. I got the feeling this was a pretty close bunch who'd worked together on a lot of stuff, and they didn't like the idea of her hiring other people. Anyway, *they* weren't on the movie, and they didn't know who was."

"Did they have any suggestions?" Matthew asked.

"One of them—the lighting man, Lew Smollet—said there are good people in Tampa, Miami and Jacksonville, but he didn't know whether Prue actually knew any of them since she usually worked out of Calusa."

"Any names?"

"No, but I can get on that if you want me to. Florida's a Right-to-Work state, and none of these guys *have* to belong to unions if they don't want to. But I know there are two different unions for all these technicians, and maybe I can get a list of active members in Florida, if you want me to go that route."

"I think we ought to know who she was working with, don't you?"

"Sure. You don't want me to track down everybody who ever made a movie in the state of Florida, though, do you?"

"Well . . ."

"Because, Matthew, that would take a long, long time. Has a date been set for the trial yet?"

"Not yet."

"When are you guessing?"

"The calendar's pretty full, we may not get on till February."

"Well, that's not too bad then. I'll get started on it, see what unions these guys might have belonged to, get a list of their people. So that's the first thing. We struck out with her crew."

"What's the second thing?"

"The second thing is crime was up seventeen percent in Calusa County this year, and my cop friends down the old station house tell me it's mostly drug related, which means there're quite a few unsolved junkie burglaries, and if the burglary at the Markham house was a junkie on the prowl who later knifed Prue and stole her pocketbook, we've got a long, tough row to hoe. I'll keep snooping around, but turning up the burglar looks very slim. Are you still listening? I've got more bad news."

Matthew sighed.

"I know just how you feel," Warren said, nodding. "But here it is, anyway. On November tenth, the moon was in the second day of its first quarter. That's a fairly good moon, Matthew. Plus it was a clear night, lots of stars."

"How about the night of the murder?"

"Four days past full moon. Full mooon was on the sixteenth.

Still pretty big on the twentieth. And another clear night, Matthew. In short . . . ."

"Excellent visibility on both nights."

"Yes."

"Wonderful," Matthew said.

"I knew you'd be thrilled. There's more."

"Spare me."

"I went to see Alan Saunders—the friend Markham was planning a fishing trip with? The guy he was supposed to've been with on the night of the burglary? From nine to eleven? Remember?"

"Yes."

"Saunders now seems sure that Markham left him at around ten, a little after ten. Which would put him back at his own house at ten-thirty or thereabouts, just when Mrs. Mason says she saw him breaking into his own kitchen."

"Terrific," Matthew said.

"You want the worst of it?"

"How much worse can it get?"

"Much," Warren said. "When you talked to Markham, did he mention anything about his first wife?"

"No. *What* first wife?"

"Lady he was married to ten years ago, when he was fresh out of college and living in New Orleans."

"What about her?"

"She was stabbed to death, Matthew."

The State Attorney's Office used to be a motel.

It sat across the street from a ball park that once was used for big-league spring training before the team moved to Sarasota. Now teams sponsored by beer companies played there. The old motel sat behind what used to be the old courthouse. You could still see the twin white towers of the old courthouse—now an office building—from the courtyard surrounded by what used to be motel units but were now offices for the State Attorney's staff. There were palm trees and bougainvillea and hibiscus in the courtyard. It was a sunny afternoon, and you expected to see sleepy-eyed lovers strolling out of the old motel rooms into the courtyard. A brown plastic sign with white lettering was fastened to the wall of one of the old motel units. It read:

PUSS IN BOOTS

OFFICE OF THE STATE ATTORNEY
TWELFTH JUDICIAL CIRCUIT
Skye Bannister
807 Magnolia Boulevard
Office Hours Monday–Friday
8:30 A.M.–5:00 P.M.

It was 3:30 P.M. when Matthew opened the door to the office and told the receptionist he had an appointment with Arthur Haggerty. She asked him to please have a seat. He took a seat on a bench and looked around. You could see where the old motel walls had been knocked down to make a bigger space. There were still marks on the ceilings and walls. An open door at the far end of the room revealed a motel bathroom beyond it: pink sink, toilet and tub. He could see ledgers stacked in the tub.

"Mr. Hope?"

"Yes?"

"Mr. Haggerty will see you now."

"Thank you," he said.

She nodded to a closed door. He went to the door and opened it. No walls knocked down this time. A single motel room disguised as an office. Big desk stacked with legal papers in blue binders, shelves crowded with reference books, a wall covered with diplomas. A law office. But you could still see the telltale tub in the bathroom.

Behind the desk stood a big red-faced man with his hand extended. Unruly brown hair and bright blue eyes. Beer belly hanging over his belt. Wearing tan slacks with brown loafers, a yellow shirt open at the throat, tie pulled down, cuffs rolled up onto his forearms. His grip was firm and dry and strong.

"Arthur Haggerty," he said, "nice to meet you. Have a seat."

Matthew sat in a wooden chair on the other side of the desk.

"What can I do for you?" Haggerty asked.

Matthew got straight to the point.

"Mr. Haggerty," he said, "when I made my demand for discovery, I specifically asked for any police reports made in connection with this case. You . . ."

"You're referring to the Markham case, of course."

"Yes, that's the case I'm handling."

"I'm handling several cases at the moment, you see," Haggerty said, and smiled. "So. How can I help you?"

"I've just come from a visit with my client," Matthew said. "He corroborates information I now have about a murder that took place in New Orleans ten years ago, on which extensive police reports were made, none of which were provided by you in your response."

"Are you referring to the knife murder of Jennifer Bowles Markham, the wife of Carlton Barnaby Markham at the time?"

"I am."

"What's your question?"

"Why wasn't I supplied with those New Orleans police reports?"

"You asked for police reports in connection with the case. By 'the case' I assumed you meant the murder of Prudence Ann Markham. That's the case you're handling, isn't it?"

"Mr Haggerty, let's not fence around here, okay?" Matthew said. "We're not in court yet, and you're not playing to a jury. My client tells me he was questioned endlessly about the murder of his former wife. He tells me that for almost a full week he was considered a suspect by the New Orleans police . . ."

"Yes, he was."

". . . but that finally the police decided he'd had nothing to do with the murder."

"Well, the case remains unsolved, if that's what you mean."

"You know exactly what I mean, Mr. Haggerty. He wasn't arrested and he wasn't charged. The murderer was never found."

"Mmm," Haggerty said.

He tented his hands and looked over them.

He waited for what seemed an extraordinarily long time.

Still playing to an absentee jury.

"You know, of course," he said at last, "that Markham never came up with a reasonable alibi for where he was while his wife was being stabbed twenty times on a deserted back street in the French Quarter."

"The New Orleans police . . ."

"Yes, well, the New Orleans police. Markham claimed he

was at the *movies*, Mr. Hope. Does that sound familiar to you?"

"He *was* at the movies."

"So he says. And so the police up there apparently accepted. Because they could find no evidence to support a homicide charge. No weapon, no bloody . . ."

"No *anything*. They were newlyweds, they'd only been married for four months, the whole damn experience was shattering to him."

"I'm sure it was. Especially since his wife was playing around with another man."

"Markham didn't know that," Matthew said, "and I don't want to argue an investigation which for good reason never resulted in an arrest. All I want to know . . ."

"Yes," Haggerty said.

Matthew looked at him.

"Yes, I *do* plan to introduce this material at the trial."

"Then why didn't you send me the New Orleans police reports?"

"A communications failure," Haggerty said, and shrugged. "I thought you were interested only in any *Calusa* documents relating to . . ."

"I'd like those reports now," Matthew said.

"Sure," Haggerty said. "I'll have them delivered by hand later this afternoon. Anything else?"

"You know, of course . . ."

"Sure. I'll be waiting for it. And then we'll let a judge decide, okay?"

6

IN THE CIRCUIT COURT OF
THE TWELFTH JUDICIAL CIRCUIT
CALUSA COUNTY, STATE OF FLORIDA

STATE OF FLORIDA,   )
     Plaintiff   )

             vs,   )   CASE NO. 84-2207-CF-A-S9

CARLTON B. MARKHAM,   )
     Defendant   )

_____

MOTION IN LIMINE

COMES NOW the Defendant, by and through his undersigned attorney, and moves this Honorable Court in limine to instruct the State and all his counsel not to mention or make reference as to the following and for the following grounds:

1.   That the Defendant at any time prior to the date of this incident was questioned by the New Orleans Police Department regarding the murder of his former wife, Jennifer Bowles Markham.

2.   That the Defendant at any time prior to this incident in the above-styled charge told the New Orleans police that he was at a movie theater on the night of the murder of his former wife, Jennifer Bowles Markham.

3.   That the Defendant's former wife, Jennifer Bowles Markham, at any time while married to the Defendant was seeing other men.

4.   That the above information is inadmissible at trial, and therefore would be highly prejudicial to the defense if such information was known to the jury, either by the State, voir dire, opening argument or by witnesses listed by the State in the above—styled cause.

5.   This motion should be granted because there is no other way this problem can be properly handled before the Court in the above—styled cause and in all probability such an attempt to do such evidence would result in a mistrial.

WHEREFORE, the above—named Defendant respectfully requests this Honorable Court to instruct the State and all his counsel not to mention, refer to, or interrogate concerning, or attempt to convey to the jury in any manner, either directly or indirectly any of the above—mentioned facts relative to the Defendant's background or former wife's background without first obtaining permission from the Court outside the presence of the jury and the hearing of the jury; and to further instruct the State and all his counsel not to make any reference to the fact that this motion has been filed and granted; and further to instruct the State and all his counsel to warn and caution each and every one of his witnesses to strictly follow these instructions.

MATTHEW HOPE, Attorney
Summerville and Hope
333 Heron Street
Calusa, Florida

BY: _Matthew Hope_

CERTIFICATE OF SERVICE

I HEREBY CERTIFY that a true and correct copy of the foregoing has been furnished to the Office of the State Attorney, 807 Magnolia Boulevard, Calusa, Florida, this the <u>10th</u> day of <u>December</u>, 1986.

Matthew Hope

Matthew Hope
Attorney for the Defendant

"Denied it, huh?" Frank said.

"Said he saw no reason why Haggerty shouldn't be allowed to introduce this material.

"What's this about the former wife playing around?"

"The New Orleans cops had evidence that she'd been dating a musician up there. They were trying to get Markham to admit he knew about it. That was their attempt at establishing motive."

"*Did* he know about it?"

"Not according to him."

"Is Haggerty going to try showing the *new* wife was playing around too?"

"I've got his list of witnesses. I don't see anything there to indicate . . ."

"How about this Mason woman who lives next door? You think *she* might testify along those lines?"

"I . . . well, that never occurred to me."

"Then why'd you ask that the material be excluded?"

"Because I didn't want a jury thinking what the New Orleans cops thought. That Markham killed a hot-pantsed wife who was cheating on him."

"Married only four months, huh?"

"Yeah."

"Messing around with a musician."

"A junkie trumpet player."

"I'd have killed her myself," Frank said.

"Which is just why I asked for exclusion."

"How about the guy living on the other side? Raddison, is that his name? You think *he's* got anything on Pru? He was pretty damn interested in everything going on next door. Maybe he spotted a boyfriend going in and out."

"I didn't ask him anything along those lines. I just found out about this New Orleans thing yesterday Frank."

"Well, if the material's going to be admitted . . ."

"Yeah, I know, I'd better ask some more questions."

The two men were silent for a moment.

"That movie alibi," Frank said.

"I know."

"Always at the movies while his wives are getting stabbed."

"I know."

They were silent again.

"The thing is . . ." Matthew said, and then stopped and shook his head.

"Yeah, what?" Frank said.

"No, nothing."

"Say it."

"The killer up there . . ."

"Yeah?"

"They never found him, Frank."

Another silence, longer this time.

"I know what you're thinking," Frank said.

Matthew shook his head again.

"You're thinking maybe Markham makes a *habit* of stabbing his wives. That's what a jury's going to think, you know. The minute Haggerty brings up the New Orleans murder . . ."

"Well, why the hell do you think I filed the motion?" Matthew said heatedly. "I *know* what a jury's going to think. The son of a bitch got away with *one* murder but he won't get away with *another* one."

"Never mind the jury," Frank said. "What do *you* think?"

Matthew sighed heavily.

"I don't know," he said.

So that's it, Warren thought.

Time to quit lollygagging around and get on the stick. Because this morning's demand for Notice of Alibi meant that he and Matthew had better come up with something damn soon or their

101

IN THE CIRCUIT COURT OF
THE TWELFTH JUDICIAL CIRCUIT
IN AND FOR CALUSA COUNTY, FLORIDA

STATE OF FLORIDA,   )
    Plaintiff   )

        vs,   )   CASE NO. 84–2207–CF–A–S9

CARLTON B. MARKHAM,   )
    Defendant   )

DEMAND FOR NOTICE OF ALIBI

COMES NOW THE STATE OF FLORIDA, by and through the undersigned Assistant State Attorney, and pursuant to Florida Rules of Criminal Procedure 3.200, and demands that the Defendant provide notice of any intent to rely on the defense of alibi in the above–styled cause and further states the following:

1. The offense committed, date, time and place of said offense is:
   a. Offense Committed: Murder in the first degree.
   b. Date of Offense: November 20, 1986.
   c. Time of Offense: 2230–2300 hours.
   d. Place of Offense: 8489 Rancher Road, Calusa, FL.

2. The State demands that Defendant provide within said notice of alibi specific information as to the place at which the Defendant claims to have been at the time of the alleged offense and, as particularly as is known to the Defendant or his attorney, the names and addresses of the witnesses by whom he proposes to establish such alibi.

I HEREBY CERTIFY that a true copy of the foregoing Demand for Notice of Alibi has been furnished by <u>hand</u> to: <u>Matthew Hope, Esq.</u>, <u>Summerville and Hope, 333 Heron Street, Calusa</u>, <u>FL</u> on this <u>12th</u> day of <u>December</u>, 1986.

SKYE BANNISTER
STATE ATTORNEY

By: *Arthur Haggerty*

Assistant State Attorney
807 Magnolia Boulevard
Calusa, Florida

man would be sent to the chair on evidence as circumstantial as that supporting Aunt Hattie's phantom lover who she claimed ran off to Kansas City with a high yeller girl named Suella Simms. Aunt Hattie believed that her long-ago lover actually existed, and as evidence of his substantiality had shown the entire family letters presumably written while he was a soldier in Italy during World War II. The letters were from someone named Abner Cross, who Warren later learned had been killed in action in the year 1945 and who couldn't possibly have run off to Kansas City or anyplace else in the year 1949. But try telling that to Aunt Hattie.

And try telling Skye Bannister, via Arthur Haggerty, that Carlton Barnaby Markham, on the night of November twentieth, coincidentally the night of his wife's brutal murder, had first been watching a movie in a theater called Twin Plaza I, in a shopping mall called South Dixie, had later wandered the mall for a bit, and had then dropped into a bar called Harrigan's where he'd watched television while sipping a single drink—*unless* you could come up with someone who could state unequivocally that he or she had actually *seen* Mr. Markham doing one or more of those things.

So that Friday night at eight-thirty P.M., thirteen days before Christmas, Warren pulled his car into the parking lot outside the mall, determined first to find a parking space—which would not be easy with all these Christmas shoppers out doing their

103

ED McBAIN

thing—and next to find someone who could positively identify Markham's photograph. This was the kind of legwork Warren had detested when he was a detective in St. Louis, the kind he *still* detested, tedious, boring, repetitive and tough on the arches. He found a parking space at last alongside a pickup truck with a shotgun on a rack across the rear window, locked his car, and went into the mall. He knew this would not be easy, and it wasn't.

He started with the young girl selling tickets at the double theater complex, Twin I and Twin II, asking her if she had been working on the night of November twentieth. The girl was chewing bubble gum. The rush of people buying tickets for the two movies that had started at eight o'clock was over and she'd been enjoying just sitting there and popping her gum until Warren walked up.

He already knew that on weekdays the movies in these particular theaters ran on a twelve-fifteen, three o'clock, five-thirty, eight o'clock, and ten-thirty schedule. Markham had told Matthew he'd caught the eight o'clock show on the night of his wife's murder, a Thursday, so at least the schedule checked out. Got out of the theater at around ten-thirty, he'd said, which also checked out. Wandered the mall a bit, then stopped for a single drink at a bar called Harrigan's, near the mall, got home at about midnight, which was a reasonable time to have made the drive to Pompano Way. But this *didn't* check out with Oscar Raddison having seen him in the backyard burying clothes and a bloody knife at eleven-fifteen. The only way Markham could have been at his house at that time was if he'd been killing his wife at ten-thirty or thereabouts, rather than doing all those other things he said he'd done.

"Who wants to know?" the girl said.

Warren flashed the St. Louis potsie.

"Routine investigation," he said.

"I work every night but Monday and Tuesday," she said. "Was this a Monday or Tuesday?"

"A Thursday," he said.

"Then I was here."

"Recognize this man?" Warren asked, and fished the eight-by-ten blowup out of its manila envelope.

Without even looking at the picture, the girl said, "You gotta be kidding."

"Take a look at it, okay?" he said.

"When did you say?"

"Thursday night, November twentieth."

"How long ago was that?"

"Three weeks ago last night," Warren said.

"And you expect me to remember somebody from *then*?"
She popped her gum.

Warren winced.

"Just take a look, okay?" he said.

The girl looked at the picture of Markham and his wife on a beach, the ocean behind them, the sky wide and blue above them.

"Both of them?" she said.

"No, just the man." And then, at once, "Why? Do you recognize the woman?"

"I don't recognize either one of them," she said. "What'd he do?"

"Nothing. Take another look."

"How many times do I have to look?"

"You didn't sell this man a ticket on Thursday night, November twentieth?"

"You know how many tickets I sell here every night?" she said. "We've got two theaters here, you know how many tickets I sell?"

"How many?" he asked.

"Millions!" she said. "All these people, they're not even *faces* to me, they're voices saying which movie they want to see, and how many tickets, and then they're hands shoving bills across the counter here, that's what all these people are."

"So you don't recognize him, huh?" Warren said.

"How many times do I have to say it?" the girl said.

"Okay to go inside and talk to the people selling popcorn?"

"You want to go inside, you got to buy a ticket," the girl said, "badge or not."

Warren bought a ticket. Never ask, never explain, he thought. Should've walked right in. He was getting old.

Older by the minute, as it turned out.

He knew he would strike out with the concessionaires, and he did.

He knew he would strike out all through the mall as well.

Markham claimed that he'd got to Harrigan's at ten to eleven. It was a five-minute drive from the mall, which meant he'd been wandering around here for fifteen minutes after the movie let out. The chances that anyone had seen him—or would *remember* having seen him even if they *had* see him—were exceedingly slim. But Warren went through the tiresome routine, anyway, consoling himself with the knowledge that he was killing time until he could cruise Harrigan's; he wanted to get there at the same time Markham claimed to have been there.

And so he checked out the entire mall, moving from store to store and fast-food joint to fast-food joint, rubbing elbows with Christmas shoppers in Bermuda shorts, T-shirts, tube tops, jeans, polyester slacks, floral-patterned short-sleeved shirts, halters, sweat suits, jogging shorts, the *haute couture* of Florida in December, flashing the picture of Markham and his wife, posing questions to people who often became indignant because he was asking them to remember all the way back to November twentieth, when here it was almost Christmas, the busiest time of the year, did he *mind*?

At a quarter to eleven, operating on the theory that regulars of any given bar generally spent the same hours there on any given night, he headed for Harrigan's.

At eleven thirty-two, he got lucky.

Depending upon how you looked at it.

Harrigan's tried to look like a genuine Irish bar on Third Avenue in New York. It succeeded in looking like a fake Irish bar in Calusa. Never mind the brass rails, and the black leather booths, and the polished mahogany, and the cut-glass mirrors, and the waiters wearing green derbies on their heads and green garters on their shirtsleeves. This was ersatz stuff, as phony as the Santa Claus who'd been shaking a bell inside the South Dixie Mall.

Markham had told Matthew he'd sat at the bar watching television and drinking just one martini before heading home at twenty to twelve, a quarter to twelve, so Warren showed his picture to all three barmaids, each of them wearing the same green derby and green-gartered shirtsleeves the waiters wore, but wearing instead of black trousers very short red skirts and red high-heeled shoes, presumably because this was the holiday season. None of the barmaids had noticed Markham in there on the night of November twentieth or on any other night, for that matter. One of them commented that Markham looked kind of cute, but she admitted she was partial to blond men. Undaunted, Warren began canvassing the patrons sitting at the bar. He got lucky, sort of, when a woman looked at the picture and said, "Oh, sure."

Warren's eyes opened wide.

"You recognize him?" he asked, astonished.

"I recognize him is right," the woman said. "Sat right next to me. Ordered a martini with two olives."

Carlton Barnaby Markham had told Matthew he'd ordered a Tanqueray martini, very dry, straight up, with two olives.

Warren closed in on her.

It was very easy to close in on her in that she weighed perhaps two hundred pounds and somewhat overspilled the stool she was sitting on. She was wearing blue slacks and a blue T-shirt with the words FAT IS BEAUTIFUL lettered on the front and back of it. Her sandaled feet were crossed on the rung of the stool. Her hair was the color of straw, falling loose over one ear, pulled back and clipped behind the other ear with a pale blue barrette. A long rhinestone earring dangled from that ear. Warren guessed she was in her mid-forties. It was sometimes difficult to tell with fat people.

"This would've been around the twentieth of November," he said. "A Thursday night."

"The twentieth is right," the woman said. "A Thursday night."

"Around ten to eleven."

"Walked in right about that time is right," the woman said, and nodded, and picked up her drink, and drank heartily from it, and then put it down and belched.

"Did he talk to you?" Warren asked.

"Nope. Just drank his martini, et the two olives, sat here watching television, paid his bill, and walked out."

"Around what time?"

"What time what?"

"Did he walk out?"

"Don't have a watch," the woman said, and showed him her naked wrist.

"Then how do you know what time he walked in?"

"*Had* a watch *then*," she said. "Had to hock it to do my Christmas shopping." She reached down for a shopping bag sitting beside the stool, hoisted it as evidence.

"You're sure this was the man?" Warren asked, and showed her the picture again.

"Positive," she said. "But he wasn't with that woman. He was alone as ice-cream."

"Ice cream?"

"Alone as ice cream is right," she said.

Uh-oh, Warren thought, and at that same moment, one of the green-derbied, green-gartered, red-shirted barmaids caught his eye and twirled her forefinger against her temple, signaling in universal sign language that the woman was nuts.

"He didn't have any stains on his clothing, did he?" Warren asked.

"Stains?"

"Yes."

"What kind of stains?"

"You tell me."

"No stains is right," she said. "Walked in nice and clean and neat and ordered a Tanqueray martini, very dry, with two olives." She swiveled on the stool, raised her hand to the barmaid who's signaled she was crazy, and said, "Let me have another one of these, please."

"That's your third one, Hannah," the barmaid said.

"What's wrong with four?" Hannah asked.

The barmaid shrugged and brought her another drink.

"Would *you* remember that?" Warren asked her.

"Remember what?" the barmaid said.

"This man ordering a Tanqueray martini, very dry, with two olives?" Warren said, and showed her the picture again.

"No, I don't remember," she said.

"Ask your friends," Warren said.

"What is this?" the barmaid said. "Are you a cop?"

"Yes," Warren said.

"What'd he do?"

They always wanted to know what a person had done. Even if you were showing a picture of a *victim*, they always asked what the person had done.

"Nothing," Warren said.

"Sure," the barmaid said skeptically. "You come in here asking about a guy supposed to have been here in November, he didn't do nothing."

"He's a friendly witness," Warren said.

"You two remember this guy ordering a Tanqueray martini, very dry, two olives?" she asked, carrying the picture to where the two other barmaids were standing near the cash register, their green-gartered arms folded across their white shirts.

"Straight up or on the rocks?" one of them asked, sarcastically, it seemed to Warren.

"Straight up," Hannah said. And then added, "Yours," and burst out laughing.

The other two barmaids were looking at the picture again.

"You remember that, do you?" Warren asked Hannah. "That he ordered the martini straight up?"

"Yep."

"A Tanqueray martini, very dry, straight up, with two olives."

"Is right," Hannah said, and nodded.

"Madam," he said, "I wonder if you . . ."

"Miss," Hannah corrected.

"Miss, excuse me," Warren said. "I wonder if I might have your full name and your address."

The barmaid was back with the picture. "Why?" she asked. "You gonna ask her out?"

"Either of them remember that martini?" Warren asked her.

"Nope." She handed back the picture. "He wants to take you out, Hannah," she said.

"Fat chance," Hanna said, and then laughed at her own unintentional pun.

"Could I have your name and address, please?" Warren said.

"Fat Hannah," the barmaid said.

"Fat Hannah is right," Hannah said.

"Fat Hannah what?" Warren said.

"Merritt," Hannah said.

Warren was already writing. "And your address?"

"Three-seventy-two Waverly."

"Here in Calusa?"

"Here in Calusa is right," Hannah said. "You want my phone number, too?"

"Please."

She gave Warren the phone number, and then winked at the barmaid. She finished what was left in her glass, belched again, struggled off the stool, said, "I better hurry on home, case my phone starts ringing." She put her hand on Warren's shoulder, gave it a friendly little squeeze, winked at the barmaid again, and walked out of the bar.

"She spent six years at Ice Cream," the barmaid told him. "Up in Tallahassee."

"Ice Cream" may have been a euphemism for "I Scream," which in itself might have been hyperbole. Both nicknames had evolved from the true and proper name with which they slant-rhymed: Iscrin. The Iscrin Institute in Tallahassee was a private mental hospital named after its founder, Dr. Theodore Iscrin. It was sometimes called "The Icepick Institute," in that an alarming number of frontal lobotomies had been performed there in the dim recent past.

A check with the facility revealed that Hannah Isabel Merritt's uncle and sole guardian had committed her to the institution in 1971. She was released in 1977, after a panel of Iscrin psychiatrists suggested to the uncle that her illness could better be controlled by drugs administered in the bosom of the family home. The uncle's name was Roger Merritt, and they found a telephone number for him in Tallahassee. He was ill himself now, scarcely audible on the telephone, but not without a wry sense of humor. He told Matthew (and Warren on the extension) that his niece's release may have been "a matter of expedient economy" on Iscrin's part since he'd fallen behind on the payment of her bills after the automobile accident that had put him in a wheelchair, debilitated his strength, and was now threatening his very life. The last time he'd seen Hannah, "poor soul," was in 1983, when she'd gone down to Calusa to take a job working in a nursery. He hoped she was okay.

"So we've got a witness who spent time in a nut house," Warren said to Matthew the moment they were off the phone. "But she damn well didn't come up with that Tanqueray martini out of a clear blue sky. What do you want to do?"

"Ask her to come in for a deposition," Matthew said. "She's all we've got."

PUSS IN BOOTS

You had to know orchids before you could love them.

Biggest of all the plant families, widest spread geographically. Ranged in height from less than an inch to eighteen feet tall. Some of them had blooms so tiny you almost couldn't see them, others had blooms ten inches across. Came in all colors except black, the good Lord knew what he was doing.

Lots of orchids blooming this time of year.

Christmas was only—well, this was already the twelfth, be Christmas in just a little while.

Lots of orchids blooming.

Most beautiful spot in the whole world was this greenhouse right here.

Beauty everywhere around him.

You walked through the greenhouse here, past the Moth Orchids, what were properly called *Phalaenopsis*, you could be anyplace they grew naturally, Formosa or India, New Guinea or the Philippines—where that *other* bitch had a million pairs of shoes. In all those shoes, had there been any boots? Red boots?

Your Moth Orchid came in reds as bright as her boots, came in oranges, too, yellows, greens, pinks. White ones with lips as red as her boots, as red as her lips. White ones with yellow lips. Spotted, striped or plain, to his mind she was the most beautiful of all the orchids.

Your Moth Orchid was very long-lasting.

He wondered how long *she* would last when he put her out.

Put her out on Christmas Day.

All these orchids should still be blooming then.

Your *Cattleya tenebrosa*. Coppery brown petal with a dusky purple lip.

Your *Cattleya* hybrids with their large white flowers and yellow lips.

Lips.

Opening wide.

Your *Cattleytonia* Rosy Jewel hanging up there in a fern basket high up in the greenhouse, nothing prettier except your Moth. Three-inch fuchsia-colored flowers in clusters of eight, nine blossoms.

The *Paphiopedilum* growing over there near the Kool-Cel unit, where the recycled water was chilly and humid. Her nickname was Lady Slipper, clear green leaves on some of them, mottled on others, big waxy flowers that looked artificial. Lady Slipper.

Your Slipper Orchid, the *Phragmepedium*, was the only one didn't remind him of a woman. Looked like an old Chinese man with a long mustache. Tall spike. Pouch instead of a lip, two long ribbonlike petals on either side of the pouch. Needed the Kool-Cel unit, too. You had to treat delicate things proper or they'd die. Beautiful things. You had to know how to take care of beauty. You couldn't abuse beauty.

He knew how much her beauty meant to her.

Long red hair—well not no more, full pouting mouth, lips as scarlet as blood, eyes as dark green and brooding as the leaves on the *Phalaenopsis schilleriana*, skin as white as the flowers of the *Amabilis*, a beautiful towering woman with pink-tipped breasts and flaring hips and long legs with white thighs and shapely calves and slender ankles, a luminous woman all red and white and pink and green, green eyes, red hair above, red hair below, red lips, pink lips, soft white skin, soft red boots, puss in boots, he didn't think she would much enjoy being ugly.

You sometimes got dazzled by your own beauty, you forgot it was God-given. He would explain that to her. It was like with orchids. You sometimes tended to overlook some of them that were ugly in appearance, you passed them by till you got to know them better, and then they took on their own characteristics and their own personalities and for all their ugliness they became interesting and beautiful in their own right.

Maybe she wouldn't mind being ugly.

7

Calusa was growing and changing, but some things remained ever and always the same.

The average annual temperature, for example, was seventy-three degrees Fahrenheit. That was something like twenty-three degrees Celsius, which only *sounded* much lower.

The average annual rainfall was fifty inches.

There were almost thirty-five miles of white sand beaches in Calusa.

Those were the constants.

Everything else was growing and changing so rapidly that a great many citizens were thinking back to ten years ago as the Good Old Days, kidding themselves into believing Calusa had been just a small fishing village when they'd moved down. Where they'd moved down from, for the most part, was Illinois, Indiana, and Ohio. Now and then you got a former New Yorker like Frank Summerville, but he was a rarity. Calusa, Florida was the American Midwest transported to the Gulf of Mexico.

More and more people kept moving down to Calusa every year.

At the time of the national census six years ago, the city's population was 48,800. Today, it stood at a bit more than 53,000. The county's population back then was 202,000. Today, it was 222,000.

Growth.

Change.

Progress.

Crime was on the increase.

This year, as Warren had reported to Matthew, it had shot up seventeen percent over the year before.

"Drug related," the cops said.

Five years ago, you could maybe buy a dime bag of heroin if you had the right connections.

Today you could buy crack right on the Whisper Key beach.

Ten years ago, the yellow pages of the Calusa telephone

directory had listed no "Escort" services. This year, there were seven of them, one of which offered Senior Discounts.

"Loose women drifting over from Miami," the citizens said.

Five years ago, there was only one topless nightclub in Calusa. It was called Club Alyce. Last year, there were two, the second one calling itself Up Front. A third topless joint had opened this year. It called itself The Naked Truth.

"We will close them all down," said Skye Bannister, the State Attorney.

On Saturda night, December 13, in the growing, changing, progressive city of Calusa, Florida . . .

George Ticknor and Mosley Jones went to The Naked Truth . . .

Matthew and Susan Hope went to the Snowflake Ball . . .

And Henry Gardella broke into the Markham house.

She wouldn't tell any of them her real name.

The name she was using for the picture was Constance Redding. Constance sounded puritanical, like Charity or Felicity, she said, which was amusing for an actress playing a woman who would screw even a squirrel. The last name referred to her flaming red hair. Constance Redding. God only knew what her real name was.

On the set, they called her Connie at first.

And then, later on, Connie Lingus.

She'd toss her red hair and smile.

Then she'd go down on Jake again.

Jake was the black guy playing the miller's son, Tom, who inherited only a cat when his father died. Connie was playing the cat. Puss in Boots. A modern-dress version, but the old fairy tale nonetheless. Jake was his real first name but his last name had been chosen by Prudence Ann Markham, *La Directrice*, as they sometimes called her, when they weren't calling her Otto, after Otto Preminger. She'd plucked the name from the pages of Hemingway's *The Sun Also Rises*. The name was supposed to be an inside joke, since Jake in the book was impotent, and Jake in their movie was insatiable. When you read the credits, you were supposed to get a chuckle out of seeing the name Jake Barnes.

After the first week of shooting, they all came up with comical names to use on the credit cards. The cinematographer wanted to call himself Seymour Hare. The gaffer wanted to call himself Wun Hung Low. The sound man decided he liked I. Kutcha Kokoff. *La Directrice* vetoed all these suggestions. She was going for class and style here, she told them. She herself had decided to use the name Martin N. Prudeaux for her director's credit, on the theory that men didn't want to see a porn flick directed by a woman, and also Prudeaux sounded French, which intimated great sexual knowledge and which also referred back to the source of the fairy tale, the writer Charles Perrault. Not all fairy tales were written by Grimm.

Tick and Mose wished now that they'd gotten Connie's real name, and also Jake's full name. They figured Prudence Ann Markham, a.k.a. Martin N. Prudeaux, was the only one who knew those names because she was the one who wrote out the weekly pay checks from the Prudent Company's account—but it so happened she was dead. They were pretty sure that Jake was Jake's real first name, but what was the rest of it? And Constance Redding was anybody's guess, flaming Connie Lingus who could engorge organs as large as the one at Radio City Music Hall.

They figured maybe she was a hooker in real life.

Otherwise, where'd she learn how to do all that stuff? Just watching her in action was like spending a month in a Chinese whorehouse. Had to've been a hooker.

So they decided that the best way to get a line on redheaded hookers in the fair city of Calusa was to cruise the topless joints here.

Such was their reasoning.

Which led them to The Naked Truth at ten-thirty P.M. that Saturday night.

At ten-thirty P.M. that Saturday night, Matthew and Susan were dancing to the strains of an orchestra called Oliver Lane and the Goldens. The Goldens were fourteen musicians who specialized in playing tunes of the Forties, sometimes known as Golden Oldies. Matthew and Susan were dancing to the Artie Shaw arrangement of "Stardust," though Oliver Lane's orchestra did not have a violin section.

The people who put together the Snowflake Ball each and

every December seemed not to realize that Calusa had during the past ten years attracted a great many young people to whom "Golden Oldies" meant tunes of the Fifties or even the Sixties. When Oliver Lane and the Goldens played "It Seems to Me I've Heard That Song Before," none of these youngsters had ever heard that song before.

Blithely unaware, the gray-haired elders who put the annual event together for the American Cancer Society assumed everyone would be thrilled to dance to "Tuxedo Junction" or "I Cried For You" or "Song of India" or even "Elk's Parade," which, to tell the truth, no one there but Oliver Lane and the Goldens knew had been a Bobby Sherwood hit way back then when you and I were young, Maggie. Oliver Lane and his splendid aggravation had played all these songs and more tonight. They were now playing "Stardust," and Matthew was holding Susan close and Susan was remarking on how beautiful and handsome everyone looked.

Everyone did indeed look beautiful and handsome.

The main ballroom of the Calusa Hyatt ("overlooking the sparkling Gulf of Mexico," the hotel's advertisements in *The New Yorker* read) had been rented for the occasion, and the Volunteer Women of the Calusa Garden Society had decorated the hall awesomely. A Christmas tree the size of the one that grew to spectacular heights in *The Nutcracker* rose in dazzlingly ornamented splendor against the far wall of the mirrored ballroom, reflecting itself in myriad twinkling images aided and abetted by the several mirrored globes that rotated overhead and sprinkled sparkling reds and yellows and greens and whites across the dance floor and out through the floor-to-ceiling windows that overlooked the sparkling Gulf of Mexico. Actually, the Gulf was rather black and ominous tonight, except for a lone, fearless sailor pushing his forty-one footer under power toward the bridge leading from the mainland to Lucy's Circle. Dark, roiling clouds moved restlessly in the sky overhead, a certain promise of rain, somewhat unusual for December.

But inside the ballroom, all was glitter and gloss.

Smaller floral replicas of the magnificent Christmas tree sat in the middle of each of the tables with their red tablecloths and green napkins, these—the trees, not the linen—to be auctioned off later for the benefit of the American Cancer Society. All the men were in tuxedos, many of them rented, and all the women were in gowns purchased expressly for the gala. The younger women seemed to favor a couture that relied heavily on slits far up the leg and swooping necklines supported only by naked breasts. The elderly ladies—those pouter pigeons who had voted for the Oliver Lane orchestra—were wearing this year an astonishingly varied assortment of sequined and beaded gowns. Frank's wife, Leona—whose firm, youthful bosom rivaled that of any of the young women who'd grown up rocking to the songs of Janis Joplin or Jimi Hendrix—was wearing a silver lamé concoction that seemed still steamingly molten and that caused her to appear more naked than if she'd been in the privacy of her own shower. She was dancing with the very same judge who'd denied Matthew's motion in limine this past Thursday, dancing very close to the old bastard, in fact. Moreover, the old bastard had his hand on her silvery ass.

"Don't touch," the girl sitting in the booth with Tick and Mose said. "Read the sign. You can look, but you can't touch."

She said this because Mose had his hand on her thigh.

"Otherwise we'll get busted," she said.

She was in her mid-twenties. Tick guessed, a not very good-looking blonde wearing a costume that wouldn't have been welcomed at the Snowflake Ball across town because her costume was her underwear.

Tick wondered where the notion had started that a woman in her underwear was sexier than a woman in just her skin. France, he guessed. *La Directrice* had dressed Connie in a startling array of underwear, coming up with variations Tick had never even seen in the pages of *Penthouse*. Connie had looked very sexy in all that underwear, but Connie would have looked sexy in a potato sack. Connie was what was known in the trade as a natural.

The blonde was wearing a black garter belt, black bikini panties, black net nylons and black high-heeled shoes. No bra. Except for her naked breasts, she did not look very natural in her underwear, nor did she look particularly sexy. She looked too heavily made up and too sleazily underdressed, and she stank of cheap perfume, and she seemed much older than her

117

twenty some-odd years, and far more hard-edged, and far more worn. She looked like a hooker.

Which Tick guessed she was.

"How long have you been doing this sort of thing?" Tick asked.

"What are you, a social worker?" the girl asked. "Hey, listen, I mean it," she said to Mose, whose hand was on her thigh again. She plucked the hand off as if it were a piece of lint. "The State Attorney has people coming in and out of here all the time, Skye Bannister, you familiar with that name?"

"No," Tick said.

"The State Attorney," she said. "He'll close us down in a minute if he thinks anything funny's going on in here, which of course it isn't."

"Of course not," Tick said. "What's your name?"

"Kim," she said.

Tick guessed there were eight million girls named Kim in the topless joints across the length and breadth of America.

"Kim, we're looking for a particular person," Mose said.

Straight to the point. Good old fucking dumb Mose.

"What's the matter with me?" Kim said. "*I* happen to think *I'm* pretty particular."

"No, I meant . . ."

"What he meant," Tick said, "is we think a friend of ours may be working in Calusa, and we'd like very much to find her."

"What are you, cops?" Kim said.

"Do I look like a cop?" Tick said.

She looked at him. "No," she said, "but who can tell nowadays? Nowadays you get cops they look more like crooks than crooks do."

"We're not cops," Mose said.

She looked at Mose.

"Then what are you?"

"Friends of this girl we're trying to find," Mose said.

"What girl?"

"A redhead," Tick said.

"What's her name? We got four redheads here, two of them on tonight. One of them's up there dancing right this minute."

They looked toward the small stage around which a dozen or

more tables were arranged. A short stout redhead was up there, flailing the air with her pendulous breasts.

"That's not her," Tick said. "The redhead we're looking for is extremely beautiful."

"*I* happen to think Cindy is extremely beautiful," Kim said.

Eight million Cindys, too, Tick thought.

"Who's knocking Cindy?" he said, looking toward the stage again, where the girl was now bending over to throw an enormous moon at a baldheaded guy watching her in open-mouthed fascination. "But this particular person we're looking for is really extraordinarily beautiful, you'd agree in a minute if you ever saw her."

"*I* happen to think *I'm* extraordinarily beautiful," Kim said, and tossed her frizzied bleached hair.

"You are, no question about it," Mose said, and put his hand on her thigh again.

"Listen, you understand English?" Kim said, and this time shoved his hand away angrily. "So what is it?" she said to Tick, figuring he was the negotiator here. "You interested in me, or you interested in giving me all this bullshit about this gorgeous redhead you're looking for?"

"We're interested in both," Tick said.

"Never mind both," Kim said, "let's talk about *me*. There's a pickup out back, and the front seat is covered with blowjobs. *If* you're interested."

"What do you get?" Tick asked.

"Twenty-five," she said.

"Here's the twenty-five," he said, reaching for his wallet, opening it, and putting two tens and a five on the table. "Just for sitting here talking to us."

"Thanks," she said, and picked up the bills and tucked them into the waistband of her garter belt. "But that doesn't mean your friend here can get handy. I'm serious about people coming in here all the time looking for something going on. If you're paying for talk, we talk. Period."

"I understand," Tick said.

"But does your *friend* understand?"

Mose was thinking he'd like to go out in the pickup *first*, and then come back in here to talk. He was thinking Tick was throwing twenty-five bucks down the toilet.

119

"Sure, I understand," he said. "Here's my hands. Right here on the table, okay?" He folded them on the tabletop. "Okay?"

"Just keep them there, okay?" she said.

"Maybe *later* we can go out to the pickup," Mose said.

"Sure, for another twenty-five," Kim said. "Right now, you bought talk." She turned to Tick. "So talk," she said.

"Long red hair," Tick said. "Green eyes. Five-ten, legs that won't quit, tits like melons. Have you seen her around?"

"She sounds like a movie star," Kim said.

Mose was about to say something, but Tick shot him a look.

"What's her name?" Kim asked.

"She was going by Connie," Tick said.

"Yeah, but what's her square handle? Is she a working girl?"

"Maybe."

"Well, don't you *know*?"

"Not for sure."

"Why do you want her?"

"Do you know her? Does she sound familiar?"

"Not really. Why do you want her?"

"Have you been working these clubs long?"

"Two years now. I did a year at Alyce, another six months at Up Front. This is the best of the lot, you ask me. Why do you want her?"

"Ever see her in any of them?"

"From the way you describe her, she doesn't sound like somebody'd be working the topless joints. You're describing a racehorse, somebody'd be working the beach in Miami, have you tried Miami?"

"We're pretty sure she's in Calusa," Tick said.

"Have you called any of the services? That's the kind of girl you're talking about, a hundred a shot. If she really looks like you say she looks. Anyway, why do you want her?"

Tick looked at Mose.

"We're not creeps," he told Kim.

"Nobody said you were. But you're looking for this gorgeous redhead, I got to wonder why? She do something to you? You want to hurt her?"

"No."

"'Cause if that's the story, it's been nice knowing you."

"Okay, I'll be perfectly honest with you," Tick said. "We owe her money."

"For what?"

"She did some work for us."

"What kind of work?"

"She entertained some businessmen for us. Up in Tampa."

"What kind of businessmen?"

"We're in the construction business," Tick said. "We had this land we were interested in, and these two guys owned it, and we wanted to make a deal with them. So Connie helped us."

"Helped you how? I thought you said you weren't sure she's a hooker."

"She entertained them. Went out to dinner with them. Whatever else happened is between her and her priest."

"So how come you owe her money?"

"She checked out the next morning. We've been trying to find her since."

"This is a fairy tale, right?" Kim said. "She checks out without collecting? And you come looking to pay her? Come on, mister."

"I'm telling you the truth."

"Sure. How much money is involved here?"

"Five bills."

"Gets better and better all the time. You know any other businessmen in Tampa? For five bills, I'll go up there and entertain them out of their minds. Boys," she said, standing up and moving out of the booth, "you're full of shit. I don't know any gorgeous redheads going by Connie, and if I did I wouldn't tell you where to find her because you sound like you want to hurt her."

"How about a big black stud named Jake?" Mose asked.

Kim looked at him.

"Hung like an Arabian stallion," Tick said.

Kim turned to him.

"Jake who?" she said.

There was knowledge in her eyes. Tick saw it there.

"Sit down," he said.

121

She moved into the booth again.

"Jake," Tick said.

"You know this five hundred you were gonna give the redhead?" Kim said. A calculating look on her face now. She was smelling real bread, more than she could earn in a month out in the pickup truck. "You want Jake, I'll take that five up front."

"Make it three," Tick said.

"No, make it five," Kim said.

"What if he isn't the Jake we're looking for?"

"I'll tell you what," Kim said, a thin smile on her face. "Is he six feet tall with shoulders like a wagon yoke and buns like bowling balls? Does he look like Stallone in black face? Has he got a weapon could choke a girl? If that's the Jake you want, then hand over the bills, baby, and we'll talk."

"Four," Tick said.

"Five," Kim said. "And make it fast, 'cause I think I see a live one across the room."

Tick hesitated.

Kim swung her legs out of the booth. "So long, boys," she said.

"What's your hurry?" Tick said, and reached for his wallet again.

Skye Bannister.

Hair the color of wheat, eyes the color of his name. Six-feet-four or -five inches tall, reedy and pale, wearing a tuxedo with black patent leather slippers, a ruffled shirt with enameled Shlumberger studs and cuff links, and a red cummerbund and tie.

Skye Bannister, the State Attorney himself, in person, here at the Snowflake Ball with whiskey on his breath and two or three sheets to the wind.

"Arthur tells me he sent you a demand for alibi," he said to Matthew.

"Got it yesterday morning," Matthew said.

Oliver Lane and the Goldens were playing Harry James's "Sleepy Lagoon." Susan was dancing with Frank. She was wearing a red gown. A green feather was in her dark hair.

Matthew watched the feather bobbing out there on the dance floor.

"I hope you come up with something, Matthew, I really do," Bannister said.

Matthew knew he hoped nothing of the sort.

"Because I like you and admire you, I really do," Bannister said.

He poured more wine from the bottle on Matthew's table, lifted the glass to his lips, sipped at it, put it down on the table again.

"A job like mine is a difficult one," Bannister said, and Matthew thought, Oh my God, he's going to make a campaign speech. "It often pits me against men I've worked with in the past, men I like and admire. Like you, Matthew. I like and admire you, Matthew. I can remember the time you and Morrie Bloom worked a number on that black man from Miami, I forget his name now . . ."

"Lloyd Davis," Matthew said.

"Very clever what you did, both of you, getting that confession out of him without making it seem like entrapment. Very clever. Interesting case, that one."

What Bloom still referred to as the "Beauty and the Beast" case, but what Matthew would always think of as the George Harper tragedy. A long time ago. Water under the bridge. Bannister had been an ally then. Now he was an adversary.

"I asked you then—do you remember, Matthew?—I asked you if you were thinking of entering the practice of criminal law, do you remember? And you said, correct me if I'm wrong, you said, 'Not particularly.'"

"I remember."

"And *I* said, correct me if I'm wrong, *I* said, 'Don't, I've got enough troubles getting convictions as it is,' or words to that effect, if I recall correctly."

"You do."

"So now you *are* practising criminal law," Bannister said, and sipped at the wine again. "And you are representing a man charged with a heinous crime, Matthew, a heinous crime, and it is my duty to send that man to the electric chair. As *much* as I like and admire you, Matthew." He shook his head morosely. "That's what's so difficult about my job."

"Don't worry," Matthew said. "You won't have to send him to the chair."

Bannister looked at him boozily, fuzzily and querulously.

"I plan to see that you don't," Matthew said.

"Ah, Matthew," Bannister said, "good, true Matthew," and recklessly threw his arm around the back of Matthew's chair and onto Matthew's shoulders. "I hope so, I sincerely hope so. Nothing would give me greater satisfaction than to have you prove we've made a grievous error here, Matthew, a grievous error. Your first important case, I know how dedicated you must be to proving your client is innocent of the crime as charged, a heinous crime." He picked up his glass again, sloshing a bit of wine onto the black silk lapel of his jacket. "But why are we talking such mordred talk, Matthew, morbid? Have some wine, let's toast the holiday season and peace on earth to men of good will. Okay, Matthew? Some wine, Matthew?" He picked up the bottle with his free hand. "No hard feelings, Matthew?"

"No hard feelings," Matthew said.

Holding his glass in one hand and the bottle in the other, Bannister sloshed wine onto the table from both glass and bottle, and finally found Matthew's glass. "There we go," he said. He put the bottle back on the table. He lifted his glass. "Here's to justice," he said.

Bullshit, Matthew thought.

"Here's to justice," he said, and drank.

For somebody who was supposed to be such a smart business-man, Henry Gardella had made a lot of mistakes.

"I don't want to be bothered with bills," he'd told her.

That was his first mistake, and his biggest one.

"We've worked out a budget," he'd said. "A hundred and seventy-five grand, including your bonus on delivery. If you bring in the movie for less than that, terrific, buy yourself a new car. I don't want to see bills, I don't want to know what you're paying your actors, or how much it's costing you at whatever lab you use, that's *your* business. *My* business is I want the film made for no more than what I'm paying for it, and I want it delivered on time. You said Christmas, I want it by Christmas.

You go over budget, you fail to deliver for one reason or another, then you don't get the twenty-five grand bonus, and I get everything you shot to turn over to somebody else to finish. That's it."

His second mistake was writing a check to the Prudent Company each and every week while she was working. He had figured this was the smartest way and the safest way to do it. He didn't want any of the Miami boys to trace back lab bills or studio bills or *any* kind of bills to Henry Gardella, who if they knew he was financing a porn flick would maybe come around to break his eyeglasses. The Prudent Company could have been anything, it didn't have to be a movie company. In fact, it sounded like an insurance company.

Also, there were laws about making pornography, and he didn't want some bright boy working in a lab someplace in Atlanta or New York looking at all those dirty though stylish moving pictures and saying to himself, Gee, these checks are coming from the Candleside Dinner Theater in Miami, Florida, and they are being signed by a Mr. Henry Gardella, so maybe I ought to drop in on him and hit him up for some change unless he wants everybody in the world to know he's violating Chapter 847 of the Florida Statutes, which is a crime punishable by up to a year in jail and a possible thousand dollar fine. Better the guy should go to Prudence Ann Markham of the Prudent Company and hit on her. Henry wanted his hands to be clean.

So each and every Friday, a check for twenty thousand and some change went out to the Prudent Company at a post office box in Calusa. If she was as honest as he thought she was—for Christ's sake, she looked like a minister's wife!—then she was shooting the film and paying her crew and her actors and her food charges and her immediate lab bills and whatever else from the checks he sent her. Which at the end of five weeks and three days came to a hundred and five thousand bucks. Before she got herself killed, he still expected to pay for all the heavy lab work when she finished her editing and turned in her cut—the mix, the blowup, the answer print, the color composite, all that technical shit. That would have come to another forty-five K, which thank God he hadn't yet given her, but which would have brought the total to a hundred and fifty thousand, which was just what he'd figured in the beginning. Plus the twenty-five bonus on delivery.

The canceled checks had come back to him in Miami:

FOR DEPOSIT ONLY
THE PRUDENT COMPANY

Prudence A. Markham

President

Plus the bank's stamp someplace on the back of each check:

CALUSA FIRST NATIONAL BANK
CALUSA, FLORIDA
PAY ANY BANK

So the checks had been deposited.

And—assuming she'd been honest, which he had to assume —then *his* weekly checks had covered the checks she wrote from the Prudent Company account to the various people she'd been working with. He did not know who these people were, but one or more of them might know what Prudence Ann Markham had done with the goddamn *film*. Was the negative still at a lab someplace? Which lab? Was she storing her workprint in a safety deposit box at Calusa First? Or some other bank? Or at the bottom of a well? Where the hell *was* it?

He didn't think it was in her house.

The police would have found it there, there would have been some mention in the newspapers or on television about a pornographic movie found in the home of the murdered lady film director. No, the film wasn't in her house, and that wasn't why he decided to break into it.

He decided to break into the house because her canceled checks, or her checkbooks, or her bank statements, or any or all of these might be someplace inside there.

He did not think the police would have confiscated anything

126

that had to do with her financial matters. Why would they need such stuff? They already had her dumb husband.

But if the canceled checks, *or* her checkbooks, *or* her bank statements were inside that house . . .

And if he could find them . . .

Why then, baby, he would have *names*.

So at eleven-forty-five that Saturday night, while the floral centerpieces were being auctioned at the Snowflake Ball, he drove out to 1143 Pompano Way.

Velma Mason was watching television when she heard the sound outside.

She was watching an old movie that had come on at midnight. Velma enjoyed mysteries of all sorts, and this movie was a mystery. Or at least it seemed to be a mystery because there was a lot of thunder and lightning at the beginning of it. There was a lot of thunder and lightning outside, too. It hadn't begun raining yet, but it was certainly fixing to do so. She heard the sound right after the last clap of thunder came from either the television set or outside the house, the thunder rumbling away into the distance, fading—and then the sound.

Velma had very good ears.

She got out of the recliner chair in front of the television set and went to the sliding glass doors at the back of the house. All the trees outside were dancing like savages. She cupped her hands to the side of her face, and peered through the glass. All she saw was blackness. Then she heard the sound again, and this time she identified it.

The sound of breaking glass.

She thought, Oh, no, not again.

She went to the window at the side of the house, and cupped her hands to her face again, and looked out. The Markham house was dark. Not a light showing.

She kept watching.

Oscar Raddison was in the bathroom peeing when he heard the sound.

He had gone to bed at nine, and this was the first of his visits to the bathroom. He would have to go again at two, he knew,

127

and again at five. You could set your watch by the times he went to the bathroom during the night.

He looked out through the bathroom window.

Couldn't see a thing, night as black as a pharaoh's tomb, trees swaying in the wind. There was a flash of lightning. It illuminated the backyards of his house and the Markham house next door. Nothing out there. A boom of thunder. And then the rain came.

Oscar went back to bed.

Henry had cut his hand breaking the window on the south side of the Markham house. Wrapped his handkerchief around it, the handkerchief soaked with blood now, he had to find a towel or something. But he didn't want to turn on his flashlight just yet. Heavy duty torch, he'd used it to break the window, but somehow he'd cut himself anyway.

He stood there in the dark, a short, stout, squat little man wearing blue trousers, a blue T-shirt, a blue windbreaker, and blue socks and sneakers. His eyes blinked behind his eyeglasses. It was pitch black in here, he didn't even know what kind of room he was in.

There seemed to be a whole hell of a lot of ticking everywhere around him. Sounded like he was inside a bomb.

He waited for it to explode or something.

Next door, Velma stood at the window facing the north side of the Markham house, watching, waiting.

Maybe she'd been mistaken.

Night like tonight, there were all kind of sounds out there. Even on a good night, the raccoons made sounds you thought were witches on broomsticks. Sometimes you heard animals you didn't know *what* they were, roaming around out there, making funny noises. There was another flash of lightning, close to the house. She flinched away from the windows just as the clap of thunder came. It was raining to beat the band out there now. She couldn't hear anything but the rain beating on the ground and on the leaves of the palms. Palm rats out there, some nights, they made funny noises, too.

She went back to the window again.

Still couldn't see anything but the blackness outside.

Behind her, on the television set, somebody was saying, "I don't like the looks of this."

She kept watching.

His eyes were adjusting to the darkness. Pupils dilating. Objects taking shape. A chair. A desk. Walls beginning to form around him. On the walls, clocks. A hundred clocks on the walls. All kinds of clocks. All of them ticking. On the wall opposite the window, an opening. Had to be a doorway. He did not turn on the flashlight. He could see pretty well now. Well enough to know that the handkerchief wrapped around his right hand wasn't showing any white at all now. Behind him, wind and rain whipped in through the broken window, causing the curtains to flap like trapped birds. He moved cautiously across the room and went through the doorway.

A living room now. He could make out a sofa and some easy chairs. Sliding doors facing the backyard, illuminated now by another flash of lightning. He hunched his shoulders against the boom of thunder. The lightning flash had also revealed a kitchen beyond the living room. Had to be a towel of some kind in the kitchen, didn't there? Dish towel? Paper towels? Something. He was starting for the kitchen when he tripped over something, goddamn hassock or something, something low, hit his shin on it, almost went flying over it until he caught his balance.

"You dumb fuck," he said to the hassock, and put down the flashlight and rubbed his shin with his left hand.

"How can I be sure you won't cheat on me again?" Susan whispered.

They were in Matthew's bedroom, in bed together, the rain lashing the windows and drumming on the roof. She was snuggled into his shoulder. They had just made love. The bed was warm, his body was warm, she had always loved that about him, the way he felt like an oven in bed. On the coldest nights, in the past, when they were still married, she would roll in against him, her feet freezing, and he would never shy away from her, would always allow her to toast by the fire of his body warmth.

"Because if it ever happened again, Matthew . . ."

129

She sighed heavily, snuggled closer, comfortable in his arms, this man she had known for so long a time, or thought she had known until that night she discovered there was another woman. Did she really know him now? He had not answered her, she noticed.

"Would you?" she said. Her voice was very small. "Cheat on me again?"

"No," he said. "Never."

The proper answer, of course. He would have been a fool to have answered otherwise. She was silent for several moments, listening to the sound of the rain. Then she said, "Do you think Leona's having an affair?"

"What?" he said.

"Leona. I think she's having an affair."

"No."

"Or looking for one."

"No, I don't think so."

"She dresses like a woman sending out signals."

"She's always dressed like that."

"She does have a good figure, I suppose. But the way she . . ."

"Yes, she does."

"Oh, you noticed."

"I noticed."

Susan was silent again. The rain drummed on the roof. The thunder and lightning were gone now, and the sound of the rain made the bedroom seem cozy and snug and safe.

"Would you go to bed with Leona?" she asked. "If the opportunity . . ."

"Of course not," he said.

"I mean, suppose she came up to you one night and said, 'Matthew, I've always had a yen for you . . .'"

"She doesn't have a yen for me."

"I'm saying suppose. Would you go to bed with her?"

"No."

"Why not? Because Frank is your partner?"

"Yes. And because . . . well, I just wouldn't."

"I think she's looking for somebody to go to bed with."

"Not me," Matthew said.

"Well, somebody."

"I hope not. It would kill Frank."

"It would kill me, too," Susan said. "If you went to bed with her."

She could barely see him in the darkness.

She sat huddled in the corner of the room. The room was cold and damp and stinking of her own waste. Patchy tufts of red hair stuck out all over her head. He had shaved her below as well. She lay cold and naked and shorn, her hands and feet still bound, he would not take off the ropes. He had stuffed a rag in her mouth and wrapped the thick band of adhesive around her mouth and her head again. He had fed her two days ago, but she'd had nothing to eat since. She wondered if he planned to starve her to death.

"You got any answer for that?" he asked. "About how I could ever be sure of you again?"

She nodded.

"You do, huh?"

She nodded again.

"You want to tell me about it? Because I think I've got an answer of my own, but it might be nice to hear your ideas."

He came across the room toward her, around the generator, stood standing over her. She tried not to seem afraid, but she was. She tried not to cower away from him into the corner, but she did.

"Don't want to hurt you when I rip off the tape," he said. "That hurts, don't it?" He smiled and reached into the back pocket of his jeans. Something in his right hand now, she peered into the darkness, trying to fathom what . . .

A pruning shears.

He slipped one cutting edge of the shears under the tape. She felt the blade cold against the back of her head. He closed the shears. The tape snapped. He peeled it away from her head and her mouth. He held his hand under her mouth.

"Spit," he said.

She spit out the rag.

"Good girl," he said.

Her mouth was dry. It tasted of the rag.

"Want to tell me now?" he said. "How I could be sure about you?"

131

"You could be sure of me," she said. Saliva was beginning to flow into her mouth again. She licked her lips.

"But how, Puss? I thought I was sure of you before, you know."

"Yes, but it would be different now."

"Because you got no hair anymore, you mean? Because men might not find you too pretty without no hair?"

"Well, my hair . . ."

"Your hair would grow back, wouldn't it?"

"Not if you . . . if you didn't want it to."

"Well, you wouldn't want to go around the rest of your life without any hair, would you?"

"No, but . . ."

"Then how could I trust you if I let your hair grow back?"

"You could trust me."

"How, Puss?"

"Please don't call me that," she said.

"Oh, you don't like that name? I thought you liked that name. You seemed to enjoy it when he called you that name."

"No, I didn't."

"You seemed to."

"But I didn't."

"Oh now, I don't really believe that, Puss."

"Look . . ."

"Yes?"

"If you'd . . . if you'd just let me . . ."

"Yes?"

"Let me out of here . . ."

"Yes?"

"I promise you'd have nothing to worry about ever again."

"I don't believe that either, Puss."

"I promise."

"No, I don't believe you."

"Please believe me. I'd never ever . . ."

"No, I think my idea is better, Puss."

"Wh . . . what idea?"

"How to make sure you won't ever cheat on me again."

"I won't, I promise."

"Oh, I know you won't."

"I won't, really. I've . . ."

"Yes?"

"I've learned my lesson, really."

"You have? You mean you'll be a good girl from now on?"

"Yes."

"Say it. Say you'll be a good girl."

"I'll be a good girl."

"From now on."

"From now on. Forever. I promise."

"I know," he said. "You're going to be a good girl forever, Puss. I'm going to make sure of that."

He smiled again.

He moved closer to her.

"Want me to cut them ropes?" he asked.

"Yes," she said. Her heart was beating wildly. Maybe, maybe . . .

"With these shears here?" he asked.

"Yes. Please cut the ropes."

"Sharp enough to cut through them ropes, that's for sure," he said.

"Then please do it," she said.

"Oh, don't you worry, I'll do it," he said, and opened the shears.

Velma saw light upstairs in the Markham house.

Upstairs where there was the two bedrooms. When Prue was alive, she'd used the smaller one as a little office. Carlton had his own little room downstairs, where he worked on his clocks. Clocks on all the walls. Fiddled with them, took them apart, made sure they kept good time before he carried them over to his shop. Light moving through the upstairs room. Had to be a flashlight, the way the light was moving around up there.

She wondered was it the police in there? Police hadn't been here in a long time now, was it possible they'd come back looking for something? Then why didn't they turn on the regular lights, 'stead of sneaking around up there with a flashlight?

The light stopped moving.

In the room Prue used as an office now.

Moved again.

Stopped again.

Couldn't be Carlton breaking into his own house again 'cause he was in jail, where he belonged. Maybe it *was* the police. Or maybe she'd made a mistake that night when she thought she'd seen Carlton breaking the glass on his kitchen door, maybe it'd been somebody else, somebody coming back now to get whatever he missed last time around, easy pickings, an empty house, the wife dead, the husband in jail . . .

No, she hadn't made any mistake that night, it'd been Carlton, all right.

Then who was it up there now?

She decided to call the police.

She went immediately to the phone and dialed 911.

But by that time, Henry Gardella had found what he was looking for, and was heading down the steps toward the front door.

"Because . . . if I *could* be sure of you," Susan said, "then I'd know what to tell Joanna when we pick her up next week."

"We don't have to tell her anything," Matthew said. "She really doesn't have to know what we're . . ."

"Oh, but she will know," Susan said. "I mean, she *already* knows *something's* different around here, she knew that before she went off to school."

"Yes, she knew that. But we don't need to explain . . ."

"Well, she'll ask. You know Joanna. I love her to death, but she's the nosiest little girl who ever . . ."

"Not so little anymore."

"No, not so little. But the thing is . . . if *I* knew where we were going . . ." She shook her head. "Do *you* know where we're going, Matthew?"

"No," he said.

"Neither do I. I mean . . . are we getting married again or something?"

"I don't know."

"Do you *want* to get married again?"

"I don't know."

"Neither do I."

She was silent for a very long time.

Then she said, "Do you love me, Matthew?"

"Yes, he said. "I love you."

134

"I love you, too," she said, and almost said, But I'm so frightened.

Because she knew that the cheapest, most expensive words in the English language were "I love you."

Came right out the front door, ran through the rain to the car where he'd parked it up the street, clutching the maroon-colored accordion file to his chest, all her canceled checks in there, all her recent checkbooks and bank statements, the mother lode.

He started the car and began driving back toward the motel.

At the intersection on U.S.41, he passed a police car going in the opposite direction. The red dome lights on the police car moved into the distance in his rearview mirror.

His hand was bleeding red through the dish towel he'd wrapped around it.

Blood was seeping through the brown paper bag.

He walked through the rain, carrying the bag down to the lake.

Had to be careful walking around the lake. Lost two dogs to the gators in the past year.

Stood on the shore in the rain.

Tossed the bag out as far as he could.

Waited.

Saw one of the gators slither off the bank into the water.

Saw the gator moving toward where the bag had sunk.

Saw the gator disappear under the surface.

He walked back to the house then, to go look at the movie again.

8

On Monday afternoon, December 15, Warren and Matthew had lunch in a Japanese restaurant on Main Street. The name of the place was Cherry Blossoms, and the owner's name was Tadasi Imura. Imura was one of only thirty-four Japanese in all Calusa County. Imura's son was nine years old, and nobody knew his proper name but everyone called him Omen II. That was because everyone believed he had drowned his six-year-old sister in the bathtub. Or allowed her to drown. There had been quite a stink about it. Big police investigation. Skye Bannister desperately searching for a way to pin either a homicide or a manslaughter rap on the kid. A case was never made. Omen II. Nine years old. Slunk around the place in a faded kimono and blue jeans, looking desperate.

Warren and Matthew sat in their socks at a low table, knees under their chins, eating vegetable tempura and drinking sake they hoped Omen II had not poisoned. Warren was telling Matthew about Saturday night's burglary at the Markham house. Omen II lurked around as if trying to pick up tips on future criminal activities.

"According to my pals down at the station house," Warren said, "there was blood all over the place. They figure the burglar cut himself going in, trailed blood all through the house."

"How'd he go in?" Matthew asked.

"Through a window in a spare room on the ground floor. Markham used it for repairing clocks."

"Is that what the burglar was after?"

"The clocks, you mean? Who knows? Markham's in jail, and nobody's asking him anything. They're playing this very cozy, Matthew, 'cause they don't want this *new* burglary casting a shadow on the *old* burglary, which they claim Markham himself did. From what I can gather, they don't think the clocks were the target. Too many expensive ones still hanging on the walls there. Of course, nobody says a junkie has to know an expensive clock from his own asshole."

"Do they think it was a junkie?"

"That's the party line, but the guy I talked to says it doesn't read like your typical junkie smash-and-grab. Prue's jewelry was still upstairs in the master bedroom, for example, and there were lots of little doodads around a junkie could hock in a minute."

"Then what *was* he after?"

"The blood trail led upstairs to a second bedroom Prue used as an office. Drawers pulled out of all the desks and filing cabinets, papers strewn all over the floor."

"Any safe up there?"

"Nope. Not according to my source. Why? What are you thinking?"

"Maybe he was after that film she was working on."

"Only ones who'd know if there was film in that office would be Prue and maybe Markham."

"I'd better go talk to Markham again, ask him what she kept in there."

"You might also ask him what the hell she was working on. And who with."

"I already did. The first time I met him."

"And?"

"He didn't know. A *film* is all he said."

"That's sort of peculiar, isn't it?"

"Not according to the guy at Anvil. He told me the same thing. Very secretive, very guarded about her work."

"Maybe she was a spy," Warren said, and grinned.

"Maybe," Matthew said. "If you need me, I'll be at the jailhouse. And later I'll be stopping by Haggerty's office. I want to see his face when I deliver a demand for discovery on the police report."

"Oh yes, oh yes," Warren said. "'Cause even if the guy only stole a roll of toilet paper, we've got a *second* break-in now, and for all we know it was the same guy pulled the *first* one."

"I'd love to know what he was after," Matthew said.

Checkbooks.

And bank statements.

And canceled checks.

Spread all over the desk in Henry's motel room.

137

A joint checking account for the Markhams, nothing of any use to him there, checks made out to Florida Power & Light, and General Telephone, and Calusa Sanitation, and Visa and MasterCard, and shops and markets all over town, the usual paper trail of a busy, active couple.

It was the Prudent Company account that interested him.

The statements for that account showed that the checks he'd sent her had been deposited every week like clockwork, but he'd already known that from the canceled checks returned to him by his own bank. He wanted to know what checks *she'd* written, and he was specifically interested in any check that might provide a clue to where the goddamn *film* was.

He found a great many checks written to a company called Techno/Industrial Labs in New York City. It seemed reasonable to believe that this was the lab Prue had been using. He did not for a moment believe she'd chosen a lab so far away because she was being cautious. He suspected her choice had been prompted by the expectation of quality work, somewhat lacking down here in the boonies. She knew, of course, just as he knew, that making porn flicks in the state of Florida—or *any* state in the Union—was against the law. The lab handling her film in New York was breaking the law of that state in the same way that she was breaking Florida's law.

But—

The specific Florida statute applying to obscenity—and Henry had studied this very carefully before embarking on his maiden movie-making venture—was Chapter 847. It stated that a person was guilty of a misdemeanor of the first degree if he had "in his possession, custody or control with intent to sell, lend, give away, distribute, transmit, show, transmute or advertise in any manner, any obscene, lewd, lascivious, filthy, indecent, sadistic or masochistic book, magazine, periodical, pamphlet, newspaper, comic book, story paper, written or printed story or article, writing, paper, card, picture, drawing, photograph, *motion picture film*"—and so on.

A misdemeanor of the first degree was punishable by a term of imprisonment not exceeding one year, and a possible thousand-dollar fine. Small potatoes when one considered the possible rewards to be reaped. Smaller potatoes when one considered the Catch-22 of most obscenity laws: the burden upon the State to *prove* that the material under consideration was indeed obscene within the meaning of the law. Section 847.07 of the Florida Statutes offered a guideline:

Considered as a whole and applying community standards, material is obscene if:

a) Its predominant appeal is to prurient interest; that is, a shameful or morbid interest in nudity, sex or excretion;

b) It is utterly without redeeming social value; and

c) In addition, it goes substantially beyond customary limits of candor in describing or representing such matters.

Such a definition might apply to two-thirds of the R-rated films showing in any American motion picture theater. That was why Henry had decided to embark on a splinter career in the producing of pornographic but classy motion pictures. First let them catch him—which would have been difficult because he'd covered his tracks so carefully. Then let them charge him, if ever it came to that. And *then*, fat chance, let them prove that the product was pornographic.

He dialed 1-212-555-1212 and got a number for Techno/Industrial in New York. He rehearsed his pitch for perhaps two minutes, and then dialed the number the operator had given him.

"Techno," a woman's voice said.

"Yes, this is Harold Gordon, accountant for the Prudent Company here in Calusa, Florida?"

"Yes, sir?"

"May I speak to one of your officers, please?"

"One moment."

Henry waited.

"Hello?" a man's voice said.

"This is Harold Gordon," Henry said, "accountant for the Prudent Company here in Calusa, Florida? Who am I speaking to, please?"

"Rudy," the man said.

"And your last name, sir?"

"Holman. Who did you say this was?"

"Harold Gordon, accountant for the Prudent Company."

"Yes, Mr. Gordon?"

"I'm closing out our books for the year, going through the checks Prudence Ann Markham wrote to your company . . ."

"Yes?"

"And I was wondering if you could help me regarding some of them."

"Help you in what way?"

"Well, I'm trying to sort this out . . . have you got a minute?"

"Sure. I guess."

"Mrs. Markham was somewhat vague as to just what specific services her checks covered . . ."

"Uh-huh," Holman said.

"For example, I'm assuming most of these checks were written for the processing and the dailies."

"Yes, including our shipping charges."

"Yes, those would have been the checks she wrote in October and early November . . ."

"Uh-huh."

"Can you tell me, Mr. Holman, were any answer prints ever sent to her?"

"I don't think she's that far along, is she?" Holman said. "I don't think the picture's locked yet, is it? I know she was still working on it when she pulled the neg. What'd she do? Decide to go with another lab?"

"I'm sorry, what do you mean?"

"For any further work she needed."

"I still don't . . . did she seem unsatisfied with the work you'd . . . ?"

"Well, when she pulled the neg . . ."

"Pulled the neg?"

"Asked us to send the negative down."

"The negative?"

"Yes, sir."

"Send it down?"

"Down to Florida."

"The *negative*?" Henry said.

"Yes, sir. I was surprised, too. I thought we'd been doing a pretty good job for her. I mean, I was hoping we'd go the full route with this picture. I mean, once she had her workprint and sound tracks cut, we planned to do the mix for her sound people, and conform the neg, and do the sixteen answer print and the thirty-five blowup . . . I mean the whole damn shebang right through to the composite. So she pulls it all away. So I've got to ask myself what for? A negative's a delicate thing, even a speck of dust can scratch it, I don't know why she wanted it down there instead of safe in our vault up here. We've got a climate-controlled vault up here. Only thing I could figure is she wanted to move to another lab. Anyway, we sent it down to her. I mean, she's the customer, right?"

"By Federal Express?"

"No, sir, by personal messenger. We don't treat negatives lightly. I wanted to make damn sure it got to her."

"And did it?"

"Yes, sir."

"When was it delivered?"

"I can check if you like," Holman said.

"Yes, would you please?"

"Hold on."

Henry waited.

He could hear papers rustling on the other end of the line. Finally, Holman's voice came back on.

"It went down by personal messenger on the seventeenth of November. We billed her for it, air fare and all, you must have her canceled check there."

"Yes, I'm . . . uh . . . sure I have," Henry said. "Where did you send it, can you tell me? The negative."

"1143 Pompano Way," Holman said. "Calusa, Florida."

Her house, Henry thought.

"Mr Holman," he said, "when you say she might have been considering a move to another lab . . ."

"Well, that's the only thing I could think of. People usually store the neg here even after they've got their release print. But all at once, she wants it back. So I have to figure another lab, am I right? The quarter-inch tapes, too. She pulled those too."

"What do you mean?"

"The sound recordings. She wanted us to send those back, too."

"Did you?"

"Sure did."

141

"By messenger?"

"Yep, in the same package."

"To the same address?"

"Yes, sir."

"Then you . . . you mean you don't have anything there at all?"

"Zilch," Holman said. "It's all in her hot little hands."

"Do you have any idea who that other lab might be? The one she was considering?"

"Nope."

"I see, I see," Henry said. "I see." He was silent for several seconds. He didn't know what else to say. He felt as if someone had kicked him in the balls. "Well . . ." he said at last, "then these . . . uh . . . checks I have . . . they're for payment in full, is that correct? There's no further balance due?"

"All squared away," Holman said.

"Well, thank you very much, sir," Henry said.

"When you see her, tell her I think she made a big mistake," Holman said, and hung up.

"Shit!" Henry said, and slammed the receiver back on the cradle, and began sorting through the checks again.

That Monday, Tick and Mose got their first genuine lead to Jake Barnes.

On Saturday night, Kim—the lady in the black lingerie at The Naked Truth—had told them his real name was Jake Delaney —which they'd immediately doubted because Delaney was Irish, wasn't it, and Jake was as black as midnight. Furthermore, he was living not in Newtown which was where most of the *black* people in Calusa lived, but instead in a house on Fatback Key, which was where a lot of the *white* people in Calusa lived.

Tick was beginning to think he'd pissed five hundred bucks into the gutter.

Kim went on to explain that Jake's aunt had been married to a white man named Fred Delaney, and that she had brought up Jake when his mother ran off to New York on the trail of a man who'd knocked her up a second time. Not the same man who'd knocked her up with Jake. A different man. In fact, Jake was ten years old at the time, handsome as rain in a dry summer, and he never saw his mother again, nor whoever his mother was carrying in the oven when she ran off. His aunt and her white husband took the kid in and gave him the name Delaney. Kim couldn't remember what his *real* name used to be, or at least the name he was born with, since people usually thought of the name you were born with as your *real* name even if you'd changed it legally when you were twelve and were now going on eighty. That was a funny thing about changing your name in America, Kim said in a sidebar, seemingly pissed off because she'd legally changed her own name to Kim Arden two years ago, and people still called her Mary Androssini, which was the name she'd been born with, but which wasn't her *real* name anymore since she had a court order to prove it. Oh well, what the fuck, she said.

Tick was beginning to believe more strenuously that his five hundred bucks would buy nothing but a long pointless monologue.

Anyway . . .

The thing was . . .

Jake was living in a house on Fatback Key because he was a chauffeur for a swinging couple that came down here from Chicago only from January to May, and the rest of the time he took care of the house for them, and took care of a lot of willing white chicks in addition to the wife when she was there, spreading them wide on the king-sized bed in the upstairs bedroom with a distant view of the Gulf and doing them the way they only before had dreamt of being done, because he was *one* sexy, handsome dude, this Jake Delaney, who could have had any girl on the beach, white, black, purple, he was that gorgeous and that talented. Kim shyly admitted that she herself had succumbed to Jake's charms, which was how she happened to know so much about him, Jake being not only gorgeous but also gregarious and garrulous.

It was during one of their sessions out at the beach that Jake mentioned he was going to star in a movie they'd be shooting right there at the Chicago couple's house on Fatback Key. Tick and Mose both knew that house well; they had lugged more damn shit in and around it for more than a month. They hadn't known, however, that Jake was caretaking the house. They thought Prue had rented it from somebody she knew. Lots of people liked to see their houses in movies, even porn flicks. It made them feel as if they were in *Architectural Digest*. This particular house was set far back from the beach and far from the main road as well. You could drive in there with a film crew for *Gone with the Wind* and nobody would notice you. Perfect for what they were doing. They were using every room in the house, shooting daytime interiors mostly, except for a few scenes where Connie blew Jake in the ocean in broad daylight. So it now looked as if Jake might have been the one who arranged through the Chicago couple for Prue to use the house while they were away in the Windy City. Which was maybe a good sign. If he'd been that close to Prue, getting the house for her and all, then maybe she'd told him where the film was before her dumb husband knocked her off.

Anyway . . .

The thing was . . .

Jake wasn't living in the Fatback Key house just now.

Tick wanted his five hundred bucks back.

"Where the fuck *is* he living?" he asked.

"Well, I don't know exactly," Kim said.

"Give me my five bills," Tick said. "Right this fucking minute."

"Hold on, will you?" Kim said. "The thing is . . ."

The thing was . . .

Back in November sometime, Jake dropped by the club and told Kim they'd finished shooting this movie they were working on, and he was going to be a millionaire. Kim figured at first that he meant he was going to be a big movie star, which wasn't too far out a possibility because he had Eddie Murphy and Billy Dee Williams beat in spades, no pun intended, and there wasn't a woman who could come within a hundred yards of him without going damp. He told her he had to go down to Mexico—

"Mexico!" Tick said.

—Mexico, Kim said, to scout out a situation for the director of the movie, and that after he got back they'd be going down there with something more precious than gold, those were his exact words, more precious than gold. She thought he was talking cocaine, but she didn't ask. The point was—

"What *is* the fucking point?" Tick said, somewhat heatedly.

—the point was he was taking the Lincoln Continental the Chicago couple left in the garage down here, and driving up through the corners of Alabama and Mississippi and then across Louisiana and through Texas, and then on across the border to he didn't say where. And because it was such a long drive, he was taking a chick with him to while away the time (please let it be me, Kim thought) and they'd be gone two, three weeks, and he'd stop in again when he came back, say hello, which meant it wasn't going to be Kim after all.

"Who *was* it?" Tick asked impatiently.

"A hooker named Amber Wilson."

"When did they get back?" Mose asked.

"Jake's still down there," Kim said. "But I heard he kicked Amber out. I think maybe he got tired of her. There's lots of Mexican girls down there in Mexico."

"Where do we find this Amber Wilson?" Tick asked.

"Well, that's the thing of it," Kim said.

"*What's* the thing of it?"

"I heard she got busted for bringing some pot back with her."

"Busted? Where?"

"Texas."

"Texas!"

"But maybe she didn't. This is all stuff I heard around."

"If she didn't get busted . . ."

"Maybe she didn't . . ."

"Then where does she live here in Calusa?"

"Newtown," Kim said.

Carlton Barnaby Markham did not seem to appreciate jailhouse life. He looked much paler than he had before, and he was also considerably more irritated.

"I think you should be agitating for bail," he said.

"I can't get you out on bail," Matthew said.

"Have you tried?"

"I've talked quietly to Judge Mancuso. He's the man who denied bail in the first place, and who also denied my motion in limine. He thinks you're a maniac."

"Terrific."

"He thinks you'll run if he gives you the slightest opportunity."

"I would," Markham said.

"Don't say that. Not even in jest."

Markham scowled.

145

"So I just sit here until February, whenever the hell, whenever we go to trial."

"I'm afraid so."

"This is Russia, right?"

"No, this is America. Mr. Markham, there are some questions . . ."

"For Christ's sake, call me Carlton. You're always so god-damn formal."

"I'm sorry."

"Don't be so goddamn *sorry*, either. Your job is to get me out of here so . . ."

"I already told you . . ."

"I'm not talking about getting me out on bail, I'm talking about getting me out *period* so I can get on with my goddamn *life*!"

"That's exactly what I'm trying to do. I already told you we've found a witness . . ."

"Sure, a fat old broad with bats in her belfry."

"But all we've got for the moment."

"A jury'll take one look at her . . ."

"Well, let me worry about the jury, okay?"

"Sure, you worry about the jury. I'll worry about the electric chair."

"I'm worried about that, too, Carlton, believe me."

Markham nodded, but he did not look convinced. "So what are these questions you have?" he said.

"Your house was broken into again last night," Matthew said.

"What?"

"Yes. Along around midnight. I don't know what was taken yet, if anything. I'll be making a demand for discovery when I leave you. But I'd like to know what Prue kept in that upstairs office of hers."

"Files, records, correspondence, that's all."

"Is there a safe up there?"

"No. Why? If he was after money . . ."

"I thought she . . ."

". . . then he was barking up the wrong tree. Prue and I weren't exactly wallowing in the stuff."

"I thought she might have kept film up there."

"Film? No."

"She was working on a film when she was murdered, so I thought maybe . . ."

"I don't see what *film* has to do with her murder."

"Well, there isn't any, you see."

"Any what?"

"Film."

"A goddamn junkie killed my wife for the few dollars in her handbag, and I'm charged with her murder, and you're talking about film. What the hell does film . . . ?"

"She was working on a *film*," Matthew said. "And now there *isn't* any film. And I have to ask myself why."

"What are you suggesting? That Prue was killed because of some dumb commercial she was . . . ?"

"Is that what she was working on? A commercial?"

"I don't know what she was working on. A commercial, a documentary, who *cares*?"

"These documentaries she made in the past? Were any of them controversial?"

"No. What do you mean? Controversial? How?"

"Could they be considered exposés of any kind? Were they investigative journalism?"

"No, no, nothing like that. She did the one on child abuse that got the prize, and another one on manatees, they're an endangered species, you know, and one on . . ."

"Did the child-abuse film ruffle any feathers?"

"It was shown in every school in the state. I told you, it won a prize."

"This new film she was working on . . ."

"I don't know what it was."

"Never mentioned it to you?"

"Never. She sometimes got like that. I didn't know about the manatee film until she'd finished it."

"*Could* it have been controversial?"

"The manatee film?"

"No, the one she was working on. She wasn't doing a film about fixing horse races, for example, or selling dope to little . . . ?"

"I told you, I don't know *what* she was working on."

"Began work in September, is that right?"

"The end of September, yes."

147

"When did she work? Daytime? Nighttime?"

"Mostly at night."

"Where?"

"I don't know."

"Who was financing the film?"

"What?"

"Who was financing it? You said a few minutes ago that you and Prue weren't exactly wallowing in money. Doesn't it cost . . . ?"

"I don't know who was financing it. I told you I don't know anything *about* the damn film!"

Matthew looked at him.

"Then you don't think there's the remotest possibility that your wife may have been working on something that someone, *anyone*, might have found threatening to his or her . . ."

"I told you," Markham said. "I do not know what she was working on. Shall I say it again? I do not know what she was working on. Nor do I see how pursuing this line of approach is going to help me one damn bit!"

Matthew kept looking at him.

"Sorry," he said at last. "Just an idea."

It was not until two days later that Tick and Mose found Amber Wilson.

She was the color of her given name, amber to be sure, a girl who—or so her neighbors had reported—referred to herself with great dignity as "black" although she could have passed for white anywhere in the world. What you'd call a mulatto. Mose guessed, or a quadroon, or an octaroon, or a nectarine, or whatever the hell. What his grandfather back in Georgia would have called a "high yeller gal."

She was sitting on a blanket on the Sabal Key beach, wearing a green maillot slit high up on the leg and slashed low between her abundant breasts. Two white boys wearing swim trunks and Duke University sweatshirts were tossing a Frisbee some ten feet from where she sat. Tick and Mose, dressed for the street, came slogging through the sand toward where she sat studiously ignoring the boys trying to get her attention.

"Miss Wilson?" Tick asked.

She looked up. Her eyes were the color of the sky, a pale,

148

bluish-gray. Somewhat slanted. Set in an oval face with high cheekbones. Mose wished he'd have been the one who took her to Mexico. He also wondered why Jake Delaney had sent her back home. Jake had seemed very intelligent otherwise.

"The lifeguard over there says you're Amber Wilson," Tick said. "Mind if we sit down and talk to you a minute?"

Tick knew she was thinking Cops.

"Okay?" he said.

Amber shrugged.

Both men sat on the blanket. The Duke Frisbee-players, probably Boggers, were wondering what she saw in these two jerks that she didn't see in them. They picked up their toy and wandered farther up the beach.

"We've been trying to find you since Monday," Tick said, figuring he'd let her go on thinking they were cops for just a little while.

"Oh?" Amber said. "How'd you find me now?"

"Lady who lives next door to you said you went to the beach."

"Well, I guess I did," Amber said, "since here I am at the beach."

"We hear you just got back from Mexico," Mose said, getting straight to the point as usual. There were times when Tick wondered why he bothered with Mose at all.

"If you heard I was busted at the border, that's bullshit," Amber said. "Are you cops or what?"

"We're looking for Jake Delaney," Tick said, ignoring the question.

"He's in Mexico, and *he* didn't do anything, either."

"We know he didn't do anything," Tick said. "But we're real anxious to talk to him."

"What about?"

He wondered if she knew Prue was dead.

"When did you go down to Mexico?" he asked.

"We left on the fifteenth," Amber said.

"Last month?"

"Well, since today's the seventeenth, and the fifteenth of *this* month would've been two *days* ago, then it couldn't have been *this* month, could it, since I'm sitting on the beach here, don't you think?"

Wise-ass nigger, Mose thought.

"You're saying it was last month," he said.

"Bright," Amber said.

Like to punch you right in your fuckin' nigger mouth, Mose thought.

Tick was thinking if she left five days before Prue got killed then maybe she didn't know about the murder. He was also trying to think whether or not this was good or bad for them. He figured he'd play it by ear a bit longer.

"Why'd Jake go down to Mexico?" he asked.

"Business," she said.

"Dope?" Mose asked.

Good old Mose.

Amber merely looked at him. Her look could have killed a cockroach.

"We're friends of his," Tick said, figuring he'd quit playing games.

"I'll bet you are," Amber said.

"We worked with him on that movie out at Fatback Key."

She studied him.

"Really," he said.

She kept studying him.

"That's what we want to talk to him about."

"I don't know anything about that movie," she said.

"'Cause we understand he went down there to scout out a situation for the director of the movie," Tick said, and watched her eyes.

She didn't even blink.

"What we want to ask him . . ."

"You're cops, ain't you?" Amber said.

"No, no," Tick said.

"Who you think you're kidding here?" Amber said. "The lady got herself juked, and now you're giving me all this jive about Jake scouting a situation for her, you're cops."

So she knows about Prue, Tick thought.

"We're not cops," he said.

She studied him again.

"Really," he said.

"We worked with him," Mose said.

"You I wouldn't believe if you told me you're wearing a red shirt," Amber said, which he was wearing.

"We're not cops, I mean it," Tick said. "All we want to know is what kind of situation he was scouting for her. We'd ask him ourselves, only he's in Mexico. He'd tell us in a minute if he was here. We're *friends* of his, for Christ's sake."

"It wasn't nothing illegal," Amber said.

"Then what was it?"

"Whyn't you go to Mexico and ask *him*?"

"Where in Mexico?" Tick asked.

"Mexico City."

"Scouting for what?"

"How much is this worth to you?" Amber asked.

It always got down to money. You talked with a hooker, it was always cash on the line. There were no hookers with hearts of gold left in the entire world. But he had learned his lesson with Kim Arden née Mary Androssini.

"All I can spare is a hundred dollars," he said.

Tick's mouth fell open.

"I mean, make it fifty," Mose said, and grinned apologetically.

"No, two hundred sounds about right," Amber said.

"What am I buying for two hundred?" Tick asked.

"You want to know what he was scouting in Mexico, don't you?"

"Something else I want to know, too."

"What's that?"

"The square handle of the girl who was in the movie with him."

Amber looked at him.

"Do you know her name?"

"I know her name," Amber said.

"Her address, too?"

"No."

"Then all it's worth is a hundred."

"Make it a bill and a half."

"You've got it," Tick said, and reached for his wallet. He counted out six twenties and three tens.

"Thanks," Amber said, and slipped the money into her beach bag.

"So?" he said.

"How do you want it?"

"First the girl's name."

ED McBAIN

"Margaret."

"What's her last name?"

"Dill."

Easy to remember, Tick thought. Like a dill pickle.

"Does she live here in Calusa?" he asked.

"Yeah, but I don't know where. I already told you I don't know her address."

Punch her right in her nigger mouth, Mose thought.

"Jake never dropped anything that would . . ."

"No. He just kept talking about her all the time. Meg this, Meg that . . ."

"He called her Meg?"

"Yeah."

"You said Margaret."

"Meg's her nickname. They were real tight, huh? I think he was making it with her even when they weren't in front of the camera. Well, you know Jake."

"So it's Margaret Dill," Tick said.

"Meg," Mose said.

"Either one," Amber said, and shrugged.

"All right, what about Jake? What's he doing down there in Mexico?"

"Like you said. Scouting for the lady directed the movie."

"Where? Mexico City?"

"Mexico City."

"What kind of scouting?"

"For bread," Amber said. "And a place to work."

"A place to work? In Mexico?"

"Yeah. She was gonna finish the movie Jake was in."

"*Puss in Boots*?"

"What's that?"

"That's the name of the movie we were shooting. Did Jake say she was going to finish *Puss in Boots*?"

"He didn't tell me the name of the movie. He said it was the movie he'd starred in, and she needed a place and the bread to finish it."

Tick looked at Mose and then turned back to Amber.

"Jake didn't have the movie with him, did he?" he asked. "He wasn't carrying reels of film, was he? Or sound tape? Anything like that?"

"No, no."

Then it's still here in Calusa, Tick thought.

"While you were down there," he said, "did you hear she'd been killed?"

"No, I only found out about that when I got back."

"Do you think Jake knows?"

"I doubt it. You ever been to Mexico? It takes a hundred years to make a call back to the States."

"Did he *try* calling her back here in the States?"

"No, 'cause he didn't yet find what he was looking for. He was still looking when he showed me the door. I had to turn four tricks to get airfare back." She smiled radiantly. "He can be a pain in the ass sometimes, Jake."

"So what was the plan?" Tick asked.

"The plan?"

"I mean, once Jake got the money and a place where she could work . . ."

"She was gonna join him down there."

"When?"

"Soon as he scored."

"How much money was he looking for?"

"Who knows? However much it takes to finish a movie."

"Does he plan to come back here?" Tick asked.

"No, I think he's gonna ship the car back to these people he works for, and then stay down there. They were gonna go in business together."

"Who? Jake and the people he works for?"

"No. Jake and the lady got killed. They were gonna make movies down there. Least, that's what he told me. He's full of shit sometimes, Jake."

"He was starting a business with Prue?"

"And her husband," Amber said.

9

Joanna Hope came running into the baggage area, long blonde hair trailing, blue eyes flashing, arms spread wide. "Mom! Dad!" she shouted, and rushed to where Susan and Matthew were standing, waiting for her, and threw her arms first around Susan, and then broke away from her and embraced Matthew, and then hugged and kissed Susan again, and then said, "Wow, it's great to see you guys, you both look terrific, what a lousy flight it was, the lady sitting next to me spilled Coke all over my blouse, does Coke stain, Mom?"

She looked marvelous.

Fourteen years old, she seemed to have added two inches to her height since she'd left in September. Blue jeans and a white shirt with an amoeba-like blot over the pocket, leather fleece-lined jacket like World War II fighter pilots used to wear—"I'd better take this off before I die from the heat" —brown leather tote bag slung over her shoulder, brown boots. She looked seventeen. She looked like a young lady. Matthew had forgotten how beautiful she was. He hugged her again.

"You look gorgeous, honey," he said.

"Oh, sure, sweet talker," she said, "I've got a zit right on the end of my nose."

"You've lost weight," Susan said.

"Soccer," she said, and flexed her muscles like Wonder Woman. "Also I've been eating that crappy food up there, can we go someplace good for dinner tonight? There's one of them, Dad," she said, "wow, that was *fast*! I'm dying to take a swim, is the pool warm enough? God, what a gorgeous day, it's been snowing for the past week up there, no, the blue one, Dad."

He yanked the bag off the luggage belt and set it down on the floor. Susan immediately pulled it back and away from the crowd of people craning and jostling. Just like old times, he thought. A team. Hope to Hope.

154

"The other one's a duffel, Dad," Joanna said, "it's full of dirty laundry."

"When are you due back?" Susan asked.

"Here's your hat, what's your hurry?" Joanna said, and laughed. "Not till the fifth, ain't that great? God, I was freezing to death all last week, do you think I can buy an electric blanket to take back up with me? There it is, Dad, the one with all the bulges and the Simms sticker. Could we go for steak tonight? At the Innside Out? I've been dying for a good, thick steak. Tommy said the first thing he was going to eat when he got home was a whole roast pig, he *loves* pork. That's Tommy I told you about, Thomas Darrow," she said, and rolled her eyes, "he lives in North Carolina, let me carry the duffel, Dad . . ."

"No, no . . ."

"Lotsa muscles, no brains," she said, and hefted the bag onto her shoulder, and began walking toward the exit door, long-legged strides, tall and beautiful and rattling on a mile a minute. "I hope the washing machine's working. I've got *tons* of stuff to do. Also, Mom, if we get a chance, can we go shopping at the Circle one day, because Tommy asked me to the Glooms, and the only formal I've got up there is the one I wore to Daisy's mother's wedding when she got married again, do you remember the one? I wore it to the Sugarcane Hop when I was flat-chested, the horrible green thing that used to have the big red flower on it that we took off and you tried to fix the bustline? And I have to do all my Christmas shopping, too, there's no place at *all* near Simms where you can buy anything decent even if you *could* rent snow-shoes to get to town, we had four feet of *snow*, can you believe it, Tommy built a fort and we had a terrific snowball fight, you guys don't know what you're missing down here."

"Yes, darling," Susan said, and glanced at Matthew.

He knew they were both thinking the same thing.

How come our darling daughter hasn't yet mentioned the somewhat startling and amazing fact that we are here *together* to pick her up?

In the car, Susan's car, the new Mercedes she'd bought this year, trading in the Mercedes she'd got in the settlement agreement, together with the house and half the state of Florida—it still rankled when he thought of the way Eliot McLaughlin, her mealy-mouthed attorney, had taken him to the cleaners because he was the "guilty" party—Matthew asked, "What's the Glooms?"

"The Glooms? Oh, the Glooms. It's a big formal thing Prescott has in February, to dispel the February Glooms, you know? You see, what it is, Simms is an all-girls school in name only, bet you didn't know that when you shipped me up there, did you, Mom? Actually, the Prescott campus is right next door, and we share classes with the boys from Prescott, and it's really like we're one school, the Simms Academy–Prescott School, which is terrific, otherwise I'd never have met Tommy. The Glooms isn't really the Glooms, either, I mean that's not what it's really called, it's really the Winter Moon Ball, but Tommy nicknamed it the Glooms, and it caught on, and now everybody calls it the Glooms, which flies in the face of tradition because it's been the Winter Moon Ball since Harriet Beecher Stowe went to school there, which she didn't, you know, but we're studying *Uncle Tom's Cabin*, which Tommy thinks is a hoot! This is new, Mom, isn't it, what'd you do with the old one? Have you still got the Ghia, Dad?"

"Yes, I . . ."

"It *smells* new, Mom. I love the smell of new leather. Boy, am I glad to be home!"

Matthew suddenly hugged her to him.

"Hi, Daddy," she said.

Checks made out to Jake Delaney, Techno/Industrial Labs, George Ticknor, Tortini Pizza, Ron Sterling, Federal Express, Mosley Jones, Jr., Terrence Blair, Alison Lewis, Repro Sound Systems, Franklin Moving & Storage, Betsy Knowles, Alfred Basilio, Palm Deli, Mark Davidson, Philippa Donnelly, Anvil Studios, Klaven Film Supplies, 7-Eleven, Florida Power & Light, General Telephone, Margaret Diehl, and Prudence Ann Markham herself.

All of them marked "For Services."

Henry had to figure a cameraman, a lighting director, a sound technician and two grips. Had to figure the rest were actors and actresses, four women and two men. Had to figure all the other checks were for buying and renting and moving and feeding and generally keeping even this small-time operation on the tracks, it staggered him to think of the headaches involved with a Hollywood production.

But the check that interested him most was a check written to a firm called Calusa Travel. Of all the checks written on the Prudent Company account, this was the only one not marked "For Services." This one was marked "Mexico."

Henry opened the Calusa telephone directory. There it was, Calusa Travel. This was a Saturday, he hoped they were open. Tuning up his Harold Gordon accountant's voice, he dialed the number.

"Calusa Travel, good morning," a woman's voice said.

"Good morning," he said, "this is Harold Gordon, accountant for the Prudent Company here in Calusa?"

"Yes, Mr. Gordon, good morning."

"Good morning," Henry said. "Who am I talking to, please?"

"Ginny Holmes," the woman said.

Henry wondered if it was Ginny or Jenny. In the Deep South, Ginny and Jenny sounded exactly the same. If somebody asked you could she borrow a pin, she didn't want something to fix her bra strap, she wanted something to write with.

"Miss Holmes," he said. "I'm closing . . ."

"Mrs. Holmes," she said.

"Mrs. Holmes, excuse me. I'm closing out the company's books, and I have a check here written by Prudence Ann Markham to your firm. I was wondering if you could fill me in on what the check was for."

"A shame what happened to her," Ginny said.

"A terrible pity," Henry said. "Which makes it all the more important that I put her books in order. For the attorneys handling the estate, you know."

"Yes, I see," Ginny said. "Just one moment while I pull the file."

Henry waited.

When she came back on the line, she said, "Yes, I have it now. What was it you wanted to know?"

"The check was a sizable one, I was wondering if you could let me know what services . . ."

"Well, we're a travel agency, you know."

"Yes, I know."

"Mrs. Markham called us for airline tickets and a hotel reservation."

"Yes," Henry said. "Airline tickets to where?"

"Mexico City," Ginny said.

"Let me just jot that down," Henry said. "Airline tickets to Mexico City."

"Yes, and a hotel reservation."

"At which hotel, please?"

"The Camino Real."

"And this was for when?"

"They planned to leave on the first."

"Of?"

"Pardon?"

"The first of?"

"Oh. December. A Monday."

"You said *they*. Who did you mean by *they*?"

"Mrs. Markham and her husband."

"Were leaving for Mexico together on the first of December?"

"Yes. But, of course, there was the trouble."

"Yes. He killed her."

"Yes."

"Yes," Henry said. "And the room you booked at the hotel . . ."

"Was a double."

"I see. For Mr. And Mrs. Markham."

"Yes."

"I see. And they were returning when?"

"They were one-way tickets."

"No return?"

"No return."

"An open return, perhaps?"

"No, just one-way tickets."

"To Mexico City. On the first of December."

"Yes."

"I see," Henry said.

"Yes. Actually, I'm happy you called, Mr. Gordon. I was wondering whether I should ask for a refund on the tickets. After the trouble . . ."

"Yes, the murder."

"Yes. *Mrs.* Markham can't make the trip, you'll forgive me, and *Mr.* Markham is in jail. So what should I do? I've been wondering."

"Send a refund, yes," Henry said.

"That's what I thought," Ginny said. "I'll notify the airline, and send my own check in refund for the full amount. Shall I make it payable to the Prudent Company?"

"Yes, please do that."

"Where shall I send the check?" Ginny asked.

"To her bank, if you will. For deposit to the Prudent Company account."

"I'll get that off on Monday," Ginny said. "I'd send it out today, but I'm all alone here."

"Monday will be fine," Henry said. "Thank you very much, Mrs. Holmes."

"A terrible shame," she said, and hung up.

A terrible shame is right, Henry thought. A terrible shame that Prudence Ann Markham was planning to skip, most likely with the film he himself had paid for, and taking her dumb husband with her besides. Why the hell had he killed her? Was he planning a cross of his own? Knock off the lady, grab the film, run down to Mexico with it, and sell it to one of the *banditos* down there? Life is very complicated, Henry thought, and truth is stranger than fiction. Meanwhile, Markham was in jail, and the film was only God knew— Christ, was it in the *house*? Had he missed the forest for the trees? Did he have to break into the house all over again, cut his hand all over again, there had to be an easier way to make a living.

Sunlight streamed through the open Venetian blinds onto the checks spread on the desk top. Damn Venetian blinds were filthy, he should have looked for a better motel, but he'd been intent on keeping a low profile.

He leafed through the checks again.

He felt fairly certain that Tortini Pizza, Federal Express, Repro Sound Systems, Franklin Moving & Storage, Palm Deli, Klaven Film Supplies, 7-Eleven, Florida Power & Light, and General Telephone would not know what Prue or her dumb husband had done with the film.

That left Jake Delaney, George Ticknor, Ron Sterling, Mosley Jones, Jr., Terrence Blair, Alison Lewis, Betsy Knowles, Alfred

Basilio, Mark Davidson, Philippa Donnelly, Margaret Diehl, and Anvil Studios.

Anvil Studios seemed like the most likely bet.

He pulled the telephone to him yet another time.

On Sunday morning, four days before Christmas, the Hope family had brunch together on the terrace of a hotel/tennis complex called Island Dream, out on Stone Crab Key. the day was sunny and bright, the waters of the Gulf calm. The buffet table was dressed with sprigs of holly and ropes of pine, but this was Florida and even the huge Christmas tree just inside the sliding glass doors leading to the terrace could not generate for Matthew any sense of holiday spirit.

This was Florida.

And in Florida, at about this time last month, a young woman had been brutally slain while leaving a film studio on Rancher Road. It was difficult to think of bloody murder on a day like today. Far simpler to concentrate on the cornucopia of culinary delights offered on the festively dressed table, far easier to listen to the chatter of smartly dressed men and women who'd come directly from church to wine and dine on the sunlit terrace where not fifty feet away the sparkling waters of the Gulf lapped gently at the white sand beach and a girl in a black bikini strolled idly by, her head ducked in thought.

Better to heap your platter high with poached eggs and sausages, roast beef and turkey, buttered green beans and home fried potatoes. Better to sip at your Bloody Mary and forget for the languid moment that Prudence Ann Markham had been killed, and that her husband had been charged with the murder, and that her husband was your client, and that he had seemed to bridle unnaturally when asked again about the film Prudence had been working on. Forget all that for now. This was Sunday. This was the twenty-first day of December, four days before Christmas, and you were here in the sunshine with your family (of sorts, in that it was no longer a family in the legal sense) and your daughter was talking again (as she had done incessantly since Friday afternoon) about Thomas Darrow, Jr., her Tommy, the love of her young life.

". . . even bigger than he is, and *he's* six-two. I mean, when I saw him coming out of the blue at Tommy, my heart jumped into my mouth. Tommy was on the thirty-yard line, I guess it was, with the ball tucked under his arm and racing for the touchdown that would've given Prescott the game, I mean there was only half a minute left before it would be over with Choate at seven and us at six. And it looked like he had a clear field, do you know? Nobody in sight until this absolute *goon* suddenly pops up out of the woodwork and goes straight for Tommy, and I thought, Oh my God he's a steamroller, he'll squash Tommy flat, they'll pick him up in pieces. But Tommy caught him out of the corner of his eye, and he did this little sort of twist, he looked like a bullfighter, I swear to God, he's *so* graceful, and the goon took a flying leap at him and landed flat on his face while Tommy ran through the goal posts and jumped in the air and threw the ball down, and bang went the gun, and Prescott had it twelve to seven, God, he's so terrific!"

"Can you two excuse me a minute?" Susan said.

"Am I talking too much?" Joanna asked.

"No, no, darling, I have to visit the ladies."

She folded her napkin near her plate, kissed Joanna on top of her head, slipped Matthew a sidelong wink, and moved off, pink pleated skirt swaying about her legs, long strides like Joanna's, pink disappearing into a sea of white and pastel blues as she passed the crowd around the buffet table.

Matthew was alone with his daughter.

"You say he lives in North Carolina?" he asked.

"Chapel Hill," Joanna said. "Dad, does this taste all right to you?"

She extended her fork. Matthew tasted the potato pancake on it.

"Uh-huh," he said. "Why? What's wrong with it?"

"I don't know, it tastes kind of funny. Maybe I've gotten so used to the crap at Simms that now anything *good* tastes weird. Tommy says the school cook must've worked in prison, he's so good at institutional food."

"How old is he?" Matthew asked.

"Tommy or the school cook?" Joanna said, grinning.

"The school cook, of course," Matthew said.

"Tommy's seventeen, but he's already a senior. He's very bright, Dad, head of the debating team, writes a column for the school newspaper, I mean in addition to being Prescott's star quarterback.''

"What does his father do?"

"He teaches philosophy at U.N.C. Tommy's not sure what he wants to do yet, he thinks he may want to be a doctor like his mother. She's a psychiatrist. Tommy says he grew up with a copy of Plato in one hand and a copy of Freud in the other.''

"What does he look like?"

"Tommy or Freud?"

"Plato," Matthew said.

"Well, let me see," Joanna said. "He's got high cheekbones and a beautiful mouth, and black hair, and *gorgeous* brown eyes, and I guess I told you he's six-two, and he weighs about a hundred and ninety, and he moved like a dancer, and he's absolutely wonderful, that's what he looks like.''

"I'm dying to meet him," Matthew said.

"I was hoping you and Mom would . . . listen, I don't know what's going on with you guys, and I really don't *want* to know, in fact I'm afraid to ask. But I thought it might be nice if you both came up for Parents' Day in March, get to meet Tommy and his parents, that'd be nice.''

"I'll ask your mother," Matthew said.

"Do you think it might be possible?"

"I think so.''

"'Cause that'd be terrific. U.N.C. has its spring break around then, so Tommy's father can get away for sure. It's a matter of his mother arranging her schedule so none of her patients'll think she's abandoning them. She's really got a heavy case-load, lots of blacks of course, but plenty of white patients, too.''

Matthew looked at her.

"Tommy's black," she said. "Didn't I tell you?"

Susan was back.

"Did I miss anything?" she asked, and sat, and put her napkin on her lap.

"My turn," Joanna said, and shoved back her chair. "Did you check out the desserts, Mom? I think I'll really pig out today." She moved off swiftly, through the open sliding doors, past the buffet table, disappearing into the crowd.

"You okay?" Susan asked.

"Guess who's coming to dinner?" Matthew said.

By five o'clock that Sunday afternoon, Henry had talked to only four of the people on his list. He had struck out at Anvil Studios yesterday, where he'd talked to a conceited little shit who thought he was running MGM and who told him he didn't know where Prue's precious film was, but it certainly wasn't there at Anvil, and he was tired of people coming around *asking* him about it. Henry wondered who these people asking about it might have been, but Michael Andrews had not amplified.

There had been no listings in the Calusa directory for George Ticknor, Mosley Jones, Jr., Terrence Blair, Alison Lewis, Alfred Basilio, or Mark Davidson.

That left Jake Delaney, Ron Sterling, Betsy Knowles, Philippa Donnelly, and Margaret Diehl.

He called the number listed for Jake Delaney and got no answer. He jotted down the address of the house on Fatback Key.

He called the number listed for Ron Sterling, and got an answering machine. He told the machine he would call back, and jotted down the address on Twelfth Street.

He called Betsy Knowles, told her he was the man producing the film Prudence Ann Markham had been working on, and made an appointment to see her at noon.

He called Philippa Donnelly and made an appointment to see her at two.

There were seven Diehls listed in the Calusa directory, none of them Margarets. He spoke to six of them. None of them had ever heard of Margaret Diehl. The only one of the Diehls he could not reach by telephone was a man named Burgess Diehl. Every time he called the number, he got a busy signal. He jotted down the address on the Timucuan Point Road, and then tried Ron Sterling again. This time Sterling himself picked up, and Henry made an appointment to see him at four.

Betsy Knowles turned out to be a creamy-complexioned, freckle-faced twenty-three-year-old with a body that could stop a charging rhinoceros. She was very happy to meet the producer of *Puss in Boots*, and told him she was available for any other films he might be thinking of making in the future. She crossed her legs recklessly, toyed with her cleavage incessantly, offered Henry a mint julep with mint fresh from her own garden, and said she'd had a marvelous time working with Jake and Ron and the other three women, Philippa, Alison and Connie. She said that doing group sex with people you didn't know could be a very trying and arduous experience, but Prue had been very patient and gentle with all of them, and she couldn't understand why the crew sarcastically called her *La Directrice* or even Otto, who was Otto Preminger, who was supposed to be a first-class prick on the set.

The crew, she told Henry, consisted of:

Mark Davidson, the cameraman, who lived in Tampa.

Terrence Blair, the gaffer, also Tampa.

Alfred Basilio, the sound technician, Tampa again.

And George Ticknor and Mose Jones, both grips, both from Tampa.

"She was using a lot of Tampa people,"Betsy said. "Alison lives in Tampa, too."

Which was why Henry hadn't been able to find any of them in the Calusa directory.

"But who's Connie?" he asked. "I don't seem to have her name."

"Connie Redding," Betsy said. "Well, Constance."

"Does she live here in Calusa?"

"I think so."

"But you're not sure?"

"No. What a nice girl, I mean it. She was the star, you know, but so sweet. And so beautiful. When I say 'star,' I mean she had most of the big scenes, we were in there just for variety, you know. She was the one did all the heavy stuff with Jake."

"Jake Delaney," Henry said.

"No, Jake Barnes," Betsy said. "Not that I envied her. I had one scene with him, where he put that enormous fucking thing in my mouth, I almost choked to death. Phew," she said, and smiled angelically.

"I've been trying to reach him," Henry said. "Would you know if he's still at this address on Fatback Key?"

"I think he's in Mexico," Betsy said.

Mexico, Henry thought.

"How about Margaret Diehl?" he said. "Do you know where I can reach her?"

"Who?"

"Margaret Diehl."

"I don't know anybody named Margaret Diehl. Did she say she was on the picture?"

"Well, I haven't talked to her. I just thought . . ."

" 'Cause if she did, she's lying. Lots of girls like to say they're in the movie business when they aren't."

"Yes," Henry said, and nodded. "Actually, the reason I called, I was wondering . . ."

"Well, I'm glad you did," Betsy said, and smiled and un-crossed her legs, and then crossed them again.

"I was wondering . . . you know what happened to Prue, of course."

"Oh, of *course*, my God I thought I'd be next."

"What do you mean?"

"Well, I thought it was some maniac had a thing about porn flicks or something. I relaxed when it turned out to be only her husband."

"Yes," Henry said. "But I was wondering . . . you worked so closely with her . . ."

"Well, it *is* a pretty close relationship," Betsy said, "you know, the camera practically inside you and all."

"Yes," Henry said.

"And Prue right in there calling the shots and making sure the lighting's right, and the exposure, and everything's in focus and all. It *is* a very close relationship."

"I'm sure," Henry said. "Which is why I thought she may have told you where she was keeping the film."

"The film?"

"Yes. The negative. Or the work print. The film."

"Gee, no, I'm sorry," Betsy said. "Would you like another julep?"

Philippa Donnelly served him martinis.

She, too, was delighted to be meeting the producer of the film she'd been acting in. She was a tall, willowy, twenty-seven-year-old blonde with Dolly Parton breasts and a Carol Channing mouth. She was wearing a kimono and high-heeled slippers when she opened the door for Henry, and the first thing she offered him was a martini. He had the feeling, as their meeting progressed, that she would have offered him the sun and the moon and the stars as well, had he been of a mind to accept such lavish gifts in promise of future work, but Henry had business on his mind.

She, too, listed everyone who'd worked on the movie, all those goddamn people he'd have to track down in Tampa if he struck out here.

She, too, told him that Connie Redding had been a dream to work with.

"There were scenes, you know, where I had to go down on her, which can be embarrassing or even disgusting if you're not a dyke, which I'm not, by the way. But she was so *sweet* . . . I mean *literally* . . . that everything was just a wonderful pleasure."

Henry wondered if she knew what the word "literally" meant.

He guessed maybe she did.

He asked her if she knew anyone named Margaret Diehl.

She said she did not.

After his second martini, he asked her if Prue might have mentioned where she was keeping the film she'd shot. Philippa was sitting on the couch, one leg casually draped over the arm of it, high-heeled slipper dangling, the kimono somewhat accidentally open to reveal a glimpse of pubic hair several shades darker than the hair on her head.

"I think she was working on it at Anvil," Philippa said. "That's where she was killed, you know."

"Yes," Henry said. "But the film isn't there."

"Well, where is it then?" Philippa asked.

"I don't know. I was hoping you might know."

"Well, no, I don't," Philippa said. "I hope it isn't lost, do you think it might be lost? 'Cause we got some really wonderful stuff. There's this one scene where Jake is ramming it into me from behind, and I'm going down on Ron . . ."

Ron Sterling was twenty years old.

He wanted to be a movie star.

He told Henry he could be the next Tom Cruise. Or Sean Penn. Or Judd Nelson. Or Emilio Estevez.

Henry had never heard of any of these people.

He told Henry that working on *Puss in Boots* had been an

enjoyable and educational experience, especially the scenes he did with Connie Redding, though most of her *big* scenes were with Jake, of course. He wondered if maybe when Henry was doing the producer's cut, he could slant the movie a bit more in his direction, show some of the really terrific *love* scenes he'd played with Connie, as opposed to the *sex* scenes, because what he was looking for was a career as a romantic lead, somebody like Rob Lowe, whom Henry had never heard of, either. Who *were* all these people?

Sterling did not know where the film was.

He thought Prue might have been keeping it at Anvil, where she'd been editing it.

"She was a total bitch, you know," he said. "How long did she expect a person to keep a hard-on?"

So at five o'clock that evening, after having talked to one person yesterday and three more today, Henry climbed back into the rented Ford he was driving, found a pay phone in a shopping mall—he wondered why there was a dearth of pay phones in the city of Calusa, Florida, didn't people make public telephone calls here?—dialed the number for Burgess Diehl again, and again got a busy signal.

As he drove across U.S.41 and onto Timucuan Point Road, he was thinking that Constance Redding had to be Margaret Diehl. Otherwise there'd have been checks made out to Constance Redding. That had probably been the name she was using on the picture, Constance Redding. Be difficult to cash checks under a phony name, though, so she'd had them made out to her real name. Margaret Diehl. Who maybe was related to the Burgess Diehl in the phone book, whose address was 3755 Timucuan Point Road.

Or maybe not.

Either way, Henry figured a nice drive in the country couldn't hurt on a beautiful day like today.

"Cat got your tongue?" he asked.

No answer from her. Lay there in the corner, naked except for the boots.

"Just as well," he said, "the things you did with that tongue of yours."

Eyes wide in her head.

167

ED McBAIN

"Never realized you were so talented, Puss."

Silence in the cold, damp cinderblock room.

"Of course, that's all behind you now, ain't it? Never going to do nothing like that ever again, are you?"

Silence.

"Thought I'd drive you up to Ananberg early Christmas morning, set you out on the sidewalk there. Think you'd like that, Puss? Set you out like a common streetwalker, maybe put a little sign around your neck, I have sinned in the Lord's eyes, think you'd like that? Tell the world what you are?"

Silence.

"Be fitting, don't you think? Get there around midnight, set you out early on the morning our Lord was born, who died for your sins, Puss, died for them. Set you out on the sidewalk for all to see, a reminder that you broke the Lord's commandments in the vilest possible way, set you out, Puss. Set you out naked and ashamed in the Lord's eyes, set you out on the sidewalk there near the manger there in the middle of town. Behold, therefore I will gather all thy lovers, with whom thou hast taken pleasure, and all them that thou hast loved, with all them that thou hast hated; I will even gather them round about against thee, and will discover thy nakedness unto them, that they may see all thy nakedness. Set you out, Puss."

He stared down at her.

"See what I brung back with me?" he said, and showed her the cleaver.

Silence.

"Wherefore, O harlot," he said, "hear the word of the Lord. Thus saith the Lord God; Because thy filthiness was poured out, and thy nakedness discovered through thy whoredoms with thy lovers, and with all the idols of thy abominations . . ."

He ran his thumb along the cutting edge of the cleaver.

"I will judge thee," he said, "as women that break wedlock and shed blood are judged, and I will give thee blood in fury and jealousy."

He nodded.

"So will I make my fury toward thee to rest," he said, "and my jealousy shall depart from thee, and I will be quiet, and will no more be angry."

168

PUSS IN BOOTS

He nodded again.

The sign outside read:

ORCHIDACEOUS
Exotic Orchids

No name. No Burgess Diehl, like in the phone book. But this was the right address, there on the post below the sign, 3755 Timucuan Point Road. Dirt road leading in off the main road. Henry made the turn.

It was a beautiful day, and the mint juleps and the martinis were still working their magic, and he felt very happy, felt almost like bursting into song as he drove past foliage that looked like a jungle in here. The road ran past a big lake. Kept on twisting and turning, full of potholes, bumpety-bumpety-bump. Henry drove along it for half a mile or so, he guessed, came at last to a house. Well now, he thought. Hothouses back there behind the house, exotic orchids, right? Little cinderblock building near them, looked like a chicken house or something. He pulled up the brake, turned off the ignition key, and got out of the car.

He was walking toward the house when a door in the cinder-block building opened. A man came out. Looked like a farmer. Big tall man with wide shoulders and muscular arms, Henry figured him to be in his early forties, craggy face, blond hair, bib overalls with no shirt under them, muddy workboots. He was carrying a bloodstained brown paper bag in his left hand. Chicken farmer, Henry thought. Out back getting his Sunday night dinner. Whap! The idea was comical somehow. Henry almost laughed.

"Mr. Diehl?" he said.

The man stared at him.

Blue eyes. Shaggy eyebrows above them. Tanned, leathery face.

"I'm Henry Gardella," Henry said.

The man said nothing. Kept staring at him.

"I'm trying to locate a woman named Margaret Diehl. I've been calling all day, thought I'd come out in person." He smiled. "Would you happen to know her?" he asked.

He still thought this was pretty funny. Big dumb chicken farmer standing there with a cleaver in one hand and his chicken dinner in a bag in the other hand.

"What do you want with her?" the man said.

"Are you the Mr. Diehl who's listed in the phone book?"

"What do you want with her?" the man said again.

"If she's the woman I'm looking for, I produced a movie she . . ."

The words scarcely left his mouth. The man's eyes flared. A sound like a mixture of pain, anger and torment burst from his mouth. He dropped the bloodstained brown paper bag. He raised the cleaver.

Holy shit, he's *coming* at me! Henry thought.

All at once, it didn't seem so funny anymore.

"Hey," he said, "listen . . ."

But the man was closing the distance between them, cleaver raised above his head, eyes blazing.

"Whoremaster!" he shouted, and Henry turned and started running.

He ran toward the lake.

He was suddenly very sober.

He could hear the man's heavy breathing behind him.

Kept running toward the lake.

Saw something lying there on the bank, long and gray and . . .

He stopped dead.

Holy . . .

A hand closed on his shoulder. He felt himself being spun around.

"No, don't," he said.

10

At ten o'clock on Tuesday morning, December 23, Cynthia Huellen came in to tell Matthew she hoped the office Christmas party this year wouldn't be as rowdy as the one last year. Cynthia was a native Floridian with long blonde hair and a glorious tan that she worked at fanatically; never a weekend went by that did not find Cynthia on a beach or a boat. Twenty-five years old, employed by the firm as a receptionist, she was easily the most beautiful person in the law offices of Summerville and Hope. Matthew and Frank kept telling her to quit the job and go to law school instead. She already had a B.A. from the University of South Florida, and they would take her into the firm the minute she passed her bar exams. Cynthia just grinned and said, "No, I don't want the hassle of school again."

Apparently she did not want the hassle of another rowdy party again, either. Matthew had left the party early last year. He did not know whether it had become rowdy or not. But here was Cynthia telling him that the otherwise staid and proper attorneys who worked here (four of them in addition to Matthew and Frank) had drunk a bit too much and had conveniently forgotten during a long afternoon of wassail that some of them (two) were married and some of them (the other two) were going steady with girls Cynthia actually *knew*. And whereas she didn't mind a little camaraderie and brotherly love, she, and the other three girls working here, didn't like being chased around desks, either.

"So maybe you can sort of drop a few hints here and there, because it can get a little embarrassing, okay?"

The party was scheduled to begin at four that afternoon.

Matthew promised he would drop a few hints.

At ten minutes to eleven, Cynthia buzzed him to say that a Mrs. Holmes from Calusa Travel was on five. "Are you planning a trip?" she asked.

"Did she say what it's about?" Matthew asked.

171

"Nope."

"I'll take it," he said, and punched a button in the base of his phone, and lifted the receiver.

"Hello?" he said.

"Mr. Hope?"

"Yes?"

"Ginny Holmes, Calusa Travel."

"Yes, Miss Holmes," he said.

"Mrs. Holmes," she said. "I'm sorry to be bothering you this way, but I don't know where to send this check."

"What check?" he said.

"It would have gone out yesterday afternoon, as I promised Mr. Gordon . . ."

"Mr. Gordon?"

"Yes, the accountant for the Prudent Company."

"The Prudent Company?"

"Yes. Mrs. Markham's company. The refund check was ready to go out yesterday afternoon, but Mr. Gordon never told me which bank to send it to."

"I'm sorry, Mrs. Holmes," Matthew said, "but I'm not following you."

"He told me to make it payable to the Prudent Company, and send it to her bank for deposit to the account. But he never said which bank it was. And I deposited *her* check back in November, so I don't have it anymore to look at."

"Her check?"

"Yes, for the airfare to Mexico City. And the hotel deposit. I'm afraid I can't get the deposit back from the Camino Real. They were supposed to be there on the first, you know, so it's a little late to be canceling now. I suppose I should have telexed them the moment I read about her getting killed and Mr. Markham being in jail. But as I explained to Mr. Gordon, I really didn't know what to do. Anyway, I have the check for the airfare, so if you'll just tell me which bank to . . ."

"Mrs. Holmes," Matthew said, "I'm still not . . ."

"This *is* Matthew Hope, isn't it?" Ginny said.

"Yes?"

"I assumed . . . I read in the paper that you're representing Mr. Markham, so I automatically assumed you were also handling Mrs. Markham's estate."

"No, I'm not," Matthew said.

"Then who is, would you know? When Mr. Gordon called, he said he was getting things in order for the attorneys handling the estate. Do you know where I can reach them? Or Mr. Gordon, either one? I'd really like to get this check off my mind."

"I'm sorry I can't help you," Matthew said.

"Harold Gordon?" she said. "An accountant?"

"No, the name isn't familiar to me."

"Could you ask Mr. Markham when you see him? Which bank her account is with?"

"I certainly will," Matthew said, and picked up a pencil. "You say this was for a trip the Markhams planned to take on January first?"

"No, December first," Ginny said.

"Tell me about this trip you'd planned," Matthew said.

They were in Markham's cell. On the wall just inside the barred door, there was a white porcelain sink with two push-button faucets. Just beyond that was the toilet bowl, no seat on it, just the white porcelain bowl and a roll of toilet paper sitting on the neck of the bowl where it was fastened to the wall. A former prisoner had inked a calendar onto the wall, and had crossed out the days he'd spent in this cell, a big x through each day. Markham had been here for almost a month now. He sat on a dirty foam rubber mattress on the wall-fastened cot opposite the sink and the toilet, his hands folded and dangling between his knees.

He sighed, looked up at Matthew, and said, "Who told you we were planning to skip?"

Matthew blinked.

Skip?

Nobody had told him that Markham and his wife had been planning to *skip*. This was news to him. He decided to run with it.

"Tell me about it," he said. "You were leaving for Mexico City on the first of December, is that it?"

"If you already know . . ."

"Do you want to go to the electric chair?" Matthew said.

Silence.

173

"Then tell me."

The silence lengthened.

"Okay, the hell with it," Matthew said, and went to the cell door. "Can you let me out of here?" he called to the corridor.

"Take it easy," Markham said.

"No, I won't take it easy," Matthew said. "Either you tell me what this is all about or I walk."

"All right, all right, calm down," Markham said.

"I'm listening," Matthew said.

"It was her idea," Markham said.

"Prue's?"

"Yes. To take the film and run. Finish it in Mexico, if she could find facilities down there and get a . . ."

"Why Mexico?"

"She figured Gardella wouldn't bother chasing us all the way down there."

"Gardella? Who's Gardella?"

"Henry Gardella. The man financing the movie."

"I thought you told me . . ."

"Yeah, well."

"No, never mind 'Yeah well.' You told me you didn't know anything *about* the movie. Now you . . ."

"Yeah, well . . ."

"You say that one more time . . ."

"I'm sorry," Markham said.

"If I'm hearing you correctly, she planned to run to Mexico with the film this Gardella person had financed . . ."

"That's right."

"Why?"

"So she'd have a *hundred* percent of it, instead of *ten* percent."

"Was that supposed to be her end? Ten percent?"

"Of the gross," Markham said. "She figured the picture might do eight, nine million theatrically. Plus God knew what on the cassette. Prue'd done all the work, she didn't see why Gardella should get the biggest piece of the pie."

"Except that he'd put up the money to . . ."

"A measly hundred and twenty-five thousand," Markham said.

On Matthew's block, a hundred and seventy-five thousand wasn't very measly.

"And he hadn't paid *all* of that yet. He'd only paid out a hundred and five by the time she was killed."

Only a hundred and five, Matthew thought.

"She figured she'd use the film as collateral," Markham said. "When we got down to Mexico. Show what she had to get the loan she needed to finish it. Find a distributor later on, cut him in for a piece of it, but nowhere near as much as Gardella would be getting if she . . ."

"Where do I find this Gardella? Is he here in Calusa?"

"Miami. Why do you want him?"

"Because I'm *still* trying to keep you out of the electric chair. If Gardella found out your wife was planning to disappear with that film . . ."

"There's no way he could have known that. Nobody knew about Mexico but the three of us."

"*What* three of us? What the hell *else* haven't you told me?"

"Me, and Prue, and Jake."

"Who's Jake?"

"Delaney. He was in the movie. But he's got connections. He went down to Mexico to see about getting the loan."

"Why didn't she go herself? Why didn't you go?"

"I told you. Jake has connections."

"What kind of connections does a person need to . . . ?"

"Well, you know."

"No, I don't know."

"He knows people who . . . you know . . . people who don't always operate within the law."

"Crooks, are you saying?"

"Well, yes, I suppose you could put it that way."

"Why did the loan have to come from people outside the law?"

"Well, it might've been difficult otherwise."

"Why?"

"Because of the nature of the film."

Matthew looked at him.

And suddenly, came the dawn.

"Was your wife making a pornographic movie?" he asked.

Markham nodded.

"Who's this Gardella?" Matthew said at once. "Mafia?"

"No, no."

175

"But someone outside the law?"

"No, he runs a dinner theater in Miami. He's a legitimate businessman."

"Who was financing a pornographic movie," Matthew said.

"Well, there's lots of money to be made in porn," Markham said.

"Why didn't you tell me all this from the beginning?"

"I thought . . ."

"Your wife was breaking the law. It's entirely possible that her murder . . ."

"I don't think so."

"Where's this Jake Delaney person? Is he back in Calusa?"

"I haven't heard from him. I think he's still down there."

"Does he know your wife's dead?"

"I don't know."

"Could *he* have killed her? And *then* gone to Mexico?"

"No. He went down there on the fifteenth."

Matthew looked him square in the eye.

"Did *you* kill her?" he asked.

The same question he'd asked at their first meeting.

"No," Markham said.

The same answer.

"How do I know that? You're telling me this film can earn eight, nine million dollars, more when you throw in the cassette. How do I . . . ?"

"I loved her. Why would I have killed her? This was our way out. That damn clock shop . . ." He shook his head. "Prue doing movies that brought in peanuts. Even the one that got the prize, what do you think she realized from that one, after all was said and done? Ten thousand? Fifteen? We figured . . . if we could pull this off . . . this would be only a beginning, do you see? She could go on doing the same kind of movies, we'd make a fortune. So why would I have killed her?"

"Maybe because you wanted it all."

"No," Markham said. "No, I loved her."

"Then why didn't you tell me all this? If you loved her so damn much, and you *didn't* kill her . . ."

"I didn't think you needed to know about the movie."

"You didn't see how that could have any possible bearing on the case, huh?"

"I didn't want it to come out."

"Why not?"

"Well, the film . . . well, it's valuable, you see."

"Yes, so you told me. It's worth eight or nine million dollars."

"Well, more."

"So you decided not to tell your attorney about it."

"Well, it had nothing to do with her murder."

"You don't know that for a fact! Why'd you withhold such important . . . ?"

"Because I . . . I thought . . . I thought if Jake could come up with the money we need down there . . . well then . . . then after the trial . . . after you got me off . . . I'd go join him. And we'd go ahead just the way we planned. Finish the movie, find a distributor . . ."

"Without Prue."

"Well, yes, without her. We could find people to finish it. Edit it, do whatever else needed to be done. We had the negative, that wasn't a problem. Prue made sure she got that back from the lab. So if they found me innocent . . ."

"Did Delaney take the film with him to Mexico?"

"Well . . . no."

"You said you planned to use it as collateral . . ."

"Once he found the right people, yes. We planned to show them the film later. When we got down there."

"You planned to take the film down with you?"

"Well . . . yes. That was the plan."

"Then you know where it is," Matthew said.

Markham said nothing.

"Do you know where the film is?" Matthew said.

Still no answer.

"*Do* you?"

Markham nodded.

"Where?" Matthew said.

He parked the Karmann Ghia in the gravel lot outside a low, white stucco building, its pristine façade broken by a row of a dozen or more red doors. There were six yellow-and-green moving vans in the lot, each decorated with the company's name —Franklin Moving & Storage—and a logo depicting a little man in knee breeches, flying a kite. Under the little man's buckled shoes was the motto FRANKLIN! FAST AS LIGHTNING! Rock music blared from inside a windowed office at the far end of the building. Matthew walked over the gravel to the red door set between the windows, opened it, and stepped into a Christmas party in full swing.

There were at least two dozen girls in the place, all of them dressed somewhat less elegantly than the women at the Snowflake Ball had been, but resplendent nonetheless in party dresses and high-heeled shoes. The men in the room, outnumbered by at least two to one, were wearing a motley assortment of clothes, some of them in suits or sports jackets, others in blue jeans and short-sleeved shirts and looking as if they'd just come off the road after a long haul from Maine. A decorated Christmas tree blinked first yellow and then green, the only lights on it, an obvious homage to the company's colors. Red and green streamers were hanging from the ceiling, stretching from corner to corner. Santa Claus cut-outs were on all the walls. On one wall was the same little man who was on the side of the trucks, wearing his little knee breeches and his little buckled shoes and flying his little kite. A bar had been set up in one corner of the office, and most of the revelers were gathered around it, pouring liberally from what appeared to be a fine selection of booze.

A bell had sounded over the door when Matthew came in. How anyone had heard it over the din was a miracle, but a woman wearing a tight green skirt and a red tube top broke away from the bar, turned to look at him, and then said, "Well, well, reinforcements."

She came to him as fast as lightning, click, click, click, click, high-heeled shoes zapping the floor, wide grin on her generous mouth, red hibiscus tucked behind one ear, blonde hair brushed back from it. Pale skin, cheeks flushed. Slender, and tall, and moving as gracefully as a dancer. Long, shapely legs, firm breasts in the shirred red tube top. He guessed she was in her early thirties. He also guessed she'd been drinking a bit.

"Whoever you are, come in," she said, "we're short of gorgeous men." She extended her hand. "Marcie Franklin," she said. "I'm the boss."

"Matthew Hope," he said, taking her hand.

"Any relation to Harry?" she said at once.

"Yes, I played Larry Slade in a college production."

"Hey," she said, "somebody literate! Tell me what you think about Bergman."

"Ingrid or Ingmar?"

"Oh, my God, I think I'm falling in love," she said. "I've been in Calusa only six months, came down from New York to take over the business when my father died, and I'm so starved for conversation, I'm ready to call Dial-a-Prayer. Are you married?"

"Divorced," he said.

"Good," she said. "Oh, wow, Santa must've brought you."

Matthew smiled.

"I'm serious," she said. "Every guy I date in this town wants to talk about football. I say, 'How'd you like *Ginger and Fred*,' they say they don't watch old musicals. I say, 'Fellini, *Fellini*,' they say they don't like Italian food unless it's the Pizza Hut. I say, 'What'd you think of *Kiss of the Spider Woman*,' they say I don't know the lady. I say, 'Okay, how about *The* goddamn *Color Purple*?,' they say I prefer red. I mean, wow! Do you like movies?"

"Yes."

"Want to go to the movies with me tonight? Think it over, don't leap to a hasty conclusion you may later regret. I'll be thirty-three next month, I like tall men with dark hair and brown eyes, I'm sensitive and intelligent, and some people think I'm gorgeous. I like expensive restaurants and fancy motorcars, Beethoven and . . ."

"You sound like a personals ad in the *Village Voice*," Matthew said.

"Oh, my God, I *am* falling in love," she said. "He knows the *Village Voice*! Are you from New York, too?"

"My partner is. He talks about it all the time."

"Where are you from?"

"Chicago."

"Pity," she said, and grinned.

She had not let go of his hand. Her green eyes danced all over his face, checking out his mouth, checking out his eyes, checking out his mouth again. Yellow and green from the Christmas tree bounced off her eyes.

His own eyes roamed her face—

179

Blink, yellow, blink, green—

Oval and pale. Orange lipstick on her mouth. High model's cheekbones—

Blink yellow—

Checking her out.

White even teeth behind the wide grin—

Blink green.

Hey, he thought.

Watch it.

"Come have a drink," she said, and—still holding his hand —led him to the bar. "Jimmy," she said to a man in shirtsleeves, "please fix a drink for Matthew Hope. What are you drinking, Matthew?"

"Well . . . uh . . . just a little gin, please, on the rocks," Matthew said.

What's happening? he thought.

"Gin on the rocks for Matthew," she said, and released his hand. She tugged at her tube top again, pulling it higher on her breasts. "I am *very* happy to meet you, Matthew," she said, and grinned again. Wide grin. Luscious mouth. "Merry Christmas."

"Merry Christmas," Matthew said, and accepted the drink Jimmy handed over the bar. "Thank you," he said. "Cheers," he said to Marcie.

"Finish your drink," she said, "and then come dance with me. Lucille!" she called across the room. "Put on something romantic! Matthew wants to dance with me!"

The music stopped abruptly. The roar of the crowd sounded louder now that it was gone. There was a delay of perhaps a minute or so—voices, laughter, ice tinkling in glasses—and then another tape started, soft and slow. Watch it, he thought.

"There you go," Marcie said, and walked into his arms.

He still had the drink in his right hand.

She moved it tight against him.

He almost spilled the drink.

He steered her toward one of the desks. His right hand behind her, the drink still in it, he put it down blindly on the desktop. She pulled him close again. More people were moving out onto the floor now; it seemed suddenly very crowded and steamy. Watch it, he thought, watch it.

"I was wondering . . ." he said.

"Me, too," she said. "Oh, Matthew, you have set me wondering."

"Is there someplace we can go to talk? It's a little loud in here."

"What did you want to talk about, Matthew?"

"Storage," he said.

"Oh my, storage," she said. "This is Christmas, Matthew, let's not talk about storage. Bah-humbug on storage. Let's talk about kissing. Dance me over to the mistletoe, Matthew."

"Seriously, could we . . . ?"

"Let's not get *too* serious, Matthew, we've only just met."

"Isn't there someplace . . . ?"

"Yes, there is definitely someplace," she said, and broke out of his arms, and reached for his right hand, tugging at the tube top again with her left, and led him to a door near the bar. She opened the door with her left hand, and pulled him into a smaller office. She closed the door behind them. And kissed him at once.

"God," she said, and melted into him again, and kissed him again.

He remembered what he had told Susan.

About never cheating on her again.

Marcie's tongue was in his mouth.

"Listen," he said, breaking away from her, trying to hold her away from him, "there's . . . really, there's something we have to talk about."

"What can we possibly find to talk about at this particular moment in time?" she said.

Her arms still around his neck.

"I'm a lawyer," he said.

"So?" she said. "Sue me."

And thrust her crotch against him.

"I'm . . . I'm here on behalf of a client," he said.

"I'll bet," she said.

"Who stored something here."

"Stored?"

"Film."

"I wouldn't be surprised," she said, and cupped his face between her hands, and lifted her mouth toward his again.

He pulled away.

"Can we talk first?" he asked.

He was trembling.

"Please," he said.

"Three minutes," she said, and took his hand and led him to a couch on the far side of the room. She sat. She folded her hands primly in her lap. The tube top was slipping again. She made no move to tug it up over her breasts. He sat beside her. "So talk," she said.

"Prudence Ann Markham," he said. "The Prudent Company."

"What about her?"

"Her husband told me she was renting a storage bin here."

"So?" Marcie said.

"Was she?"

"This is the girl who got killed, isn't it?"

"Yes."

"Yes, she was renting a bin here."

"Air-conditioned, her husband said."

"They're *all* air-conditioned," Marcie said.

"One key, her husband said."

"That's all I give is one key. I don't know what people store here, and I don't ask. For all I know, half the cocaine in the state of Florida is behind those little red doors out there. One key is all I give. You give two keys, you've got two people. If you've got two people, you've also got trouble." She grinned. "As with us, Matthew. Big trouble, Matthew. From minute one. Has this ever happened to you before? This kind of heat lightning? I'm trying very hard to keep my hands off you, Matthew. Has this ever happened to you before?"

He tried to remember.

Had it been this way in the beginning with Aggie, long, long ago, the first time he'd ever cheated on a contract in his life? This kind of immediate reaction? Eyes meeting, hands touching? He had made a new contract with Susan, a contract of sorts, but a contract nonetheless. Yet sitting here with a woman he'd met not ten minutes ago, he was thinking he wanted to rip that damn tube top off her breasts. He suddenly wondered what had happened to all those fine new promises he'd made to Susan.

"Would you? Cheat on me again?"

"No. Never."

182

He wondered if he was merely a no-good philandering bas-tard.

Hey, hold it, he thought, I'm not *married*!

Then why was he sitting here feeling guilty?

I'm in trouble, he thought. Big trouble.

She was right.

"Let's finish talking," he said.

And when we finish talking? he wondered.

"Is there a master key?" he asked.

"There is."

"Can you let me into the bin she was renting?"

"Nope."

"Why not?"

"'Cause you're not the key holder. I only let key holders . . ."

"I can ask for a warrant," Matthew said.

"So ask for it."

"This is a murder case I'm defending."

"This is the right to privacy *I'm* defending."

"Oh, are *you* a lawyer, too?"

"Don't go smart-ass on me, Matthew. You've got two minutes left."

"But who's counting?"

"I am."

"Marcie, there's something in that bin that may . . ."

"No, there's nothing in it," she said.

"What do you mean?"

"Somebody cleaned it out."

"How do you know that?"

"I saw the van."

"What van? When?"

"The night she was murdered."

Matthew looked at her.

"A van was here on the night she was murdered?"

"Yes. A man unlocked the bin, took everything out of it, and put it in a van."

"What kind of van?"

"One of these little delivery vans."

"You saw him doing this?"

"I did."

"Where were you?"

"Working right here in the office."

"What time was this?"

"Around midnight, somewhere in there. I work hard, Matthew."

"So do I."

Eyes meeting again.

She clenched her hands in her lap.

That mouth.

"What did the man look like?" he asked.

"Big blond guy wearing overalls."

"Blond?"

"Blond."

"Would you recognize him if you saw him again?"

"Sure. You've got one minute, Matthew."

"Opened the door with a key?"

"With a key."

"Had to be Prue's key," Matthew said, thinking out loud.

"Whoever's," Marcie said, and shrugged, threatening the tube top's tenuous hold.

"You said you only give one key . . ."

"That's not all I give, Matthew. Forty seconds."

"So it had to be hers. Why didn't you call the police?"

"About what? Somebody taking something from one of the bins? Is that a crime?"

"It is if the somebody just killed . . ."

"I didn't see a murder, Matthew. I saw somebody emptying a bin. Thirty seconds."

"Emptying it into a van."

"A van."

"What kind of van?"

"A white one."

"What make?"

"I don't know. He was probably a musician or something."

"A musician? You said he was wearing overalls."

"Maybe he plays at barn dances. Twenty seconds."

"What makes you think he was a musician?"

"Because of what was lettered on the side of the van. In pink."

"What was lettered on the van?"

"Ten seconds."

"What was lettered there?"

"Orchestrations. Nine . . ."

"Orches . . . ?"

"Eight. Orchestrations, right."

"You saw that on the side of the van?"

"Orchestrations. Seven."

"Anything else?"

"Just that."

"That doesn't make sense."

"Six."

"No name or anything? Just . . ."

"Orchestrations. Five . . ."

"Marcie . . ."

"Four . . ."

"You've had a little bit too much to drink . . ."

"No, I haven't. Three . . ."

"And I have to get back to my . . ."

"Two . . ."

". . . office."

"One," she said. "Now kiss me again before I die."

"Marcie . . ."

"You said you weren't married . . ."

"I'm not."

"Are you gay?"

"No."

"Then kiss me. I know you want to."

"I do."

"Then do it."

Green eyes wide.

"Please," she said.

God, that mouth.

"Kiss me," she said.

"I'm sorry," he said.

He rose, moved swiftly toward the door.

"I'm sorry," he said again.

"So am I," she said. "You're breaking my heart, do you know that? I've known you for fifteen goddamn minutes, and you're already breaking my heart."

He looked at her.

Long and hard and wonderingly.

"Marcie . . ." he said.

"Oh, go the hell back to your office," she said, and buried her face in her hands.

He looked at her a moment longer, and then opened the door and sidled out, and closed it immediately behind him.

11

It was Christmas Eve.

Ever since Monday, Tick and Mose had been running down every damn Dill in the Calusa telephone directory—eight of them in all—with no luck whatsoever. They were both exhausted. Mose wanted to go out and get drunk. This was at eleven o'clock in the morning. Tick wanted to find Margaret Dill. He said they had to go see Amber Wilson again. Mose said maybe Amber Wilson would like to go out and get drunk with them, and the hell with Margaret Dill. Mose had no head at all for business. Mose didn't realize, as Tick did, how much money they could make on that movie, if they could find it.

But first they had to find Amber Wilson again.

They went back to the crumby little apartment she was living in down there in Newtown, and her talkative next door neighbor—a big fat black woman who looked like Aunt Jemima, complete with a red bandanna on her head—told them she hadn't seen Amber since early yesterday morning, heard she was out on a boat with some people. Tick took this to mean that she was out on a boat entertaining fishermen. He asked the neighbor if she knew which boat Amber was on, and the neighbor said when Amber usually went out on a boat it was through Opus Charters, operating out from behind the Hyatt. Tick and Mose thanked her and then drove south on 41 to the Hyatt.

Opus Charters rented everything from fishing boats to yachts. The owner of the operation, a man named Charlie Oppenheimer, told Tick and Mose that Amber and two other girls had gone out yesterday on a thirty-six-foot Grand Banks with some men down from Clearwater. The captain of the boat had told Charlie they were heading down for Venice, planned to spend the night out on the water—the boat slept six comfortably in air-conditioned cabins. Charlie expected they'd be back sometime this afternoon. He told them all this when he thought Tick and Mose were interested in a similar excursion. Only later did he think they might have been cops. The thought would keep him awake all night while he was waiting for Santa to come down the chimney.

At two o'clock that afternoon, Tick and Mose were sitting in the Hyatt bar, overlooking the dock and the Gulf of Mexico. Mose was drinking mimosas. Tick kept kidding him about a mimosa being a fag drink. He himself was drinking something called a Banana Dynamite, which had seven different kinds of rum in it and a little bit of banana cordial. On the Gulf, the sailors were out in earnest. It was a fine bright day, and there was a good wind and no chop at all.

"We don't find Connie today," Mose said, "I want to go back to Tampa. I don't want to spend Christmas in this shitty town."

"I was thinking," Tick said, "we don't find her today, we go back up and give those two girls a ring we met last month."

"Yeah, Revlon," Mose said.

"I still got her number, the blonde's," Tick said.

"What was her name again?" Mose said.

"Rachel," Tick said.

"No, the redhead's. Revlon's."

"Gwen," Tick said.

"Yeah, Gwen," Mose said, and licked his lips. "That's a good idea, we give them a call."

"Christmas Eve, they'll probably be busy."

"Worth a shot," Mose said. "Maybe we oughta call from here, set it up."

"Well, let's see we can't find Connie first."

"I was Connie, the money she got for that movie, I'd be up in New York right this minute, spending it."

"She didn't get all that much," Tick said.

"How do you know what she got?"

"I'm just guessing. Two bills a day maybe?"

"New York's great around Christmas," Mose said. "Florida sucks around Christmas."

"That must be it now," Tick said, and nudged Mose.

A boat was pulling into the dock. Two men in Hawaiian-print sports shirts jumped ashore and began doing things with ropes.

A third man in the same kind of shirt kept waving directions to them.

"There's Amber," Tick said.

She was standing on the bow, wearing a yellow wraparound skirt that flapped open to reveal the long line of her leg. With one hand, she was clutching a straw hat to her head. In the other hand, she was carrying a beach bag, the same one she had slipped Tick's hundred and fifty bucks into for giving him information about a woman who didn't exist.

"Let's go," Tick said.

He looked at the check, put several bills on the bartop, and shoved back his stool.

Out on the dock, the men in the Hawaiian-print shirts were giving the girls last-minute holiday hugs and farewell kisses. Three girls. Two of them white, the other one Amber, who could've passed for white. The girls waved ta-ta to each other and went off in opposite directions, the two white girls heading for the bar where maybe they hoped to drum up a bit more trade, giving Tick and Mose the once-over as they passed them, Amber heading for the angled wooden walkway that led toward the roundabout in front of the hotel. Tick and Mose fell into step beside her.

"Hello, Amber," Tick said.

"Well, well," Amber said.

"Ain't no Margaret Dill in Calusa," Mose said, straight to the point.

"Gotta be," Amber said, unruffled. "Jake told me she lives here."

"*Where* here?" Tick said. "We checked every damn Dill in the phone book."

"Maybe she's unlisted."

"Jake must've given you a clue," Tick said.

"No clue a'tall. Just her name. Margaret Dill. Or Meg. You pays your money and you takes your choice."

They were at the roundabout now, under the hotel marquee. She looked up toward 41. Mose figured he'd break her nigger arm if she tried to get in a taxi before telling them what they needed to know.

"You sure he said Dill?" Tick asked.

"Dill, Dill," Amber said. "Margaret Dill." She turned to a

189

uniformed bellhop who came out of the hotel. "Think I'll be able to get a taxi here?" she asked. "Or should I call for one?"

"They come by every five minutes," the bellhop said.

"I've been here five minutes already," she said.

The bellhop shrugged. Amber looked up toward 41 again.

"Think," Tick said. "Something he might've said. Like the mainland, or one of the keys, or out toward . . ."

"He didn't say nothing but her name."

"Margaret Dill," Tick said.

"How many time you have to hear it?" Amber said. "Margaret Dill, that's right. Dill, *Dill*."

It was dumb Mose who finally tipped, not for nothing had he come along in the fair state of Georgia.

"Are you saying *Deal*?" he said.

"Dill is what I'm saying," she said. "Right."

"Like when somebody says it's a good deal?"

"A good dill, right."

"Like deal the cards?" Mose said.

"Dill the cards, right," she said. "Margaret Dill."

They can't even talk straight, Mose thought.

There were thirteen names listed under ORCHESTRAS & BANDS in the Calusa directory's yellow pages:

Ambrose Herb Orchestra

BALLARD JOE ORCHESTRA

ALL OCCASION MUSIC

* CLUB DATES *

* WEDDINGS * PARTIES *

Experienced and Professional

Calusa Symphony Society

Condon Richard & The Commissioner's
Jazz Band

ESTIES MARTY ORCHESTRA

Wedding Receptions – Country Club Dances –

House Parties – Cocktail Trio – Keyboard
Soloist – Strolling Musicians – Guitarist

FRANCO BOBBY – ENTERTAINMENT

Performed at the Governor's
Inaugural Ball
A Specialist on All Styles & Sounds
MUSIC "DESIGNED" FOR "YOUR" SOCIAL EVENTS
Weddings * Cocktail Parties * Club Dances
3-20 Men from Maine to Florida

KING RONNIE BIG BAND

Florida's Leading Big Swing Band

MELLOW MUSIC BY ROXANNE

"ONE GAL" BAND
PRIVATE PARTIES
MELLOW SOUNDS
While You Chit & Chat
Grand Openings * Recep
Office Retirement Parties
ROXANNE DAVIES

MUSIC MAKERS THE

PRODUCTION STYLES UNLIMITED, INC.

Entertainment Agency
SPECIALIZING IN CORPORATE FUNCTIONS
Kurt Meyers – Entertainment Consultant

SEARS JOHNNY MUSIC STUDIO

Tampa Symphony Society

BILL WADDELL & HIS RECORD MACHINE

Jazz – Rock – Contemporary

Warren Chambers took a deep breath.

Christmas Eve, he thought.

Try to find a musician on Christmas Eve.

They were alone together for the first time since Joanna came home last Friday.

It was three o'clock in the afternoon on the day before Christmas, and they were decorating the tree in the house Matthew used to share with Susan and his daughter, who was out delivering Christmas gifts to friends up the street. The radio was tuned to WUSF. They were listening to Christmas carols. Everything felt right. Just like old times. But everything felt wrong.

He had not yet mentioned his close encounter yesterday.

Nor had either of them mentioned the fact that fourteen-year-old Joanna seemed to be head over heels in love with a black boy named Thomas Darrow, Jr.

Matthew wasn't sure he wished to broach either subject.

He remembered a frantic telephone conversation he'd had with his daughter when she'd learned that Susan was planning to send her off to the Simms Academy:

"She says it'll be good for me. She says St. Mark's is getting rundown. She says . . . you won't like this, Daddy."

"Tell me."

"She says too many black kids are infiltrating the school. That was the word she used."

And not ten minutes later, in a somewhat more frantic telephone conversation:

"Daddy? What Mom said, actually—about the infiltration—what she said was 'niggers.' Two black kids've been admitted to the school."

"Terrific," Matthew had said. His former wife from Chicago, Illinois, was turning into a Florida redneck.

A Christmas ornament fell from his hand. It bounced on the carpet, miraculously intact. He picked it up and looked at his watch.

"Got a taxi waiting?" Susan asked.

"I was hoping to hear from Warren by now. I gave him the number here, just in case."

"Warren?" she said.

"Chambers," he said. "A private eye I've got working for me."
He hesitated.

The moment seemed ripe.

"He's black," he said.

"Is he good?" Susan asked.

"Very," Matthew said.

He wondered if he should tell her he had enjoyed kissing Marcie Franklin yesterday. He wondered if he should tell her he'd debated calling Marcie Franklin today. He wondered if she'd really used the word "niggers" to describe those two black kids who'd been admitted to St. Mark's. He wondered if he was spoiling for a fight. He wondered if he wanted out.

"Susan," he said, and took a deep breath.

"I don't know how I feel about it," she said.

My wife, the mind reader, he thought. Excuse me, *former* wife.

"We're talking about Tommy, right?"

"Who else?" Susan said. "How do *you* feel about it?"

"She's fourteen," he said. "This, too, shall pass."

"Suppose it doesn't?"

"So?"

"I'm asking *you*, Matthew. Don't put *me* on the spot."

"A long time ago," he said, "before I met you, I dated a black girl named Ophelia Blair. I was in high school. She was in my English class. Ophelia Blair."

"Is this confession time?" Susan asked.

An edge to her voice. Maybe *she* was the one spoiling for a fight.

"A bright beautiful girl. I dated her only once. Kissed her a lot, tried to get in her pants, told her I loved her . . ."

"Matthew, I really . . ."

"Begged her to go all the way because I'd never done it with a black girl."

"If you're suggesting that Joanna . . ."

"Let me finish this, may I?"

"Not if you think Joanna and that boy . . ."

"This has nothing to *do* with Joanna!"

"Then why are you telling it? And please spare me any more quaint adolescent expressions, okay? Get in her pants, go all the way . . ."

"Damn it, I *was* an adolescent! I'd never done it with a *white* girl, either, I'd never done it with *anyone*! The point is . . ."

"Yes, Matthew, please get to the point."

"The point is I robbed her of her uniqueness, Susan. To me, she was only a black girl. To her, she was Ophelia Blair. She never dated me again."

"Is that the end of the story?"

"That's the end of it."

"Thank God. Would you mix me a martini, please?"

He went to the bar, took out a bottle of Beefeater gin and a bottle of vermouth, and mixed a pitcher of very dry, very cold martinis. He carried hers back to where she was sitting on the sofa, head tilted, examining the tree for spots bare of ornaments, places they had missed.

"Thanks," she said, and raised the glass. "Merry Christmas."

"Merry Christmas," he said. "Are we about to have a fight?"

"I thought we just had one," she said, and drank.

"What I think I'm saying, Susan . . ."

"I know what you're saying. You're saying Thomas Darrow, Jr., may be a very special individual in his own right . . ."

"*Is* a very special individual, according to Joanna."

"*Is*, fine. A very special individual who *also* happens to be black."

"Which upsets you."

"Yes. It upsets me."

"Why?"

"Matthew, don't ask stupid questions. Joanna's fourteen years old. She doesn't need the kind of trouble even *adults* can't handle."

"Some adults handle it just fine."

"I'm sure."

"Susan, I have to ask you something. When you decided to pull Joanna out of St. Mark's . . . did you use the word 'niggers' in reference to . . ."

"I've never used that word in my *life*!" Susan said.

"Not even when you were referring to the two black kids who . . . ?"

"Never! What the hell's wrong with you?"

"Joanna said you did."

"Joanna was lying."

194

"She told me . . ."

"She would have told you *anything* to keep from being sent away! How can you ever *think* . . . ?"

"On the phone later, you said you were pulling her out because the school was being overrun by inferior students."

"It was. Look at it now. Would you be happy if Joanna was still . . . ?"

"Did you mean *black* students, Susan?"

"I did not."

"Back then, when I asked you that same question, you said, 'We're in Florida.' What did you mean, Susan?"

"Is this a court of law?" she said. "If so, I'd like an attorney, please."

"Did you mean that black students in Florida are somehow inferior to . . . ?"

"I don't remember the conversation, and I don't know *what* I meant. If it was one of our *usual* conversations, we were probably yelling at each other . . ."

"The way we are now," Matthew said.

"You started it," she said.

There was a deep and ominous silence.

"I'm going to ask her to stop seeing him," Susan said.

"I wish you wouldn't."

"I don't think she knows the kind of trouble . . ."

"She's happier than I've ever . . ."

"I'm *not!*" Susan shouted. "The very thought of . . ."

She stopped the sentence.

"Of what?" Matthew asked.

Susan shook her head.

"I'm sure they kiss," he said, "if that's . . ."

"Don't!" she said.

Another silence. Longer this time.

"I'm sorry," she said. "But you were talking about my daughter."

"My daughter, too," he said.

"Well, if you know this bothers me, you shouldn't . . ."

"I think you'd be making a big mistake if you . . ."

"Can you please *stop* this?" she said. "Can't you see . . . ? Can't you . . . ? How can you *possibly* suggest that Joanna and this boy . . . ?"

"They're kids, Susan! What the hell do you think kids do? They neck, they pet, they even . . ."

"Damn you, shut *up!*" she said, and hurled her drink into his face.

On the radio, a choral group began singing "Silent Night."

He took out his handkerchief and dabbed at his face. His shirt was wet down the front. He looked at his shirt as if wondering how it had got all wet. He kept staring at his shirt. He was about to tell her he had kissed someone yesterday. And enjoyed it.

The telephone rang.

On the radio, the singers were telling the world that all was calm, all was bright.

The telephone kept ringing.

Susan got up and walked into the kitchen. She snatched the receiver from the wall phone. "Hello," she said icily. She listened. "Just a moment, please," she said, and came back into the living room.

"For you," she said. "Warren Chambers. And then you can go, please."

Bad enough when she was only kissing him.

That was in the beginning.

Early on in the movie.

The *real* fairy tale, the one he'd read when he was a kid, was about a miller who when he died left his mill to his oldest son, and his donkey to the middle son, and his cat to the youngest son, whose name was Tom. Tom figured all he could do with the cat was make a pie of him and then sell his skin. But the cat started talking, told him all he needed was a pair of high boots, and a fine hat with a feather, and a small sack, and he'd make young Tom rich. So Tom got him all these things, and through a lot of lying and finagling the cat pretended first that Tom was a marquis or something—a baron, maybe a count, this was a long time ago when he'd read the story—and tricked the king into thinking Tom was rich and finally Tom married the king's daughter and lived happily ever after.

That was the fairy tale.

In the movie . . .

But thou hast played the harlot with many lovers . . .

PUSS IN BOOTS

In the movie, this nigger just out of jail meets a girl is a harlot, and he dresses her up in high red boots and fine clothes and she lies and connives with two other girls and a young white boy, and in the end the nigger is rich and the harlot is a movie star.

Meg.

A movie star.

Bad enough at the beginning of the movie.

Only kissing him then. Kissing the nigger. Mouth open wide to receive his mouth, promising him diamonds and gold, only buy me the boots, baby, lips meeting, and a fine hat with a feather on it, and silky underwear, opening her mouth to him, her blouse to him, showing him her breasts. Yet I had planted thee a noble vine, wholly a right seed; how then art thou turned into the degenerate vine of a strange plant before me?

Later on in the movie . . .

The things she did with the nigger and the three other women, the boy, the things she did.

Was the nigger bothered him most.

For though thou wash thee with nitre, and take thee much soap, yet thine iniquity is marked before me.

Sitting in the living room of the main house, he watched the flickering images on the screen, watched them over and over again, over and over.

And I brought you into a plentiful country, he thought, to eat the fruit thereof and the goodness thereof; but when ye entered ye defiled my land, and made mine heritage an abomination.

"I think you got it wrong," Tick said. "I think maybe she meant Dill, after all."

"No, she was saying Deal," Mose said. "I know how niggers talk, she was saying *Deal*."

"Then how come we called every fucking Deal in the phone book, eleven Deals altogether and none of them ever heard of a Margaret Deal? You got it wrong, Mose."

"I got it right," Mose insisted.

"I want to go back over the Dills again," Tick said. "Maybe we missed one."

"I'm telling you it's *Deal*!"

"Where's that phone book?" Tick said.

"You'll be wasting your time looking at all those Dills again."

"I wasted my time looking at all the *Deals* too."

"Wasn't no Margaret *Dill*, either. All those numbers we called, nobody knew of any Margaret Dill."

"'Cause maybe we missed one. Where's that book?"

He opened the directory again to the page starting with Dieckmann at the top and ending with Diners Club/Carte Blanche at the bottom.

"Check these off on your list," he said.

"I'm telling you we got them all."

"Check them off *anyway*," Tick said, and began reading. "Dill, Abner."

"Got it."

"Dill, Bernard."

"Right."

"Dill, Evan."

"Right."

"Dill, Roger."

"Yeah."

"Dill, Rosalie."

"Uh-huh."

"Dill, Samuel."

"Yes."

"Dill, Thomas."

Mose sighed.

"You got a Dill, Thomas?"

"I got a Dill, Thomas."

"Dill, Victor."

"Yes. That's all of them," Mose said.

"That's all of them, yeah," Tick said.

He was starting to turn back to the page the Deals were on, thinking maybe they might've missed one or more of the Deals, had his hand ready to turn back the page, when his eye fell on the first listing at the top of the page. *Dieckmann Frank*, and his eye and his hand hesitated, his eye drifted several names down the page to where first one name, and then six other names popped out of the page at him:

Diehl Andrew

Diehl Bertram

Diehl Burgess

Diehl Candace

Diehl Carl

Diehl Joseph

Diehl Randolph

"Well, well, well," he said to Mose.

It was almost six o'clock.

Some four blocks away from Warren's office on the corner of Ross and Cameron, the First Congregational Church chimed the hour three minutes too early. Matthew looked at his watch. Warren looked at his watch.

"There are thirteen people listed under Orchestras and Bands," he said, "I managed to reach only eight of them."

"In person or on the phone?"

"Three in person, the rest on the phone. I had to do a bit of tightrope dancing, Matthew, 'cause I couldn't come right out and say, Hey, you didn't happen to clean out a storage bin rented by a lady was killed back in November, did you? What I said was I was looking to rent a van to transport some instruments in, and I heard you had such a van, and if you do I sure could use it on New Year's Eve for this gig in Sarasota. None of them had a van, none of them I spoke to anyway."

"So where do we go from here?" Matthew asked.

"Let it go till tomorrow, I guess, though I doubt we'll have any better luck on Christmas Day."

"Which ones did you cover?"

"Well, take a look," Warren said, and opened the telephone book to the yellow pages, and leafed past NURSES AND OFFICE and OILS and OPTOMETRISTS, until he came to the page listing ORCHESTRAS & BANDS. "The ones with the check marks after them are the ones I got to."

"Did you look under Music?"

"No," Warren said. "Shit, why didn't I think of that?"

He was starting to turn the pages back, when Matthew said, "Wait a minute."

The last listing under ORCHESTRAS & BANDS was:

BILL WADDELL & HIS RECORD MACHINE
Jazz - Rock - Contemporary

Under that, there was a new heading:

▶ **ORCHID GROWERS**

Elite Orchids, Inc.
Franco's Orchid Farm
Graham Orchids
Green Orchid The
Michael's Orchids
Orchidaceous

"There it is," Matthew said.

Tick was driving.

Mose was complaining.

"We should've used the phone," he said.

"Sure. A lot of luck we had already with the phone," Tick said.

"Those last two guys didn't think too kindly of us stopping by on Christmas Eve."

"Fuck 'em," Tick said. "What's that address again?"

"Thirty-seven fifty-five."

"Take a look at the next mailbox, tell me what it says."

He slowed the car as they approached a mailbox on the right side of the road.

"Thirty-six forty-three," Mose said.

"Almost there," Tick said. "Let me do all the talking this time, okay?"

"You did all the talking last time," Mose said.

"No, you were the one who said we were looking for a girl worked on a movie with us."

"So? What was wrong with that?"

"They thought we were lying is what was wrong."

The sky behind them was turning red.

"Pretty sunset coming," Tick said.

"I wish we were back in Tampa," Mose said.

"Let's find Connie first," Tick said. "Or Margaret. Or whoever the hell she is."

The car kept moving along Timucuan Point Road, heading east.

This scene now . . .

The nigger unzipping his fly.

Meg on her knees.

Looking up at him, angelic smile on her face.

Oooo, she says.

No sound on the film. He had to read their lips. Knew it by heart now, anyway.

Take it, he says.

All that? she says.

For starters, he says, and grins.

He sat in the darkness of the living room, shotgun on the floor beside the easy chair, anybody else came around looking for her, sniffing after her, they'd find the wrath of God. Wanted to pick up the shotgun right this minute, blow the nigger off the screen, blow him to hell and gone. *Wherefore* will ye plead with me . . .

Looks up at him.

Tastes like milk chocolate, she says.

Takes him in her mouth again.

Lifts her head.

And honey, she says.

In her mouth again.

Mmmm, she says.

Lifts her head.

Do you come white? she asks.

Smiles.

Takes it again.

Mmmm.

Moves her mouth off it. Looks at it. Admires it. Rolls her eyes again. Licks it. Closes her eyes. Says, Mmmmmm. Takes it in her mouth again, the mouth of the just bringeth forth wisdom, but the froward tongue shall be cut out. Her hand moving on it. Her lips moving on it.

Don't let up, he says.

She murmurs something around it.

That's it, Puss.

She moans around it.

Don't stop, Puss.

Mmm, she says.

Now, he says.

He giveth snow like wool, he scattereth the hoarfrost like ashes.

Oh baby, baby, he says, black hands in her red hair.

Mmm, she says.

Rolls her eyes again.

You like that, Puss?

Mmmmm.

"There it is," Tick said.

"There it is, for sure," Mose said.

They were crouched outside the window of the house, peering in under the bottom three inches of the drawn shade. They were looking at Jake Delaney milking himself on Connie's lips.

A man sat watching the movie.

Big blond guy in overalls.

Eyes fixed on the screen.

Like he was in a trance.

On the screen . . .

Think you can make me hard again?

Well, why don't we just try, honey?

They knew those words by heart.

Slow steamy smile.

Well, why don't we just try, honey?

They'd shot this scene the next day, but it looked like it followed immediately after the cum shot, made Jake look like a superman who could get another erection in the wink of an eye. Connie teasing him with her tongue and her lips, rolling him over her cheeks and her closed eyes, taking him between her breasts, stroking him against the cleft of her ass, closing both hands on him, tugging him gently, yanking him hard, letting up, rolling those green eyes, smiling that slow steamy smile again, hand stroking him gently again, head bending swiftly to him, tongue darting, and then straddling him, spreading herself wide to him, camera in for the close shot, rolling off him, going at him with her mouth again, playing, teasing, camera on her tongue, tight close shot, teasing, playing, driving Jake wild till he turned into a human battering ram again, sixty seconds flat, and only a day late.

"What do we do?" Mose asked.

"Why, we ask the man for our movie," Tick said.

He reached for the shotgun the moment the knock sounded at the door.

He snapped off the projector.

"Who's there?" he said.

"Mr Diehl?"

A man's voice.

Ye all have transgressed against me.

"What do you want?" he asked.

"Mr Diehl, we'd like to talk to you about that movie."

He raised the gun, turned it toward the door.

"Come in," he said. "It's open."

They made the right turn at the Orchidaceous sign, drove up the potholed road in Matthew's Ghia, Matthew at the wheel, Warren sitting beside him, his knees crowding him in the small car. The sky to the west was purple now, darker here over the land surrounding the lake, a bluish-black, night falling rapidly, silent night, holy night.

It was five hours before Christmas.

There was a house up ahead.

Dark.

Behind the house, two looming buildings with rounded tops.

"Must be the greenhouses there," Warren said.

Matthew nodded.

Angled toward the greenhouses, over to one side, a cinderblock structure.

They could hear noises out on the lake.

Thrashing.

Up ahead, in the car's headlights, a door opened in the cinderblock building.

A man appeared in the doorframe, his back to them.

He was dragging something.

"Hey now," Warren said.

Matthew stopped the car.

The man in the doorframe turned. Just his head. Arms still extended in front of him, bent over, holding something. Blond hair caught in the beams of the headlights. Warren was already getting out of the car. The man dropped whatever it was he was dragging. Matthew got out of the car on his side. The man reached inside the door. When he turned again, his whole body this time, a shotgun was in his hands.

"Down!" Warren shouted, and Matthew threw himself flat on the ground as a blast from the shotgun ripped yellow on the blue-black night. Warren was running toward the man. Warren had a pistol in his hand.

"Drop it!" Warren shouted, and the man fired again.

Warren took a quick step to the right, miraculously dodging the blast, twisted to face the man again, pistol in both hands now, a policeman's crouch. "Freeze!" he shouted, but the man came at him, holding the shotgun by the barrel, swinging the stock as if it were a club, the stock flailing the air, striking nothing but the night.

Warren fired.

His first shot took the man in the shoulder.

The man kept coming.

Warren fired lower this time, taking the man in the right leg, knocking him off his feet.

The man twisted and groaned in the dirt.

Warren came over to him.

"Okay?" he said, breathing hard. "Enough?"

The man tried to get to his feet.

"Mister, you're gonna be dead," Warren said.

And the man fell forward onto his face.

"Bingo," Warren said.

Matthew was walking toward the cinderblock building. Warren knelt beside the unconscious man, nodded, and then slipped the pistol back into his shoulder holster. Matthew was still walking toward the cinderblock building.

The Ghia's headlights illuminated the open doorway.

Matthew looked down at what was just inside the door.

"Oh, Jesus," he said, and turned away.

Warren ran to him.

"What . . . ?"

"Oh, Jesus," Matthew said again.

PUSS IN BOOTS

Warren looked down at the torn and mutilated body in the red leather boots, a garland of bloodred orchids around her neck. An instant of pain knifed his eyes, but that was all. It came, and it was gone, and he was once again a cop who had seen this before, had seen worse before.

Matthew had never seen anything like it in his life.

Matthew was bent over double, vomiting into the dirt road.

12

The Q and A took place in Burgess Diehl's room at Good Samaritan Hospital. Present with the stenographer and Diehl were State Attorney Skye Bannister, Assistant State Attorney Arthur Haggerty, Detective Morris Bloom of the Calusa P.D., Detective Ralph Sears of the Calusa Sheriff's Department, and Attorney Matthew Hope.

"Roll it," Haggerty said to the stenographer.

Date, time, place, people present, Haggerty read the routine information into the microphone. When he read Diehl the Miranda warnings, Diehl said, "I don't need no lawyer."

"And do you understand that even if you don't have a lawyer present, you still have the right to stop answering questions at any time?"

"I do."

"And you also have the right to stop answering at any time until you talk to a lawyer, if you decide later on you want to talk to one. Do you understand that?"

"Yes, I understand."

"Because this is America," Skye Bannister said.

"Very well then," Haggerty said. "Mr. Diehl, before I begin the questioning, is there anything you'd like to tell us about what happened? If you'd like to tell us in your own words . . ."

And he told them.

I knew about the movie, of course, knew she was working on a movie. I just didn't know what *kind* of movie.

A year and a half ago, must've been, she worked with this woman before. The woman was doing some kind of school movie about child abuse, and Meg was working at a day-care center at the time, she's very good with children, Meg. The good Lord never saw fit for us to have our own children, but she gave her heart to these other children day in and day out. That's where she met this woman for the first time. When they were doing scenes at the day-care center.

So she told me, Meg did, that this woman was doing another educational movie, and she wanted her to help out with the costumes on it, Meg's good with a needle and thread, too. Said it would only be from the end of September till early in November sometime, be a good opportunity to earn a few extra pennies.

So I said yes.

I mean, she'd never lied to me ever, she'd never withheld things from me ever.

But then I found the checks.

Four checks. Each for fifteen hundred dollars. The first one dated October third, the last one dated October twenty-fourth. She hadn't deposited them yet, I guess she was still trying to figure out where she could deposit them, how she could keep all this money from me. They were in the top drawer of her bureau, in back, under her panties. I forget what I was looking for in her drawer where she kept her panties.

Where are you getting this kind of money, I asked her, what are you doing to earn this kind of money? For Services, the checks read, what *kind* of services I asked her, where'd you get these, I asked her, what're these checks for? What does For Services mean?

And she said I shouldn't be going through her drawers, anyway, she said her drawers were private. So I said why is this Prudent Company paying you fifteen hundred dollars a week for services? She said I *knew* she was working for this woman who was making an educational movie, I've been doing costumes for her, I told you all about it. I'm doing wardrobe for her. That's why I'm gone five days a week, I've been doing wardrobe on this movie, you never listen when I tell you anything, you're so busy with your orchids all the time.

I said that seems like a lot of money for stitching and sewing.

She said well, movies pay a lot of money, movies are a big business.

I said I wanted to see them making this movie she was working on, and she said no, you can't do that, it's a closed set. I didn't know what that meant, a closed set. She told me the director of the movie, the woman who was paying her to make the costumes, was a very temperamental lady who didn't like anyone hanging around while she was working, that was what a closed set meant.

She kissed me then and told me not to worry, they'd be finished shooting on the fifth of November, which was only a bit more than a week away, and then she'd be home every day, and we'd have all this extra spending money.

The night she kissed me, I didn't know where her mouth had been.

On Halloween night—this was four days later, four days after we'd talked about her doing costumes—she told me that they had to shoot this scene at night, it was a big costume party scene, she had to be there at night. I said sure, fine. But I followed her. She drove the VW out to Fatback Key, me behind in the van, keeping a safe distance behind her, I wanted to see what she was doing to earn fifteen hundred dollars a week.

I could have killed them all that very minute, the things I spied that night. For all nations have drunk of the wine of the wrath of her fornication, and the kings of the earth have committed fornication with her, and the merchants of the earth are waxed rich through the abundance of her delicacies. And I heard another voice from heaven saying, "Come out of her, my people, that ye not be partakers of her sins, and that ye receive not of her plagues. For her sins have reached unto heaven, and God hath remembered her iniquities." And I beheld another beast coming out of the earth, and he had two horns like a lamb, and he spake as a dragon. And I saw three unclean spirits like frogs come out of the mouth of the dragon, and out of the mouth of the beast, and out of the mouth of the false prophet. I could have killed them all. Standing outside there in the dark, looking in at them, spying what they were doing, I could have killed them all, God forgive me.

And yet . . .

Forgive them, for they know not what they do.

But . . .

The false prophet knew.

The woman, you see. The blonde woman telling them what to do. And they worshipped the dragon which gave power unto the beast. She knew.

I followed her home that night.

Didn't even know her name at the time.

Prudence Ann Markham.

Didn't even know her name.

208

That was the first time I followed her.

They finished the movie on the fifth day of November, same as Meg had told me they would. Nothing to worry about anymore, she said. She'd be home every day now, no more going out to stitch and sew her *costumes*, oh no, little Puss in Boots safe at home now.

I was still following Prudence Ann Markham.

Because I figured . . .

This is a *movie*.

This is something people will *see*, Meg naked and unashamed, doing vile things with the beast and the others, the three other women and the young boy. I didn't know yet what I was going to do about Meg, had no plans for her yet, but I knew I had to get that movie, had to keep people from seeing that movie, had to make sure nobody saw what I didn't want them to see, what it was wrong for them to see, what the good Lord had never intended anyone to see, had to get that movie, destroy that movie, burn that movie.

She was working on it at a studio out on Rancher Road. Drove to the storage bin each night, took cans of film out of it, carried them with her to the studio, drove back to the bin again when she was finished there each night. Had a key to the storage bin.

I figured I had to get that key.

Had to get that key to get the movie.

Destroy the movie.

Followed her each night from the storage place to her house on Pompano Way. Followed her. And they worshipped the dragon which gave power to the beast. Had to destroy the movie. Had to destroy the dragon responsible for the movie, responsible for what Meg had become.

Still didn't know what I was going to do about Meg.

That only came to me later.

I'm not dumb, I'm not a stupid person. I knew I had to destroy this woman so I could get the film she carried with her each night to the studio, get the key to the storage bin where maybe there was more film, destroy the movie. But how would it serve the Lord if I destroyed myself at the same time? No, no, I'm not stupid.

She was married, I knew that by then, I'd seen her husband at the house there on Pompano Way, knew she was married, what kind of a man allowed his wife to do such things? To spew such filth upon the earth? So the idea came to me, it occurred to me that I could kill two birds with one stone, three birds if you counted the movie, destroy the woman and her husband both and then destroy the movie.

I broke into the house on the tenth of November, watched the house till they were both gone, knew the house would be empty. Stole his clothes and the knife. Some other things, too, so they wouldn't know what I was after. Stole some of *her* clothes, too, I still have them, they're in Meg's bureau where she used to keep her things before I burned them. I still look at the woman's clothes sometimes, I look at them. Wonder what kind of a woman could do such things. Look at her clothes and wonder. Still wonder.

Gave myself a little time after I broke into the house. Figured I'd wait a week so nobody'd make any connection. Then decided ten days'd be better. Followed her to the studio. Waited outside for her. She come out, it must've been twenty to eleven, around then. It didn't take more'n a minute to do it to her. Got my clothes—*his* clothes—all covered with the filth of her blood while I was doing it. Took the cans of film and tape in this aluminum carrying case and her pocketbook and her keys. It wasn't no more'n ten minutes from Rancher Road to my house, another ten minutes to shower and change my clothes—I'd already locked Meg in the generator room by then, though I still didn't know what I was going to do with her. I wrapped the bloody clothes and the knife in a plastic garbage bag, left the house around eleven it must've been, took me fifteen minutes or so to get to Pompano Way. I must've got there around a quarter past eleven, thereabouts. I buried the bloody clothes and the knife in the backyard, behind the house, in the flower bed. Then I went to the storage bin and opened it with her key, and took what was inside there. Got there around midnight, I guess. Took everything was inside the bin.

I watched that movie a lot.

Still do.

Never saw anything in my life like what's in that movie.

People shouldn't be allowed to see movies like that.

I'll burn it one day.

For wickedness burneth as the fire.

"Mr Diehl," Haggerty said, "I show you this Polaroid photo taken by the Sheriff's Department at 3755 Timucuan Point Road earlier tonight. Is this your wife, Margaret Diehl?"

"But the wicked shall be cut off from the earth," Diehl said, "and the transgressor shall be rooted out of it."

"Sir? Is this photograph I show you, this picture of a woman in red boots . . . is this your wife Margaret Diehl, sir?"

"For the husband is the head of the wife, even as Christ is the head of the church," Diehl said.

"Is this your wife, sir?"

"Therefore, as the church is subject unto Christ, so let the wives be to their own husbands in every thing."

"Mr. Diehl, can you tell us what happened to your wife? To this woman in the photograph. *Is* this your wife, sir?"

"What?"

"Your wife. Is this woman your wife?"

"*Was* my wife."

"*Was* your wife? Do you mean she's no longer your wife because she's dead, sir?"

"Dead? No, no."

"Sir . . . this woman in the photograph. Sir, her arms have been amputated . . ."

"Yes, I know."

"Do you know who amputated her arms, sir? And mutilated her breasts?"

"I did."

"Then, Mr. Diehl . . . did you kill your wife, Margaret?"

"No. Kill her? No, no. I was gonna put her out tonight. On the street. Near the manger."

"Put her body out on the street?"

"Put *her* out on the street. For all to see her shame. For it is a shame even to speak of those things which are done of them in secret."

"But your wife is dead, sir. The Medical Examiner . . ."

"No, sir."

"Mr. Diehl, the Medical Examiner estimates that she's been dead for quite some . . ."

"Then who've I been talking to? Speak not in the ears of a fool, for he will despise the wisdom of thy words."

"Did you cut off her arms, Mr. Diehl?"

211

"The fingers."

"Sir?"

"I started with the fingers. To punish her for what she'd done with her hands. For what evil is in mine hand? And when ye spread forth your hands, I will hide mine eyes from you . . ."

"Mr. Diehl . . ."

"Yeah, when ye make many prayers, I will not hear. Your hands are full of blood."

"When you say you started with the fingers . . ."

"That's a lie."

"Sir?"

"I cut off her hair first. Everywhere. All over her body. Her head, down there . . . everywhere."

Silence.

Haggerty turned to Bannister.

"Skye? You want to take this?" he said.

"Mr. Diehl," Bannister said, "I'm Skye Bannister, the State Attorney. I wonder if I might be able to help you make yourself a bit more clear. As I understand this, you cut off your wife's fingers, and then her arms . . ."

"First her hair."

"Then her fingers . . ."

"No, then her tongue. I cut out her tongue. But the tongue can no man tame. It is an unruly evil, full of deadly poison. And the tongue is a fire, a world of iniquity. So is the tongue among our members, that it defileth the whole body and setteth on fire the course of nature, and it is set on fire of hell."

"You cut out her tongue . . ."

"Let the woman learn in silence with all subjugation."

"And then her fingers, and her hands . . . her arms . . ."

"His own hands shall bring the offerings of the Lord made by fire, the fat with the breast, it shall he bring, that the breast may be waved for a wave offering before the Lord. They'll see her tonight, when I put her out beside the manger. See her naked, the whore, except for the boots. I stitched her mouth shut, too, with nylon sail thread, so she'd never be able to use it again for the things she done. Stitched her shut down there, too, for a whore is a deep ditch and a strange woman is a narrow pit."

Skye Bannister sighed.

It was eleven-thirty on Christmas Eve, and outside in the hospital parking lot a Christmas tree blinked red and green to a starry night.

"Mr. Diehl," he said, "is there anything you'd like to add to what you've already told us?"

"You'll find something in the water," Diehl said.

"Sir?"

"How much more abominable and filthy is man, which drinketh iniquity like water?"

"Mr. Diehl, is there anything you'd like to change or correct in what you've . . . ?"

"Nothing," Diehl said. "I don't want to change nothing I done."

Bannister looked at his watch.

"Time completed, twenty-three hundred hours, thirty-one minutes," he said into the microphone, and then, to the stenographer, "It's a wrap."

They left Diehl's room.

In the corridor outside, Bannister said, "Meese's people were right."

"What?" Matthew said.

"The Attorney General's Commission on Pornography. They were right. Pornography leads to violence."

Matthew said nothing.

On Christmas morning, he wondered what he was supposed to do.

He had already informed Markham that the charge against him was being dropped. He was a free man. Free to get on with his goddamn life, as he'd once called it.

"What about the film?" Markham asked.

"What about it?" Matthew said.

"When do I get the film back?"

"I'm sure they'll need it for Diehl's trial," Matthew said. "To establish motive."

"What about after the trial? I was counting on that film for . . ."

"You'll have to ask Bannister about that."

"Bannister? What the hell does . . . ?"

"He may want to burn it," Matthew said.

And now, at a little before ten o'clock on Christmas morning, he wondered what he was supposed to do. He had not heard from Susan since she'd asked him to leave her house last night. He had planned to spend Christmas with her and Joanna. Open presents together. Just like old times. Maybe the man was right, he thought. Maybe you can't go home again. He lifted the phone and dialed her number.

Joanna answered the phone.

"Hi, Dad," she said. "Merry Christmas."

"Merry Christmas, honey," he said.

"Mom tells me you won't be coming over today."

"Oh?"

"What happened?"

"Well . . . I'm not sure," he said.

"You guys are very confusing," Joanna said.

"That's for sure," Matthew said, and then hesitated. "Joanna . . . if anyone tells you to stop seeing Thomas . . ."

"Who would tell me that?"

"Well, if anyone should . . ."

"I can't imagine anyone . . ."

"Honey . . . no one has the right to censor your mind or your heart."

"Huh?" she said.

"Just remember that."

"Well, sure," she said. "Shall I get Mom?"

"Please," he said, and hoped he'd made himself clear.

When Susan picked up the phone, it was indeed like old times. He used to wonder which Susan he'd be talking to on any given day, the Witch or the Waif. On Christmas, he was sort of expecting the Waif. Instead, he got . . .

"Matthew, I don't think you ought to come over today, do you? I've been doing a lot of thinking about last night, and it seems to me we've been rushing into something perhaps neither of us is quite ready for. The argument last night was too reminiscent of painful times in the past, and quite frankly I'm not eager to cover the same ground all over again. I know you're eager to see Joanna, this *is* after all Christmas, but perhaps you can spend tomorrow with her, exchange your gifts then, if that's all right with you. I think it might be worse for her if all three of us spent the day together, considering the uncertain climate between us just now. Don't you agree?"

"Sure," he said.

"So," she said.

"So," he said.

There was a long silence.

Then she said, "Matthew, don't you . . . ?"

And paused.

And said plaintively, "Matthew, don't you think I'm right? I mean, what's the use of . . . oh, shit, I just don't know."

"Neither do I," he said.

"Can we give it a little time?"

"Sure."

Another silence.

"And I won't say anything to Joanna," she said.

"About?"

"Her boyfriend."

"Oh."

"I'll give *that* a little time, too."

"Good," Matthew said.

"So," she said again.

"So," he said.

"Merry Christmas," she said.

"Merry Christmas," he said.

There was a click on the line.

He put the receiver back on the cradle.

He went out into the living room.

He mixed himself a martini. Ten o'clock in the morning.

The telephone rang.

Susan, he thought. A change of heart.

Or Joanna. In tears.

He walked to the kitchen counter, picked up the phone.

"Hello?" he said.

"Matthew?"

A woman's voice.

"Yes?"

"This is Marcie Franklin."

"Oh, hi," he said.

"Merry Christmas," she said.

"Merry Christmas."

"I wanted to apologize for the other day. I guess I *did* have one too many, I'm not normally that brazen."

215

Silence.

"I'm glad this is the right number," she said. "I got it from last year's phone book."

More silence.

"Well," she said, "I know you must be busy, this is Christmas Day, I just wanted to . . ."

"Are you free for lunch?" he said.

"I thought you'd never ask," she said.

Lady Killer

The city in these pages is imaginary.
The people, the places, are all fictitious.
Only the police routine is based on established
investigatory technique.

1

WERE YOU
A CRANK
THIS WEEK ? ? ? ?

A crank is a person who calls Frederick 7–8024 and says, "I don't want to have to tell you about that Chinese laundry downstairs again. The owner uses a steam iron, and the hissing keeps me awake. Now, will you please arrest him?"

A crank is a person who addresses a letter to the 87th Precinct and writes: "I am surrounded by assassins. I need police protection. The Russians know that I have invented a supersonic tank."

Every police precinct in the world gets its share of crank calls and letters every day of the week. The calls and letters range from the sincere to the idiotic to the sublime. There are people who have information about suspected Communists, kidnappers, murderers, abortionists, forgers, and high-class whorehouses. There are people who complain about television comedians, mice, landlords, loud phonographs, strange ticking sounds in the walls, and automobile horns that play, "I'll be down to getya inna taxi, honey." There are people who claim to have been exhorted, extorted, duped, threatened, libeled, slandered, beaten, maimed, and even murdered. The classic call at the 87th was from a woman who claimed to have been shot dead four days ago, and why hadn't the police yet found her murderer?

There are, too, mysterious and anonymous calls that flatly and simply state, "There is a bomb in a shoe box at the Avon Theater."

Crank calls can be terrifying. Crank calls and letters cost the city a lot of time and expense. The trouble is, you see, that you can't tell a crank from a noncrank without a programme.

WERE YOU
A CRANK
THIS WEEK ? ? ? ?

It was Wednesday, July 24th.

The city was hot, and the muster room of the 87th Precinct was probably the hottest place in the city. Dave Murchison sat behind the high desk to the left of the entrance doorway and wished that his underwear shorts would stop riding up his buttocks. It was only eight o'clock in the morning, but the city had been building a blast-oven temperature all the preceding day, and the night had brought no relief. And now, with the sun barely up, the city was still wilted. It was difficult to imagine any further wilting, but Dave Murchison knew the muster room would get hotter and hotter and hotter as the day wore on, and he knew the small rotating fan on the corner of the high desk would not help to cool the room, and he also knew his undershorts would continue to ride up his buttocks.

At 7.45 A.M., Captain Frick, the commanding officer of the precinct, had inspected the handful of uniformed policemen who had not relieved their colleagues on post. He had then sent them out into the streets and turned to Murchison.

"Going to be a scorcher, huh, Dave?" he had asked.

Murchison had nodded bleakly. He was fifty-three years old, and had lived through many a suffocating summer in his day. He had learned over the years that comments about the weather very rarely changed the weather. The thing to do was sit it out quietly. It was his own belief that all this heat was caused by those damn H-bomb explosions in the Pacific. Human beings had begun messing around with the stuff best left to God, and this was what they got for it.

Surlily Dave Murchison tugged at his underwear.

He barely looked at the boy who mounted the stone steps before the station house and walked into the muster room. The kid glanced at the sign requesting all visitors to stop at the desk.

He walked to the sign and stood before it, laboriously working out the words.

"What do you want, sonny?" Murchison asked.

"You the desk sergeant?"

"I'm the desk sergeant," Murchison said. He reflected on the virtues of a job that made it necessary to justify yourself to a snotnose.

"Here," the kid said, and he handed Murchison an envelope. Murchison took it. The boy started out of the building.

"Just a second, kid," Murchison said.

The kid didn't stop. He kept walking, down the steps, out onto the sidewalk, into the city, into the world.

"Hey!" Murchison said. Hastily he looked around him for a patrolman. He had never seen it to fail. There never was a cop around when you needed one.

Sourly he tugged at his undershorts and opened the envelope. He read the single page inside the envelope. Then he folded the page, put it back into the envelope, and shouted, "Is there another damn cop in this building besides me?"

A patrolman poked his head from behind one of the doors on the ground floor.

"Something wrong, Sarge?" he asked.

"Where the hell *is* everybody?"

"Around," the patrolman said. "We're around."

"Take this letter up to the squadroom," Murchison said. He handed the envelope over the desk.

"A *billet-doux*?" the patrolman asked. Murchison did not reply. It was too hot for half-assed attempts at humor. The patrolman shrugged and followed the pointing DETECTIVE DIVISION sign to the second floor of the building. He walked down the corridor, stopped at the slatted rail divider, pushed open the gate in the railing, walked to the desk of Cotton Hawes, and said, "Desk sergeant said to bring this up here."

"Thanks," Hawes said, and he opened the letter.

The letter read:

2

Detective Hawes read the letter, and then read it again. His first reaction was "Crank."

His second reaction was "Suppose not?"

Sighing, he shoved back his chair and walked across the squadroom. He was a tall man, six feet two inches in slipper socks, and he weighed one hundred and ninety pounds. He had blue eyes and a square jaw with a cleft chin. His hair was red, except for a streak over his left temple where he had once been knifed and where the hair had curiously grown in white after the wound healed. His straight nose was clean and unbroken, and he had a good mouth with a wide lower lip. His fists were huge. He used one of them now on the lieutenant's door.

"Come!" Lieutenant Byrnes shouted.

Hawes opened the door and stepped into the corner office. A rotating fan swept air across the lieutenant's desk. Byrnes sat behind the desk, a compact man in shirt sleeves, his tie pulled down, his collar open, the sleeves rolled up over his biceps.

"The newspapers say rain," he said. "Where the hell's the rain?" Hawes grinned. "You bringing me trouble, Hawes?"

"I don't know. What do you think?" He put the letter on Byrne's desk.

Byrnes read it rapidly. "It never fails," he said. "We always get the cuckoos when the temperature's in the nineties. It drives them out of the woodwork."

"Do you think it's a crank, sir?"

"How the hell do I know? It's either a crank, or it's legit." He smiled. "That's a phenomenal bit of deduction, isn't it? It's no wonder I'm a lieutenant."

"What do we do?" Hawkes asked.

"What time is it?"

Hawes looked at his watch. "A little past eight, sir."

"That gives us about twelve hours—assuming this is legit— to stop a potential killer from knocking off 'the lady,' whoever she is. Twelve hours to find a killer and a victim in a city of eight

223

million people, with nothing more to go on than this letter. *If it's legit.*"

"It may be, sir."

"I know," Byrnes said reflectively. "It may also be somebody's idea of a joke. Nothing to do? Time growing heavy on your hands? Write a letter to the cops. Send them off on a wild-goose chase. It could be that, Cotton."

"Yes, sir."

"Don't you think it's time you started calling me Pete?"

"Yes, sir."

Byrnes nodded. "Who's handled this letter, outside of you and me?"

"the desk sergeant, I imagine. I didn't touch the surface, sir . . . Pete . . . if you're thinking of latents."

"I am," Byrnes said. "Who's on the desk?"

"Dave Murchison."

"He's a good man, but I'll bet his prints are all over this damn thing. How was he to know what was inside the envelope?" Byrnes thought for a moment. "Let's play it safe, Cotton. When we send this over to the lab, we'll shoot a copy of your prints, mine, and Dave's with it. It might save Grossman's boys a lot of time. Time looks like the one thing we can use."

"Yes, sir," Hawes said.

Byrnes picked up his phone, pressed the intercom button twice, and waited.

"Captain Frick," a voice answered.

"John, this is Pete," Byrnes said. "Can you—?"

"Hello, Pete," Frick said. "Going to be a scorcher, huh?"

"Yeah," Byrnes said. "John, can you relieve Murchison at the desk for an hour or so?"

"I suppose so. Why?"

"And get a man set up with the roller and pad. I want some prints taken right now."

"Who'd you pick up, Pete?"

"Nobody."

"Well, whose prints do you want?"

"Mine, Hawes's, and Murchison's."

"Oh, I see," Frick said, completely bewildered.

"I'll need a squad car with a siren, and a man you can spare. I'll also want to question Murchison."

"You sound pretty mysterious, Pete. Want to . . . ?"

"We're coming down now to get printed," Byrnes said. "Will you be ready for us?"

"Sure, sure," Frick said, mystified.

"'Bye, John."

The three men were printed.

The prints and the letter were put together into a large manila envelope, and the package was entrusted to a patrolman. The patrolman was instructed to drive directly to Headquarters downtown on High Street, using his siren all the way. He would deliver the package to Sam Grossman, the lieutenant in charge of the police laboratory there, and then he would wait while Sam's men photographed the letter. He would bring the photograph back to the 87th, where the detectives would study it while Grossman's laboratory technicians performed their various tests on the original. Grossman had already been called and informed that speed was essential. The patrolman knew this, too. When the squad car pulled away from the curb in front of the station house, the tyres were squealing and the siren was beginning its high wail.

Inside the precinct, in the detective squadroom, a cop named Dave Murchison was being questioned by Byrnes and Hawes.

"Who delivered the letter, Dave?"

"A kid," Murchison said.

"Boy or girl?"

"Boy."

"How old?"

"I don't know. Ten? Eleven? Somewhere around there."

"What color hair?"

"Blond."

"Eyes?"

"I didn't notice."

"How tall?"

"Average height for a kid that age."

"What was he wearing?"

"Dungarees and a striped tee shirt."

"What colour stripes?"

"Red."

"That ought to be easy," Hawes said.

"Any hat?" Byrnes asked.

"No."

"What kind of shoes?"

"I didn't see his feet from behind the desk."

"What did he say to you?"

"He asked if I was the desk sergeant. I told him I was. He handed me the letter."

"Did he say who it was from?"

"No. He just handed it to me and said. 'Here.'"

"What then?"

"He walked out."

"Why didn't you stop him?"

"I was alone with the desk, sir. I yelled for him to stop, but he didn't. I couldn't leave the desk, and nobody else was around."

"What about the desk lieutenant?"

"Frank was having a cup of coffee. I couldn't stick with the switchboard and also go chasing a kid."

"Okay, Dave, don't get excited."

"I mean, what the hell, Frank wants a cup of coffee, that's his business. He only went upstairs to Clerical. How the hell were we supposed to know this would happen?"

"Don't get excited, Dave."

"I'm not excited. I'm just saying there was nothing wrong with Frank getting a cup of coffee, that's all. In this heat you got to make allowances. A man sits behind that desk, he begins to—"

"Okay, Dave, okay."

"Look, Pete," Murchison said, "I'm sorry as hell. If I'd known this kid was going to be important—"

"It's all right, Dave. Did you handle the letter much?"

Murchison looked at the floor. "The letter and the envelope both. I'm sorry, Pete. I didn't think this would be—"

"It's all right, Dave. When you get back to the switchboard, turn on your radio, will you? Give a description of this kid to all cars in the precinct. Get one car to cruise and alert every foot patrolman. I want the kid brought in as soon as he's located."

"Right," Murchison said. He looked at Byrnes. "Pete, I'm sorry if I—"

Byrnes clapped him on the shoulder. "Forget it," he said. "Get those calls out, will you?"

The maximum pay for a patrolman in the city that cradled the 87th Precinct was $5,015 a year. That is not a lot of money. In addition to that $5,015, the patrolman received $125 for the annual maintenance of his uniforms. That is still not a lot of money.

It becomes even less money when the various deductions are made every two weeks on payday. Four bucks comes out automatically for hospitalization, and another buck and a half is deducted for the precinct bed tax. This tax pays the salary of police widows who make up the dozen or so precinct beds that are used in emergencies when two shifts are on duty—and that are sometimes used by anyone wanting to catch a little shut-eye, emergency or no. Federal income tax takes another bite. The Police Benevolent Association, a sort of union for the law enforcers, gets its cut. The *High Street Journal*, the police publication, is usually subscribed to, hence another bite. If the cop has been decorated, he donates to the Police Honor Legion. If he's religious, he donates to the various societies and the various charities that visit the precinct each year. His pay check, after it has been divided and subdivided, usually comes to $130 every two weeks.

That amounts to sixty-five bucks a week no matter how you slice it.

If some cops take graft—and some cops *do* take graft—it maybe because they're slightly hungry.

A police force is a small army, and as with any military organization, the orders must be obeyed no matter how ridiculous they may sound. When the foot patrolmen and the radio motor patrolmen of the 87th received their orders that morning of July 24th, they thought the orders were rather peculiar. Some shrugged. Some cursed. Some simply nodded. All obeyed.

The orders were to pick up a ten-year-old boy with blond hair who was wearing dungarees and a red-striped tee-shirt.

It sounded simple.

At 9:15 A.M. the photograph of the letter came back from the lab. Byrnes called a meeting in his office. He put the letter in

227

the centre of his desk, and he and three other detectives studied it.

"What do you make of it, Steve?" he asked. He asked Steve Carella first because of many reasons. To begin with, he thought Carella was the best cop on his squad. True, Hawes was beginning to shape up, even though he'd made a bad start shortly after his transfer to the precinct. But Hawes, in Byrnes's estimation, had a long way to go before he would equal Carella. Secondly, and quite apart from the fact that Carella was a good cop and a tough cop, Byrnes felt personally attached to him. He would never forget that Carella had risked his life, and almost lost it, trying to crack a case in which Byrnes's son had been involved. In Byrnes's mind, Carella had become almost a *second* son. And so, like any father with a son in the business, he asked for Carella's opinion first.

"I've got my own theories about guys who send letters like this," Carella said. He picked up the photograph and held it to the light streaming through the windows. He was a tall, deceptively slender man, giving an impression of strength without the slightest hint of massive power. His eyes were slightly slanted and, together with his clean-shaven look, they gave him a high-cheeked, somewhat Oriental appearance.

"What's your idea, Steve?" Byrnes asked.

Carella tapped the photograph. "The first question I ask is, Why? If this joker is about to commit homicide, he sure as hell knows there are laws against it. The obvious way to do murder is to do it secretly and quietly and try to escape the law. But no. He sends us a letter. Why does he send us a letter?"

"It's more fun for him this way," said Hawes, who had been listening intently to Carella. "He's got a double challenge—the challenge of killing someone, and the challenge of getting away with it after he's raised the odds."

"That's one way to look at it," Carella said, and Byrnes watched the interplay between the two cops and was pleased by it. "But there's another possibility. He *wants* to get caught."

"Like this Heirens kid in Chicago, a few years back?" Hawes said.

"Sure. The lipstick on the mirror. Catch me before I kill again." Carella tapped the letter. "Maybe *he* wants to get caught, too. Maybe he's scared stiff of killing and wants us to catch him before he *has* to kill. What do you think, Pete?"

Byrnes shrugged. "It's a theory. In any case, we still have to catch him."

"I know, I know," Carella said. "But if he wants to get caught, then the letter isn't just a letter. Do you follow me?"

"No."

Detective Meyer nodded. "I get you, Steve. He's not just warning us, he's tipping us."

"Sure," Carella said. "If he wants to get caught, if he wants to be stopped, this letter'll tell us just how to stop him. It'll tell us who and where." He dropped the letter on Byrnes's desk.

Detective Meyer walked over to it and studied it. Meyer was a very patient cop, and so his scrutiny of the letter was careful and slow. Meyer, you see, had a father who was something of a practical joker. The senior Meyer, whose name was Max, had been somewhat startled and surprised when his wife had announced she was going to have a change-of-life baby. When the baby had been born, Max had played his little joke on humanity and incidentally on his son. He had given the baby the name of Meyer, which added to the surname of Meyer, had caused the infant to emerge as Meyer Meyer. The joke had doubtless been a masterpiece of hilarity. Except perhaps to Meyer Meyer. The boy had grown up as an Orthodox Jew in a predominantly Gentile neighborhood. The kids on the block had been accustomed to taking out their petty hatreds on scapegoats, and what better scapegoat than one whose name presented a ready-made chant: "Meyer Meyer, Jew-on-Fire!" In all fairness, they had never put Meyer Meyer to the stake. But he had suffered many a beating in the days of his youth, and faced with what seemed to be the overwhelming odds of life, he had developed an attitude of extreme patience toward his fellow man.

Patience is an exacting virtue. Perhaps Meyer Meyer had emerged unscarred and unscathed. Perhaps. He was nonetheless completely bald. There are a lot of men who are completely bald. But Meyer Meyer was only thirty-seven years old.

Patiently, exactingly, he studied the letter now.

"It doesn't say a hell of a lot, Steve," he said.

"Read it," Byrnes told him.

"'I will kill The Lady tonight at eight,'" Meyer quoted. "'What can you do about it?'"

"Well, it tells us who," Carella said.

"Who?" Byrnes asked.

"'The Lady,'" Carella said.

"And who's she?"

"I don't know."

"Mmmm."

"It doesn't tell us how," Meyer said, "or where."

"But it does give a time," Hawes put in.

"Eight. Tonight at eight."

"You really think this character wants to get caught, Steve?"

"I really don't know. I'm just offering a theory. I do know one thing."

"What's that?"

"Until we get a report from the lab, we'd better start with what we've got."

Byrnes looked at the letter.

"Well, what the hell do we have?"

"The Lady," Carella answered.

3

Fats Donner was a stool pigeon.

There are stool pigeons and there are stool pigeons, and there is no law in the city that prevents you from getting your information from whomever you want to. If you like Turkish baths, there is no better stool pigeon than Fats.

When Hawes had worked with the 30th Squad, he had had his own coterie of informers. Unfortunately, his tattletales had all been highly specialized men who were hip only to the crimes and criminals within the 30th Precinct. Their limited scope did not extend to the brawling, sprawling 87th. And so at 9:27 A.M. that morning, while Steve Carella went to see his own preferred stoolie—a man named Danny Gimp—and while Meyer Meyer checked the Lousy File for any female criminals who might have used "The Lady" as an alias, Cotton Hawes spoke to Detective Hal Willis, and Willis told him to look up Donner.

A call to Donner's apartment drew a blank.

"He's probably at the baths," Willis said, and he gave Hawes the address. Hawes checked out a car and drove downtown.

The sign outside the place read:

REGAN BATHS
Turkish
Steam
Galvanized

Hawes walked in climbed a flight of wooden steps leading to the second floor of the building, and stopped before a desk in the lobby. The climb had already brought perspiration to Hawes's forehead. He wondered why anyone would go to a Turkish bath on a day like today, and then he further wondered why anyone would go swimming in January, and then he thought the hell with it.

"What can I do you for?" the man at the desk asked. He was

a small man with a sharp nose. He wore a white tee shirt upon which the name REGAN BATHS was stencilled in green. He also wore a green eyeshade.

"Police," Hawes said, and he flashed the tin.

"You got the wrong place," the man said. "This is a legit bath. Somebody steered you wrong."

"I'm looking for a man named Fats Donner. Know where I can find him?"

"Sure," the man said. "Donner's a regular. You got no beef with me?"

"Who are you?"

"Alf Regan. I run this joint. Legit."

"I only want to talk to Donner. Where is he?"

"Room Four, middle of the hall. You can't go in like that, mister."

"What do I need?"

"Just your skin. But I'll give you a towel. Lockers are back there. Anything valuable, you can leave here at the desk. I'll put it in the safe."

Hawes unloaded his wallet and watch. He debated for a moment, and then unclipped his service revolver and holster and put them on the desk.

"That thing loaded?" Regan asked.

"Yes."

"Mister, you better—"

"It's got an internal safety," Hawes said. "It can't go off unless the trigger is pulled."

Regan looked at the .38 sceptically. "Okay, okay," he said, "but I wonder how many people accidentally get shot by guns that got internal safeties."

Hawes grinned and headed for the lockers. While he was undressing, Regan brought him a towel.

"I hope you got a thick hide," he said.

"Why?"

"Donner likes them hot. I mean *hot*."

Hawes wrapped the towel around his middle.

"You got a good build," Regan said. "Ever do any boxing?"

"A little."

"Where?"

"In the Navy."

"Any good?"

"Fair."

"Take a punch," Regan said.

"What?"

"Throw a punch at me."

"What for?"

"Go ahead, go ahead."

"I'm in a hurry," Hawes said.

"Just take a swing. I want to see something." Regan put up his hands in a fighting stance.

Hawes shrugged, feinted with his left, and then crossed a right at Regan's jaw, pulling the punch just before it hammered home.

"Why'd you pull it?" Regan demanded.

"I didn't want to knock your head off."

"Who taught you that feint?"

"A lieutenant j.g. named Bohan."

"He taught you good. I manage a couple of fighters on the side. You ever think of going into the ring?"

"Never."

"Think about it. This country could use a heavyweight champ."

"I'll think about it," Hawes said.

"You'd make a hell of a lot more than the city pays you, you can bet your ass on that. Even doing tankers, you'd make a hell of a lot more."

"Well, I'll think about it," Hawes said. "Where's Donner?"

"Down the hall. Listen, take my card. You ever decide to take a whack at it, give me a ring. Who knows? Maybe we got another Dempsey here, huh?"

"Sure," Hawes said. He took the card Regan offered him, and then looked down at the towel. "Where do I put the card?" he asked.

"Oh. Oh, yeah. Well, give it to me. I'll catch you on the way out. Donner's right down the hall. Room Four. You can't miss it. There's enough steam in there to move the *Queen Mary*."

Hawes started down the corridor. He passed a thin man who looked at him suspiciously. The man was naked, and his suspicion was bred by the towel Hawes wore. Hawes passed the man guiltily, feeling very much like a photographer in a nudist colony. He found Room Four, opened the door, and was hit in

233

the face by a blast of heat that almost sent him reeling back down the corridor. He tried to see through the layers of shifting steam in the room, but it was impossible.

"Donner?" he called.

"Here, man," a voice answered.

"Where?"

"Over here, man. Sittin'. Who is it?"

"My name's Cotton Hawes. I work on Hal Willis' squad. He told me to contact you."

"Oh, yeah. Come on in, man, come on in," the bodiless voice said. "Close the door. You're lettin' steam out and draughts in."

Hawes closed the door. If he had ever wondered how a loaf of bread feels when the oven door seals it in, he now knew. He worked his way across the room. The heat was suffocating. He tried to suck air into his lungs, found only heat passing into his throat. A figure suddenly materialized in the shifting hot fog.

"Donner?" Hawes asked.

"Ain't nobody here but us chickens, boss," Donner answered, and Hawes grinned despite the heat.

Fats was truly fat in the plural. He was city-wide, he was state-wide, he was continental. Like a giant, quivering bowl of white flesh, he sat on the marble bench against the wall, languishing in the fetid air, a towel draped across his crotch. Each time he breathed, layers of fat shook and trembled.

"You're a cop, ain't you?" he asked.

"Sure."

"You said Willis' squad, but that coulda meant like other things. Willis gave me the nod, huh?"

"Yes," Hawes said.

"Good man, Willis. I saw him dump a guy who musta weighed four hundred pounds right on his ass. Judo. He's a judo expert. You reach for him and push-pull-click-click! your arm's in a plaster cast. Man, we in danger." Donner chuckled. When he chuckled, everything he owned chuckled with him. The motion was making Hawes a little seasick.

"So what do you want to know?" Donner asked.

"Know anybody called The Lady?" Hawes said, figuring it was best to come straight to the point before he collapsed of heat prostration.

"The Lady," Donner said. "Fancy handle. She in the rackets?"

"Maybe."

"I knew a dame called The Lady Bird in St. Louis. She was a stoolie. Damn good one, too. So they called her The Lady Bird. Pigeon, bird, you dig?"

"I dig," Hawes said.

"She knew everything, but everything, man, *every*thing! You know how she got the dope?"

"I can imagine," Hawes said.

"Well, it don't take much imagination. That's exactly how she got it. She could get information from the Sphinx, I swear to God. Right in the middle of the desert, she'd—"

"She's not in this city, is she?"

"No. She's dead. She got information from a guy it was very unhealthy to get information from. An occupational hazard. Bam! No more Lady Bird."

"He killed her because she stooled on him?"

"That, and also one other thing. Like it seems she also gave him the clap. This guy was a very clean fellow, personal habits, I mean. He didn't appreciate what she give him. Bam! No more Lady Bird." Donner thought for a moment. "Come to think of it, she wasn't such a lady, huh?"

"I guess not. What about the lady we want?"

"You got a hint?"

"She's going to be killed tonight."

"Yeah? Who's gonna kill her?"

"That's what we're trying to find out."

"Mmm. A tough nut, huh?"

"Yeah. Listen, do you think we could step outside and talk there?"

"What's the matter? You got a chill? I can ask them to turn up the—"

"No, no, no," Hawes said hastily.

"The Lady, huh?" Donner asked, thinking. "the Lady."

"Yes."

It seemed to be getting hotter. While Donner sat and thought, the temperature in the room seemed to mount steadily. Each second of thought seemed to bring a corresponding second of increased heat. Hawes was gulping in air through his mouth, gasping for breath. He wanted to take off the towel, wanted to take off his skin and hang it on a peg. He wanted a glass of ice-cold water. He wanted a glass of cool water. He would accept a glass of lukewarm water. He'd settle for hot water, which, he was certain, would be cooler than the temperature of the room. Sweating from every pore, he sat while Donner thought. The seconds ticked by. The perspiration trickled down his face, poured from his wide shoulders, streamed down his backbone.

"There was a colored dancer at the old Black and White Club," Donner said.

"She around now?"

"No, she does a strip in Miami. They called her The Lady. She did a very delicate strip. For those who got the Shy Young Thing Fetish combined with the Colored Fetish. She was a big hit. But she's in Miami now."

"Who's here?"

"I'm trying to think," Donner said.

"Can you think a little faster?"

"I'm thinking, I'm thinking," Donner said. "There was a pusher called The Lady. But I think she went to New York. That's where all the junkie money is these days. Yeah, she's in New York."

"Well, who's here?" Hawes asked irritably, wiping his sweaty face with a sweaty hand.

"Hey, I know," Donner said.

"Who?"

"The Lady. A new hooker on Whore Street. You familiar?"

"Vaguely."

"She works for Mama Ida. You know the place?"

"No."

"The boys on the squad will. Look her up. The Lady. At Mama Ida's."

"Do you know her?" Hawes asked.

"The Lady? Only professionally."

"Whose profession? Yours or hers?"

"Mine. I got some info from her a couple of weeks back. Jesus, I shoulda thought of her right away. Only I never call her The Lady. That's for the trade. Her real name is Marcia. She's a peacheroo."

"Tell me about her."

"Not much to tell. You want the straight story, or the story on the Street? I mean, you want to know about Marcia—or about The Lady?"

"Both."

"Okay. Here's the way Mama Ida tells it. She's parlayed this thing into a fortune, believe me. Anybody comes down to the Street, they look for Mama Ida's joint. And once they find it, they're itching to tackle The Lady."

"Why?"

"Because Mama Ida's got a good imagination. Here's the legend. Marcia was born in Italy. She's the daughter of some Italian count who's got a villa on the Mediterranean. During the war, Marcia—against the wishes of her father—married a guerrilla who was fighting Mussolini. She took about ten thousand dollars in jewels with her and went to live in the hills with him. Picture this flower of nobility, a kid who knew how to ride before she knew how to walk, living in a cave with a band of bearded men. Well, one day her husband got killed in a raid on a railroad. Second in command claimed Marcia as his own, and pretty soon the entire band of cutthroats was getting in on the act. One night Marcia took off. They chased her through the hills, but she escaped.

"Her jewels bought her passage to America. But she was an enemy alien and had to stay in hiding. Barely able to speak the language, unable to get a job, she drifted into prostitution. She's still in the racket, but she loathes it. Goes about it in a ladylike fashion, and every time she's had, it's like rape. That's The Lady, and that's the way Mama Ida tells it."

"What's the real story?" Hawes asked.

"Her name's Marcia Polenski. She's from Scranton. She's been a hooker since she was sixteen, has the shrewdness of a viper, and a good ear for dialect. The Italian accent is as phony as the rape scenes."

"Any enemies?" Hawes asked.

"How do you mean?"

"Anybody who'd want to kill her?"

"Probably every other hooker on the Street wants to kill her. But I doubt if any of them would."

"Why?"

"Hookers are nice people. I like them."

237

"Well," Hawes said noncommittally. He rose. "I'm getting out of here."

"Will Willis take care of me?" Donner asked.

"Yeah. Talk to him about it. So long," Hawes said hastily. "Thanks."

"*De nada*," Donner replied, and he leaned against the steam.

After Hawes had dressed and listened to a dissertation by Regan on the big money to be made in boxing, accompanied by Regan's card and an admonition to keep it in a safe place, he went out into the street and called the squad. He got Carella.

"You back?" he asked.

"Yeah. I was waiting for your call."

"What'd you get?"

"Danny Gimp tells me there's a hooker named The Lady working on the Street. She may be our baby."

"I got the same from Donner," Hawes said.

"Good. Let's look her up. This may turn out to be simpler than we thought."

"Maybe so," Hawes said. "Want me to come back to the squad?"

"No, I'll meet you on the Street. Jenny's, do you know it?"

"I'll find it," Hawes said.

"What time have you got?"

Hawes looked at his watch. "10:03," he said.

"Can you meet me at 10:15?"

"I'll be there," Hawes said, and he hung up.

4

La Vía de Putas was a street in Isola that ran north and south for a total of three blocks. Over the course of years, the street had changed its name many times, but never its profession. It had changed its name only to accommodate the incoming immigrant groups, translating "Whore Street" into as many languages as there were nations. The profession, as solidly economic a profession as undertaking, had steadfastly defied the buffeting of time, tide, and policemen. In fact, the policemen were in a sense part of the profession. Whore Street, you see, was not a secret. Trying to keep the Street a secret would have been like trying to keep the existence of Russia a secret. There was hardly a citizen, and barely a visitor, who had not heard of La Vía de Putas, and many citizens had first-hand knowledge of the practices plied there. And if the citizenry know of something, the police—as slow-witted as they sometimes are—know of it, too.

It was here that the oldest profession clasped hands with the neophyte profession. And during the clasping of hands, bills of various denominations were exchanged so that the Street could continue its brisk trade without interference from the Law. Things got difficult for the 87th's cops when the Vice Squad decided to get puritanical. But even then, it didn't take cops long to realize that the green stuff could be divided and then subdivided. There was plenty of it to go all the way around, and there was certainly no reason to get stuffy about something as universal as sex.

Besides, and here was rationalization of the most sublime sort, was it not better to have most of the precinct's hookers contained in an area three blocks long rather than scattered all over the streets? Of course, it was. Crime was something like information for a thesis. So long as you knew where to find it, you were halfway home.

The uniformed cops of the 87th knew where to find it—and they also knew how to lose it. Every now and then they would stop by and chat with the various Mamas who ran the brothels. Mama Luz, Mama Theresa, Mama Carmen, Mama Ida, Mama Inez (from the song of the same name), were all bona fide madams and could all be counted on for the discreet payoff. In turn, the cops looked the other way. Sometimes, on a sleepy afternoon when the streets were quiet, they dropped into the cribs for a cup of coffee and things. The madams didn't mind too much. After all, if you ran a pushcart you expected the cop on the beat to take an apple every now and then, didn't you?

The detectives of the 87th rarely got a piece of the long green that shuttled from customer to hooker to madam to patrolman. The detectives had bigger things going for them, and everybody has to eat. Besides, they knew the Vice Squad was getting its cut, and they didn't want the pie sliced too many ways lest the bakery close shop altogether. Out of professional courtesy, they, too, looked the other way.

On Wednesday, July twenty-fourth, at 10:21 A.M., Carella and Hawes looked the other way. Jenny's was a tiny dump on the corner of Whore Street. Most of the payoffs took place in Jenny's, but Carella and Hawes were not looking for payoffs. They were discussing The Lady.

"From what I understand," Carella said, "we may have to wait in line to see her."

Hawes grinned. "Why don't you let me handle this one alone, Steve?" he said. "After all, you're a married man. I don't want to corrupt—"

"I've been corrupted," Carella said. He looked at his watch. "It isn't even ten thirty yet. If this works out, we're nine and a half hours ahead of our killer."

"*If* it works out," Hawes said.

"Well, let's go see her." He paused. "You ever been in one of these joints?"

"We had a lot of high-class callhouses in the Thirtieth," Hawes said.

"These ain't high-class, son," Carella said. "These are very low-class. If you've got a clothespin, put it on your nose."

They paid their bill and went into the street. Halfway up the block, a radio motor-patrol car was at the curb. Two patrolmen were on the sidewalk talking to a man and a woman, surrounded by kids.

"Trouble," Carella said. He quickened his pace. Hawes fell into step beside him.

"Now, take it easy," the patrolman was saying, "just take it easy!"

"Easy?" the woman shouted. "Why I should take it easy? This man—"

"Pipe down!" the second patrolman yelled. "You want the goddamn commissioner to drive up?"

Carella pushed his way through the knot of kids. He recognized the patrolmen at once, walked to the nearest one and said, "What's up, Tom?"

The woman's face burst into a grin. "Stevie!" she said. "*Dio gracias*. Tell these stupids—"

"Hello, Mama Luz," Carella said.

The woman he addressed was a fat woman with alabaster-white skin and black hair pulled into a tight bun at the back of her neck. She wore a loose silk kimono, and her swelling bosom moved fluidly in the open neck. Her face was exquisitely carved, angelic, patrician. She was one of the most notorious madams in the entire city.

"What's up?" Carella asked the patrolman again.

"This guy don't want to pay," the patrolman said.

This guy was a little man in a seersucker suit. Standing alongside Mama Luz, he seemed thinner than he actually was. He had a small paintbrush mustache under his nose, and his black hair fell despondently onto his forehead.

"What do you mean?" Carella asked.

"He don't want to pay. He's been upstairs. Now he's tryin' to beat the check."

"Get *dinero* first, I always tell them," Mama Luz said, clucking "*Dinero* first, then *amor*. No. This stupid, this new one, she forgets. So see what happens? Tell him, Stevie. Tell him I get my money."

"You're getting careless, Luz," Carella said.

"Yes, yes, I know. But tell him I get my money, Stevie. Tell this *Hitler*!"

Carella looked at the man, noticing the resemblance for the first time. The man had said nothing so far. With his arms folded across his chest, he stood beside Mama Luz, his lips pursed beneath the ridiculous paintbrush mustache, his eyes glaring heatedly.

"Are you a detective?" he asked suddenly.

"I am," Carella said.

"And you permit this sort of thing to go on in this city?"

"What sort of thing?" Carella asked.

"Open prostitution."

"I don't see any prostitution," Carella said.

"What are you, a pimp or something? A collection agency for every madam in the city?"

"Mister—" Carella started, and Hawes gently touched his arm. There was imminent danger in the situation, and Hawes recognized it immediately. It was one thing to look the other way. It was another thing to openly condone. Whatever Carella's relationship with Mama Luz, Hawes did not feel this was a time for him to be sticking his neck out. An irate call to Headquarters and there could be trouble, big trouble.

"We've got somebody to see, Steve," he said.

Carella's eyes met Hawes's and plainly asked him to keep the hell out of this.

"Were you upstairs, mister?" he asked the little man.

"Yes."

"Okay, I don't know what you did up there, and I'm not asking. That's your business. But I judge from that wedding band on your finger—"

The man pulled his hand back sharply.

"—that you wouldn't appreciate the idea of being hauled into court to testify on the open prostitution permitted in this city. I'm busy as hell, mister, so I'll leave the entire thing to your conscience. Come on, Cotton," he said.

He started up the street. Hawes caught up to him. As they walked, Hawes glanced over his shoulder.

"He's paying," he said.

Carella grunted.

"You sore?" Hawes asked.

"A little."

"I was only thinking of you."

"Mama Luz is a co-operative madam. Aside from that, I like her. Nobody asked that guy to come into the precinct. He came, he had a meal, and I think it's justice that he should pay for it. The girl he was with isn't in this for kicks. She works a hell of a lot harder than a five-and-dime clerk."

"Then why doesn't she become a five-and-dime clerk?" Hawes asked logically.

"*Touché*," Carella said, and he smiled. "Here's Mama Ida's."

Mama Ida's looked just like any of the other tenements lining the street. Two kids sat on the front stoop playing tic-tac-toe with a piece of chalk.

"Get off the stoop!" Carella said, and the kids scattered. "This is what burns me up," he said to Hawes. "The kids seeing all this. What a way to be brought up."

"A little while ago, you sounded as if you thought it was an honest profession," Hawes said.

"Are you looking for an argument?"

"No. I'm trying to find out what makes you tick."

"Okay. Crime isn't honest. Prostitution is crime, or at least it's crime in this city. Maybe the law's right, and maybe it isn't, and it's not for me to question it, it's only for me to enforce it. Okay. In this precinct, and maybe in every damn precinct, for all I know, prostitution is a crime that isn't a crime. Both those patrolmen are getting paid by every madam on the street. They keep trouble away from the madams, and the madams in turn run things clean. No muggings, no rollings. A clear act of commerce. But the guy who tried to cheat Luz was committing a crime, too, wasn't he? So where does the cop go from there? Does he turn his back on all crime, or just some crimes?"

"No," Hawes said. "Only on the crimes for which he's been paid off."

Carella faced Hawes levelly. "I've never taken a dime all the time I've been on the force. Remember that."

"I didn't think you had."

"Okay," Carella said. "A cop can't do everything by the book. I've got a sense of right and wrong that has nothing whatever to do with the law. I thought Hitler was committing a wrong back there. No tickee, no shirtee. Basic. Maybe I stuck my neck out, maybe I didn't. I say it's Spam, and I say the hell with it."

"Okay," Hawes said.

"Are *you* sore now?"

"Nope. Just enlightened."

"There's one other thing," Carella said.

"What's that?"

"The kids surrounding that scene. Was it better to have them taking it all in? Or better to break it up?"

"You could have broken it up without forcing the guy to pay."

"You're a marksman today," Carella said, and they entered the building. Only one bell button in the hall panel worked. Carella rang it.

"Mama Ida's a bitch," he said. "She thinks she owns the street *and* the city. You've got to be rough with her."

The inside door opened. A woman with a hairbrush in her hand stood just inside the jamb. Her black hair was hanging loose around her face. The face was narrow, with piercing brown eyes. The woman wore a light-blue sweater and a black skirt. She was barefooted.

"What now?" she said.

"It's me. Carella. Let us in, Ida."

"What do you want, Carella? Are the bulls getting in the act now?"

"We want to see a girl you call The Lady."

"She's busy," Ida said.

"We'll wait."

"She may be a while."

"We'll wait."

"Wait outside."

"Ida," Carella said gently, "get the hell out of that doorway."

Ida moved back. Carella and Hawes stepped into a dim corridor.

"What do you want with her?" Ida asked.

"We want to ask her some questions."

"What about?"

"Police business," Carella answered.

"You're not going to take her away, are you?"

"No. Just some questions."

Ida smiled radiantly. There was a gold tooth at the front of her mouth. "Good," she said. "Come in. Sit down."

She led them into a small, cheerless parlor. There was the smell of incense in the room, and the smell of perspiration. The perspiration won out.

Ida looked at Hawes. "Who's this one?" she asked.

"Detective Hawes," Carella said.

"Handsome," Ida said unenthusiastically. "What happened to your hair? How'd you get that white hair?"

"I'm getting old," Hawes said, touching the streak.

"How long will she be?" Carella asked.

"Who knows? She's slow. She's hard to get. She's The Lady, don't you know? Ladies have to be treated gently. Ladies have to be talked to."

"You must lose a lot of money with her."

"She costs three times more than the rest," Ida said.

"Is she worth it?"

She shrugged. "If you have to pay for it, I guess she's worth it." She looked at Hawes again. "I'll bet you never had to pay for it."

Hawes studied her blandly. He knew the woman was only talking in terms of her trade. He had never known a whore or a madam who did not discuss sex as simply as the average woman discussed clothes or babies. Nonetheless, he did not answer her.

"How old do you think I am?" she asked him.

"Sixty," he answered flatly.

Ida laughed. "You bastard," she said. "I'm only forty-five. Come around some afternoon."

"Thanks."

"Sixty," she scoffed. "I'll show you sixty."

Upstairs, a door opened and closed. There were footsteps in the hallway. Ida looked up.

"She's finished," she said.

A man came down the steps. He looked sheepishly into the parlor, and then went out the front door.

"Come on," Ida said. She watched Hawes as he stood up. "A big one," she said, almost to herself, and then she led the detectives onto the stairway. "I really ought to charge you for her time."

"We can always take her to the squadroom," Carella said.

"I'm joking, Carella," Ida answered. "Don't you know when I'm joking? What's your first name, Hawes?"

"Cotton."

"Doesn't your friend know when I'm joking, Cotton?" She

paused on the steps and looked down at Hawes. "Are those sixty-year-old legs?" she asked.

"Seventy," Hawes answered, and Carella burst out laughing.

"You bastard," Ida said, but she could not suppress the chuckle that came to her throat. They passed into the upstairs corridor. In one of the rooms, a girl in a kimono was sitting on the edge of her bed, polishing her nails. The other doors along the corridor were closed. Ida went to one of the closed doors and knocked on it.

A soft voice answered, '*Si?* Who ees it?"

"Ida. Open up."

"One minute, *per piacere.*"

Ida pulled a face and waited. The door opened. The girl standing in the doorframe was at least thirty-two years old. Black hair framed a tranquil face with deep-set brown eyes. There was sadness on the face and around the edges of the mouth. There was nobility in the way the girl held her head, in the way she kept her shoulders pulled back, one hand clutched daintily, protectively, to the neck of the kimono, holding it closed over the thrust of her breasts. There was fear in her eyes, as if she dreaded what was coming next.

"*Si?*" she said.

"Some gentlemen to see you," Ida said.

She looked to Ida plaintively. "Again?" she said. "Please, *signora*, not again I beg you, I am so—"

"Knock it off, Marcia," Ida said. "They're cops."

The fear left Marcia's eyes. The hand dropped from the neck of the kimono. The kimono fell open, revealing the first rise of her breasts. All nobility left her face and her carriage. There were hard lines about her eyes and her mouth.

"What's the beef?" she asked.

"None," Carella said. "We want to talk to you."

"You sure that's all?"

"That's all."

"Some cops come in here and expect—"

"Can it," Hawes said. "We want to talk."

"In here? Or downstairs?"

"Call your own shot."

"Here," she said. She stepped back. Carella and Hawes entered the room.

"You need me?" Ida asked.

"No."

"I'll be downstairs. Want a drink before you leave, Cotton?"

"No, thanks," Hawes said.

"What's the matter? You don't like me?" She cocked her head saucily. "I could show you a few things."

"I love you," Hawes said, grinning, and Carella looked at him in surprise. "I'm just afraid the exertion would kill you."

Mama Ida burst out laughing. "You bastard," she said, and she went out of the room. In the hallway he heard her mumble chucklingly, "The exertion would *kill* me!"

Marcia sat, crossing her legs in a most unladylike manner.

"Okay, what is it?" she asked.

"You been working here long?" Carella said.

"About six months."

"Get along?"

"I get along fine."

"Have any trouble since you've been here?"

"What do you mean?"

"Any arguments? Fights?"

"The usual. There's twelve girls here. Somebody's always yelling about using somebody else's bobby pins. You know how it is."

"How about anything serious?"

"Hair pulling? Like that?"

"Yes."

"No. I try to steer clear of the other girls. I get more money than they do, so they don't like it. I'm not looking for trouble. This is a cushy spot. Best I ever had it. Hell, I'm star of the show here." She pulled the kimono up over her knees, "Hot, ain't it?" she asked.

"Yes," Carella said. "Did you ever have any trouble with one of the customers?"

Marcia began flapping the kimono about her legs, using it as a fan. "What's this all about?" she asked.

"Did you?"

"Trouble with the customers? I don't know. Who the hell remembers? What's this all about?"

"We're trying to figure out whether or not somebody wants to kill you," Hawes said.

247

Marcia stopped fanning her legs with the kimono. The silk dropped from her fingers. "Come again," she said.

"You heard it the first time."

"*Kill* me? That's crazy. Who'd want to kill me?" She paused, then proudly added, "I'm a good lay."

"And you never had any trouble with a customer?"

"What kind of trouble could I—" She stopped. Her face went pensive. For a moment it took on the quiet nobility of her role as The Lady. When she spoke, the moment was gone. "You think it could be *him*?" she asked.

"What do you mean?"

"You're sure somebody wants to kill me? How do you know?"

"We don't know. We're guessing."

"Well, there was this guy . . ." She stopped. "Naw, he was just talking."

"Who?"

"Some jerk. A sailor. He kept trying to place me all the while he was here. Finally, he done it. Remembered me from New London. I was working there during the war. The submarine base, you know. Good pickings. He remembered me and claimed he got cheated, wanted his money back. Said I wasn't no Italian count's daughter, I was just a plain phony. I admitted I come from Scranton, but I told him he got what he paid for, and if he didn't like it, he could take a flying leap. He told me he'd come back. He said when he came back, he'd kill me."

"When was this?"

"About a month ago, I guess."

"Do you remember his name?"

"Yeah. I don't usually, except this guy raised a fuss. They all tell me their names, you know. First thing. Right off the bat. I'm Charlie, I'm Frank, I'm Ned. You'll remember me, won't you, honey? Remember them! Jesus! I have a hard enough time trying to *forget* some of them."

"But you remember this sailor, do you?"

"Sure. He said he was gonna kill me. Wouldn't you remember? Besides, he had a goofy name."

"What was it?"

"Mickey."

"Mickey what?"

248

"That's what I asked him. I said, "What is it? Mickey Mouse?" It wasn't Mickey Mouse at all."

"What was it?"

"Mickey Carmichael. I can remember him saying it. Mickey Carmichael. Firecontrolman Second Class. That's just the way he said it. As if he was saying, 'His Majesty, the King of England.' A nut. A real nut."

"Did he say where he was based?"

"He was on a ship. This was his first liberty in the city."

"Which ship?"

"I don't know. He called it a tin can. That's a battleship, ain't it?"

"That's a destroyer," Hawes said. "What else did he say about the ship?"

"Nothing. Except he was glad to be off it. Wait a minute. A strike? Something about a strike?"

"A striker?" Carella asked. He turned to Hawes. "That's a Navy term, isn't it?"

"Yes, but I don't see how it would apply to a noncommissioned officer. He *did* say Firecontrolman Second Class, didn't he?" He didn't say Seaman Second? Firecontrolman striker?"

"No, no, he was a sergeant or something. He had red stripes on his sleeve."

"*Two* red stripes?"

"Yeah."

"He was a second-class petty officer," Hawes said. "She's right, Steve." He turned to the girl. "But he said something about a strike?"

"Something like that."

"A mutiny?"

"Something like that. A strike or something."

"A strike," Hawes said, half to himself. "Strikers, picket lines—" He snapped his fingers. "A picket! Did he say his ship was a picket ship?"

"Yeah," Marcia said, her eyes widening. "Yeah. That's exactly what he said. He seemed pretty proud of *that,* too."

"A picket destroyer," Hawes said. "That shouldn't give us much trouble. Mickey Carmichael." He nodded. "Anything else you want to ask her?"

"I'm finished."

"So am I. Thanks, Miss."

"You think he's *really* gonna try to kill me?" Marcia asked.

"We'll find out," Hawes said.

"What should I do if he comes here?"

"We'll get to him before then."

"But suppose he gets past you?"

"He won't."

"I know. But suppose he does?"

"Try hiding under the bed," Carella said.

"Wise guy," Marcia said.

"We'll call you," Carella said. "If he's our man and you're his target, we'll let you know."

"Look, do me a favor. Let me know even if I *ain't*. I don't want to sit here trembling every time there's a knock on the door."

"You're not scared, are you?"

"Damn right I am," Marcia said.

"It should help your act," Carella answered and they left.

The administration building for the Naval District that bound-aried the city had its offices downtown on Worship Avenue. When Carella and Hawes got back to the squad, Hawes looked up the number in the phone book and dialled it.

"Naval Administration," a voice answered.

"This is the police," Hawes said. "Let me speak to your commanding officer."

"One moment, please." There was a pause and then some clicking on the line.

"Ensign Davis," a voice said.

"Are you the commanding officer?" Hawes asked.

"No, sir. May I help you?"

"This is the police. We're trying to locate a sailor from a—"

"That would fall into the province of the Shore Patrol, sir. One moment, please."

"Look, all I want to—"

The clicking on the line interrupted Hawes.

"Yes, sir?" the operator asked.

"Put this call through to Lieutenant Jergens in Shore Patrol, would you?"

"Yes, sir."

More clicking. Hawes waited.

"Lieutenant Jergens, Shore Patrol," a voice said.

"This is Detective Cotton Hawes," Hawes answered, figuring he'd throw a little rank around among all this brass. "We're looking for an enlisted man named Mickey Carmichael. He's aboard a—"

"What'd he do?" Jergens asked.

"Nothing yet. We want to stop him before—"

"If he didn't do anything, we wouldn't have any record of him. Is he connected with this building?"

"No, he's—"

"Just a moment, I'll get you Personnel."

"I don't want—"

The clicking cut him off again.

"Operator?" Jergens said.

"Yes, sir."

"Put this through to Commander Elliot in Personnel."

"Yes, sir.

Hawes waited.

Click-click.

Click-click.

"Commander Elliot's office," a voice said.

"Is this Commander Elliot?"

"No, sir. This is Chief Yeoman Pickering."

"Let me talk to the commander, Pickering."

"I'm sorry, sir, he's not in right now, sir. Who's calling, please, sir?"

"Let me talk to his superior, will you?" Hawes asked.

"His superior, sir, is commanding officer here, sir. Who's calling please, sir?"

"This is Admiral Hawes!" Hawes shouted. "Connect me with your commanding officer at once!"

"Yes, sir, Admiral. Yes, sir!"

The clicking was frantic now.

"Yes, sir?" the operator asked.

"Put this through to Captain Finchberger," Pickering said. "On the double."

"Yes, sir!"

The clicking clicked again.

"Captain Finchberger's office," a voice said.

"Get me the Captain! This is Admiral Hawes!" Hawes said, enjoying himself immensely now.

"Yes, sir!" the voice snapped.

Hawes waited.

The voice that came onto the line wasn't having any damned nonsense.

"Admiral *who*?" it shouted.

"Sir?" Hawes asked, recalling his Navy days and remembering that he was talking to a Naval captain, which is very much different from an Army captain, a Naval captain being a very high rank, indeed, full of scrambled eggs and all sorts of highly polished brass. Considering this, Hawes turned on the oil. "I'm sorry, sir, your secretary must have misunderstood. This is Detective Hawes of the Eighty-seventh Precinct here in the city. We were wondering if we could have the Navy's assistance on a rather difficult problem."

"What is it, Hawes?" Finchberger said, but he was weakening.

"Sir, we're trying to locate a sailor who was in the city a month ago, and who is perhaps still here. He was off a picket destroyer, sir. His name is—"

"There was a picket destroyer here in June, that's right," Finchberger said. "The U.S.S. *Perriwinkle*. She's gone now. Left on the fourth."

"All hands aboard, sir?"

"The commanding officer did not report anyone A.O.L. or A.W.O.L. The ship left with its full complement."

"Have there been any other picket destroyers in port since then, sir?"

"No, there haven't."

"*Any* destroyers at all?"

"We've got one scheduled for the end of the week. Coming up from Norfolk. That's all."

"Would it be the *Perriwinkle*, sir?"

"No, it would not. It would be the *Masterson*."

"Thank you, sir. Then there is no possibility that this sailor is still in the city or scheduled to arrive in the city?"

"Not unless he jumped ship in the middle of the Atlantic," Finchberger said. "The *Perriwinkle* was headed for England."

"Thank you, sir," Hawes said. "You've been very kind."

"Don't pull that admiral routine again, Hawes," Finchberger said, and he hung up.

"Find him?" Carella asked.

Hawes replaced the phone in its cradle.

"He's on his way to Europe," He said.

"That lets him out," Carella said.

"It doesn't let our hooker friend out," Hawes answered.

"No. She might still be the target. I'll call her and tell her not to worry about the sailor. In the meantime I'll ask Pete for a couple of uniformed men to watch Ida's joint. If she *is* the target, our boy won't try for her with cops around."

"We hope."

Hawes looked up at the white-faced clock on the squadroom wall. It was exactly 11 o'clock in the morning.

In nine hours, their killer—whoever he was—would strike.

From somewhere across the street in Grover Park, the sun glinted on something shiny, blinking its rays through the grilled window of the squadroom, flashing momentarily on Hawes's face.

"Draw that shade, will you, Steve?' he asked.

5

Sam Grossman was a police lieutenant, a laboratory technician, and the man in charge of the Police Laboratory at Headquarters on High Street, downtown.

Sam was a tall, loosely jointed man who moved with angular nonchalance and ease. He was a gentle man with a craggy face, a man who wore glasses because too much reading as a child had ruined his eyesight. His eyes were blue and mild, guileless eyes that denied the fact that their owner used them to pry into the facts of crime and violence—and very often death. Sam loved lab work, and when he was not busy with his test tubes in an effort to prove the lab's effectiveness in crime detection, he could be found talking to the nearest detective, trying to impress upon him the need for co-operation with the lab.

When the letter from the 87th Precinct had arrived by messenger that morning, Sam had put his men to work on it immediately. The phone call preceding it had urged speed. His men had photographed the letter and sent the photo back to the 87th at once. And then they had begun the task of scrutinizing the letter and the envelope for latent fingerprint impressions before beginning their other tests.

The original letter was handled with the utmost care. Sam sourly reflected that half the cops in the city had probably handled it already, but he had no desire to compound the felony. Carefully, methodically, his men put a very thin, uniform layer of a ten per cent solution of silver nitrate onto the letter, passing the sheet of paper between two rollers that had been moistened with the solution. They waited while the sheet of paper dried, and then they put it under the ultra-violet light. In a few seconds, the prints appeared.

This is what the letter looked like:

There were a lot of fingerprints all over the letter. Sam Grossman had expected as much. The letter had been created by snipping words from newspapers or magazines and pasting them to a sheet of paper. Sam expected that the pasting process would have left fingermarks all over the page, and such was exactly the case. Each snip of paper had been pressed to the

255

page so that it would stick. Each word on the page carried its own full complement of prints.

And each print on the page was hopelessly smeared or blurred or overlaid with another print—except for two thumbprints. These thumbprints were on the left hand side of the page; one close to the top, the other just a little below center. Both were good prints.

Both—unfortunately—belonged to Sergeant Dave Murchison.

Sam sighed. It was a crying shame. He always had to make his point the hard way.

Hawes took the call from Grossman in the Interrogation Room, where he had gone to study the photo of the letter. The call came at 11:17.

"Hawes?" Grossman said.

"Yes."

"Sam Grossman at the lab. I've got a report on that letter. Since there's a time element on this, I thought I'd give it to you on the phone."

"Shoot," Hawes said.

"Not much help on the prints," Grossman said. "Only two good prints on the letter itself, and they're your desk sergeant's."

"This is the front of the letter?"

"Yes."

"How about the back?"

"Everything smeared. The letter was folded. Whoever folded it ran his bunched fist along the crease. Nothing there, Hawes. I'm sorry."

"And the envelope?"

"Murchison's prints—and yours. Nothing else except some good prints left by a child. Did a child handle the envelope?"

"Yes."

"Well, I've got a good batch of his prints, in case you need them for comparison. Want me to send them over?"

"Please," Hawes said. "What else have you got?"

"On the letter itself, we dug up a few items that might help you. The paste used was five-and-dime stuff put out by a company called Brundy's. They manufacture it in a jar and in a tube. We found a microscopic blue-metallic-paint scraping stuck to one corner of the letter. Their tube is blue, so chances are your letter writer used the tube. That's no help, though. He could have bought the paste anywhere. It's a common item. The paper, though . . ."

"Yes, what about that?"

"It's a good-rag-content bond, manufactured by the Cartwright Company in Boston, Massachusetts. We checked our watermark file. The catalogue number on the paper is 142-Y. It costs about five and a half bucks a ream."

"But it's a Boston company, huh?"

"Yes, but distributed nationally. There's a distributor in this city. Want the name?"

"Please."

"Eastern Shipping. That's on Gage Boulevard in Majesta. Want the phone number?"

"Yes."

"Princeton 4–9800."

Hawes jotted it down. "Anything else?"

"Yes. We know where the letter writer got his words."

"Where?"

"The tip-off was the *T* in the word *tonight*. That *T* is famous, Hawes."

"It's the *New York Times*, isn't it?"

"Exactly. Distributed here, as in every city in the country. I'll confess our newspaper and magazine file doesn't go back too far. But we try to keep abreast of the major dailies and all the big publications. We sometimes get parts of bodies wrapped in newspapers or portions of newspapers. Every once in a while it helps to have a file."

"I see," Hawes said.

"This time we were lucky. Using that *New York Times T* as a springboard, we looked through what we had and pinpointed the sections of the *Times* he used, and the date."

"And they were?"

"He used the magazine section and the book section of the *Times* for Sunday, June twenty-third. We've located enough of the words he's used to eliminate coincidence. For example, *The Lady* came from the book section. Snipped from an ad for the Conrad Richter novel. The word *can* was from an ad in the magazine section for Scandale. That's a woman's undergarment trade name."

"Go ahead."

"The figure eight was obvious, again from the magazine section. An ad for Ballantine beer."

"Anything else?"

"The word *kill* was easy. Not many advertisers use that word unless it's pertinent to their product. This ad said something about killing bathroom odours. "Kill bathroom odours with—" and the name of the product. In any case, there's no doubt in our minds. He used the June twenty-third *Times*."

"And this is July twenty-fourth," Hawes said.

"Yeah."

"In other words, he planned this thing as long as a month ago, made up his letter, and then held it until he'd decided on the date for the murder."

"It would seem that way. Unless he used an old paper that was around."

"It would also seem to eliminate a crank."

"It looks legit to me, Hawes," Grossman said. "I was talking to our psychologist upstairs. He didn't seem to think a crank would wait a month between composing a letter and delivering it. He also feels the delivery of the letter was an act of compulsion. He thinks the guy *wants* to be stopped, and he further thinks the letter will give you a clue about *how* to stop him."

"How?" Hawes asked.

"He didn't say."

"Mmmm. Well, have you got anything else for me?"

"That's it. Oh, wait. The guy smokes cigarettes. There were a few grains of tobacco in the envelope. We tested them, but they could have come from any of the major brands."

"Okay, Sam. Thanks a lot."

"Don't mention it. I'll send that kid's prints over. So long."

Grossman hung up. Hawes lifted his copy of the letter from the desk, opened the door, and started for Lieutenant Byrnes's office. It was then that he noticed the chaos in the squadroom.

It was the noise that first attracted him, the sound of shrill voices raised in protest, speculation, and wonder. And then his eyes were assailed with what seemed like an overly patriotic display, a parade for the dead-and-gone. Fourth of July. The squadroom was bursting with red, white, and blue. Hawes blinked. Crowding the slatted rail divider, lined up against the desks and the file cabinets and the windows and the bulletin boards, slouched into every conceivable corner of the room, were at least eight thousand kids in blue dungarees and red-and-white-striped tee shirts.

"Shut up!" Lieutenant Byrnes shouted. "Now, just knock off all this chatter!"

The room modulated slowly into silence.

"Welcome to the Grover Park Nursery School," Carella said to Hawes, smiling.

"Jesus," Hawes said, "we sure as hell have an efficient bunch of patrolmen in this precinct."

The efficient bunch of patrolmen had followed their orders to the letter, rounding up every ten-year-old kid wearing dungarees and a red-striped shirt. They had not asked for birth certificates, and so the kids ranged from seven to thirteen. The tee shirts, too, were not all tee shirts. Some of them sported collars and buttons. But the patrolmen had done their job, and a hasty count of the kids revised Hawes's earlier estimate of eight thousand. There were only seven thousand. Well, at least three dozen, anyway. Apparently there had been a run on red-striped tee shirts in the neighborhood. Either that, or a new street gang was forming and they had decided upon this as their uniform.

"Which of you kids delivered a letter to this precinct this morning?" Byrnes asked.

"What kinda letter?" one asked.

"What difference does it make? Did you deliver it?"

"Naw," the kid answered.

"Then shut up. Which one of you delivered it?"

Nobody answered.

"Come on, come on, speak up," Byrnes said.

An eight-year-old kid, obviously impressed by the Hollywood effort, piped, "I wanna call my lawyer."

The other kids all laughed.

"Shut up!" Byrnes roared. "Now, listen, you're not in any trouble. We're only trying to locate the man who gave you that letter, that's all. So if you delivered it, speak up."

"What'd he do, this guy?" a twelve-year-old asked.

"Did you deliver the letter?"

"No, I just wanna know what he done, this guy."

"Any of you deliver the letter?" Byrnes asked again. The boys were all shaking their heads. Byrnes turned to Murchison. "How about it, Dave? Recognize one of them?"

"Hard to say," Murchison said. "One thing for sure, he was a blond kid. You can let all the dark-haired kids go. We've got a couple of redheads in there, too. They're no good. This kid was blond."

"Steve, keep only the blonds," Byrnes said, and Carella began walking through the room, tapping boys, telling them to go home. When he'd finished the culling process, the room had thinned down to four blond boys. The other boys idled on the other side of the slatted rail divider, watching.

"Beat it," Hawes said. "Go home."

The boys left reluctantly.

Of the four blonds remaining, two were at least twelve years old.

"They're too old," Murchison said.

"You two can go," Byrnes told them, and the boys drifted out. Byrnes turned to one of the remaining two.

"How old are you, sonny?" he asked.

"Eight."

"What do you say, Dave?"

"He's not the kid."

"How about the other one?"

"Him neither."

"Well, that's—" Byrnes seemed suddenly stabbed with pain. "Hawes stop those other kids before they get past the desk. Get their names, for Christ's sake. We'll put them on the radio. Otherwise we'll be getting the same damn kids in here all day long. Hurry up!"

Hawes went through the railing and sprinted for the steps. He stopped some of the kids in the muster room, rounded up the rest on the sidewalk, and sent them all back into the precinct. One kid sighed reluctantly and patted a huge German shepherd on the head.

"You wait, Prince," he said. "I gotta handle this again," and then he walked into the building.

Hawes looked at the dog. The idea clicked into his mind. He

ran into the building, climbed the steps, and rushed into the squadroom.

"A dog!" he said. "Suppose it's a dog!"

"Huh?" Byrnes asked. "Did you stop those kids?"

"Yes, but it could be a dog!"

"*What* could be a dog?"

"Lady! The Lady!"

Carella spoke instantly. "He could be right, Pete. How many dogs named Lady do you suppose there are in the precinct?"

"I don't know," Byrnes said. "You think the nut who wrote that letter . . . ?"

"It's a possibility."

"All right, get on the phone. Meyer! Meyer!"

"Yah, Pete?"

"Start taking these kids' names. Jesus, this place is turning into a madhouse!"

Turning, Byrnes stamped into his office.

Carella's call to the Bureau of Licenses revealed that there were thirty-one licensed dogs named Lady within the precinct territory. God alone knew how many unlicensed dogs of the same name there were.

He reported his information to Byrnes.

Byrnes told him that if a man wanted to kill a goddamn lady dog, that was his business and Byrnes wasn't going to upset his whole damn squad tracking down every bitch in the precinct. They'd find out about it the minute the dog was killed, anyway, and then they might or might not try to find the canine killer.

He suggested that in the meantime Hawes call Eastern Shipping in an attempt to find out whether or not any shops in the precinct carried the paper the letter was pasted on.

"And close the goddamn door!" he shouted as Carella left.

6

It was 11:32 A.M.

The sun was climbing steadily into the sky and now was almost at its zenith, its rays baking the asphalt and the concrete, sending shimmering waves of heat up from the pavements.

There was no breeze in the park.

The man with the binoculars sat atop a high outcropping of rock, but it was no cooler there than it was on the paths that wound through the park. The man wore blue-gabardine trousers and a cotton-mesh short-sleeved sports shirt. He sat in cross-legged Indian fashion, his elbows resting on his knees, the binoculars trained on the police precinct across the street.

There was an amused smile on the man's face.

He watched the kids streaming out of the police station, and the smile widened. His letter was bringing results. His letter had set the precinct machinery in motion, and he watched the results of that motion now, and there was a strange pulsing excitement within him as he wondered if he would be caught.

They won't catch me, he thought.

But maybe they will.

The excitement within him was contradictory. He wanted to elude them, but at the same time he relished the idea of a chase, a desperate gun battle, the culminating scene of a carefully planned murder. Tonight he would kill. Yes. There was no backing away from that. Yes. He had to kill, he knew that, there was no other way, that was it, yes. Tonight. They could not stop him, but maybe they would. They could not stop him.

A man was leaving the precinct, coming down the stone steps.

He focused the binoculars tightly on the man's face. A detective, surely. On business his letter had provoked? His grin widened.

The detective had red hair. The hair caught the rays of the brilliant sun. There was a white streak over one temple. He followed the detective with his binoculars. The detective got

262

into an automobile, an unmarked police car, undoubtedly. The car pulled away from the curb quickly.

They're in a hurry, the man thought, lowering the binoculars. He looked at his wrist watch.

11:35.

They haven't got much time, he thought. *They haven't got much time to stop me.*

The bookshop was unusual for the 87th Precinct neighborhood. You expected all the reading matter to be in drugstore racks, and you expected sadistic mysteries like *I, the Hangman*, historical novels like *See My Bosom*, dramas of the Old West like *Sage-brush Sixgun*.

The shop was called Books, Incorporated. It huddled in one of the side streets between two tenements, below street level. You passed through an old iron gate, walked down five steps, and were face to face with the plate-glass window of the shop and its display of books. A sign in the window said, "We Stock Spanish-language books." Another sign said, "*Aqui habla Español.*"

In the right-hand corner of the window, lettered onto the glass in gold gilt, were the words CHRISTINE MAXWELL, PROP.

Hawes walked down the steps and opened the screen door of the shop. A bell over the door tinkled. The shop instantly touched something deep in his memory. He felt he had been here before, had seen the dusty racks and shelves, had sniffed of the musty bookbindings, the intimate smell of stored knowledge. Had he browsed in such a shop on a rainy day in the side streets fringing The Quarter downtown? Was this *The Haunted Bookshop* come to life, a stationary "Parnassus on Wheels"? He remembered the Morley books from his youth, and he wished he had time to browse, wished that time were not so important right now. There was a friendliness and warmth to the shop, and he wanted to soak it up, sponge it into his bones, and he wished his visit were not such an urgent one, wished he had come for information that had nothing to do with sudden death.

"Yes?" the voice said.

He broke off his thoughts abruptly. The voice was gentle, a voice that belonged in the shop. He turned.

The girl stood before the shelves of brown-backed books, stood in an almost mistilike radiance, fragile, tender, gentle, against the musty cracked brown. Her hair was blond, whisper-like tendrils softly cradling the oval of her face. Her eyes were blue and wide, the soft blue of a spring sky, the delicate blue of a lilac. There was a tentative smile on her full mouth, a mouth kissed by the seasons. And because she was a human being and because it was a hot day in July, there was a thin film of perspiration on her upper lip. And because she was a human being and not a memory and not a dream and not a maiden from some legendary Camelot, Hawes fell in love with her instantly.

"Hello," he said. There was surprise in his voice, but it was not a wise guy's "Hell-*lo*!" It was more an awed whisper, and the girl looked at him and again said, "Yes?"

"Perhaps you can help me," Hawes said, reflecting on the fact that he fell in and out of love too easily, musing upon the theory that all true love was love at first sight, in which case he had been truly in love a great many times, but nonetheless studying the girl and thinking, *I love her, so the hell with you.*

"Were you looking for a book, sir?" the girl asked.

"Are you Miss Maxwell?" he asked.

"*Mrs.* Maxwell," she corrected.

"Oh," he said. "Oh."

"Was there a book you wanted?"

He looked at her left hand. She was not wearing a wedding band. "I'm from the police," he said. "Detective Hawes, Eighty-seventh squad."

"Is something wrong?"

"No. I'm trying to track down a piece of stationery. Eastern Shipping says you're the only store in the precinct that carried the paper."

"Which paper is that?" Christine asked.

"Cartwright 142-Y."

"Oh, yes," she said.

"Do you carry it?"

"Yes?" She made it a question.

"Run this shop with your husband, do you?" Hawes asked.

"My husband is dead," she said. "He was a Navy pilot. He was killed in the Battle of the Coral Sea."

"I'm sorry," Hawes said genuinely.

"Please don't," she said. "It's been a long time. A person can't live in the past, you know." She smiled gently.

"You don't look that old," he said. "I mean, to have been married during World War Two."

"I got married when I was seventeen," she said.

"Which makes you?"

"Thirty-three," she said.

"You look much younger."

"Thank you."

"I'd say you were barely twenty-one."

"Thank you, but I'm not. Really."

They looked at each other silently for a moment.

"It seems strange," Hawes said. "To find a shop like this. In this neighborhood, I mean."

"I know. That's why it's here."

"What do you mean?"

"Well, there's enough deprivation in this neighborhood. It needn't extend to books."

"Do you get a lot of people coming in?" Hawes asked.

"More now than in the beginning. Actually, the stationery supplies are what keep the shop going. But it's better now than it was. You'd be surprised how many people want to read good books."

"Are you afraid of the neighborhood?"

"Should I be?" she asked.

"Well . . . a pretty girl like you. I mean, this isn't the best neighborhood in the world."

The girl seemed surprised. "The people here are poor," she said. "But *poor* isn't necessarily synonymous with *dangerous*"

"That's true," he said.

"People are people. The people who live here are no better, no worse, than the people who live in swanky Stewart City."

"Where do you live, Miss—*Mrs*. Maxwell?"

"In Isola."

"Where?"

"Why do you want to know?"

"I'd like to see you sometime," Hawes said.

Christine was silent for a moment. She looked at Hawes penetratingly, as if she were trying to read his mind and his motives.

Then she said, "All right. When?"

"Tonight?" he asked.

"All right."

"Wait a minute," he said. He thought for a moment. "Well, it'll be over by eight o'clock either way," he said. "Yes, tonight is fine."

"What'll be over by eight?"

"A case we're working on."

"How do you know it'll be over by eight? Do you have a crystal ball?"

Hawes smiled. "I'll tell you about it tonight. May I pick you up at nine? Is that too late for you?"

"Tomorrow's a working day," she said.

"I know. I thought we'd have a drink and talk a little."

"All right," she said.

"Where?" he asked.

"711 Fortieth Boulevard. Do you know where that is?"

"I'll find it. That's lucky. Seven-eleven."

Christine smiled. "Shall I dress?"

"We'll find a quiet cocktail lounge," he said. "If that's all right with you."

"Yes, that's fine. Air-conditioned, please."

"What else?" he said, spreading his hands.

"Are you sensitive about the white streak in your hair?"

"Not at all."

"If you are, I won't ask."

"You can ask. I got knifed once. It grew back this way. A puzzle for medical science to unravel."

"Knifed? By a person, do you mean?"

"Sure," he said.

"Oh." It was a very tiny "Oh."

Hawes looked at her. "People do . . . well, people do get knifed, you know."

"Yes, of course. I imagine a detective . . ." She stopped. "What was it you wanted to know about the stationery?"

"Well, how much of it do you stock?"

"All my paper supplies come from Cartwright. The 142-Y

comes in reams and also in smaller packages of a hundred sheets."

"Do you sell a lot of it?"

"Of the smaller packages, yes. The reams move more slowly."

"How many smaller packs have you sold in the past month?"

"Oh, I couldn't possibly say. A lot."

"And the reams?"

"The reams are easier to check. I got six reams at the beginning of June. I can count how many are left."

"Would you, please?" he asked.

"Certainly."

She walked to the back of the shop. Hawes pulled a book from the shelf and began leafing through it. When Christine returned he said, "That's one of my favorites. Have you read it?"

"Yes. A long time ago."

"I read it when I was still a girl." She smiled briefly, put the book out of her mind, and said, "I have two reams left. I'm glad you stopped in. I'll have to reorder."

"That means you sold four, correct?"

"Yes."

"Would you remember to whom?"

"I know to whom I sold two of them. The others I couldn't say."

"Who?" Hawes asked.

"A young man who comes in here regularly for 142-Y. He buys at least a ream a month. He's one of the chief reasons I keep it in stock."

"Do you know his name?"

"Yes. Philip Bannister."

"Does he live in the neighborhood?"

"I imagine so. Whenever he's come into the shop, he's been dressed casually. He came in once wearing Bermuda shorts."

"Bermuda shorts?" Hawes asked, astonished. "In *this* neighborhood?"

"People are people," the girl reminded him.

"You don't know where he lives, though?" Hawes said.

"No. It must be close by, though."

"What makes you say that?"

"He's often come in with shopping in his arms. Groceries, you know. I'm sure he lives close by."

"I'll check it," Hawes said. "And I'll see you tonight at nine."

"At nine," Christine said. She paused. "I'm—I'm looking forward to seeing you again," she said.

"So am I," he answered.

"Goodbye," she said.

"Goodbye."

The bell over the door tinkled when he left.

The telephone directory listed a Philip Bannister at 1592 South Tenth. Hawes called the squad to let Carella know where he was going, and then he drove to Bannister's place.

South Tenth was a typical precinct street, crowded with tenements and humanity, overlooked by fire escapes cluttered with the paraphernalia of life. The fire escapes were loaded today. Today every woman in the neighborhood had said to hell with cleaning the house. Today every woman in the neighborhood had put on her lightest clothing and stepped out onto the fire escape in the hope of catching any breeze that might rustle through the concrete canyon. Radios had been plugged into extension cords that trailed back into the apartments, and music flooded the street. Pitchers of lemonade, cans of beer beaded with cold sweat, milk bottles full of ice water, rested on the fire escape. The women sat and drank and fanned themselves, their skirts pulled up over their knees, some of them sitting in shorts and halters, some of them sitting in slips, all of them trying desperately to beat the heat.

Hawes pulled the car to the curb, cut the engine, mopped his brow, and stepped from his small oven into the larger oven that was the street. He was wearing light-weight trousers and a cotton sports shirt open at the throat, but he was sweating nonetheless. He thought suddenly of Fats Donner and the Turkish bath, and felt immediately cooler.

1592 was a dowdy gray tenement set between two similarly dowdy and similarly gray tenements. Hawes climbed the front stoop, walking past two young girls who were discussing Eddie Fisher. One of them couldn't understand what he'd seen in Debbie Reynolds. She herself was built better than Debbie

Reynolds, and she was sure Eddie had noticed her that time she'd got his autograph outside the stage door. Hawes went into the building wishing he could sing.

A small neatly-lettered white card told him that Philip Bannister lived in Apartment 21. Hawes wiped sweat from his lip, and then climbed to the second floor. Every door on the floor was open in an attempt to produce a cross-current circulation of air. The attempt failed miserably. Not a breeze stirred in the hallway. The door to Apartment 21 was open, too. From somewhere inside the apartment, Hawes heard the unmistakable chatter of a typewriter. He knocked on the door-jamb.

"Anybody home?" he called.

The typewriter continued its incessant jabbering.

"Hey! Anybody home?"

The clatter of the keys stopped abruptly. "Who is it?" a voice shouted.

"Police," Hawes said.

"*Who?*" The voice was utterly incredulous.

"Police."

"Just a second."

Hawes heard the typewriter start up again. It went furiously for some three and a half minutes and then stopped. He heard a chair being scraped back, heard the pad of bare feet through the apartment. A thin man in undershirt and striped undershorts came into the kitchen and walked to the front door. He cocked his head to one side, his bright brown eyes gleaming.

"Did you say *police*?" he asked.

"Yes, I did."

"It can't be Grandfather because he's dead. I know Dad drinks a bit, but what kind of trouble can he be in?"

Hawes smiled. "I'd like to ask you a few questions. That is, if you're Philip Bannister."

"The very same. And you are?"

"Detective Hawes, Eighty-seventh Squad."

"A real cop," Bannister said appreciatively. "A real live detective. Well, well, enter. What's the matter? Am I typing too loud? Did that bitch complain about it?"

"What bitch?"

"My landlady. Come in, make yourself homely. She's

threatened to call the cops if I type at night again. Is that what this is?"

"No," Hawes said.

"Sit down," Bannister said, indicating one of the chairs at the kitchen table. "Want a cold beer?"

"I can use one."

"So can I. When do you think we'll get some rain?"

"I couldn't say."

"Neither could I. Neither can the weather bureau. I think they get their forecasts by reading yesterday's forecast in the newspapers." Bannister opened the icebox door and pulled out two cans of beer. "Ice melts like hell in this weather. You mind drinking it from the can?"

"Not at all."

He punctured both cans and handed one to Hawes.

"To the noble and the pure," he toasted, and he drank. Hawes drank with him. "Ahhhhh, good," Bannister said. "The simple pleasures. Nothing like them. Who needs money?"

"You live here alone, Bannister?" Hawes asked.

"Entirely alone. Except when I have visitors, which is rarely. I enjoy women, but I can't afford them."

"You employed?"

"Sort of. I'm a free-lance writer."

"Magazines?"

"I am currently working on a book," Bannister said.

"Who's your publisher?"

"I have no publisher. I wouldn't be living in this rat trap if I had a publisher. I'd be lighting cigars with twenty-dollar bills and I'd be dating all the high-class fashion models in the city."

"Is that what successful writers do?"

"That's what this writer is going to do when he's successful."

"Did you buy a ream of Cartwright 142-Y recently?" Hawes asked.

"Huh?"

"Cartwright 14—"

"Yeah," Bannister said. "How the hell did you know that?"

"Do you know a prostitute called The Lady?"

"Huh?"

"Do you know a prostitute called The Lady?" Hawes repeated.

"No. What? What did you say?"

"I said—"

"Are you kidding?"

"I'm serious."

"A prost—Hell, no!" Bannister seemed to get suddenly indignant. "How would I know a prost—? Are you kidding?"

"Do you know *anyone* called The Lady?"

"The Lady? What is this?"

"The Lady. Think."

"I don't have to think. I don't know anybody called The Lady. What is this?"

"May I see your desk?"

"I don't have a desk. Listen, the joke has gone far enough. I don't know how you found out what kind of typing paper I use, and I don't particularly care. All I know is that you're sitting there drinking my good beer which costs me money Dad works hard to earn, and asking me foolish questions about prost— Now, what is this, huh? What is this?"

"May I see your desk, please?"

"I don't have a goddamn desk! I work on a table!"

"May I see that?"

"All right, all right, be mysterious!" Bannister shouted. "Be a big-shot mysterious detective. Go ahead. Be my guest. The table's in the other room. Don't mess up anything or I'll call the goddamn commissioner."

Hawes went into the other room. A typewriter was on the table, together with a pile of typed sheets, a package of carbon paper, and an opened box of typing paper.

"Do you have any paste?" Hawes asked.

"Of course not. What would I be doing with paste?"

"What are your plans for tonight, Bannister?"

"Who wants to know?" Bannister asked, pulling back his shoulders dignifiedly, looking the way Napoleon must have looked in his underwear.

"I do," Hawes said.

"Suppose I don't care to answer you?"

Hawes shrugged. The shrug was very meaningful. Bannister studied the shrug and then said, "Okay, I'm going to the ballet with Mother."

"Where?"

"The City Theater."

"What time?"

"It starts at eight-thirty."

"Your mother live here in the city?"

"No. She lives out on Sand's Spit. The East Shore."

"Is she well-fixed, would you say?"

"I would say so, yes."

"Would you call her a suburban lady?"

"I would," Bannister admitted.

"A lady?"

"Yes."

Hawes hesitated. "Do you get along with her?"

"With Mother? Of course, I do."

"How does she feel about your writing?"

"She feels I have great talent."

"Does she like the idea of your living in a slum neighbor-hood?"

"She would rather I lived home, but she respects my wishes."

"The family's supporting you, is that right?"

"That's right."

"How much?"

"Sixty-five a week."

"Mother ever oppose this?"

"The money, you mean? No. Why should she? I spent much more than that when I was living at home."

"Who paid for the ballet tickets tonight?"

"Mother."

"Where were you this morning at about eight o'clock, Bannister?"

"Right here."

"Anybody with you?"

"No."

"Anybody see you here?"

"The typewriter was going," Bannister said. "Ask any of my neighbors. Unless they're all dead, they heard it. Why? What am I supposed to have done at eight o'clock this morning?"

"What paper do you read on Sundays?" Hawes asked.

"The *Graphic*."

"Any out-of-town papers?"

"Like what?"

"Like the *New York Times*?"

"Yes. I buy the *Times*."

"Every Sunday?"

"Yes. I like to see what pap is on the best-seller list each week."

"Do you know where the station house is?"

"The police station, you mean?"

"Yes."

"It's near the park, isn't it?"

"Is it, or isn't it?" Hawes asked.

"Yes, it is. I still don't understand—"

"What time are you meeting your mother?"

"Eight," Bannister said.

"Eight tonight. Do you own a gun?"

"No."

"Any other weapon?"

"No."

"Have you had any arguments with your mother recently?"

"No."

"With any other woman?"

"No."

"What do you call your mother?"

"Mother."

"Anything else."

"Mom."

"Any nicknames?"

"Sometimes I call her Carol. That's her name."

"Ever call her The Lady?"

"No. Are we back to that again?"

"Ever call *anybody* The Lady?"

"No."

"What do you call your landlady, the bitch who said she'd call the cops if you typed at night?"

"I call her Mrs. Nelson. I also call her The Bitch."

"Has she given you a lot of trouble?"

"Only about the typing."

"Do you like her?"

"Not particularly."

"Do you hate her?"

"No. I hardly ever think about her, to tell the truth."

"Bannister . . ."

"Yes?"

"A detective will probably follow you to the ballet tonight. He'll be with you when—"

"What do you mean? What am I supposed to have done?"

"—when you leave this apartment, and when you meet your mother, and when you take your seat. I'm telling you this in case—"

"What the hell is this, a police state?"

"—in case you had any rash ideas. Do you understand me, Bannister?"

"No, I don't. The rashest idea I have is buying Mother an ice-cream soda after the show."

"Good, Bannister. Keep it that way."

"Cops," Bannister said. "If you're finished, I'd like to get back to work."

"I'm finished," Hawes said. "Thank you for your time. And remember. There'll be a cop with you."

"Balls," Bannister said, and he sat at his table and began typing.

Hawes left the apartment. He checked with the three other tenants on the floor, two of whom were willing to swear (like drunken sailors!) that Bannister's damn machine had been going at eight o'clock that morning. In fact, it had started going at six-thirty, and hadn't stopped since.

Hawes thanked them and went back to the squad.

It was 12:23.

Hawes was hungry.

7

Meyer Meyer had raised the shade covering the grilled window facing the park, so that sunshine splashed onto the desk near the window where the men were having lunch.

From where Carella sat at the end of the desk facing the window and the park, he could see out across the street, could see the greenery rolling away from the stone wall that divided the park from the pavement.

"Suppose this isn't a specific lady?" Meyer asked. "Suppose we're on the wrong track?"

"What do you mean?" Carella asked biting into a sandwich. The sandwich had been ordered at Charlie's Delicatessen, around the corner. It nowhere compared with the sandwiches Carella's wife, Teddy, made.

"We're assuming this nut has a particular dame on his mind," Meyer said. "A dame called The Lady. This may not be so."

"Go ahead," Hawes said.

"This is a terrible sandwich," Carella said.

"They get worse all the time," Meyer agreed. "There's a new place, Steve. The Golden Pot. Did you see it? It's on Fifth, just off Culver Avenue. Willis ate there. Says it's pretty good."

"Does he deliver?" Carella asked.

"If he doesn't, he's passing up a gold mine," Meyer said. "With all the *fressers* in this precinct."

"What about The Lady?" Hawes asked.

"On my lunch hour he wants me to think, yet," Meyer said.

"Do we need that shade up?" Carella asked.

"Why not?" Meyer said. "Let the sunshine in."

"Something's blinking in my eyes," Carella said.

"So move your chair."

Carella shoved back his chair.

"What about—" Hawes started.

"All right, all right," Meyer said. "This one is eager. He's bucking for commissioner."

"He's liable to make it," Carella said.

"Suppose you were pasting up this damn letter?" Meyer asked. "Suppose you were looking through the *New York Times* for words? Suppose all you wanted to say was, 'I'm going to kill a woman tonight at eight. Try and stop me.' Do you follow me so far?"

"I follow you," Hawes said.

"Okay. You start looking. You can't find the word *eight*, so you improvise. You cut out a Ballantine-beer thing, and you use that for the figure eight. You can't find the words *I'm going*, but you do find *I will*, so you use those instead. Okay, why can't the same thing apply to The Lady?"

"What do you mean?"

"You want to say a *woman*. You search through the damn paper, and you can't find those words. You're looking through the book section, and you spot the ad for the Conrad Richter novel. Why not? you say to yourself. Woman, lady, the same thing. So you cut out *The Lady*. It happens to be capitalized because it's the title of a novel. That doesn't bother you because it conveys the meaning you want. But it can set the cops off on a wild-goose chase looking for a capitalized Lady when she doesn't really exist."

"If this guy had the patience to cut out and paste up every letter in the word *tonight*," Carella said, "then he knew exactly what he wanted to say, and if he couldn't find the exact word he created it."

"Maybe, maybe not," Hawes said.

"There are only so many ways to say *tonight*," Meyer said.

"He could have said *this evening*," Carella said. "I mean, using your theory. But he wanted to say *tonight*, so he clipped out every letter he needed to form the word. I don't buy your theory, Meyer." He moved his chair again. "That damn thing is still blinking in the park."

"Okay, don't buy it," Meyer said. "I'm just saying this nut may be ready to kill *any* woman, and not a *specific* woman called The Lady."

Carella was pensive.

"If that's the case," Hawes said, "we've got nothing to go on. The victim could be any woman in the city. Where do we start?"

"I don't know," Meyer said. He shrugged and sipped at his coffee. "I don't know."

"In the Army," Carella said slowly, "we were always warned about . . ."

Meyer turned to him. "Huh?" he asked.

"Binoculars," Carella said. "Those are binoculars."

"What do you mean?"

"In the park," he said. "The blinking. Somebody's using binoculars."

"Okay," Meyer said, shrugging it off. "But if the victim *is* any woman, we've got about a chance in five million of stopping—".

"Who'd be training binoculars on the precinct?" Hawes asked slowly.

The men fell suddenly silent.

"Can he see into this room?" Hawes asked.

"Probably," Carella said. Unconsciously their voices had dropped to whispers, as if their unseen observer could also hear them.

"Just keep sitting and talking," Hawes whispered. "I'll go out and down the back way."

"I'll go with you," Carella said.

"No. He may run if he sees too many of us leaving."

"Do you think—?" Meyer started.

"I don't know," Hawes said, rising slowly.

"You can save us a lot of time," Carella whispered. "Good luck, Cotton."

Hawes emerged into the alley that ran behind the precinct just outside the detention cells on the ground floor. He slammed the heavy steel door shut behind him, and then started through the alley. Idiotically, his heart was pounding.

Easy does it, he told himself. We've got to play this easy or the bird will fly, and we'll be left with The Lady again, or maybe Anywoman, Anywoman in a city teeming with women of all shapes and sizes. So, easy. Play it easy. Sprinkle the salt onto the bird's tail, and if the bastard tries to run, clobber him or shoot him, but play it easy, slow and easy, play it like a "Dragnet" copy, with all the time in the world, about to interrogate the slowest talker in the United States.

He ran to the alley mouth and then cut into the street. The sidewalk was packed with people sucking in fetid air. A stickball game was in progress up the street, and farther down toward the end of the block, a bunch of kids had turned on a fire hydrant and were romping in the released lunge of water, many of them fully clothed. Some of the kids, Hawes noticed, were wearing dungarees and striped tee shirts. He turned right, putting the stickball game and the fire hydrant behind him. What does a good cop do on the hottest day of the year? he wondered. Allow the kids to waste the city's water supply and cause possible danger should the fire department need that hydrant? Or use a Stillson wrench on the hydrant and force the kids back into a sweltering, hot inactivity, an inactivity that causes street gangs and street rumbles and possibly more danger than a fire would cause?

What does the good cop do? Side with the madam of a whorehouse, or side with the good citizen trying to cheat her?

Why should cops have to worry about philosophy, Hawes wondered, worrying about philosophy all the while.

He was running.

He was running, and he was sweating like a basement cold-water pipe—but the park was dead ahead, and the man with the binoculars was in that park somewhere.

"Is he still there?" Meyer asked.

"Yes," Carella said.

"Jesus, I'm afraid to move. Do you think he tipped to Hawes?"

"I don't think so."

"One good thing," Meyer said.

"What's that?"

"With all this action, my sandwich tastes better."

The man in the park sat cross-legged on the huge rock, the binoculars pointed at the precinct. There were two cops seated at the desk now, eating sandwiches and talking. The big red-headed one had got up a few minutes ago and leisurely walked away from the desk. Perhaps he'd gone for a glass of water, or maybe a cup of coffee? Did they make coffee inside a precinct? Were they allowed to do that? In any case, he had not come out of the building, so he was still inside somewhere.

Maybe he'd been called by the captain or the lieutenant or whoever was his superior. Maybe the captain was all in a dither about the letter and wanted action instead of men sitting around having lunch.

In a way, their having lunch annoyed him. He knew they had to eat, of course—*everybody* has to eat, even cops—but hadn't they taken his letter seriously? Didn't they know he was going to kill? Wasn't it their job to stop someone from killing? For Christ's sake, hadn't he warned them? Hadn't he given them every possible chance to stop him? So why the hell were they sitting around eating sandwiches and chatting? Was this what the city paid cops for?

Disgustedly, he put down the binoculars.

He wiped sweat from his upper lip. His lip felt funny, swollen. Cursing the heat, he pulled a handkerchief from his back pocket.

"It's gone," Carella said.

"What! What!"

"The blinking. It's gone."

"Can Hawes be there already?" Meyer asked.

"No, it's too soon. Maybe the guy's leaving. Goddamnit, why didn't we—"

"There it is! The blinking, Steve. He's still there!"

Carella sighed heavily. His hands were clenched on the desktop. He forced himself to pick up his coffee container and sip it.

Come on, Cotton, he thought. *Move!*

He ran along the park's paths, wondering where the man with the binoculars was. People turned to look at him as he hurried by. It was strange to see a man running at any time, but especially strange on a day as hot as this one. Invariably the passers-by looked behind Hawes to see who was chasing him, fully expecting a uniformed cop with a drawn gun in hot pursuit.

A high spot, he figured. If he's able to see the second floor of the precinct, it had to be from a high spot. The brow of a hill, or a big rock, but something high, something close to the street where the park ground slopes up to meet the pavement.

Is he armed?

If he's going to kill someone tonight, he's probably armed

279

right now, too. Unconsciously, Hawes touched his back hip pocket, felt the reassuring bulge of his .38. Should he take the gun out now? No. Too many people on the paths. A gun might panic them. One of them might think Hawes was on the opposite side of the law and get heroic, try to stop an escaping thief. No. The gun stayed where it was for now.

He began climbing into the bushes, feeling the slope of the ground beneath his feet. Somewhere high, he thought. It has to be high, or the man can't see. The ground was sharply sloping now, gently rolling grass and earth giving way to a steeply pitched outcropping of rock. Is this the rock? Hawes wondered. Is this the right rock? Is my bird up here?

He drew his .38.

He was breathing hard from the climb. Sweat stained his armpits and the back of his shirt. Small pebbles had found their way into his shoes.

He reached the top of the rock. There was no one there.

In the distance, he could see the precinct.

And off to the left, sitting on another high rock, he could see a man crouched over a pair of binoculars.

Hawes's heart unexpectedly lurched into his throat.

"What do you see?" Meyer asked.

"Nothing."

"He's still there?"

"The sun's still on the binoculars."

"Where the hell is Hawes!"

"It's a big park," Carella said charitably.

Sitting on the rock, the man with the binoculars thought he heard a sound in the bushes. Slowly he turned, lowering the glasses. Barely breathing, he listened.

He could feel the hackles at the back of his neck rising. Suddenly he was drenched with sweat. He wiped beads of perspiration from the swollen feel of his upper lip.

There was an unmistakable thrashing in the woods.

He listened.

Was it a kid?

Lovers?

Or a cop?

Run, his mind shrieked. The thought ricocheted inside his skull, but he sat riveted to the rock. They'll stop me, he thought.

But so soon? So soon? After all the planning? To be stopped so soon?

The noise in the woods was closer now. He saw the glint of sunlight on metal. Goddamnit, why hadn't he taken the gun with him? Why hadn't he prepared for something like this? His eyes anxiously scanned the barren surface of the rock. There was a high bush at the base of the stone surface. Crawling on his belly, the binoculars clutched in his right hand, he moved toward the bush. The sunlight caught at something bright, something non-metallic this time. Red. Red hair! The cop who'd left the desk! He held his breath. The thrashing in the woods stopped. From where he crouched behind the bush, he could see the red hair and only that. And then the head ducked, and then reappeared. The cop was advancing. He would pass directly in front of the bush.

The man with the binoculars waited. His hand on the metal was sweating. He could see the cop plainly now, advancing slowly, a gun in his right hand.

Patiently he waited. Maybe he wouldn't be seen. Maybe if he stayed right where he was, he wouldn't be discovered. No. No, that was foolish. He had to get out of this. He had to get out of it, or be caught, and it was too soon to be caught, too damned soon.

Hefting the binoculars like a mace, he waited.

From where Hawes advanced through the bushes, he could hear no sound. The park seemed to have gone suddenly still. The birds were no longer chattering in the trees. The sound of muted voices, which hung on the air like a swarm of insects, drifting over the paths and the lake and the trees, had suddenly quieted. There was only the bright sun overhead and the beginnings of the sloping rock, a huge bush on Hawes's left, and the frightening sudden silence.

He could feel danger, could sense it in every nerve ending, could feel it throbbing in every bone marrow. He had felt this way the time he'd been knifed, could remember the startling appearance of the blade, the naked light bulb glinting on metal, the hurried, desperate lunge for his back pocket and his revolver.

He could remember the blurred swipe of the blade, the sudden warmth over his left temple, the feel of blood gushing onto his face. And then, unable to reach his gun before the slashing knife was pulled back, he had struck out with his fists, struck, repeatedly until the knife had clattered to the hallway floor, until his assailant had been a blubbering quivering hulk against the wall, and still he had hit him, hit him until his knuckles had bled.

This time he had a gun in his hand. This time he was ready. And still, danger prickled his scalp, rushed up his spinal column with tingling ferocity.

Cautiously he advanced.

The blow struck him on his right wrist.

The blow was sharp, the biting impact of metal hitting bone. His hand opened, and the .38 clattered to the rock surface. He whirled in time to see the man raise the binoculars high. He brought his hands up to protect his face. The binoculars descended, the lenses catching sunlight, glittering crazily. For a maniacal, soundless moment he saw the man's frenzied, twisted face, and then the binoculars struck, smashing into Hawes's hands. He felt intense pain. He clenched his fists, threw a punch, and then saw the binoculars go up again and down, and he knew they would strike his face this time. Blindly he clutched at them.

He felt metal strike his palms, and then he closed his hands and wrenched at the glasses with all his strength, pulling at them. He felt them come free. The man stood stock-still for just a moment, surprise stamped on his face. Then he broke into a run.

Hawes dropped the glasses.

The man was in the bushes by the time Hawes retrieved the .38.

He picked up the gun and fired into the air. He fired into the air again, and then he thrashed into the bushes after the man.

When Carella heard the shots in the squadroom, he shoved back his chair and said, "Let's go, Meyer."

They found Hawes sitting on a patch of grass in the park. He'd lost their man, he said. They examined his wrist and his hands. There didn't seem to be any broken bones. He led them back to the rock where he'd been ambushed, and again he said, "I lost him. I lost the bastard."

"Maybe you didn't," Carella said.

Spreading a handkerchief over his palm, he picked up the binoculars.

8

At the police lab, Sam Grossman identified the glasses as having been made by a firm named Pieter-Vondiger. The serial number told him the glasses had been manufactured sometime during 1952. The air-glass surfaces were not anti-reflection coated, and so the binoculars had not been made for the Armed Forces, as many of the firm's glasses had been during that time. A call to the company assured Sam that the model was no longer being sold in retail stores, having been replaced by more recent, improved models. Nonetheless, he prepared a chart on the glasses for the cops of the 87th, while his men went over the glasses for fingerprints. Sam Grossman was a methodical man, and it was his contention that the smallest, most insignificant-seeming piece of information might prove valuable to the men investigating a case. And so he wrote down every particular of the field glasses.

Magnification: 8 diameters
Objective lenses: 30 mm.diameter
Angular field: 7° 44′
Pupilary distance: 48 to 72 mm.
Exit pupil: 3.5 mm.
Relative brightness: 12.3
Field at 1,000 yards: 135 yds.
Length closed: 4¼″
Length extended: 4⅝″
Weight: 18oz.

The glasses were central focusing, right ocular adjustable individually. The price of the glasses when new, sold together with a stiff sole leather casing and straps, was $92.50.

There were two sets of prints on the glasses. One belonged to Cotton Hawes. The other, which—because of the very way in which binoculars must be held—consisted of fairly good thumb and finger impressions for both hands, had been left on the glasses by Hawes's assailant. Photos were taken of the prints. One photo was sent immediately to the Bureau of Criminal Identification. The other was photo-transmitted to the Federal Bureau of Investigation in Washington. Each agency was asked for extreme speed in making a possible identification from the prints.

Sam Grossman prayed that the man who'd left the prints on the glasses had also left a record of those prints somewhere in the United States.

It was 1:10 P.M.

Lieutenant Byrnes spread the newspaper on the desk. "How about this, Hawes?" he asked.

Hawes looked at the page, his eye running down it until he found the ad. The ad said:

> *Appearing now at the Brisson Roof!*
> *Jay "Lady" Astor*
> *Piano-stylings and Songs*
> *in the*
> *Lady Astor manner*

There was a picture of a dark-haired girl in a skin-tight evening dress, smiling.

"I didn't know she was in the city," Hawes said.

"Ever hear of her?"

"Yes. She's pretty popular. Sophisticated stuff, you know. Cole Porter, like that. And lots of special material with off-color lyrics in impeccable taste."

"How's your wrist?"

"Fine," Hawes said, feeling it with his left hand.

"Do you want to look her up?"

"Sure," Hawes said.

The phone on Byrnes's desk rang. He picked it up.

"Byrnes here," he said. He listened. "Sure, put him on, Dave." He covered the mouthpiece. "The lab," he said to Hawes. He uncovered the mouthpiece and waited. "Hello, Sam," he said, *"wie gehts?"* Hawes listened, Byrnes listened, interjecting an occasional "Uh huh" into the phone. He listened

285

for about five minutes. Then he said, "Thanks a lot, Sam," and hung up.

"Anything?"

"A good set of prints on the glasses," Byrnes said. "Sam's already sent copies to the I.B. and to Washington. Keep your toes crossed. He's sending a written report back with the glasses. They're 1952 vintage, discontinued for the later models. Once we get them, I'll have Steve and Meyer start checking the hockshops. How about this Lady Astor? Think she's the target?"

Hawes shrugged. "I'll check her out."

"It could be," Byrnes said, returning the shrug. "What the hell? Person in the public eye. Maybe some jerk doesn't like the dirty songs she sings. What do you say?"

"I say it's worth a try."

"Make it fast," Byrnes said. "Don't stop to listen to any of her songs. We may have a few other tries to make before eight tonight." He looked at his watch. "Jesus, the time flies," he said.

A call to the Brisson Roof told Hawes that Jay Astor's first show went on at eight P.M. The roof manager refused to divulge her address even when Hawes told him he was a detective. He insisted that Hawes give him a number to call back. Hawes gave him the Frederick 7 number, and the manager called back immediately, apparently satisfied after talking to the desk sergeant and being transferred to the Detective Division that he was talking to a bona fide cop and not one of Miss Astor's great unwashed. He gave Hawes the address, and Hawes left for the apartment immediately.

It seemed odd that Miss Astor was not staying at the hotel where she was performing, but perhaps she didn't like to mix business with pleasure. Her apartment was in uptown Isola, in the swank brownstone neighborhood on the south side, some thirty blocks below the first street in the 87th-precinct territory. Hawes made the drive in ten minutes. He left the car at the curb, climbed the twelve steps to the front door, and entered a small, immaculate lobby. He scanned the mailboxes. There was no Jay Astor listed on any of the boxes. He stepped outside, and standing on the front stoop once more, checked the address again. It was the right address. He went into the lobby again

286

and rang for the superintendent. He could hear the loud bell sounding somewhere beyond the curtained inner-lobby door. He heard a door opening and closing, heard footsteps, and then the curtained door opened.

"Yes?" the man said. He was an old man wearing house-slippers and a faded blue basque shirt.

"I'd like to see Miss Jay Astor," Hawes said.

"There's no Miss Astor here," the man answered.

"I'm not a fan or a reporter," Hawes said. "This is police business." He took out his wallet and opened it to his shield.

The man studied it. "You're a detective?" he asked.

"Yes."

"She's not in any trouble, is she?"

"She might be," Hawes said. "I'd like to talk to her."

"Just a minute," the man said. He went inside, leaving the curtained lobby door open, and also leaving the door to his ground-floor apartment ajar. Hawes could hear him dialing a phone. Upstairs, Hawes heard a phone ringing. The ringing stopped abruptly, and Hawes heard the old man talking. In a few minutes the old man came back.

"She said you should go up. It's Apartment 4A. That's the one she uses for the entrance. She's got the whole top floor, actually. That's 4A, 4B, and 4C. But she uses 4A for the entrance, got the other ones blocked off from inside with furniture. 4A. You can go right on up."

"Thank you," Hawes said. He moved past the old man into the hallway. Carpeted steps led from the inner hallway upstairs. An ornately carved banister was on one side of the steps. The hallway was suffocatingly hot. Hawes climbed the steps, thinking of Carella and Meyer hitting the hockshops. Would Byrnes ask for interprecinct assistance on this one? Or did he expect the 87th to hit every hockshop in the city? No, he'd ask for the other men. He'd have to.

There was a small placard set in a brass rectangle screwed to the doorjamb of Apartment 4A. The placard simply read, ASTOR.

Hawes pressed the buzzer.

The door opened so rapidly that Hawes suspected Jay Astor had been standing just inside it.

"You the detective?" she asked.

"Yes."

"Come in."

He walked into the apartment. If anything, Jay Astor was a disappointment. She had appeared sexy, slinky, and seductive in her newspaper photo, the skin-tight gown molding the abundant curves of a naturally endowed body. Her eyes had been provocative, and her smile had held the flash of promised evil, the tantalizing challenge of a mysterious woman. Here, in person, there was no challenge and no promise.

Jay Astor wore shorts and a halter. Her bosom was full and rich, but her legs were somewhat muscular, the legs of a tennis player. Her eyes were slightly squinted, but he realized instantly that the squint was a result of myopia and not sexuality. Her teeth revealed by her smile were rather large, giving her the appearance of a benevolent horse. Or perhaps he was being too cruel. He supposed, unprepared by the photo, he would have considered Miss Astor an attractive woman.

"The living room's air-conditioned," she said. "Come on in there, and we'll close the door."

He followed her into a room done in extreme modern. She closed the door behind him and said, "There. Isn't that better? This heat is the most. I came up from a South American tour two weeks ago, and believe me it wasn't as hot down there. What can I do for you?"

"We received a letter this morning," Hawes said.

"Oh? What about?" Jay Astor went to the bar lining one side of the long room. "Would you like a drink? A gin rickey? A Tom Collins? You call it."

"Nothing, thanks."

Her face expressed mild surprise. Unperturbed, she began mixing herself a gin and tonic.

"The letter said, 'I will kill The Lady tonight at eight. What can you do about it?'" Hawes said.

"Nice letter." She pulled a face and squeezed a lime into the drink.

"You don't seem particularly impressed," Hawes said.

"Should I be?"

"You *are* known as The Lady, aren't you?"

"Oh! Oh!" she said. "Oh, yes. The Lady. I will kill The Lady tonight. I see. Yes. Yes."

"Well?"

288

"A crank," Jay said.

"Maybe. Have you had any threatening letters or calls?"

"Recently, do you mean?"

"Yes."

"No, not recently. I get them every now and then. Jack the Ripper types. They call me smutty. They say they will kill me and cleanse the world in the blood of the lamb, and like that. Buggos. Cranks." She turned from the bar, grinning. "I'm still alive."

"You seem to take all of it pretty lightly, Miss Astor."

"Call me Jay," she said. "I do. If I had to worry about every buggo who writes or calls, I'd become a buggo myself. There's no percentage in that."

"All the same, you *may* be the person indicated in this letter."

"So what do we do about it?"

"First of all, if you don't mind, we'd like to give you police protection tonight."

"All night?" Jay asked, raising an eyebrow coquettishly, her face expressing for a fleeting instant the promise and the challenge that was in the newspaper photo.

"Well, from when you leave the apartment until your show is over."

"My last show is at two," she said. "Your cop'll be busy. Or will the cop be you?"

"No, he won't," Hawes said.

"Worse luck," Jay answered, and she pulled at her drink.

"Your first show goes on at eight, is that right?"

"That's right."

"The letter says—"

"That could be a coincidence."

"Yes, it could. What time do you generally leave for the Brisson?"

"About seven."

"I'll have a patrolman stop by for you."

"A handsome Irish cop, I trust."

"We have a lot of those," Hawes said, smiling. "In the meantime, can you tell me whether or not anything has happened recently that would—"

"—cause someone to want me dead?" Jay thought for a moment. "No," she said.

"Anything at all? An argument? A contract dispute? A disgruntled musician? Anything?"

"No," she said pensively. "I'm easy to get along with. That's my rep in the trade. An easy lady," She grinned. "I didn't mean that to sound the way it did."

"How about the threatening letters and calls you mentioned? When was the last time you got one of those?"

"Oh, before I went to South America. That was months ago. I've only been back two weeks, you know. I doubt if the buggos know I'm around. When they hear my new album, they'll begin their poison penmanship again. Have you heard it?" She shook her head. "But of course you haven't. It hasn't been released yet."

She went to a hi-fi unit, opened one of the cabinets, and pulled a record album from the top shelf. On the album cover, Lady Astor was riding a white horse, naked. Her long black hair had been released so that it cascaded over her breasts, effectively covering her. There was the same malevolent, mischievous, inviting gleam in her eyes as had been in the newspaper photo. The album was titled, "Astor's Pet Horse."

"It's a collection of cowboy songs," Jay explained, "with the lyrics jazzed up a bit. Would you like to hear a little of it?"

"Well, I—"

"It won't take a minute," Jay said, moving to the hi-fi and putting the record on the turntable. "You'll be getting a sneak preview. What other detective in the city can make that statement?"

"I wanted to—"

"Sit," Jay said, and the record began.

It began with the customary corny cowboy guitar, and then Lady Astor's insinuatingly chic voice came smoothly over the speaker.

"Home, home in the slums," she sang.

"Full of pushers, and junkies, and bums.

"Where seldom is heard

"Mating call of the bird,

"And the zip guns play music like drums . . ."

The record went on and on. Hawes thought it only mildly funny. He was too close to the reality to find the parody amusing.

At the end of "Home on the Range," a parody of "Deep in the Heart of Texas" began.

"This one is a little rough," Jay said, "full of innuendo. A lot of people won't like it, but I don't give a damn. Morality is a funny thing, do you know?"

"How do you mean?"

"I came to the conclusion a long time ago that morality is strictly personal. The hardest thing any artist can attempt is to reconcile his own moral standards with those of the great unwashed. It can't be done. Morality is morality, and mine's mine and yours is yours. There are things I accept matter-of-factly, and these same things shock the hell out of the Kansas City housewife. That's a trap the artist can fall into."

"What trap?"

"Most artists—in show business, anyway—live in the big cities. That's where the business is, you know, so that's where you have to be. Well, urban morality is pretty different from morality in the sticks. The stuff that goes with the city slickers just won't go with the guy mowing a field of wheat—or whatever the hell you do with wheat. But if you try to please everybody, you go buggo. So I try to please myself. If I use my own good taste, I figure the morals will take care of themselves."

"And do they?"

"Sometimes, yes—sometimes, no. Like I said, things I consider absolutely pure and simple don't seem quite so pure or quite so simple to the farmhand."

"Things like what?" Hawes asked innocently.

"Things like—would you like to go to bed with me?"

"Yes, I would," he answered automatically.

"Then let's," she said, putting down her drink.

"Right now?" he asked.

"Why not? It's as good a time as any."

He felt ridiculous answering what he had to answer, but he plunged ahead, anyway. "I haven't the time right now," he said.

"Your letter-sender?"

"My letter-sender."

"You may have lost your golden opportunity," she said.

"Those are the breaks," Hawes said, shrugging.

"Morality is a question of the means and the opportunity," Jay said.

"Like murder," Hawes answered.

"If you want to get morbid, okay. All I'm trying to say is that I would like you to make love to me now. Tomorrow I may not feel the same way. I may not even feel the same way ten minutes from now."

"Now you've spoiled it," Hawes said.

Jay raised an eyebrow inquisitively.

"I thought it was me. Instead, it's just your whim of the moment."

"What do you want me to do? Undress you and burp you?"

"No," Hawes said, rising. "Give me a rain check."

"It hasn't rained for weeks," Jay said.

"Maybe it will."

"And to quote an old sawhorse, lightning never strikes twice in the same place."

"I'll tell you," Hawes said, "I'm just liable to go out and shoot myself."

Jay smiled. "You're pretty damned sure of yourself, aren't you?"

"Am I?" he asked.

For a moment they faced each other. There was none of the photographic sensuality on her face now. Neither was there the fury of a woman scorned. There was only the somewhat pathetic loneliness of a little girl living in a vast top-floor apartment with an air-conditioner in the living room.

Lady Astor shrugged.

"What the hell," she said. "Give me a call sometime. The whim may return."

"Expect that cop," Hawes said.

"I will," she answered. "He may beat your time."

Hawes shrugged philosophically. "Some guys have all the luck," he said, and he left the apartment.

9

Some guys, too, have all the misfortune.

Meyer Meyer and Steve Carella had their share that blistering day. By 1:40 P.M. the sidewalks were baking, the buildings were ready to turn cherry red with contained heat, the people were wilting, automobile tires were melting, and it was obvious even to the neophyte science-fiction fan that the earth had somehow wandered too close to the sun. It would surely be consumed by fire. This was the last day, and Richard Matheson had called the tune, and the world would end in molten fire.

Undramatically speaking it was damn hot.

Meyer Meyer was a sweater. He sweated even in the wintertime. He didn't know why he sweated. He supposed it was a nervous reaction. But he was always covered with perspiration. Today he was drowning in it. As the two detectives wandered from hockshop to hockshop on sleazy Crichton Avenue, wandered from open door to open door, passed rapidly from one trio of gold balls to the next, Meyer thought he would die in a way unbefitting a heroic cop. He would die of heat prostration, and the obits would simply say COP FLOPS. Or perhaps, if the news was headlined in *Variety,* SOPPY COP DROPS.

"How do you like this *Variety* headline announcing my death by heat prostration?" he said to Carella as they entered another hockshop: "Soppy cop drops."

"That's pretty good," Carella said. "How about mine?"

"In *Variety*?"

"Sure."

"Let me hear it."

"SOPPY WOP COP DROPS."

Meyer burst out laughing. "You're a prejudiced bastard," he said.

The owner of the hockshop looked up as they approached his cage.

"Yes, sir, gentlemen," he said, "what can I do for you, sirs?"

"We're from the police," Carella said. He plunked the binoculars down on the countertop. "Recognize these?"

The hockshop owner examined them. "A beautiful pair of glasses," he said. "Pieter-Vondiger. Have they figured in a crime, perhaps?"

"They have."

"Was the perpetrator carrying them?"

"He was."

"Mmmm," the owner said.

"Recognize them?"

"We sell a lot of field glasses. That is, when we have them to sell."

"Did you have *these* to sell?"

"I don't think so. The last Pieter-Vondigers I had was in January. These are 8 x 30. The pair I had were 6 x 30. These are better glasses."

"Then you didn't sell these glasses?"

"No, sirs, I didn't. Are they stolen?"

"Not according to our lists."

"I'm sorry I can't help you, sirs."

"That's all right," Carella said. "Thanks."

They walked out onto the blistering sidewalk again.

"How many other cops are on this?" Meyer asked.

"Pete asked for a pair from each precinct. Maybe they'll come up with something."

"I'm getting tired. Do you suppose that damn letter is a phony?"

"I don't know. If it is, we ought to lock the bastard up, anyway."

"Hear, hear," Meyer said, in a burst of enthusiasm rare for the heat.

"Maybe we'll get a make on the prints," Carella said.

"Sure, maybe," Meyer agreed. "Maybe it'll rain."

"Maybe," Carella said.

They walked into the next shop. There were two men behind the counter. Both grinned as Meyer and Carella crossed the room.

"Good afternoon," one said, smiling.

"A pleasant day," the other said, smiling.

"I'm Jason Bloom," the first said.

"I'm Jacob Bloom," echoed the other.

"How do you do?" Carella answered. "We're Detectives Meyer and Carella of the Eighty-seventh Squad."

"A pleasure, gentlemen," Jason said.

"We're trying to trace the owner of these binoculars," Carella said. He put them on the counter. "Do you recognize them?"

"Pieter-Vondiger," Jason said.

"Excellent glasses," Jacob said.

"Superb,"

"Magnificent."

Carella broke into the lavish praise. "Recognize them?"

"Pieter-Vondiger," Jason said. "Didn't we—?"

"Precisely," Jacob said.

"The man with the—"

And the brothers burst out laughing together. Carella and Meyer waited. The laughter showed no signs of subsiding. It was reaching heights of hysteria, unprecedented hurricanes of hilarity, fits of festivity. Still, the detectives waited. At last the laughter subsided.

"Oh, my God," Jason said, chuckling.

"Do we remember these glasses?"

"Do we?" Jason said.

"Oh, my God," Jacob said.

"Do you?" Carella asked. He was hot.

Jason sobered instantly. "*Are* these the glasses, Jacob?" he asked.

"Certainly," Jacob said.

"But are you sure?"

"The scratch on the side, don't you remember? See, there is the scratch. Don't you remember he complained about the scratch? We reduced the glasses a dollar and a quarter because of the scratch. And all the while he was—" Jacob burst out laughing again.

"Oh, my God," Jason said, laughing with him.

Meyer looked at Carella. Carella looked at Meyer. Apparently the heat in the shop had grown too intense for the brothers.

Carella cleared his throat. Again the laughter subsided.

"Did you sell these glasses to someone?" he asked.

"Yes," Jason said.

"Certainly," Jacob said.

295

"Who?"

"The man with the lollipop!" Jason said, bursting into a new gale of hysteria.

"The man with the lollipop!" Jacob repeated, unable to keep his laugh from booming out of his mouth.

"This man had a lollipop?" Carella asked, deadpanned.

"Yes, yes! Oh, my God!"

"He was sucking on it all the while we haggled over the . . . the . . ."

". . . the glasses," Jason concluded. "Oh, my God. Oh, my good Lord! When he left the shop, we couldn't stop laughing. Do you remember, Jacob?"

"Yes, yes, how could I forget? A red lollipop! Oh, was he enjoying it! Oh, no child ever enjoyed a lollipop more! It was wonderful! Wonderful!"

"Magnificent!" Jason said.

"Fantastically—"

"What was his name?" Carella asked.

"Who?" Jason asked, sobering.

"The man with the lollipop."

"Oh, what was his name, Jacob?"

"I don't know, Jason."

Carella looked at Meyer. Meyer looked at Carella.

"Isn't there a bill of sale, Jacob?"

"Certainly, Jason."

"When was he here?"

"Two weeks ago, wasn't it?"

"A Friday?"

"No, a Saturday. No, you're right, it was a Friday."

"When was that? What date?"

"I don't know. Where's the calendar?" The brothers busied themselves over a calendar on the wall.

"There," Jacob said, pointing.

"Yes," Jason agreed.

"Friday," Jacob said.

"July twelfth."

"Would you check your bills?" Carella asked.

"Certainly."

"Of course."

The brothers moved into the back room.

"Nice," Meyer said.

"What?"

"Brotherly love."

"Um," Carella answered.

The brothers returned with a yellow carbon copy of the bill.

"Here it is," Jason said.

"July twelfth, just as we thought."

"And the man's name?" Carella asked.

"M. Samalson," Jason said.

"No first name?"

"Just the initial," Jason said.

"We only take the initial," Jacob corroborated.

"Any address?" Meyer asked.

"Can you read this?" Jason asked, indicating the writing on the line printed *Address*:

"It's your handwriting."

"No, no, you wrote it," Jason said.

"You did," Jacob told him. "See how the *t* is crossed. That is your handwriting."

"Possibly. But what does it say?"

"That's a *t*, for sure," Jacob said.

"Yes. Oh, it's Calm's Point! Of course! That's Calm's Point."

"But what's the address?"

"31–63 Jefferson Street, Calm's Point," Jason said, in a deciphering burst.

Meyer copied down the address.

"A lollipop!" Jason said.

"Oh, my God," Jacob said.

"Thank you very much for . . ." Carella started, but the brothers were laughing to beat the band, so the two detectives simply left the shop.

"Calm's Point," Carella said when they were outside. "Clear the hell over on the other end of the city."

"It would be that way," Meyer said.

"We'd better get back to the squad. Pete may want to put a Calm's Point precinct on it."

"Right," Meyer said. They walked back to the car. "You want to drive?"

"I don't care. You tired?"

"No. No. I just thought you might want to drive."

"Okay," Carella said.

They got into the car.

"Think those reports on the prints are back yet?"

"I hope so. Might save us a call to Calm's Point."

"Um," Meyer said.

They set the car in motion. They were silent for a while. Then Meyer said, "Steve, it's hot as hell today."

The reports from the Bureau of Criminal Identification and the F.B.I. were waiting at the office when Carella and Meyer returned. Both agencies had reported that they were unable to find fingerprints in their vast files corresponding to the ones taken from the binoculars.

Hawes walked into the squadron as the men were reading the reports.

"Any luck?" he asked.

"No make," Carella said. "But we got the name of the guy who bought those binoculars. That's a break."

"Pete want to pick him up?"

"I haven't told him yet."

"What's his name?"

"M. Samalson."

"You'd better tell Pete quick," Hawes said. "I got a good look at the guy who slugged me. If it was Samalson, I'll know it."

"And we've also got the prints to compare, in case your memory's faulty," Carella said. He paused. "How'd you make out with Lady Astor?"

Hawes winked and said nothing.

Carella sighed and went into Byrnes's office.

The closest Calm's Point precinct to M. Samalson's home address was the 102nd. Byrnes put in a call to the detective squad there and asked them to pick up and deliver Samalson as soon as possible.

At 2:00 P.M. a new batch of kids in dungarees and red-striped tee shirts was trotted into the precinct squadroom. Dave Murchison was brought up from the desk. He looked the kids over, stopped before one of them, and said, "This is the kid."

Byrnes walked over to the boy.

"Did you deliver a letter here this morning?" he asked.

"No," the boy said.

"He's the kid," Murchison insisted.

"What's your name, son?" Byrnes asked.

"Frankie Annuci."

"Did you bring a letter here this morning?"

"No," the kid said.

"Did you come into the building and ask for the desk sergeant?"

"No," the kid said.

"Did you hand a letter to this man here?" Byrnes said, indicating Murchison.

"No," the kid said.

"He's lying," Murchison said. "This is the kid."

"Come on, Frankie," Byrnes said gently. "You did deliver that letter, didn't you?"

"No."

There was fear in the boy's wide blue eyes, fear of the law, a fear deeply ingrained in the mind of every precinct citizen.

"You're not in any trouble, son," Byrnes said. "We're trying to find the man who gave you that letter. Now, you did deliver it, didn't you?"

"No," the kid said.

Byrnes turned to the other detectives, his patience beginning to wear thin. Hawes walked to the boy, joining Byrnes.

"You've got nothing to be afraid of, Frankie. We're trying to find the man who gave you that letter, do you understand? Now, where did you first meet him?"

"I didn't meet anybody," the kid said.

"Get rid of the rest of these kids, Meyer," Byrnes said. Meyer began shutting the other boys out of the room. Frankie Annuci watched their departure, his eyes growing wider.

"How about it, Frankie?" Carella asked. Unconsciously he had drifted into the circle around the boy. When Meyer had got rid of the other boys, he came back to stand with Byrnes, Hawes, and Carella. There was something amusing about the scene. The ridiculousness of it struck each of the detectives at the same moment. They had automatically assumed the formation for intense interrogation, but their victim was a boy no older than ten, and they felt somewhat like bullies as they surrounded him, ready to fire their questions in machine-gun bursts. And yet, this boy was a possible lead to the man they were seeking, a lead that might prove more fruitful than the thus far phantom name of M. Samalson. They waited, as if unwilling to begin the barrage until their commanding officer gave the signal to fire.

Byrnes opened it.

"Now, we're going to ask some questions, Frankie," he said gently, "and we want you to answer them. All right?"

"All right," Frankie said.

"Who gave you the letter?"

"Nobody."

"Was it a man?"

"I don't know."

"A woman?" Hawes asked.

"I don't know."

"Do you know what the letter said?" Carella asked.

"No."

"Did you open it?" Meyer said.

"No."

"But there *was* a letter?"

"No."

"You did deliver a letter?"

"No."

"You're lying, aren't you?"

"No."

"Where'd you meet the man?"

"I didn't meet anybody."

"Near the park?"

"No."

"The candy store?"

"No."

"One of the side streets?"

"No."

"Was he driving a car?"

"No."

"There *was* a man?"

"I don't know."

"Was he a man or a woman?"

"I don't know."

"The letter said he was going to kill somebody tonight. Did you know that?"

"No."

"Would you like this man or this woman to kill somebody?"

"No."

"Well, he's going to kill somebody. That's what the letter said. He's going to kill a lady."

"She may be your mother, Frankie."

"Would you like this man to kill your mother?"

"No," Frankie said.

"Then tell us who he is. We want to stop him."

"I don't know who he is!" Frankie blurted.

"You never saw him before today?"

Frankie began crying. "No," he said. "Never."

"What happened, Frankie?" Carella asked, handing the boy his handkerchief.

Frankie dabbed at his eyes and then blew his nose. "He just came over to me, that's all," he said. "I didn't know he was gonna kill anybody. I swear to God!"

"We know you didn't know, Frankie. Was he on foot or in a car?"

"A car."

"What make?"

"I don't know."

"What color?"

"Blue."

"A convertible."

"No."

"A sedan?"

"What's a sedan?"

"Hardtop."

"Yes."

"Did you see the license number?"

"No."

"What happened, Frankie?"

"He called me over to the car. My mother said I should never get in cars with strangers, but he didn't want me to get in the car. He asked me if I wanted to make five bucks."

"What did you say?"

"I said how?"

"Go ahead, Frankie," Byrnes said.

"He said I should take this letter to the police station around the corner."

"What street were you on, Frankie?"

"Seventh. Right around the corner."

"Okay. Go ahead."

"He said I should come in and ask for the desk sergeant and then give it to him and leave."

"Did he give you the five dollars then or later?"

"Right then," Frankie said. "With the letter."

"Have you still got it?" Byrnes asked.

"I spent some of it."

"We wouldn't get anything from a bill, anyway," Meyer said.

"No," Byrnes said. "Did you get a good look at this man, Frankie?"

"Pretty good."

"Can you describe him?"

"Well, he had short hair."

"Very short?"

"Pretty short."

"What color eyes?"

"Blue, I think. They were light, anyway."

"Any scars you could see?"

"No."

"Mustache?"

"No."

"What was he wearing?"

"A yellow sports shirt," Frankie said.

"That's our man," Hawes put in. "That's who I tangled with in the park."

"I want a police artist up here," Byrnes said. "Meyer, get one, will you? If this Samalson doesn't work out, we may be able to use a picture to show around." He turned sharply. The phone in his office was ringing. "Just a second, Frankie," he said, and he went into the office and answered the phone.

When he returned, he said, "That was the Hundred and Second. They checked Samalson's home address. He isn't there. His landlady says he works in Isola."

"Where?" Carella asked.

"A few blocks from here. A supermarket called Beaver Brothers, Inc. Do you know it?"

"I'm halfway there," Carella said.

On the telephone, Meyer Meyer said, "This is the Eighty-seventh Squad. Lieutenant Byrnes wants an artist up here right away. Can you—?"

Cotton Hawes knew the instant Carella brought the man into the squadroom that he was not the man who'd assaulted him in the park.

Martin Samalson was a tall, thin man wearing the white apron of a supermarket clerk, the apron somehow emphasizing his gauntness. His hair was blond and wavy and worn long. His eyes were brown.

"What do you say, Cotton?" Byrnes asked.

"Not him," Hawes said.

"Is this the man who gave you the letter, Frankie?"

"No," Frankie said.

"What letter?" Samalson asked, wiping his hands on the apron.

Byrnes picked up the binoculars, which were resting on Carella's desk. "These yours?" he asked.

Samalson looked at them in surprise. "Yeah! Hey, how about that? Where'd you find them?"

"Where'd you lose them?" Byrnes asked.

Samalson seemed suddenly aware of the situation. "Hey, now wait a minute, just wait a minute! I lost those glasses last Sunday. I don't know why you dragged me in here, but if it's got something to do with those glasses, just forget it! Boy, get off that kick fast." He shook the air with one outstretched palm, wiping the slate clean.

"When did you buy them?" Byrnes asked.

"About two weeks ago. A hockshop on Crichton. You can check it."

"We already have," Byrnes said. "We know all about the lollipop."

"Huh?"

"You went into the shop sucking a lollipop."

"Oh." Samalson looked sheepish. "I had a sore throat. It's good to keep your mouth wet when you got a sore throat. That's why I had the lollipop. There's no law against that."

"And you had these glasses until last Sunday, is that right? And last Sunday you claim you lost them."

"That's right."

"Sure you didn't loan them to anybody?"

"Positive. Last Sunday I went on a boat ride. Up the Harb. That's when I musta lost them. I don't know what them damn glasses have been doing since, and I don't care. You can't tie me up with them after last Sunday. Damn right!"

"Slow down, Samalson," Hawes said.

"Slow down, my ass! You drag me into a police station and—"

"I said slow down!" Hawes said. Samalson looked at his face. Instantly he shut up.

"What boat were you on last Sunday?" Hawes asked, the menace still in his voice and on his face.

"The S.S. *Alexander*," Samalson said pettishly.

"Where'd it go?"

"Up the River Harb. To Paisley Mountain."

"When'd you lose the glasses?"

"It must've been on the way back. I had them while we were at the picnic grounds."

"You think you lost them on the boat?"

"Maybe. I don't know."

"Did you go anywhere afterward?"

"How do you mean?"

"After the boat docked?"

"Yeah. I was with a girl. The boat docks right near here, you know. On North Twenty-fifth. I had my car parked there. So we drove down to a bar near the supermarket. I stop there every now and then on my way home from work. That's how come I was familiar with it. I didn't feel like tracking all over the city looking for a nice place."

"What's the name of the bar?"

"The Pub."

"Where is it?"

"It's on North Thirteenth, Pete," Carella said. "I know the place. It's pretty nice for this neighborhood."

304

"Yeah, it's a nice bar," Samalson agreed. "I took the girl there, and then we drove around for a while."

"Did you park?"

"Yes."

"Where?"

"Near her house. In Riverhead."

"Could you have lost the glasses then?"

"I suppose so. I think I lost them on the boat, though."

"Could you have lost them in this bar?"

"Maybe. But I think it was the boat."

"Come here, Steve," Byrnes said, and both men walked toward Byrnes's office. In a whisper, Byrnes asked, "What do you think? Should we hold him?"

"What for?"

"Hell, he may be an accomplice in this thing. That lost-glasses story stinks to high heaven."

"It doesn't read like a pair, Pete. I think our killer is a single."

"Still, the killer may know him. May head for this guy's place after the murder. Put a tail on him. O'Brien's sitting at his desk doing nothing. Use him." Byrnes walked back to Samalson. Carella walked over to where Bob O'Brien was typing a report at the other end of the squadroom. He began talking to him in a whisper. O'Brien nodded.

"You can go, Samalson," Byrnes said. "Don't try to leave the city. We may want to question you further."

"Would anyone mind telling me what the hell this is about?" Samalson said.

"Yes, we would," Byrnes said.

"Boy, some goddamn police department in this city," Samalson said, fuming. "Can I have my glasses back?"

"We're finished with them," Byrnes said.

"Thanks for nothing," Samalson said, seizing the glasses. Hawes led him to the railing and watched as he went down the steps, still fuming. O'Brien left the squadroom a moment later.

"Can I go, too?" Frankie asked.

"Not yet, son," Byrnes said. "We're going to need you in a little while."

"What for?" Frankie asked.

"We're going to draw a picture," Byrnes said. "Miscolo!" he yelled.

From the clerical office outside the railing, Miscolo's head appeared. "Yo?" he said.

"You got any milk in there?"

"Sure."

"Get this kid a glass, will you? And some cookies. You want some cookies, Frankie?"

Frankie nodded. Byrnes tousled his hair and went back into the corner office.

10

At 2:39 P.M. the police artist arrived.

He did not look at all like an artist. He did not wear a smock or a floppy bow tie, and his fingers were not stained with paint. He wore rimless eyeglasses, and he looked like a bored salesman for an exterminating service.

"You jokers send for an artist?" he asked at the railing, resting his leather case on the wood.

Hawes looked up. "Yes," he said. "Come on in."

The man pushed his way through the gate. "George Angelo," he said, extending his hand. "No relation to Michel, either family-wise or talent-wise." He grinned, exposing large white teeth. "Who do you want sketched?"

"A ghost," Hawes said. "This kid and I both saw him. We'll give you the description, you make the picture. Deal?"

"Deal," Angelo said, nodding. "I hope you both saw the same ghost."

"We did," Hawes said.

"And can both describe him the same way. I sometimes get twelve eyewitnesses who each saw the same guy twelve different ways. You'd be surprised how cockeyed the average citizen is." He shrugged. "But you're a trained observer, and kids are innocent and unprejudiced, so who knows? Maybe this'll be a good one."

"Where do you want to set up?" Hawes asked.

"Anyplace you got light," Angelo answered. "How about that desk near the window?"

"Fine," Hawes said. He turned to the boy. "Frankie, want to come over here?"

They walked to the desk. Angelo opened his case. "This going into the newspapers?"

"No."

"Television?"

"No. We haven't got time for that. We just want copies run off for the men trying to track down this guy."

"Okay," Angelo said. He reached into the case for a sketch pad and pencil. Then he took out a stack of rectangular cards. He sat at the desk, looked up at the sunlight once, and then nodded.

"Where do you want to start?"

"Pick the shape of the face from the shapes on this card," Angelo said. "Square, oval, triangular, they're all there. Look them over.

Hawes and Frankie studied the card. "Something like this, don't you think?" Hawes asked the kid.

"Yeah, something like that," Frankie agreed.

"The oval?" Angelo asked. "Okay, we'll start with that."

Quickly he sketched an egg-shaped outline on the pad. "How about noses? See anything here that looks like his nose?" He produced another card. Hawes and Frankie looked at the profusion of smellers that covered the card.

"None of them look just like his nose," Frankie said.

"Any of them come close?"

"Well, maybe this one. But not really."

"The idea in this is simplicity," Angelo said to Hawes. "We're not trying for a portrait that'll hang in the Louvre. We want a likeness that people can identify. Shade and shadow tend to confuse. I try to stick to line, blacks and whites, a feeling of the person rather than a photographic representation. So if you'll try to remember the characteristics that struck you most about this man, I'll try to get them on paper—simply. We'll refine as we go along. This is just the beginning; we'll draw and we'll draw until we get something that looks like him. Now—how about those noses? Which one is the closest to his?"

"This, I guess," the kid said. Hawes agreed.

"Okay." Angelo began sketching. He produced another card. "Eyes?"

"He had blue eyes, I remember that," Hawes said. "Sort of slanted, downward."

"Yeah," the kid said. Angelo kept nodding and drawing.

The first sketch looked like this:

"That don't look like him at all," the kid said when Angelo showed it.

"All right," Angelo said mildly. "Tell me what's wrong with it."

"It just don't look like the guy, that's all."

"Well, where is it wrong?"

"I don't know," the kid said, shrugging.

"He's too young, for one thing," Hawes said. "The guy we saw is an older man. Late thirties, maybe early forties."

"Okay. Start with the top of the picture and work your way down. What's wrong with it?"

"He's got too much hair," the kid said.

"Yes," Hawes agreed. "Or maybe too much head."

Angelo began erasing. "That better?"

"Yeah, but he was going bald a little," the kid said, "like up here. On the forehead."

Angelo erased two sharp wings into the black hair on the man's forehead. "What else?"

"His eyebrows were thicker," Hawes said.

"What else?"

"His nose was shorter," the kid said.

"Or maybe the space between his nose and his mouth was longer, either one," Hawes said. "But what you've got doesn't look right."

"Good, good," Angelo said. "Go on."

309

"His eyes looked sleepier."

"More slanted?"

"No. Heavier lids."

They watched as Angelo sketched. Putting an overlay of tracing paper onto the erased drawing, he began to move his pencil rapidly, nodding to himself as he worked, his tongue peeking from one corner of his mouth. At last he looked up.

"This any better?" he asked.

He showed them the second drawing.

"It still don't look like him," Frankie said.

"What's wrong?" Angelo asked.

"He's still too young," Hawes said.

"Also, he looks like a devil. His hair is too sharp," Frankie said.

"The hairline, you mean?"

"Yeah. It looks like he got horns. That's wrong."

"Go ahead."

"The nose is about the right length now," Hawes said, "but it's still not the right shape. He had more of a—this middle thing, whatever you call it, the thing between the nostrils."

"The tip of his nose? Longer?"

"Yes."

"How are the eyes?" Angelo asked. "Better?"

"The eyes look right," Frankie said. "Don't touch the eyes. Don't them eyes look right?"

"Yes," Hawes said. "The mouth is wrong."

"What's wrong with it?"

"It's too small. He had a wide mouth."

"And thin," the kid said. "Thin lips."

"Is the cleft chin right?" Angelo asked.

"Yeah, the chin looks okay. But that hair . . ." Angelo was beginning to fill in the hairline with his pencil. "That's better, yeah, that's better."

"A widow's peak?" Angelo asked. "Like this?"

"Not as pronounced," Hawes said. "He had very close-cropped hair, receding above the temples, but not as pronounced as that. Yes, now you're getting it, that's closer."

"The mouth longer and thinner, right?" Angelo asked, and his pencil moved furiously. Working with a new sheet of tracing paper, he began to transpose results of the collaboration. It was very hot at the desk where he worked. His sweating fist stuck to the flimsy tracing paper.

The third version of the suspect looked like this:

There was a fourth version, and a fifth version, and a tenth version, and a twelfth version, and still Angelo worked at the desk in the sunlight. Hawes and the boy kept correcting him,

311

often changing their minds after they had seen their verbal description take shape on paper. Angelo was a skilled technician who transposed their every word into simple line. Their reversals of opinion did not seem to disturb him. Patiently he listened. And patiently he corrected.

"It's getting worse," the kid said. "It don't look at all like him now. It looked better in the beginning."

"Change the nose," Hawes said. "It had a hook in it. Right in the middle. As if it had been broken."

"More spaces between the nose and the mouth."

"Shaggier eyebrows. Heavier."

"Lines under the eyes."

"Lines coming from his nose."

"Older. Make him older."

"Make his mouth a little crooked."

"No, straighter."

"Better, better."

Angelo worked. There was sweat clinging to his forehead. They tried turning on the fan once, but it blew Angelo's papers all over the floor. From time to time, cops from all over the precinct drifted over to where Angelo was working at the desk. They stopped behind him, looking over his shoulder.

"That's pretty good," one of them said, never having seen the suspect in question.

The floor was covered with sheets of rumpled tracing paper now. Still Hawes and Frankie fired their impressions of the man they had seen, and Angelo faithfully tried to capture those impressions on paper. And suddenly, after they had lost count of the number of drawings, Hawes said, "Hold it! That's it."

"That's him," the kid said. "That's the guy!"

"Don't change a line," Hawes said. "You've got him! That's the man." The kid grinned from ear to ear and then shook hands with Hawes.

Angelo sighed a heavy sigh of relief.

This was the picture they felt resembled the man they had both seen:

Angelo began packing his case.

"That's very neat," the kid said.

"That's my signature," Angelo replied. "Neat. Forget this Angelo stuff. My real name is Neat, with a capital N." He grinned. He seemed very happy it was all over.

"How soon can we get copies?" Hawes asked.

"How soon do you need them?"

Hawes looked at his watch. "It's 3:15," he said. "This guy is going to kill a woman at eight tonight."

Angelo nodded seriously, the cop in him momentarily replacing the artist. "Send a man with me," he said. "I'll run them off the minute I get back."

At 4:05 P.M., armed with pictures the ink on which was still wet, Carella and Hawes left the precinct simultaneously, Carella headed for a bar on North Thirteenth, a bar named The Pub, the bar to which Samalson had taken his girl on the preceding Sunday. Carella went there solely to show the picture to the bartender in the hope he might identify the suspect.

Hawes went directly around the corner from the precinct to Seventh Street, where Frankie Annuci had said he had met the man who'd given him the letter. It was Hawes's plan to start with Seventh and work his way east, heading uptown, going as far as Thirty-third if he had to. He would then double back, working north and south. If the man lived anywhere in the neighborhood, Hawes meant to find him. In the meantime, a copy of the picture had been sent to the I.B. in the hope of getting a make from the photos in the files in case none of the investigating cops struck paydirt.

At 4:10 P.M. Meyer and Willis left the squadroom with their copies of the picture. Starting with Sixth Street, their plan was to work westward from the precinct, going down past First and into the named streets below First until they hit Lady Astor's street.

At 4:15 P.M. a squad car was called back to the precinct. Copies of the picture were dumped into the car, and then distributed to every motorized and foot patrolman in the precinct. Copies were delivered to the neighboring 88th and 89th precincts, too. The immediate area adjacent to the precinct, starting with Grover Avenue and going into Grover Park, was flooded with detectives from the 88th and the 89th (which precincts handled the actual park territory), in the event the suspect might return in search of his binoculars. It was a big city, and a big, teeming precinct—but the precinct was fortunately smaller than the city.

Hawes, stopping at every store, stopping at every tenement, talking to shop owners and superintendents, talking to the kids in the streets, who were sometimes the shrewdest observers around, did not connect until he reached Twelfth Street.

It was late afternoon by this time, but the streets had not cooled down at all. Hawes was still hot, and he was beginning to feel the first disgruntled disappointment of defeat. How the hell would they ever stop this guy? How the hell would they ever find him? Dispiritedly he began working his way up the street, showing the picture. No, they did not know the man. No, they did not recognize him. Was he from the neighborhood?

At the fifth tenement from the corner, he showed the picture to a landlady in a flowered cotton housedress.

"No," she said instantly. "I never—" And then, she stopped. She took the picture from Hawes's hands. "Yeah, that's him," she said. "That's the way he looked this morning. I saw him when he was coming down. That's the way he looked."

"Who?" Hawes said. He could feel the sudden surge of energy within him as he waited for her answer.

"Smith," she said. "John Smith. A weird duck. He had this—"

"What apartment?' Hawes said.

"Twenty-two. That's on the second floor. He moved in about two weeks ago. Had this—"

But Hawes was already moving into the building, his gun drawn. He did not know that his conversation with the landlady had been viewed from a second-floor window. He did not know that his red hair had instantly identified him to his observer. He did not know until he was almost on the second-floor landing, and then he knew instantly.

The explosion thundered in the small, narrow corridor. Hawes fell to the floor at once, almost losing his footing on the top step, almost hurtling backward down the stairwell. He fired a shot into the dimness, not seeing anything, but wanting John Smith to know he was armed.

"Get out of here, cop!" the voice shouted.

"Throw your gun down here," Hawes said. "There are four cops with me downstairs. You haven't got a chance."

"You're a liar," the man shouted. "I saw you when you got here. You came alone. I saw you from the window."

Another shot exploded into the hallway. Hawes ducked below the top step. The bullet ripped plaster from the already chipped plaster on the wall. He squinted his eyes, trying to see into the dimness, cursing his position. Wherever Smith was, he could see Hawes without in turn being seen. Hawes could not move from his uncomfortable position on the steps. But perhaps Smith couldn't move, either. Perhaps if he left wherever he was, he would be seen. Hawes waited.

The hall went utterly still.

"Smith?" he called.

A fusillade of shots answered him, angry shots that whined across the hallway and ripped at the plaster. Chalk cascaded onto Hawes's head. He clung to the steps, cursing tenement hallways and would-be killers. From the street below, he could hear excited yells and screams, and then the repeated, shouted word "Police! Police! Police! Police!"

"Do you hear that, Smith?" he shouted. "They're calling the cops. The whole damn precinct'll be here in three minutes. Throw your gun down."

315

Smith fired again. The shot was lower. It ripped a splinter of wood from the landing near the top step. Hawes reared back and then instantly ducked. He heard a clicking at the other end of the hallway. Smith was reloading. He was about to sprint down the corridor when he heard a clip being slammed into the butt of an automatic. Quickly he ducked down behind the top step again.

The hallway was silent again.

"Smith?"

There was no answer.

"Smith?"

From the street below, Hawes heard the high whine of a police siren.

"You hear that, Smith? They're here. They'll be—"

Three shots exploded into the hallway. Hawes ducked and then heard a man scuffling to his feet, caught a glimpse of a trouser leg as Smith started up the stairway. Hawes bounded into the hallway, triggering a shot at the retreating figure. Smith turned and fired, and Hawes dropped to the floor again. The footsteps were clattering up the steps now, noisily, excitedly, hurriedly. Hawes got to his feet, ran for the steps, charged up them two at a time. Another shot spun into the hallway. He did not duck this time. He kept charging up the steps, wanting to reach Smith before he got to the roof. He heard the roof door being tried, heard Smith pounding on it, and then heard a shot and the spanging reverberation of metal exploding. The roof door creaked open and then slammed shut. Smith was already on the roof.

Hawes rushed up the remaining steps. A skylight threw bright sunshine on the landing inside the roof door. He opened the door, and then closed it again rapidly when a bullet ripped into the jamb, splashing wood splinters onto his face.

Goddamn you! he thought. *You goddamn son of a bitch, goddamn you!*

He threw open the door, fired a blind fusillade of shots across the roof, and then followed his own cover out onto the melting tar. He saw a figure dart behind one of the chimney pots and then rush for the parapet at the roof's edge. He fired. His shot was high. He was not shooting to warn or to wound now. He was shooting to kill. Smith rose for an instant, poised on the

316

edge of the roof. Hawes fired, and Smith leaped the air-shaft between the buildings, landing behind the parapet on the adjoining roof. Hawes started after him, his shoes sticking in the tar. He reached the edge of the roof. He hesitated just an instant, and then leaped the airshaft, landing on his hands and knees in the sticky tar.

Smith had already crossed the roof. He looked back, fired at Hawes, and then rushed for the ledge. Hawes levelled his revolver. Smith climbed onto the ledge, silhouetted against the painful blue of the sky, and Hawes steadied the revolver on his left arm, taking careful aim. He knew that if Smith got onto that next roof, if Smith maintained the lead he now had, he would get away. And so he took careful aim, knowing that this shot had to count, watching Smith as he raised his arms in preparation for his jump across the airshaft. He aimed for the section of trunk that presented the widest target. He did not want to miss.

Smith stood undecided on the ledge for a moment. His body filled the fixed sight on Hawes's gun.

Hawes squeezed the trigger.

There was a mild click, a click that sounded shockingly loud, a click that thundered in Hawes's surprised ears like a cannon explosion.

Smith leaped the airshaft.

Hawes got to his feet, cursing his empty pistol, reloading as he ran across the roof to the airshaft. He looked across it to the next roof. Smith was nowhere in sight. Smith was gone.

Swearing all the way, he headed back for Smith's apartment. There had been no time to reload until it was too late, and once it's too late, there's nothing to be done about it. Walking with his head down, he crossed the sticky tar.

Two shots rang out into the stillness of the summer roof-tops, and Hawes hit the tar again. He looked up. A uniformed cop was standing on the edge of the opposite roof ahead, taking careful aim.

"Hold your fire, you dumb bastard!" Hawes yelled. "I'm on your side."

"Throw your gun away," the cop yelled back.

Hawes complied. The cop leaped the airshaft and approached

Hawes cautiously. When he saw his face, he said, "Oh, it's you, sir."

"Yes, it's me, sir," Hawes said disgustedly.

The landlady was having none of Cotton Hawes. The landlady was screaming and ranting for him to get out of her building. She had never had trouble with the cops, and now they came around shooting, what was going to happen to her tenants, they'd all move out, all because of him, all because of that big red-headed stupid jerk! Hawes told one of the uniformed cops to keep her downstairs, and then he went into Smith's apartment.

The bed had been slept in the night before. The sheets were still rumpled. Hawes went to the single closet in the bedroom and opened it. There was nothing in the closet except the wire hangers on the rod. Hawes shrugged and went into the bathroom. The sink had been used sometime during that day. Soap was still in the basin, clotted around the drain. He opened the medicine cabinet. A bottle of iodine was on the top shelf. Two bars of soap were on the middle shelf. A pair of scissors, a straight razor, a box of Band-Aids, a tube of shaving cream, a toothbrush and toothpaste, were all crowded onto the lowest shelf. Hawes closed the door, and left the bathroom.

In the bedroom again, he checked through Smith's dresser. *Smith*, he thought, *John Smith*. The phoniest name anybody in the world could pick. The dresser was empty of clothing. In the top drawer, six magazines for an automatic pistol rested in one corner. Hawes lifted one of them with his handkerchief. Unless he was mistaken, the magazine would fit a Luger. He collected the magazines and put them into his pockets.

He went into the kitchen, the sole remaining room in the apartment. A coffee cup was on the kitchen table. A coffee pot was on the stove. Bread crumbs were scatterd near the toaster. John Smith had apparently eaten here this morning. Hawes went to the icebox and opened the door.

A loaf of bread and a partially used rectangle of butter were on one of the shelves. That was all.

He opened the ice compartment. A bottle of milk rested alongside a melting cake of ice.

The lab boys would have a lot of work to do in Smith's apartment. But Hawes could do nothing more there at the moment except speculate on the absence of clothing and food, an absence that seemed to indicate that John Smith—whatever his real name—did not actually live in the apartment. Had he rented the place only to carry out his murder? Had he planned to return here after he'd done his killing? Was he using this as a base of operations? Because it was close to the precinct? Or because it was close to his intended victim? Which?

Hawes closed the door to the ice compartment.

It was then that he heard the sound behind him.

Someone was in the apartment with him.

11

His gun was in his hand before he whirled.

"Hey!" the woman said. "What's that for?"

Hawes lowered the gun. "Who are you, miss?"

"I live across the hall. The cop downstairs said I should come up here and talk to the detective. Are you the detective?"

"Yes."

"Well, I live across the hall."

The girl was unattractive, a brunette with large brown eyes and a very pale skin. She spoke from the side of her mouth, a mannerism that gave her the appearance of a Hollywood gun moll. She was wearing only a thin pink slip, and the one disconcertingly attractive thing about her was the bosom that threatened the silk.

"Did you know this John Smith character?" Hawes asked.

"The few times he was here, I seen him," the girl said. "He only moved in a couple of weeks ago. You know, you noticed him right away."

"How often has he been here since he moved in?"

"Only a couple of times. I came in one night he was here—to introduce myself, you know? Neighborly. What the hell?" The girl shrugged. Her breasts shrugged with her. She was not wearing a brassiere, and Hawes found this disconcerting, too. "He was sitting right there at the kitchen table, cutting up newspapers. I asked him what he was doing. He said he kept a scrapbook."

"When was this?"

"About a week ago."

"He was cutting up newspapers?"

"Yeah," the girl said. "Goofy. Well, he looked goofy, anyway. You know what I mean."

Hawes bent to examine the kitchen table. Studying it closely, he could see traces of paste on the soiled oilcloth covering. Then Smith had composed the letter here, and it had been only a week ago, and not on the Sunday of June 23rd. He had simply used an old newspaper.

320

"Was there paste on the table?" Hawes asked her.

"Yeah, I think so. A tube of paste. Well, for his scrapbook, I guess."

"Sure," Hawes said. "Ever talk to him again after that night?"

"Just in the hall."

"How many times?"

"Well, he was here one night after that. Last week, I mean. And then he was here last night."

"Did he sleep here last night?"

"I guess so. How should I know?" The girl seemed suddenly aware that she was wearing only a slip. She crossed one arm over her abundant bosom.

"What time did he get here last night?"

"Pretty late. After midnight, it must've been. I was listening to the radio. It was very hot last night, you know. It's almost impossible to get any sleep in these apartments. They're just like ovens. The door was open, and I heard him down the hall, so I went out to say hello. He was putting the key in the lock, looking just like a Russian spy, I swear to God. All he needed was a bomb, and that would be the picture."

"Did he have anything with him?"

"Just a bag. Groceries, I guess. Oh yeah. Glasses. You know. Opera glasses. I asked him was he just getting back from the opera."

"What did he say?"

"He laughed. He was a hot sketch. Smith. John Smith. That was funny, don't you think?"

"What was funny about it?" Hawes asked.

"Well, the cough drops and all, you know. He was a hot sketch. I guess he won't be coming back after today, huh?"

"I guess not," Hawes said, trying to keep up with the somewhat vague conversation.

"Is he a crook or something?"

"We don't know. Did he ever tell you anything about himself?"

"No. Nothing. He didn't talk so much. Anyway, he was only here those few times. And even then, he always seemed in a hurry. I asked him once if this was his summer place. You know, like a joke. He said yeah this was his retreat. A hot sketch. Smith." She laughed at the name.

"But he never told you where he worked. Or even *if* he worked?"

"No." The girl crossed her other arm over her bosom. "I better go put something on, huh?" she said. "I was taking a little nap when all the shooting started. I got so excited when it was over, I run downstairs in my slip. I'm a real sight, ain't I?" She giggled. "I better go put something on. It was nice talking to you. You don't seem like a bull at all."

"Thank you," Hawes said, and then wondered if he was being complimented.

The girl hesitated at the door. "Well, I hope you get him, anyway. He shouldn't be too hard to find. How many like him can there be in the city?"

"How many Smiths, do you mean?" Hawes asked, and the girl thought this was hysterical.

"You're a hot sketch, too," she answered. He watched her as she went down the hall. He shrugged, closed the apartment door behind him, and went downstairs to the street. The landlady was still screaming.

Hawes told one of the patrolmen to keep everybody out of Apartment Twenty-two until the lab boys had gone over it.

Then he went back to the precinct.

It was 5:00 P.M.

Carella was sitting at one of the desks drinking coffee from a container when Hawes walked in. Willis and Meyer had not yet returned. The squadron was silent.

"Hello, Cotton," Carella said.

"Steve," Hawes answered.

"Understand you got into a little fracas on Twelfth?"

"Umm."

"You all right?"

"I'm fine. Except I keep losing people."

"Have some coffee. The desk was really jumping downstairs. Must have got fifty calls about the shooting. He got away again, huh?"

"Umm," Hawes said.

"Well." Carella shrugged. "Cream? Sugar?"

"Little of each."

Carella fixed the coffee and handed the cup to Hawes. "Relax. We can use a rest."

"I want to make a call first."

"Where?"

"Pistol permits." He emptied his pockets onto the desk. "I picked these up in his apartment. Do they look like Luger magazines to you?"

"They damn well couldn't be anything else," Carella said.

"I want to check on permits for Lugers in the precinct. Who knows? We may get a break."

"That's the easy way," Carella said. "Nothing ever comes the easy way, Cotton."

"It's worth a try," he said. He looked up at the wall clock. "Jesus," he said. "Five already. Three hours to go."

He pulled the phone to him and made his call. When he'd finished, he picked up the coffee container.

"They'll call me back," he said to Carella. He put his feet up on the desk. "Ahhhhhhhhh."

"Think this damn heat'll ever break?"

"God, I hope so."

In the silence of the squadron, the two men sipped at their coffee. There was, for the moment, no need for communication. They sat with the afternoon sunlight filtering through the grilled windows, marking the floor with long golden rectangles. They sat with the hum of the electric fans rotating limpid air. They sat with the hushed, faraway street noise below them. They sat, and for the moment they were not policemen working on a difficult case on the hottest day of the year. They were simply two friends having a cup of coffee together.

"I've got a date tonight," Hawes said.

"Nice?" Carella asked.

"A widow," Hawes said. "Very pretty. I met her this afternoon. Or was it this morning? Well, before lunch, anyway. A blonde. Very pretty."

"Teddy's a brunette," Carella said. "Black hair. Very black."

"When do I get to meet her?" Hawes asked.

"I don't know. Name it. I'm supposed to take her to a movie tonight. She's a remarkable lip-reader. She enjoys the movies as much as anyone who can hear."

It no longer surprised Hawes to hear Carella talk about the

handicap of his wife, Teddy. She had been born a deaf-mute, but this didn't seem to hinder her in the pursuit of happiness. From what other detectives on the squad had told him, Hawes had pieced together the picture of a lively, interesting, vivacious, and damned beautiful girl, and his mental picture couldn't have been more correct. Too, because he liked Carella, he was predisposed toward liking Teddy, and he really did want to meet her.

"You say you're going to a movie tonight?" Hawes asked.

'Mmm," Carella said.

Hawes balanced the pleasure of meeting Teddy against the pleasure of entertaining Christine Maxwell alone. Christine Maxwell won out, proving the age-old adage, Hawes mused, that gentlemen prefer blondes.

"This is a first date," he said to Carella. "After I get to know her, we'll make it a double, okay?"

"Anytime you say," Carella said.

Again the squadron fell silent. From the clerical office down the hall, they could hear the steady rat-tat-tat of Miscolo's typewriter. They sat drinking their coffee silently. There was something peaceful about these few minutes of relaxation, these few minutes of suspended time, this breathing spell in the race with the clock.

The moments ended.

"What's this? A country club?" Willis called from the railing.

"Look at them, willya?" Meyer said. "We're shagging ass all over town, and they're taking their tea and crumpets."

"Blow it out," Carella said.

"How do you like this?" Willis went on, refusing to let it go. "I hear you got shot, Cotton," he said. "The desk sergeant tells me you're a hero."

"No such luck," Hawes replied, regretting the sudden rupture of silence. "He missed."

"Too bad, so sad," Willis said. He was a small detective with the fine-boned body of a jockey. But Fats Donner had told the truth about him; Willis was not a man to fool with. He knew judo the way he knew the Penal Code, and he could practically break your arm just by looking at you.

Meyer pulled a chair up to the desk. "Hal, go get us some coffee, will you? Miscolo's probably got a pot going."

Willis sighed. "Man, I—"

"Come on, come on," Meyer said. "Respect your elders."

Willis sighed again, and departed for the clerical office.

"How'd you make out at the bar, Steve?" Meyer asked.

"Huh?"

"The Pub. Wasn't that the name of it? Anybody make the picture?"

"No. It's a nice bar, though. Right on Thirteenth. Stop in if you're in the neighborhood."

"Did he set up a few for you?" Meyer asked.

"Naturally," Carella said.

"You drunken bastard."

"All I had was two beers."

"That's more than I've had since breakfast," Meyer said. "Where the hell is Willis with that coffee?"

The telephone rang. Hawes picked it up.

"Eighty-seventh Squad, Hawes." He listened. "Oh, hello, Bob. Just a second." He handed the phone to Carella. "It's O'Brien. For you, Steve."

"Hello, Bob," Carella said into the phone.

"Steve, I'm still with this Samalson guy. He just left the supermarket. He's in a bar across the street, tilting one before he heads home, I guess. You still want me to stick with him?"

"Hold on, Bob."

Carella pressed the hold button on the phone and buzzed the lieutenant's office.

"Yes?" Byrnes said.

"I've got O'Brien on the wire," Carella said. "Do you still want that tail on Samalson?"

"Is it eight o'clock yet?" Byrnes asked.

"No."

"Then I still want the tail. Tell Bob to stick with him until he goes to sleep. In fact, I want him watched all night. If he's in this thing, the goddamn shooter may come to him."

"Okay," Carella said. "You going to relieve him later, Pete?"

"Oh, hell, tell him to call me as soon as Samalson gets to the apartment. I'll have a cop from the Hundred and Second relieve him."

"Right," Carella clicked off, pressed the extension button,

and said, "Bob, stick with him until he's in his apartment. Then call Pete, and he'll get somebody from the Hundred and Second to spell you. He wants this to be an all-night plant."

"Suppose he doesn't head home?" O'Brien asked.

"What can I tell you, Bob?"

"Shit! I'm supposed to go to a ball game tonight."

"I'm supposed to go to a movie. Look, this thing'll be over by eight."

"It'll be over for the shooter, sure. But Pete figures he may be tied in with Samalson, doesn't he?"

"He doesn't really believe that, Bob. But he's trying to cover every angle. Samalson's story was a little thin."

"You think the killer's going to seek a guy who's already been interrogated by the cops? That's faulty reasoning, Steve."

"It's a hot day, Bob. Maybe all of Pete's cylinders aren't clicking."

"Sure but where does—Oh-oh, the bastard's on his way. I'll call in a little later. Listen, do me a favour, will you?"

"What's that?"

"Crack this by eight. I want to see that ball game."

"We'll try."

"He's moving. So long, Steve." O'Brien hung up.

"O'Brien," Carella said. "He's beefing about the tail on Samalson. Thinks it's ridiculous. I think so, too. Samalson didn't have the smell on him."

"What smell?" Meyer asked.

"You know the smell. Every thief in the city gives it off. Samalson didn't have it. If he's tied in with this, I'll eat his goddamn field glasses."

The phone rang again.

"That's probably Samalson," Hawes said, "complaining about O'Brien tailing him."

Smiling, Carella picked up the receiver. "Eighty-seventh Squad, Detective Carella," he said. "Oh, sure." He covered the mouthpiece. "Permits. You want me to take it down?"

"Go ahead."

"Shoot," Carella said to the mouthpiece. He listened for a moment, then turned to Hawes. "Forty-seven registered Lugers in the Precinct. You want them all?"

"I just thought of something," Hawes said.

"What?"

"They take your fingerprints for the back of a pistol-licence application. If—"

"Never mind," Carella said into the phone. "Forget it. Thanks a lot." He hung up. "If our boy," he concluded for Hawes, "had a permit, the fingerprints would be on file at the I.B. *Ergo*, our boy ain't got a permit."

Hawes nodded. "You ever have a day like that, Steve?"

"Like what?"

"Where you're just plain stupid," Hawes said despondently.

"I knew you were calling Permits, didn't I?" Carella asked. "Did I try to stop you?"

Hawes sighed and stared through the window. Willis came back with the coffee.

"Here you are, sir," he said to Meyer. "I hope everything is satisfactory, sir."

"I'll leave a big tip," Meyer said, and he picked up the coffee cup and then cleared his throat.

"I've got a tip for you," Willis said.

"What's that?"

"Never become a cop. The hours are long and the pay is low, and you have to do all sorts of menial chores for your colleagues."

"I'm getting a cold," Meyer said. He reached into his back pocket and pulled out a box of cough drops. "I always get summer colds. They're the worst kind, and I always get them." He put a cough drop on his tongue. "Anybody want one of these?"

Nobody answered. Meyer returned the box to his back pocket. He picked up his coffee and began sipping at it.

"Quiet," Willis said.

"Yeah."

"You think it really is a *specific* lady?" Hawes asked.

"I don't know," Carella said. "But I think so, yes."

"He used the name John Smith," Hawes said. "When he moved into this apartment. No clothes there. No food."

"John Smith. *cherchez la femme*," Meyer said. "*Cherchez* Pocohontas."

"We've been *cherchez*-ing *la femme* all day," Hawes said. "I'm getting weary."

"Stick it out, kid," Carella said. He looked up at the wall clock. "It's 5:15. It'll all be over soon."

And then it started.

12

It started with the fat woman in the housedress, and her arrival at the slatted rail divider seemed to trip off a train of events none of which had any immediate bearing on the case. It was terribly unfortunate that the events intruded upon the smooth progress of the investigation. None of the 87th's cops would have had it that way if there had been a choice. They were, after all, rather intent upon preventing a murder that night. But the men of the 87th were working stiffs doing a job, and the things that happened within the next fifty minutes were not things that fit into place like the pieces of a jig-saw puzzle. They followed no pat line of development. They brought the cops not an iota closer to finding The Lady or the man who had threatened to kill. The train of events started at 5:15 in the late afternoon of Wednesday, July 24th. They did not end until 6:05 P.M. in the evening of that same day.

All they did was consume the most valuable commodity the detectives had: time.

The woman in the housedress puffed up to the slatted rail divider. She was holding the hand of a ten-year-old blond kid in dungarees and a red-striped tee shirt. The kid was Frankie Annuci. The woman was controlling a rage that threatened to burst her seams. Her face was livid, her eyes were sparkling black coals, her lips were compressed tightly into a narrow line that held back the flow of her anger. She charged up to the railing as if she would batter it down by sheer momentum, and then stopped abruptly. The steam building inside her pushed past the thin retaining line of her lips. Her mouth opened. The words came out in a roar.

"WHERE'S THE LIEUTENANT HERE?"

Meyer almost spilled his coffee and swallowed his cough drop. He whirled around in his chair. Willis, Carella, and Hawes stared at the woman as if she were the ghost of Criminals Past.

"THE LIEUTENANT!" she shouted. "THE LIEUTENANT! Where is he?"

Carella rose and walked to the railing. He spotted the boy and said, "Hello, Frankie. What can I do for you, ma'am? Is there—"

"Don't say hello to him!" the woman shouted. "Don't even look at him! Who are you?"

"Detective Carella."

"Well, Detective Carella, I want to talk—" She stopped. "*Tu sie'taliano?*"

"*Si*," Carella said.

"*Bene. Dove il tenente? Voglio parlare con—*"

"I don't understand Italian too well," Carella said.

"You don't? Why not? Where's the lieutenant?"

"Well, can I help you?"

"Did you have Frankie in here this afternoon?"

"Yes."

"Why?"

"To ask him some questions."

"I'm his mother. I'm Mrs. Annuci. Mrs. Rudolph Annuci. I'm a good woman, and my husband is a good man. Why did you have my son in here?"

"He delivered a letter for somebody this morning, Mrs. Annuci. We're looking for the man who gave him the letter, that's all. We just asked him some questions."

"YOU HAD NO RIGHT TO DO THAT!" Mrs. Annuci shouted. "HE IS NOT A CRIMINAL!"

"Nobody said he was," Carella answered.

"THEN, WHAT WAS HE DOING IN A POLICE STATION!"

"I just told you . . ."

A phone began ringing somewhere in the squadroom. It synchronized with what Mrs. Annuci screamed next so that all Carella heard was:

"WELL I WAS NEVERRRRRRING SO EMBRRRRR-RING IN MY LIFE!"

"Now, now, *signora*," Carella said.

Meyer picked up the phone. "Eighty-seventh Squad, Detective Meyer."

"Don't *signora* me, I'm not your old grandmother! Humiliated! Humiliated! *Vergogna, vergogna!* He was picked up by one of the Snow Whites. Right in the street! Standing with a

330

bunch of boys, and the Snow White pulls to the curb and two cops get out and grab him. Like—"

"What?" Meyer said.

Mrs. Annuci turned to him. "I said two cops—" and then she saw he was talking to the phone.

"Okay, we'll move!" Meyer said. He hung up rapidly. "Willis, come on! Holdup in progress on Tenth and Culver. The guy's shooting it out with the beat cop and two squad cars!"

"Holy Jesus!" Willis said.

They ran through the gate in the railing, nearly knocking Mrs. Annuci down.

"Criminals!" she said as they rushed down the stairs. "You deal with criminals. You take my son into the police station, and you mix him with thieves. He's a good boy, a boy who—" She stopped suddenly. "Did you beat him? Did you use a hose on him?"

"No, no, of course not, Mrs. Annuci," Carella said, and then he was distracted by a sound on the metal steps outside. A man in handcuffs appeared at the top of the steps, and then another man stumbled in behind him, his face oozing blood. Mrs. Annuci turned, following Carella's gaze, just as the patrolman came into view behind the pair. The patrolman shoved at the man with the handcuffs. Mrs. Annuci gasped.

"Oh, my God!" she said. "Jesus, Mary, and Joseph!"

Hawes was already on his feet, walking toward the railing.

"Mrs. Annuci," Carella was saying, "why don't we sit down here on the bench where we can—"

"What've you got?" Hawes asked the patrolman.

"His head! Look at his head!" Mrs. Annuci said, her face going white. "Don't look, Frankie," she added, contradicting herself.

The man's head was indeed a sorry-looking mess. The hair was matted with blood, which trickled onto his face and neck, staining his white tee shirt. There was an open cut on his forehead, too, and the cut streamed blood onto the bridge of his nose.

"This son of a bitch used a baseball bat on him, sir," the patrolman said. "The guy bleeding is a pusher. Desk lieutenant thought there might be a dope angle to this, figured you should question him."

"I ain't no pusher," the bleeding man said. "I want him sent to prison! He hit me with a bat!"

"You'd better get him to a hospital," Hawes said, looking at the bleeding man.

"No hospital! Not until he's in prison! He hit me with a ball bat! This son of a bitch—"

"Ohhhh," Mrs. Annuci said.

"Come on outside," Carella said. "We'll sit on that bench, all right? I'll explain everything that happened with your son."

Hawes pulled the man with the handcuffs into the room. "Get in there!" he said. "Take off the cuffs, Alec," he said to the patrolman. "You better get to the hospital, mister," he said to the bleeding man.

"No hospital!" the man insisted. "Not until he's booked and sent to jail."

The patrolman took the cuffs off the other man.

"Get some wet rags for this guy's head," Hawes said, and the patrolman left. "What's your name, mister?"

"Mendez," the bleeder said. "Raoul Mendez."

"And you're no pusher, huh, Raoul?"

"I never pushed junk in my life. That's a crock, believe me. This guy just came over—"

Hawes turned to the other man. "What's your name?"

"—you!" the man said.

Hawes looked at him steadily.

"Empty your pockets on that desk."

The man did not move.

"I said—"

The man suddenly lunged at Hawes, his fists swinging wildly. Hawes clamped one hand into the man's shirt collar and rammed the other clenched fist into his face. The man staggered back several paces, bunched his fists again, and came at Hawes once more. Hawes chopped a quick right to his gut, and the man doubled over.

"Empty your pockets, punk," Hawes said tightly.

The man emptied his pockets.

"Now. What's your name?" Hawes asked, as he went through the accumulation that had been in the man's trousers.

"John Begley. You hit me again, you son of a bitch, and I'll—"

"Shut your mouth!" Hawes snapped.

Begley shut up instantly.

"Why'd you go at him with a ball bat?"

"That's my business," Begley said.

"It's mine, too," Hawes answered.

"He tried to kill me," Mendez said. "Assault! First-degree assault! That's Section 240. Assault with intent to kill!"

"I didn't try to kill him," Begley said. "If I wanted to kill him, he wouldn't be walking around right now!"

"You're familiar with the Penal Law, huh, Mendez?" Hawes asked.

"I hear guys talking about it in the neighborhood," Mendez said. "Hell, everybody knows Section 240. Assault is common."

"240's first-degree assault, Begley," Hawes said. "You can get ten years for that. 242 is assault in the second degree. No more than five years and a fine, maybe just the fine. Which are you trying for?"

"I didn't try to kill him."

"Is he a pusher?"

"Ask him."

"I'm asking you."

"I'm no stoolie. I don't know what the hell he is. I didn't try to kill him. I just wanted to bust a couple of arms and legs. Legs, especially."

"Why?"

"He's been chasing my wife."

"What do you mean?"

"What the hell do you think I mean?"

"How about that, Mendez?"

"He's crazy. I don't even know his wife."

"You lying son of a bitch!" Begley said, and he started for Mendez.

Hawes shoved him away. "Cool off, Begley, or I'll knock you on your ass!"

"He knows my wife!" Begley shouted. "He knows her too goddamn good! I'll get that bastard! If I go to jail, I'll get him when I get out!"

"He's crazy, I told you!" Mendez said. "Crazy! I was standing on the corner minding my own business, and he came up with the ball bat and started swinging."

"All right, all right, keep quiet," Hawes said.

The patrolman came back with the wet cloths.

"We won't need those, Alec," Hawes said. "Get this man to a hospital before he bleeds to death right here in the squadroom."

"Not until *he* goes to prison!" Mendez shouted. "I ain't leav—"

"You want to go to prison yourself, Mendez?" Hawes said. "For resisting an officer?"

"Who's—?"

"Get the hell out of here! Your pusher smell is stinking up the squadroom!"

"I'm no pusher!"

"He's a pusher, sir," the patrolman said. "He's been put away twice, already."

"Get the hell out, Mendez," Hawes said.

"A pusher? You got me wrong—"

"And if I ever catch you with any junk on you, I'll take a ball bat to you myself! Now clear out! Get him to the hospital, Alec."

"Come on," the patrolman said, taking Mendez's arm.

"A pusher," Mendez mumbled, as they went through the railing. "Man, a guy takes one fall, right way he's labelled."

"*Two* falls," the patrolman corrected.

"Okay, two, two," Mendez said, as they went down the steps.

Mrs. Annuci swallowed.

"So you see," Carella said to her, "all we did was ask some questions. Your son is something of a hero, Mrs. Annuci. You can tell that to your neighbors."

"And have this killer come after him next? No, thank you, no, thank you."

In the squadroom, Hawes said, "Were you trying to kill him, Begley?"

"I told you. No. Look—"

"What?"

Begley's voice trailed to a whisper. "This is only second-degree assault. The guy was making it with my wife. I mean, what the hell, suppose it was your wife?"

"I'm not married."

"Okay, but suppose. You going to send me to jail for protecting my home?"

"That's up to the judge," Hawes said.

Begley's voice went even lower. "Let's judge it ourselves, huh?"

"What?"

"What'll it cost? Three bills? Half a century?"

"You've got the wrong cop," Hawes said.

"Come on, come on," Begley said, smiling.

Hawes picked up the phone and buzzed the desk. Artie Knowles, the sergeant who'd relieved Murchison at 4:00 P.M., answered.

"Artie, this is Cotton Hawes. You can book this bum. Make it second-degree assault. Send somebody up for him, will you?"

"Right!" Knowles said.

"You kidding?" Begley asked.

"I'm serious," Hawes said.

"You're turning down five hundred bucks?"

"Are you offering it? We can add that to the charge."

"Never mind, never mind," Begley said hastily. "I ain't offering nothing. Boy!"

He was still "Boy"-ing when the patrolman led him downstairs, passing Bert Kling in the hallway. Kling was a tall and youthful blond detective. He was wearing a leather jacket and dungarees. His denim shirt under the jacket was stained with sweat.

"Hi," he said to Hawes. "What's up?"

"Assault," Hawes said. "You finished for the day?"

"Yeah," Kling said. "This waterfront plant is for the birds. I'll never learn anything. There isn't a guy on the docks who doesn't know I'm a cop."

"Have they really tipped to you?"

"I guess not, but nobody's talking about heroin, that's for sure. Why the hell doesn't Pete leave this to the Narcotics Squad?"

"He's trying to get a jump on the precinct pushers. Wants to know where the stuff's coming in. You know how Pete feels about dope."

"Whose hand is Steve holding outside?"

"Hysterical mother," Hawes said, and then he heard Meyer's voice coming up the stairway. Kling took off his jacket.

"Brother, I'm hot," he said. "You ever try unloading a ship?"

"Nope," Hawes said.

"Get in there, you rotten hood," Meyer said, "and don't give me any back talk." He glanced at the woman on the bench only cursorily, and then shoved at his prisoner. The man he shoved was wearing handcuffs. The cuffs were tight on his wrists.

A pair of police handcuffs resembles the five-and-dime stuff purchased for kids, except the police stuff is for real. They are made out of steel, forged into a slender, narrow, impervious, portable jail. The movable arm is bolted into the body of the cuff. The movable arm has a saw-tooth edge that, when engaged with the body, catches and holds there. Like blood travelling through a vein, the saw-tooth edge cannot reverse its course; it can only move forward. It can, in fact, move completely through the body of the cuff itself, completing a full circle, so that a key is not necessary to open the wristlet before it is clamped onto the wrist. The arresting officer simply squeezes the movable arm into and through the body of the cuff until the arm emerges on the other side. He then clamps it onto the wrist and wedges it shut again. The wrist prevents the movable arm from making the full circle again. To take the cuff off the wrist, a key is necessary.

A trio of metal links attaches one wristcuff to the other. The cuffs are not at all comfortable. If they are placed on the wrists with care, it is possible to keep them from biting into the flesh. But the average arresting officer squeezes the cuff to snap the movable arm into its open position, and then hastily clamps the cuff onto the wrist and squeezes again until the metal collides with flesh and bone. When a pair of handcuffs is taken off a prisoner, the prisoner's wrists are usually raw and lacerated—and sometimes bleeding.

Not very much delicacy had been used on the man Meyer led into the squadroom. He had just been shooting it out with a gang of policemen, and when they had finally collared him, they'd clamped the cuffs onto his wrists with barely controlled ferocity. The metal was biting into his flesh and paining him. Meyer shoved him into the room, and the metal cuffs bit further as he moved his arms trying to maintain his balance.

"Here's a big man," Meyer said to Hawes. "Tried to hold off half the precinct, didn't you, big man?"

The prisoner did not answer.

336

"The jewelry store on Tenth and Culver," Meyer said. "He was inside with a gun when the beat patrolman spotted him. Brave man. A daytime holdup. You're a brave man, aren't you?"

The prisoner did not answer.

"He started shooting the minute he saw the patrolman. A cruising squad car heard the shots and joined the battle, and then radioed for another car. The second car called back here for help. A regular hero's siege, huh, big man?" Meyer asked.

The prisoner did not answer.

"Sit down, big man," Meyer said.

The prisoner sat.

"What's your name?"

"Louis Gallagher."

"You been in trouble before, Gallagher?"

"No."

"We'll check it, so don't start with a snow job."

"I've never been in trouble before," Gallagher said.

"Miscolo got any coffee?" Kling asked, and he started down the corridor. Carella was just returning from the steps. "Get rid of her, Steve?"

"Yeah," Carella said. "How were the docks?"

"Hot."

"You plan on going home?"

"Yeah. Soon as I have some coffee."

"You'd better stick around. We've got a nut loose."

"What do you mean?"

"A letter. Going to kill a dame at eight tonight. Stick around. Pete may need you."

"I'm bushed, Steve."

"No kidding?" Carella said, and he walked into the squad-room.

"You've got a record, haven't you, Gallagher?" Meyer asked.

"No. I told you once already."

"Gallagher, we've got a lot of unsolved holdups in this neighborhood."

"That's your problem. You're the cops."

"You do them?"

"I held up the store today because I need dough. That's all.

This is the first time I ever did anything like this. How about taking the cuffs off and letting me go?"

"Oh, brother, you slay me," Wilis said. He turned to Hawes. "He tries to shoot us, and then he cops a plea."

"Who's copping a plea?" Gallagher said. "I'm asking you to forget the whole thing."

Willis stared at the man as if he were a dangerous lunatic ready to begin slashing passers-by with a razor. "It must be the heat," he said unblinkingly.

"Come on," Gallagher said. "How about it? How about giving me a break?"

"Look—"

"What the hell did I do? Shoot a little? Did I hurt anybody? Hell, I gave you a little excitement. Come on, be good guys. Take off these cuffs and send me on my way."

Willis mopped his brow. "He isn't kidding, you know that, don't you, Meyer?"

"Come on, Meyer," Gallagher said, "be a sp—" and Meyer slapped him across the face.

"Don't talk to me, big man. Don't use my name, or I'll ram it down your throat. This your first holdup?"

Gallagher looked at Meyer with hooded eyes, nursing his hurt cheek. "You I wouldn't give the sweat off my—" he started and Meyer hit him again.

"How many other holdups you pull in this precinct?"

Gallagher was silent.

"Somebody asked you a question, Gallagher," Willis said.

Gallagher looked up at Willis, including him in his hatred.

Carella walked over to the group. "Well, well, hello, Louie," he said.

Gallagher looked at him blankly. "I don't know you," he said.

"Why, Louie," Carella said, "your memory is getting bad. Don't you remember me? Steve Carella. Think, Louie."

"Is this guy a bull?" Gallagher asked. "I never seen him before in my life."

"The bakery, Louie? Nineteen forty-nine? South Third? Remember, Louie?"

"I don't eat cake," Gallagher said.

"You weren't there buying cake, Louie. You were sticking

up the joint. I happened to be walking by. Remember now?"

"Oh," Gallagher said. "That."

"When'd you get out, Louie?" Carella asked.

"What difference does it make? I'm out."

"And back at the old pushcart," Meyer said. "When'd you get out?"

"You got ten years for armed robbery, Gallagher," Carella said. "What happened? Parole?"

"Yeah."

"When did you get out?" Meyer repeated.

"About six months ago," Gallagher said.

"I guess you enjoyed your stay with the state, huh?" Meyer asked. "You're itching to get back."

"Come on, let's forget the whole deal," Gallagher said. "Whattya wanna be rotten guys for, huh?"

"Why do *you* want to be a rotten guy, Gallagher?"

"Who, me? I don't want to be rotten," Gallagher said. "It's a compulsion."

"Now I've seen everything," Meyer said. "Psychiatrist thieves! It's too much, too much. Come on, bum, the lieutenant's gonna want to talk to you. On your feet. Come on."

One of the phones rang. Hawes picked it up.

"Eighty-seventh Squad, Hawes," he said.

"Cotton, this is Sam Grossman."

"Hello, Sam, what've you got?"

"Nothing much. Prints that match up with the ones on the glasses, but . . . Well, let's face it, Cotton. We haven't got time to give that apartment the going-over it should get. Not before eight o'clock, anyway."

"Why? What time is it?" Hawes asked.

"It's past six already," Grossman said, and Hawes looked up at the wall clock and saw that it was exactly five minutes past six. Where had the last hour gone?

"Yeah. Well . . ." he started, and then he couldn't think of anything to say.

"There's just one thing that might help you," Grossman said. "Maybe you saw it already."

"What's that?"

"We picked it up in the kitchen. On the window sill over the sink. It has the suspect's prints on it, so maybe he used it. In any case, he handled it."

"What, Sam?"

"A card. You know, a business card."

"What's the business?" Hawes asked, picking up a pencil.

"It's a card for the Jo-George Diner. That's two words, hyphenated. No *e* on the *Jo*."

"Address?"

"336 North Thirteenth."

"Anything else on the card?"

"Right-hand corner of the card says 'Fine Food.' That's it."

"Thanks, Sam. I'll get right over there."

"Sure. Maybe the suspect eats there, who knows? Or maybe he's one of the owners."

"Jo or George, huh?"

"It could be," Grossman said. "You don't figure this joker lived in that apartment, do you?"

"No. Do you?"

"A few signs of habitation, but all recent. Nothing prolonged. My guess is that he used it as a *pied à terre*, if you'll pardon the Japanese."

"That's what I figure, too," Hawes said quickly. "Sam, I'd love to throw the bull with you, but it's getting late. I'd better hit that diner."

"Go ahead," Grossman said. "Good luck."

13

The Jo-George Diner was on The Stem at Thirteenth Street. Because the diner's entrance was on the side street rather than the avenue, the address was 336 North Thirteenth. There were no trucks parked outside it, but Hawes formed no opinions about the quality of the food. Perhaps trucks would have been there were there not parking regulations against them.

The diner looked like any other diner in the city, or perhaps even every other diner in the world. Metallically glistening in the sun still lingering in the sky, it squatted on the corner, a large sign across its top announcing the name JO-GEORGE DINER.

It was 6:15 P.M. when Hawes climbed the steps and opened the front door. The diner was packed.

The juke box was blaring, and there was the persistent hum of conversation bouncing off the walls and the ceiling. There were several waitresses scurrying back and forth between the booths and the counter. Two men were behind the counter, and Hawes could see beyond the pass-through into the kitchen, where three more men worked. The Jo-George Diner was a thriving little spot, and Hawes wondered which of the men were the owners.

He looked for a stool at the counter, but they were all occupied. He went to stand alongside the cash register at one end of the counter. The waitresses scurried past, ignoring him, picking up their orders. The men behind the counter dashed from customer to customer.

"Hey!" Hawes said.

One of the men stopped. "There'll be a short wait, sir," he said. "If you'll just stand over there near the cigarette machine, away from the door, somebody'll get up and you—"

"Jo around?" Hawes asked.

"It's his day off," the man said. "You a friend of—?"

"George here?"

The man looked puzzled. He was a man in his late fifties with

341

iron-grey hair and blue eyes. He was heavily built, his shirt sleeves rolled up over muscular biceps. "*I'm* George," he said. "Who are you?"

"Detective Hawes. Eighty-seventh Squad. Is there any place we can talk, Mr. . . . ?" He let the sentence trail.

"Laddona," George said. "George Laddona. What's this about?"

"Just a few questions, that's all."

"What about?"

"Can we talk some place besides here?"

"You sure picked a hell of a time. I got my big supper-crowd here right now. Can't you come back later?"

"This can't wait," Hawes said.

"We can talk in the kitchen, I guess."

Hawes listened to the sounds emanating from the bustling kitchen, the orders being shouted, the pots and pans being thrown around, the dishes being washed.

"Any place quieter?"

"The only other place is the men's room. It's okay with me if it's okay with you."

"Fine," Hawes said.

George came from behind the counter, and they walked to the other end of the diner. They opened a door that had no lettering on it, just the figure of a man in a top hat. The ladies' room featured a woman with a parasol. When they were inside, Hawes locked the door.

"What's your partner's name?" he asked.

"Jo Cort. Why?"

"Is that his full name?"

"Sure."

"The Jo, I mean."

"Sure. Jo. J-o. Why?"

Hawes pulled the police drawing out of his pocket. He unfolded it and showed it to George.

"This your partner?"

George looked at the picture. "Nope," he said.

"You sure?"

"Don't I know my own partner?"

"Ever see this man in the diner before?"

George shrugged. "Who knows? You know how many people

342

I get in here? Take a look outside. That's how busy it is every night at this time. Who recognizes individuals?"

"Take another look," Hawes said. "He may be a regular."

George looked at the picture again. "There's something familiar about the eyes," he said. He looked at it more closely. "Funny, I . . ." He shrugged. "No. No, I don't place him, I'm sorry."

Disappointedly, Hawes folded the picture and returned it to his pocket. The card looked like another false lead. The picture was certainly not a drawing of George, and George had just now said it wasn't his partner, either. Where did he go now? What did he ask next? What time was it? How long before the bullet from a Luger crashed into the body of an unsuspecting woman? Was a cop with the prostitute known as The Lady? Did Jay Astor have her police protection yet? Had Philip Bannister left to meet his mother at the ballet? Where was John Smith now? Who was John Smith? What do I ask now?

He pulled the business card from his wallet.

"Recognize this, George?" he asked.

George took the card. "Sure. That's our card."

"You carry them?"

"Sure."

"Jo carry them?"

"Sure. Also, we leave them on the counter. There's a little box for them. People pick them up all the time. Word-of-mouth advertising. It works, believe me. You saw how packed it was out there." He seemed to suddenly remember his customers. "Look, is this going to take much longer? I got to get back."

"Tell me about your setup here," Hawes said, unwilling to leave just yet, unwilling to let go of a lead that had taken him here to this diner, a card found in the apartment of the man who'd called himself John Smith, a man who was not George Laddona and not Jo Cort, but where had the man got the card? Had he eaten here? Hadn't George said there was something familiar about the eyes? Could the man have eaten here? *Dammnit, where was he? Who was he? I'm losing my grip,* Hawes thought.

"Regular partnership setup," George said, shrugging. "It's the same all over. Jo and me are partners."

"How old is Jo?"

"Thirty-four."

"And you?"

"Fifty-six."

"That's a big difference. Know him long?"

"About eleven years," George said.

"You get along with him?"

"Fine."

"How'd you meet?"

"At the 52-20 Club. You were in the service, weren't you?"

"Sure."

"Remember when you got out, they had this thing where the state gave you twenty bucks a week for a maximum of fifty-two weeks. A sort of rehabilitation thing. Until you found work."

"I remember," Hawes said. "But you weren't in the service, were you?"

"No, no, I was too old."

"Was Jo?"

"He was 4-F during the war. Had a punctured eardrum or something."

"Then how'd you meet at the Fifty-two—"

"We were both working there. For the Welfare Board, you know. Jo and me. That's how we met."

"What happened then?"

"Well, you know, we got friendly. I'd trust him with my right arm. Straight from the beginning. It was just one of those friendships. You know, we hit it off right away. It started with us stopping for a few brews on the way home from work. We still do it. Whenever we work together, we stop for a few brews. Place down the street. Jo and me, the guzzlers." George smiled. "The guzzlers," he repeated fondly.

"Go ahead," Hawes said. He looked at his wrist watch. He had the oddest feeling that he was wasting precious time listening to this fraternal account. "Go ahead," he said again, more impatiently this time.

"Well, we got to discussing our dreams and ambitions. I had a little dough socked away, and so did Jo. We talked about opening a little business. First we thought we'd open a bar, but it costs a lot of money to equip one, you know, and then there's the liquor licence and all. We just didn't have that kind of dough."

"So you decided on a diner instead."

"Yeah. We got a loan from the bank, and together with what we had, that was enough to start the business. Partners. Me and Jo. Fifty-fifty split. And it works, believe me. You know why?"

"Why?"

"Because we've got ambition. Both of us. Ambition to get ahead, to make something of ourselves. In a few years we'll be opening another diner, and then later on another. Ambition. And trust." George's voice dropped to a more confidential tone. "Listen, I trust that kid . . . I trust him like he was my own son." He began chuckling. "Hell, you have to, in my position."

"What do you mean?"

"I'm an orphan, all alone in the world. Jo's the only one I've got. And this is a partnership. That kid's as good as gold. I wouldn't trade him for the world."

"Where is he today?" Hawes asked.

"Wednesday. His day off. We both work Saturdays and Sundays, and we each take a day during the week. We're building, you know. Toward the big string of diners." George smiled.

"You think Jo might have given your card to the man whose picture I showed you?"

"He might have. Why don't you show him the picture?"

"Where can I reach him?"

"I'll give you his phone number. You can call him at home. If he's not there, he's probably with his girlfriend. A nice girl. Her name's Felicia. He'll probably marry her someday."

"Where does he live?" Hawes asked.

"In a nice apartment downtown. One of these hotel apartments. Very nice. He likes to live nice. Me, any hole in the wall'll do. But not Jo. He's . . . You know, a smart kid. Likes nice things."

"Give me the number," Hawes said.

"You can make the call right here, in the kitchen. There's a phone on the wall. Listen, can we get out of here? Besides my customers, it's getting hot as hell in this cubbyhole."

He opened the door, and they started walking toward the kitchen.

"It's like this every night," George said. "Jam-packed. We

give them quality, and it pays off for us. But, boy, it's a lot of work. This won't begin slacking off until seven thirty, eight o'clock. Busy. Busy all the time. Knock wood," he added, rapping on the counter.

Hawes followed him back to the kitchen. The kitchen was very hot, hot with the heat of the day and the heat of the stoves, and hot with hurried, frantic speech.

"Phone's over there," George said. "The number's Delville 2–4523."

"Thanks," Hawes said.

He walked to the phone, and deposited a dime. Then he began dialing. He waited.

"Riverdix Hotel," the voice said.

"Jo Cort, please," Hawes said.

"I'll try his apartment, sir. One moment, please."

Hawes waited. The operator rang.

"I'm sorry, sir. He doesn't seem to be answering."

"Try it again," Hawes said.

"Yes, sir." She tried it again. And again. And again and again. "I'm sorry, sir," she told him. "There's still no answer."

"Thank you," Hawes said, and he hung up.

He went out front and found George.

"He's not home."

"Oh. Too bad. Try his girlfriend. Felicia Pannet. She's in Isola, too."

"Where?" Hawes asked.

"I don't know the address. Midtown someplace. Or just above the Square, I think. Yeah, that's it. On the north side." George turned to a customer. "Yes, sir," he said, "would you care to see a menu."

"Just give me a bacon and tomato on toast," the man said. "And a cup of coffee."

George turned to the pass-through leading to the kitchen. 'BT down," he shouted. "Draw one!" He turned back to Hawes. "Will I be glad when *this* day is over. Know what I'm going to do?"

"What?" Hawes said.

"As soon as this crowd thins out, half hour or so from now, I'm going for a brew. Right down the street. Maybe two brews. Maybe I'll sit there and drink all night. I'm so thirsty I could drink a keg of the stuff. I can't wait. Half hour or so, *whizzz*, I'm out of here."

He had mentioned time, the enemy, and so Hawes unconsciously looked at his wrist watch. It was three minutes to seven.

An hour to go.

"Thanks," he said to George, and he left the diner.

Outside, he wondered what to do. The girl lived in midtown Isola, above the Square. Should he go there? Was it worth it? Suppose Jo wasn't there? Or suppose he *was* there and couldn't identify the picture? Or suppose he *could* identify the picture, would there be time to stop the killer? He looked at his watch again.

Seven o'clock.

Was there time?

Could they stop him now? Could they stop him from killing the woman, whoever she was?

Well, what else was there to do? Go back to the precinct squadroom and wait for the hour to pass? Sit there with the boys while a killer took aim at his target, while a Luger was brought to bear and then fired?

What the hell else was there to do? If he hurried, if he put on the siren and cleared the streets, he could be there in ten minutes. Another ten to talk to Jo—if he was there—and then ten to get back to the precinct. He could be in the squadroom by 7:30, and maybe Jo *would* identify that picture. Maybe, maybe, *maybe* . . .

Hawes walked into a drugstore and directly to the phone booths. He looked up Felicia Pannet's address, got it, and then decided to call her first. If Jo Cort wasn't there, she would tell him so and save him a trip.

He repeated the number to himself, went into the booth, and dialed it.

The busy signal clicked in his ear.

He hung up and waited. Then he dialed again.

Still busy.

Dammit, he was wasting time. If the phone was busy, *somebody* was home! And he sure as hell couldn't spend the next precious hour in a phone booth. He left the drugstore and walked back to the police sedan.

He gunned away from the curb, and turned on the siren.

14

Nathan Hale Square divided the island of Isola almost exactly in two. Dominated by the huge statue of the patriot, it was the hub of a bigger square of city commerce. Swank shops, bookshops, drugstores, automobile showrooms, hotels, and the new giant sports arena surrounded the square with their bustling activity. The heat had in no way diminished the bustle, or the hustle accompanying it. The heat very rapidly affects pursuit of the long green.

And yet, seeming to typify a more gracious time when the only thing people had to worry about was revolutions, Nathan Hale complacently looked out at the commercialism surrounding him, seemed in fact to look above and beyond it. And like dutiful subjects, a smattering of citizens sat on the benches circling the statue, feeding the pigeons, or reading newspapers, or just watching the girls in their thin summer frocks go by. Watching the girls in their summer frocks was a favorite city pastime, and another thing the heat could not affect.

Stopped for a moment by the maze of traffic in the square, Hawes watched the girls in their thin dresses. The traffic broke, the siren erupted, the car gunned forward, the girls were behind him. He swung around the square, heard a motorist curse behind him, and then headed east, taking the corner into Felicia Pannet's block on two wheels. He pulled the sedan to the curb, yanked the keys from the ignition, slammed out of the car, and took the front-stoop steps two at a time to the entrance lobby.

Felicia Pannet, the card in the bell panel read. Hawes pushed the button. He waited, his hand on the knob of the inner door. The door clicked, the lock sprang. Hawes pushed open the door and stepped into the ground-floor lobby. An elevator was at the rear of the lobby. He started for it, then remembered he hadn't looked at Felicia's apartment number. Cursing, muttering proverbs about haste making waste, he went back to the entrance door, opened it, braced it with one foot, and leaned into the lobby to read the apartment number in the bell panel. Sixty-three.

He went back inside to the elevator, pushed the *down* button and waited. The indicator told him the elevator was on the seventh floor. He waited. Either the indicator was broken, or the elevator was not moving. He pushed the button again. The elevator stayed on the seventh floor.

He could visualize two fat matrons discussing their arthritis, one of them holding the elevator door open while the second fumbled for her apartment keys in her purse. Or perhaps a delivery boy shuttling a month's supply of groceries from the elevator to some apartment, having wedged the door open with the shopping cart. He pushed the button again. Adamantly the damned elevator refused to move. Hawes looked at his watch and then took the steps.

He was winded and dripping wet when he reached the sixth floor. He looked for Apartment Sixty-three, found it, and pushed the black buzzer button in the doorjamb. No one answered. He pushed it again. As he was pushing it, he heard the hum of the elevator, saw the lighted car pass on its way downward to the street.

"Who is it?" a voice from within the apartment asked. The voice was low and cool, a woman's voice.

"Police," Hawes said.

Footseps padded toward the door. The peephole flap grated metal against metal when it swung back. The peephole presented only a mirrored surface to whoever was standing outside the doorway. The woman inside could see out, but Hawes could not see in.

"I'm not dressed," the voice said. "You'll have to wait."

"Please hurry," Hawes said.

"I'll dress as quickly as I know how," the voice said, and Hawes felt he had been reprimanded. The peephole flap grated shut again. Hawes leaned against the wall opposite the doorway, waiting. It was hot in the corridor. The collected smells of the day had merged with the cooking smells of the evening, and these in turn had merged with the heat to form an assault wave on the nostrils. He pulled out his handkerchief and blew his nose. It didn't help.

He realized all at once that he was hungry. He had not eaten since noontime, and he'd done a lot of chasing around since then, and his stomach was beginning to growl.

It'll soon be over, he thought, one way or the other. Then you can go home and shave and put on a clean white shirt and a tie and the grey tropical, and you can pick up Christine Maxwell. You didn't promise her dinner, but you'll buy her dinner, anyway. You'll have some long, tall drinks rammed full with ice. You'll dance to the air-conditioned rhythms of Felix Iceberg and his Twelve Icicles, and then you'll escort Miss Maxwell home and discuss Antarctica over a nightcap.

It sounded delightful.

I wish I worked for an advertising agency, Hawes thought. I'd leave the office at five and by this time I'd be immersed in a tub of marti—

Time.

He looked at his watch.

Good God, what the hell was taking her so long? Impatiently he reached for the buzzer again. He was about to press it when the door opened.

Felicia Pannet was easily the coolest-looking person he had seen all day. All week. All year. There was no other word for her. She was cool. She was, as a few junkies he knew might put it, the coolest, man.

She had straight black hair clipped in what he supposed the coiffure con men called a Spider Cut or a Bedbug Cut or some sort of an insect cut. Whatever they called it, it was extremely short except for the tendrils, which, insect-like, swept over her forehead.

Her eyes were blue. They were not a warm blue. They were the blue you sometimes find on a very fair-skinned blonde or an Irish redhead. But fair hair softens the harshness of the blue in those cases; Felicia Pannet's hair had been poured from an inkwell, and it dropped the temperature of the blue eyes to somewhere far below zero.

Her nose, like her hair, had been bobbed. The job was an excellent one, but Hawes could spot a nose bob at a hundred paces. Felicia's nose was a properly American, properly supperclub, properly martini-glass-in-hand-spouting-latest-best-seller-talk nose. A cool nose for a cool woman. And her mouth, without lipstick, was thin and bloodless. For a moment, Hawes thought of Charles Addams. The moment passed.

"I'm sorry I kept you waiting," Felicia said. Her voice expressed no regret whatever.

"That's quite all right," Hawes said. "May I come in?"

"Please."

She did not ask for identification. He followed her into the apartment. She was wearing an ice-blue sweater and a black skirt. The thongs of pale-blue sandals passed through the spaces alongside her big toes. Her toenails were painted a bright red, as were her long, carefully manicured fingernails.

The apartment was as cool as the woman. Hawes was not an expert on modern furniture, but he knew the stuff in this apartment had not been purchased on Crichton Avenue. This was nine-months-wait, special-order furniture. It had the look and the feel of luxury.

Felicia sat.

"What's your name?" she said.

Her voice had the peculiarly aloof nasal twang Hawes had always identified with Harvard men. He had always assumed that the speech instructor at Harvard was a man who spoke through his nose and, emulated by his students, produced a generation of young men whose voices emerged through their nostrils rather than their mouths. He was surprised to hear the affected speech pattern and tone in a woman. He was half tempted to ask her if she was a Harvard graduate.

"My name's Hawes," he said. "Detective Hawes."

"Do I call you Detective Hawes or Mr. Hawes? Which?"

"Whichever you like. Just don't—"

"Just don't call me late for dinner," she completed unsmilingly.

"I was going to say," Hawes said flatly, annoyed that she thought he'd been about to use the old saw, "just don't waste any more of my time."

The rebuff produced nothing more on the face of Felicia Pannet than a slight lifting of her left eyebrow. "I had no idea your time was so valuable," she said. "What do you want here?"

"I've just come from the Jo-George Diner," Hawes said. "Do you know George?"

"I've met him, yes."

351

"He told me that you're his partner's girlfriend. Is that right?"

"Are you referring to Jo?"

"Yes."

"I suppose you might say I'm his girlfriend."

"Do you know where I can locate him, Miss Pannet?"

"Yes. He's out of town."

"Where?"

"He went upstate to do some fishing."

"When did he leave?"

"Early this morning."

"What time this morning?"

"About one o'clock."

"You mean this *afternoon*, then, don't you?"

"No, I mean this morning. I rarely say anything I don't mean, Detective Hawes. I mean this morning. One o'clock this morning. He worked late at the dinner last night. He stopped by here to have a nightcap, and then he left for upstate. It must have been about one o'clock." She paused. Emphatically she added, "In the *morning*."

"I see. Where did he go upstate?"

"I don't know. He didn't say."

"When will he be back?"

"Either late tonight or early tomorrow morning. He's due back at the diner tomorrow."

"Will he call you when he gets back?"

"He said he would."

"Are you engaged to him, Miss Pannet?"

"In a sense, yes."

"What does that mean?"

"It means I don't date any other men. But I haven't got his ring. I don't want it yet."

"Why not?"

"I'm not ready to marry him yet."

"Why not?"

"When I get married, I want to stop working. But I want to live the way I live now. Jo makes a decent amount of money. The diner's a going business, and he splits everything fifty-fifty with George. But he still doesn't make as much money as I do."

"Where do you work, Miss Pannet?"

"For a television packaging outfit. Trio Productions. Have you heard of it?"

"No."

Felicia Pannet shrugged. "Three people," she said. "A writer, a director, and a producer. They banded together and formed their own producing company. We package shows for a good deal of the industry. The 'Pennsylvania Coal Hour' is one of our shows. Surely, you've seen that."

"I don't own a television set," Hawes said.

"Don't you believe in art?" she asked. "Or can't you afford one?"

Hawes let the remark pass. "And what do you do with Trio Productions?" he asked.

"I'm one of the original three, one of the trio. I'm the producer."

"I see. And this pays well, does it?"

"It pays extremely well."

"And Jo's cut of the business doesn't pay as well?"

"No."

"And you're not going to marry him until you can stay home and knit booties and raise a family on his earnings, is that—?"

"Until I can live the way I'm living now, yes," Felicia said.

"I see." Hawes took the folded picture from his pocket. Slowly he unfolded it and handed it to Felicia. "Ever see this man before?" he asked.

Felicia took the picture. "Is this your subtle way of getting my fingerprints?" she asked.

"Huh?"

"By handing me this picture?"

"Oh." Hawes smiled, beginning to dislike Miss Plannet intensely now, beginning to dislike Trio Productions, and beginning to dislike the "Pennsylvania Coal Hour" even though he had never seen the damned show. "No. I'm not trying to get your fingerprints. Would I have reason to want them?"

"How would I know?" she said. "I still don't know why you're here."

"I'm here to identify this man," Hawes said. "Do you know him?"

She looked at the picture. "No," she said. She handed it back to Hawes.

"Never saw him before?"

"Never."

"Possibly with Jo? Would he be one of Jo's friends?"

"All of Jo's friends are my friends. I never saw him with that man. Unless it's a bad likeness.

"It's a pretty good likeness," Hawes said. He folded the picture and put it in his pocket. His last chance seemed to have evaporated. If Jo Cort was on a fishing trip, there was no way to reach him before eight o'clock tonight. There was no way to show him the picture. There was no way to identify the potential killer. Hawes sighed. "A fishing trip," he said disgustedly.

"He likes fishing."

"What else does he like?"

For the first time since he'd been in the apartment, Hawes saw Felicia smile. "Me," she said.

"Mmm," Hawes answered, refusing to comment on the taste that makes horse races and ball games. "Where'd you meet him?" he asked.

"He picked me up," she said.

"Where?"

"On the street. Does that shock you?"

"Not particularly."

"Well, that's the way it happened. Are you familiar with The Quarter?"

"Downtown? Yes."

"I was walking there one Wednesday. Our big show is Tuesday night, the 'Coal Hour.' It's our only live show. We sort of relax right after it, generally take Wednesdays off unless there's a crisis in the office. I went down there that Wednesday to buy some jewelry. They have these unusual jewelry shops down there, as you may know."

"Yes," Hawes said. He looked at his watch. Why was he wasting time here? Why didn't he get back to the squadroom, where the company was congenial and pleasant?

"I was looking in one of the shop windows at a beautiful gold bracelet when I heard a voice behind me. It said, 'Would you like me to buy that for you?' I turned. A rather pleasant-looking man with a mustache and chin whiskers was standing behind me."

"Jo Cort?" Hawes asked.

"Yes. At first, I thought he was a Quarter artist. Because of the mustache and beard, you know. I said to him, 'Can you afford it?' He went into the shop and bought it for me. It cost three hundred dollars. That was the beginning of our relationship."

It figured, Hawes thought, and he began to form his own impressions of Jo Cort, a bearded jerk who'd spent three hundred dollars to pick up a girl like Felicia Pannet.

"He always wear this beard?" he asked, thinking of bearded men he had known in the past. One had grown the chin brush to hide the lack of a jaw. Another—

"Always," Felicia said. "He grew it when he was eighteen, and he's kept it ever since. I imagine he grew it because he was 4-F. A punctured eardrum. The beard made him feel more manly, I supposed. At a time when all of his friends were pretending to be men because of their uniforms. It's really quite attractive." She paused. "Have you ever been kissed by a man with a beard?"

"No," Hawes said. "I prefer my men with long sideburns instead." He rose. "Well, thanks a lot, Miss Pannet," he said.

"Is there anything you want me to tell Jo when I see him again?"

"By the time you see him again," Hawes said, "it'll be all over."

"*What* will be all over?"

"It," he said. "You might tell him that he picked an inconvenient time to go fishing. He might have been able to help us."

"I'm sorry," Felicia said, and again her voice indicated no regret.

"Yeah, well don't lose any sleep over it."

"I shan't."

"I didn't think you would."

"May I ask a personal question?" Felicia said.

"Sure. Go ahead."

"That white streak in your hair. Where did you get it?"

"Why do you want to know?"

"I'm attracted by oddities."

"Like Jo Cort's beard and mustache?"

"I'll admit his beard attracted me."

355

"That and the three-hundred-dollar bracelet," Hawes said.

"It was a very unusual approach," Felicia said. "I don't usually allow myself to be picked up on the street." She paused. "You still haven't answered me."

"I got stabbed once," Hawes said. "They shaved the hair to get at the wound. When it grew back, it was white."

"I wonder why," she said, expressing real interest.

"It probably turned white from fright," Hawes said. "I've got to be going."

"If you ever want television work—" she started.

"Yes?"

"You'd make a good menace. In a spy story. The streak in your hair is loaded with intrigue."

"Thanks," Hawes said. At the door, he paused. "I hope you, and Mr. Cort, and the beard are very happy together."

"I'm sure we will be," Felicia Pannet said.

From the way she said it, he didn't doubt a word of it.

15

It was 7:35 P.M.

In twenty-five minutes The Lady would become a target. In twenty-five minutes the threat would become a reality, a potential killer would become a real killer.

It was 7:36 P.M.

In twenty-four minutes a Luger would spit bullets into the night. A woman would fall. A phone would ring, and the desk sergeant would say, "Eighty-seventh Precinct," and the call would be transferred upstairs, and Homicide North and Homicide South and police headquarters and lab technicians and assistant medical examiners would be called in to deal with a fresh homicide.

It was 7:37 P.M.

A pall of gloom had settled over the squadroom. Bert Kling was anxious to get home. He'd had a trying day at the waterfront, but he waited now with his leather jacket slung over his arm, waited for something to break, waited for Byrnes to pop out of his office and shout, "Bert! I need you!"

It was 7:38 P.M.

They sat around the desk looking at the letter again, Meyer, Carella, and Hawes. Meyer was sucking cough drops. His throat was worse, and he blamed it on the heat.

I WILL KILL THE LADY TONIGHT AT 8.

WHAT CAN YOU DO ABOUT IT?

The answer was in each of the detectives' minds.

NOTHING.

We can do nothing about it.

"Maybe it *is* a dog," Meyer said, sucking on his cough drop. "Maybe it's a dog called Lady."

"And maybe it isn't," Hawes said.

"Or maybe it's that hooker," Carella said. "Marcia. The Lady. If it's her, we're okay. She's covered, isn't she?"

"She's covered," Hawes said.

"Lady Astor, too?"

"She's covered," Hawes said again.

"Pete didn't send anybody to the ballet, did he?"

"No," Hawes said. "Bannister's clean. He didn't look anything like that damn picture."

"And nobody at the diner could identify it, huh?" Meyer asked. He swallowed and reached for another cough drop.

"I only saw one of the partners," Hawes said. "The other one's out of town." He paused. "The first one had the right idea, all right."

"Anybody want one of these?" Meyer asked, extending the box.

The other man ignored him. "What idea was that?" Carella asked.

"He was heading for a beer as soon as the eating crowd thinned. A place right down the street, he said. That's for me, too. As soon as I get out of here. You fellows join me? I'm buying."

"Where's the diner?" Carella asked, interested.

"Huh?"

"The diner."

"Oh. Thirteenth and The Stem."

"Near that bar, isn't it?"

"What bar?"

"The Pub. The bar where Samalson might have lost the glasses. The Pub. That was on North Thirteenth and Amberly."

"You think there's a connection?" Hawes asked.

"Well," Carella said, "if the guy ate at the Jo-George Diner, maybe he stopped for a drink at The Pub down the street. Maybe that's where he found Samalson's binoculars."

"Where does that lead us?"

"Noplace," Carella admitted. "But maybe it rounds out the picture." He shrugged. "I'm just batting it around."

"Yeah," Hawes said.

It was 7:40 P.M.

"This guy at the diner couldn't identify it, though, huh? The picture?" Meyer asked.

"No. It was a bum lead. All George wanted to talk about was how much he loved his partner, Jo. A son to him, that kind of kick. George is an orphan, all alone in the world. He's attached himself to this kid."

"Kid?" Carella asked.

"Well, he's thirty-four. But that's a kid to George. George is fifty-six."

"Funny partnership," Carella said.

"They met a long time ago."

"The usual partnership setup?"

"What do you mean?"

"In case of death, where there are no relatives, the surviving partner gets the business."

"I suppose so," Hawes said. "Yes. George mentioned that it was the usual partnership setup."

"Then if George kicks off, his partner inherits the diner, right? You said George was all alone in the world, didn't you? No relatives to make claims?"

"That's right," Hawes said. "What are you thinking?"

"Maybe Jo is getting itchy for George to drop dead. Maybe he's going to help him along tonight at eight."

Mention of the time caused each of the men to look up at the clock. It was 7:42 P.M.

"Well, that's a nice theory, Steve," Hawes said. "Except for a couple of items."

"Like?"

"Like . . . does *George* sound like a *lady*?"

"Mmm," Carella said.

"And most important, we showed that picture to both George and the girlfriend of Cort. Neither of them recognized it. Our killer ain't Jo Cort."

"What made you think George was a lady, Steve?" Meyer asked. "The heat getting you?"

"Is he a queer or something?" Carella asked, refusing to drop it. "This George character?"

"Nope. I'd recognize it, Steve. He was legit."

"I was thinking . . . you know . . . some tie-in with The Lady." He tapped the letter. "But if he's not . . . well . . ." He shrugged.

"No, no," Hawes said, "you're on the wrong track."

"Yeah, you're right," Carella said. "I just thought . . . well, the motive looked damn good."

"It's too bad it doesn't fit with the other facts," Meyer said, smiling. "Maybe we can change them to fit your theory, huh, Steve?"

Carella grinned. "I'm getting weak. This has been a busy day."

"You coming for a beer?" Hawes asked. "When this is all over?"

"Maybe."

"He had the right idea, George did," Hawes said. "As soon as his place cleared out, he was heading for *this*." Unconsciously his finger tapped the Ballantine sign that had been used to form the figure 8 in the letter. And then his finger stopped.

"Hey!" he said.

"The eight," Carella said.

"You think . . . ?"

"I don't know."

"But . . ."

"Is the killer telling us? Is he telling us *where*?"

"A bar? At eight? Is that it?"

"Holy Jesus, Cotton, do you think so?"

"I don't know. Steve . . ."

"Hold it, Cotton. Now hold it."

The men were sitting on the edge of their chairs. The clock on the wall read 7:44 P.M.

"If it's a bar—could it be The Pub?"

"It could. But who?"

"The Lady. It said The Lady. But if this damn eight had a hidden meaning . . . The Lady. The Lady. Who?"

The men were silent for a moment. Meyer took another cough drop and threw the box onto the desk.

"George may be headed for The Pub," Carella said. "He said a bar down the street, didn't he? And that's where Samalson lost the glasses. Maybe George *is* the victim. Cotton, I can't see it any other way."

"The Lady? How the hell can George Laddona be The Lady?"

"I don't know. But I think we—"

"Holy . . . !"

"What?" Carella stood up. "What?"

"Oh, Jesus. Translate it! You're Italian, Steve. Translate Laddona. The Lady! The Lady!"

"*La donna!*" Carella said. "Oh, my aching . . . then he wants to be stopped. Goddamnit, Cotton, the killer *wants* to be stopped! He's told us who and where. The killer—"

"But who's the killer?" Hawes asked, rising. And then his eye fell on the cough-drop box on the desk, and he shouted "Smith! Smith!"

And then they ran like hell out of the squadroom because the clock on the wall read 7:47 P.M.

16

Standing on top of the garbage can in the alley alongside The Pub, the man could see into the small window directly to the table where George Laddona was sitting.

He had not been wrong, then. He had known George's habits well enough to realize that he would stop at The Pub again tonight on the way home from the diner, would sit at his regular table, and would order a large schooner of beer. And when that was consumed, he would order another . . . except that tonight he would not order another, he would never order another glass of beer again because at eight o'clock he would die.

The man looked at the luminous dial of his watch. It was 7:52.

In eight minutes, George Laddona would die.

He felt a sudden sadness. It was a thing he had to do, of course. It was the only way he could see. And he had planned it very well, had planned it so that he would be in the clear, so that even if he was suspected of motive, the facts would never tie in with him, the facts would never tie in with the man who'd be seen running down the street after the shooting.

And then to his own apartment. And then, tomorrow morning back to work, unchanged, seemingly the same. Except that he would have committed a murder.

Would they stop him?

Had his letter been too subtle? Well, of course, he could not *tell* them, could he have come right out and *told* them? But hadn't there been enough hints, hadn't he cleverly indicated what was going to happen, and shouldn't they have figured it out?

They had certainly figured out the rest. They hadn't been laggard about that, by God. He thought of the apartment he'd rented on Twelfth Street, the sleazy dump where he'd planned to spend the night, a place within walking distance of the shooting. He could no longer do that. They had found the apartment, had almost captured him. He could still remember shooting it out with the red-headed cop. That had been exciting, exhilarating. But now he couldn't use the apartment; he'd have

362

to return to his own apartment. Was that wise? Suppose some-one saw him? Should he simply wander the streets tonight? Should he put on the—

He stopped his thoughts abruptly and looked at his watch again. 7:55.

He reached into his pocket, felt something soft and warm, was surprised for an instant, and then remembered. And then his hand closed on something cold and hard, and he pulled it from his pocket, and the dim moon in the already dark sky illuminated the Luger with a deadly glitter.

He checked the magazine. It was a full clip.

Those magazines he had left in the apartment. Could they be traced? It didn't matter. He didn't have a licence for the gun. Would they trace it to the man from whom he'd bought it? No, that was unlikely. He'd bought it in the neighborhood, and he was sure it was a stolen gun. The man he'd bought it from had had all sorts of things to sell. This was some neighborhood, all right, some neighborhood, and still it had been good to him. It would be even better to him. After tonight it would be better.

He clicked off the safety.

It was 7:57.

He rested the Luger on the window sill, and carefully took aim at the back of George Laddona's head. On his left wrist, the second hand of his wrist watch moved, and moved, and moved. The minute hand suddenly lurched. He saw it move, actually saw it move. It was 7:58. Would they stop him? He doubted it. The fools. The stupid fools.

Carefully he kept his hand steady, and waited.

At 8 o'clock, just as he was going to fire, Cotton Hawes burst into the alley mouth.

"Hey!" he shouted. "You!"

The gun went off, but the killer's hand had yanked back an instant before he'd fired. Hawes lunged at him. The man turned, the Luger in his fist. Hawes leaped.

The gun went off again, and then the garbage can and the man rolled down clatteringly onto the alley floor. The gun was coming up again, turning to point at Hawes, a graceful weapon with a lethal discharge. Hawes swung. The gun went off wide. He swung again. He felt his fist collide with the man's face, and again he struck. And now the day's punishment, the heat, and

363

the chase, and the seeming futility of the senseless desperation welled up in Hawes, exploded into his fists so that he battered the man until he was senseless.

And then, sighing heavily, he dragged him out of the alley mouth.

Inside The Pub, George Laddona was still trembling. The bullet had whacked into the tabletop, missing his head by perhaps two inches. He sat with a puzzled expression on his face, and his hands shook, and his lips shook as Hawes tried to explain.

"It was your partner," he said. "Jo Cort. It was your partner who shot at you, Mr. Laddona."

"I don't believe it," George said. "I just don't believe it. Not Jo. Jo wouldn't try to kill me."

"He would if he had a money-hungry girlfriend," Hawes said.

"You mean . . . you mean *she* was behind this?"

"Not actually," Hawes said. "At least, I don't think so. She didn't *tell* him to kill you, if that's what you mean. Felicia Pannet isn't the kind of girl who'd spend the rest of her life with a murderer. But she let him know what she wanted, and this probably seemed to him the only way he could get it for her."

"No," George said. "Not Jo," and he seemed ready to weep.

"Remember that picture I showed you today?" Hawes asked.

"Yes! That wasn't Jo! That was someone else. That's the man—"

"Wasn't it?" Hawes asked. He took the picture and a pencil from his pocket, and hastily went to work on it. "Wasn't it Jo Cort?" he asked George, and he showed him the changed picture.

"Yes," George said. "Yes, that's Jo."

"Believe me," Hawes said. "He tried to kill you."

George brushed at his eyes. "He succeeded," He said.

In the police sedan, with the prisoner between Meyer and Carella on the back seat, Hawes drove leisurely back toward the precinct.

"Why'd you shout 'Smith!' when we were leaving?" Carella asked.

"Because I was looking at Meyer's damn box of cough drops, and all of a sudden I remembered."

"What'd you remember?"

"I remembered a landlady saying, *'That's the way he looked this morning.'* It didn't make sense at the time, but actually it meant he looked different this morning than he had looked on other mornings. And then this girl who lived across the hall from him. She said he'd reminded her of a *Russian spy.* All he needed was a bomb. And she thought it was funny that his name was Smith. When I asked her why, she said, *'Well, the cough drops and all, you know.'* I thought she was nuts at the time. But tonight, when I saw Meyer's box of Smith Brothers Cough Drops, it all clicked into place. Cort had shaved in the apartment the night before. That's what the scissors and straight razor were doing in that medicine cabinet."

"It figures," Carella said. "He's had that beard since he was eighteen. He thought he wouldn't be recognized without it."

"And he wasn't," Hawes said. He stopped for a traffic light. "But what I don't understand is how he planned to go back to the diner tomorrow morning? He'd be identified immediately."

"Maybe this'll help you," Carella said. "I found it in his pocket."

He flipped a soft furry object onto the front seat. Hawes picked it up. "A false mustache and beard!" he said. "I'll be a son of a bitch!"

"I guess he planned to wear that until the real McCoy grew back," Carella said.

"He can grow a real long beard where he's going," Meyer said. "Anybody want a cough drop?"

Carella and Hawes burst out laughing.

"Man, I'm weary," Carella said.

"I guess O'Brien gets to see his ball game, huh?"

The traffic light changed. On the back seat Cort stirred into consciousness. He blinked and then mumbled, "You stopped me, didn't you?"

"Yeah," Carella said. "We stopped you."

"You've got the light, Cotton," Meyer said. "Let's go."

"What's the hurry?" Hawes asked. "We've got all the time in the world."